Charity—a beautiful, cold-blooded prostitute who had contemptuously used men for profit, and now found herself the helpless victim of an Indian's hate-maddened lusts.

Elizabeth—a cavalry officer's young wife who had despised the desires of the flesh, until defenses that could not be taken by storm were melted by one man's irresistible passionate siege.

Kate—a lovely, idealistic girl who committed the greatest of all sins for a white woman—falling in love with the Cheyenne who had carried her off.

Three women . . . each with her own struggle for survival . . . each with her own heartbreaking choice when her moment of liberation came. . . .

SWEETWATER SAGA

SWEETWATER SAGA

Roxanne
Dent

A SIGNET BOOK

NEW AMERICAN LIBRARY

SIGNET, SIGNET CLASSIC, MENTOR, PLUME, MERIDIAN AND NAL
BOOKS *are published by New American Library,*
1633 Broadway, New York, New York 10019

FIRST PRINTING, SEPTEMBER, 1979

  5 6 7 8 9 10 11 12 13

With much love,

To David Dunham for supporting, sharing, and caring.

SWEETWATER
SAGA

1

1845

It was unusually hot for late fall in Minnesota. The merciless early-morning sun beat down on the dry, parched earth, sending up layers of steam. Nothing moved; not a bird, not an insect, nor an animal. Not even a blade of brown grass stirred. In the distance, a cloud of dust could be seen rising from the road that led into the town of Sweetwater. The dust was caused by four silent, wary travelers who were heading toward the town. The sweat plastered their shirts to their backs and burned their eyes. No one thought to complain. Every once in a while, one of the younger men would glance over at the older man uneasily. The older man's gaze never wavered. He kept his blue eyes fixed straight ahead and his lips set in a grim line. By the time the sun had reached its zenith, he would have satiated his lust for revenge. As a result of his actions, he would set in motion a chain of irrevocable events that would wipe the flourishing town of Sweetwater off the map before another day had dawned. As a man, he was no better or worse than his fellows. It was his unique capacity as a catalyst that set him apart from the rest. If he had not played out the part, in time another would have risen to do so.

In the town of Sweetwater feelings of hate, greed, revenge, and fear had been rapidly building to a crescendo for four long years.

As the travelers neared the town, they heard none

of the usual signs of life. There was no laughing, no shouting, none of the hustle and bustle that usually occurred on a Monday morning. There was only the pounding heat and the same silence that had characterized the four men. It was a silence that was charged with electricity and fraught with tension. The streets were deserted. If it were not for the pungent odor of fear that permeated the dry air, a stranger would have imagined the town to be abandoned.

As though on cue, as soon as the four men had reached the middle of town the male population of Sweetwater slowly emerged onto the streets, carrying rifles and guns. One man, much larger than the rest, with a thick neck, a ruddy complexion, and massive shoulders that immediately put one in mind of his profession as the town's blacksmith, moved into the middle of the street and blocked the riders' way. He looked about fifty, had small dark eyes, a broken nose from innumerable barroom brawls, and thick black beetle brows that were drawn together in a frown as he stared up into the face of the older man. "We should have left already," he muttered sullenly.

Joseph Mallory stared at Carl Gomber with obvious distaste.

When he spoke, his voice was tinged with scorn. "We'll leave when I say so." If there was one thing he hated more than an Indian, it was a child beater. Ever since Gomber's wife had run away with another man, some three years ago, Carl had taken to mistreating his now twelve-year-old daughter. Lorrie was a good little girl who minded her manners and did as she was told. No matter how hard she tried to please her brutal father, he always found fault with her. Lorrie jumped when her father entered the room and trembled when he looked at her. She had good cause, too, Joseph Mallory thought angrily. On more than one occasion Lorrie's father had beaten her senseless. Several citizens of Sweetwater, whom Joe Mallory had gotten together, tried to have Lorrie taken away from him. So far, they had been unsuccessful. When the judge questioned Lorrie, she surprised everyone by adamantly insisting her father hadn't unduly punished her. She wanted to remain with him. Mallory was sure Carl Gomber had browbeaten his daughter into telling such a lie.

Carl Gomber flushed and clenched his hands. Before he could argue the point, another man joined them. Ben Haskell was only three years younger than the two men he faced, but he looked at least fifteen years their junior. He was a little under average height, with a wiry, sunburned body, wide shoulders, and a narrow waist. His hair was still thick and fair, with only faint traces of gray running through it. His eyes were a deep blue and his brows were still so fair that he gave the appearance of having none. Ben was neatly dressed, his boots polished to a high sheen, and he smelled of shaving lotion. In his younger days he was jokingly referred to as "The Dandy." Despite his outward appearance and deceiving smile, Ben was not a soft man. He had worked hard in the early days, and had fought against outlaws, Indians, and the elements. He had conquered all. Now he possessed one of the largest spreads in Minnesota and had recently married one of the prettiest widows in the area. In spite of the fact that he was one of the richest men in Sweetwater and had a reputation as a sharp dealer and a hard boss, Ben was generally well-liked. If he lost his temper, he soon forgot what triggered it. When one of his hands took sick, he made sure he was well taken care of. He didn't overpay his workers, but he didn't underpay them either. His only fault was greed. Ben could never possess enough land or enough cattle to satisfy his craving. That, and the fact that five years ago the Cheyenne had murdered his first wife and only son while he was away getting supplies, was why he decided to join forces with his old friend Joseph Mallory. He despised Carl Gomber as much as Mallory did. But he knew that now wasn't the time for squabbling among themselves. He smiled, showing white even teeth, and said pleasantly, "See you brought your boys along, Joe. Good idea. It'll do them good to see some action." He paused and added apologetically, "We *should* be on our way, unless you want to rest up a minute."

Before Joseph Mallory could answer, his son Timothy replied a little too quickly, "Ben is right. Our horses are tired and . . ." He stopped in mid-sentence, flushing to the roots of his fair hair as his brown eyes met his father's cold blue ones.

"We have fresh horses waiting for us," Joseph Mallory said stiffly after an uncomfortable silence, and looked away from the one son he found it difficult to feel affection for.

Timothy Mallory was the second eldest of four boys. Despite his weak chin, he possessed the acknowledged Mallory good looks. Timothy was aware of his father's feelings and constantly strove to gain his approval and love. All his efforts went unrewarded. It seemed the harder he tried, the more distant and uncommunicative his father became. His youngest brother, Sean, often told him that he tried too hard. His brother Michael didn't understand why he cared if their father approved of him or not. Michael didn't have to care, Timothy thought resentfully. He was his father's favorite. No matter what he did, his father always forgave him and even seemed to admire him for doing it. Timothy was always the outsider, the son his father never talked about to neighbors unless he was asked first. He often imagined that if he disappeared one day, his father wouldn't even send out a search party to look for him. Life would go on as it had before. He wouldn't even be missed. Timothy frowned. It wasn't fair. And yet, he thought miserably, it had always been that way, ever since he could remember. There was that time several years ago when he awoke startled one night to hear his parents arguing, something they seldom did. His mother's voice was raised in anger.

"You're not being fair to Timmy. You don't spend time with him like you do with the others. You're neglecting him as a father. Sometimes I think you care more for a total stranger than you do for your own son."

"It's not my fault that I don't spend more time with him," Joseph Mallory shouted. "He's *your* son. He always was. You've kept him tied to your apron strings ever since he was born. *Hell*, he spends more time in the kitchen gossiping to you than Katie does."

"He was a sickly child and he needed me," Ellen Mallory retaliated defensively.

"Well, he's no longer a baby. He's a grown man and he's weak. *You've* made him weak."

The argument had happened well over six years ago, but Timothy still flinched when he recalled the incident. That was the trouble, all right, he thought bitterly. He *was* weak. His father had been right. He was a coward. He flushed with shame and stared at the ground. That was why he had deliberately volunteered to join his father and brothers on the Indian attack. If his father saw that he could be brave just once, maybe then Timothy would see something else besides disappointment and scorn reflected in his father's face. Maybe then he'd be proud of him as he was of his other sons.

As the Mallorys dismounted and changed to fresh horses, Joseph Mallory's gaze rested on his favorite son, Michael, and it softened perceptibly. Michael was by far the best-looking of the Mallory boys. He had thick, curly golden hair, dark blue eyes that were always laughing, and an engaging dimple in his left cheek. He was an inch shorter than his father, and at twenty, strong as an ox. Michael was quick, bright, and loaded with charm. Unlike Timothy, he had a devil-may-care attitude about life. Michael wanted to be the first to do anything, especially if it was danger-

ous. That was part of the reason Joseph Mallory loved
him the best. If his father yelled at him, he laughed or
listened respectfully. He never trembled or failed to
meet his father's eyes as Timothy did.

Michael, unlike Timothy, was anxious to be off. He
had pleaded with his father to allow him to accompany them when they made a surprise attack on the
two camps of Cheyenne. He was bored with ranch
duties and itched to see some real action. The attack
on the Cheyenne would afford him ample opportunity
to revenge his mother's brutal death. He smiled, his
blue eyes sparkling with excitement. Michael was too
good-natured to possess a cruel streak. But the Indians
had butchered his mother, and like his father, he hated
them and felt it was his right to take revenge. Automatically he ran his hand over the smooth butt of the
rifle his father had given him last Christmas. He was
going to show those savages a thing or two.

Watching Michael's eager face instilled grave misgivings in Mallory. Michael was still young, and although a good shot, inexperienced in combat. He
frowned. The boy was reckless. Still, Mallory thought
proudly, his face clearing, there was always a first
time for every boy when he becomes a man. Just to be
on the safe side, though, he would keep an eye on
Michael in the battle, to make sure he didn't lose all
sense of caution.

If Michael was Joseph Mallory's favorite and Timothy the one he despised, his eldest son, John, who
was twenty-five, ran a close second to Timothy with
one exception. His father grudgingly admitted that although John might be the stupidest, most pigheaded
and prudish person he had ever known, he commanded respect, if not admiration. John lived his life
the way he saw fit, and nobody, not even his strong-
willed father, could sway him from a path once
chosen.

John was the tallest of the boys and bore the closest
resemblance to his father in his younger days, which

irritated the older man considerably. He had dark gold hair, a thin blond well-groomed mustache, and his father's cold blue eyes, which, unlike the latter's, never lit up with laughter or amusement. John prided himself on his abstinence and never permitted a drop of Satan's liquor to pass his lips. He refused to participate in the dancing provided on occasion by his church and wouldn't allow his meek, timid wife, Nora, to do so either.

As he so often put it, "Dancing, drinking, and idleness are the ruination of mankind. They break down a man's morals and leave him with a continuous thirst for the pleasures of the flesh. Once that occurs," John would sniff, "we are surely on the way to damnation, as were those unfortunate citizens of Sodom and Gomorrah."

"Yes, dear!" Nora always obediently replied.

John's reasons for joining the party were twofold. "I feel it is my Christian duty to help rid the area of savages that daily threaten our welfare," he patiently explained to Nora, his most avid listener.

"But, John," Nora replied apologetically, a frown of puzzlement on her usually placid face, "the Indians didn't attack us first. It's not as if we were at war with them."

John smiled indulgently and patted his wife's small hand patronizingly. "You must remember, Nora dear, that Indians are primitive beings who are subject to whims and might at any moment, for no particular reason, attack and murder us unaware. They are not like Christian folks. They haven't got a conscience. They're just biding their time until they are strong enough to strike. We must be the ones to strike first."

John's second reason, which he kept to himself, was more in keeping with his materialistic outlook. With the majority of the Indians dead and the remainder removed to reservations in other states, their land would be open for settlement. John was living on land his fa-

ther had given him as a wedding present. He wanted
more—his own land. The Cheyenne had some of the
best grazing land available. Since he considered the Indians devils without souls, he felt perfectly justified in
murdering them, suffering not the slightest twinge of
conscience.

Besides the three sons who accompanied him, Mallory had another son, who had remained at home in
ignorance of their mission. He frowned as he thought
of his youngest son. Sean was only fifteen, and in
many ways he took after Michael. He resembled him
in physical appearance and had his independent manner and fearless spirit. Unlike Michael, he also
possessed an insatiable curiosity. At first Joseph Mallory had smiled indulgently at the boy's eagerness for
knowledge. But recently he had found out that his
own son was out making friends with the Indians.

"What in blazes are you doing associating with
heathens when you know your own ma was butchered by them?" he demanded. He watched Sean's chin
set in that defiant way he had that greatly resembled
his brother John, and felt his uneasiness increase.

"The war is over, Dad. Both sides lost friends and
family, not just us. It's time we exchanged ideas, time
we learned more about each other. That way, we
won't have another war. You're always talking about
the threat of an Indian uprising. Well, if you and the
other ranchers made friends with the Cheyenne,
maybe peace could be secured once and for all instead
of everybody holding their breath."

"Peace will never be secured, so long as there is one
Indian left alive," Mallory retorted in disgust at the
boy's ignorance. "And I want you to give up this
foolishness and promise me you won't go near any
more Indians."

Sean had refused to promise him anything. He
didn't lie or hedge, he simply squared his shoulders
and refused point-blank. Mallory had yelled at the
boy, threatened him with various dire punishments,

and finally resorted to thrashing him. Sean had still seemed far from compliant. Joseph Mallory's eyes darkened and his grip on his rifle tightened. That's all he needed in the family, he thought bitterly, an Injun lover. What really rankled was that he knew it was all his daughter's fault. Katie had taken over at the ranch after her ma had died, and she and Sean were close, too close. Sean listened to her advice and got his love of reading and curiosity from her. Mallory's mouth twisted into a grimace. He knew how his only daughter felt about Indians. They had argued often enough since her ma's death. Katie insisted it was wrong to dwell in the past and nurse a hatred for a people he didn't understand. She pointed out that the Cheyenne had lost mothers, brothers, and husbands too. And it was *their* land we had taken away.

Their land! Mallory turned red with anger. As though *we* had no claim to it. Well, he had the deed to prove it belonged to him. His own children were turning against him, he thought glumly.

Despite his daughter's radical beliefs concerning Indians, Mallory had a soft spot for Katie and seldom pressed his views. He knew she would argue with him until he was too tired to keep his eyes open. The fact that she greatly resembled her mother, with her long auburn hair and green eyes that flashed fire when she was angry, caused him to avoid the one topic that upset her. But he couldn't have a son who hung around with savages. Pretty soon he'd learn their language, and if the family wasn't careful, he'd wind up murdering them all while they slept.

He remembered the story of a boy who was captured by the Sioux and lived with them for ten years. When he came back, he couldn't speak a word of English and preferred the floor to a bed. One night he attacked and wounded his own father and one of his brothers before they could tie him down. That wasn't going to happen in his family, he muttered to himself grimly. He'd see to that! He'd see that Sean stayed away from Katie. After he returned from the raid, after it was all over, he'd hold a big celebration and invite all their neighbors from miles around to attend, especially the eligible men. Katie was eighteen and mighty attractive. He'd hate to lose her. He sighed. On the other hand, he reasoned sensibly, why keep her isolated at the ranch where she could poison Sean's mind until he grew up and turned against his own kind.

"Everybody's ready," Ben Haskell said quietly, studying his friend's face for a clue to his thoughts.

Mallory's face betrayed none of the personal problems that troubled him. As for the attack, he wasn't worried. It would go well. There was the element of surprise involved. He smiled for the first time and wiped the sweat from his brow with the edge of his shirtsleeve. "Then what the hell are we waiting for, Ben?"

As the four hundred men left Sweetwater armed and hell-bent on annihilating the unsuspecting Cheyenne, the sheriff, whose duty it was to alert the soldiers to such hostile action on the part of the citizens, turned his back.

Sheriff Davis had only just discovered the plot that morning. It had been too late to warn the soldiers of the surprise attack on the Indian villages. When the soldiers demanded to know why he hadn't reported it, he would tell them he had been completely ignorant of it. That was at least partially true. He knew the majority of Sweetwater would back him up. Secretly he hoped that the Indians would all be killed, every last man, woman, and child. Davis had been one of the first settlers in Minnesota, and he had seen what the red devils could do. His own brother had been found tied to a burning wagon wheel and would have been unrecognizable except for a gold cross with his name on it that the savages had neglected to steal. His brother's wife and their infant baby had also perished at the hands of the Cheyenne. The baby's head had been smashed against a nearby elm tree. Nancy had been raped and beaten to death. Sheriff Davis still trembled when he permitted himself to recall those painful memories. He took several slugs of the whiskey he kept in his left-hand drawer. Maybe then, maybe after the savages were all dead, there would be some real peace in Sweetwater. At least there wouldn't be the constant threat of an Indian uprising hanging over their heads like a goddamn ax.

Not all the residents of Sweetwater were in favor of the deliberate slaughter of a people who had as yet done nothing to deserve such brutality. But they were few in number and felt it was best to keep silent.

There were, however, a few unfortunate souls who were unaware of the events that were rapidly gathering speed to drastically change the future destinies of them all.

Frank and Martha Tilby, owners of the general store, belonged to the former list of silent protesters. Martha Tilby was a favorite with the townspeople. She was plump, with rosy cheeks, blue eyes, and fair hair. She never had a harsh or unkind word to say about anybody, and her kindness to those less fortunate than herself often caused her indignant husband to cynically remark to his children that the reason they never made any profit was because their mother preferred *giving* their supplies away. On this morning, Martha's usual cheerful smile was replaced by a frown as she watched the riders depart. "I still think we ought to have done something to stop them," she said, displaying slight traces of a German accent.

A stab of pain shot through Frank Tilby's nervous stomach and caused him to wince before replying defensively, "I told the sheriff, didn't I? What would you have had me do, stop four hundred armed men at gunpoint?"

Martha turned away from the window, her blue eyes troubled. "Why hasn't the sheriff done anything,

Frank? He ought to have left for the fort as soon as you informed him what was happening. Why hasn't he gone?"

"How do I know?" Frank muttered, avoiding her searching gaze. "That's his business. I told him. Now it's up to him."

"Maybe he didn't understand how serious it was," Martha continued. "You might not have put it to him right. Sometimes you don't explain things clearly. Why don't you try again?" she urged.

"Sheriff Davis understood me perfectly," Frank assured his wife dryly.

"Then if he's too busy to go, why don't you go, Frank? Leslie and I could look after the store while you're gone."

"I'm not going anywhere," Frank shouted, his usually pale face flushing with guilt. "It's not *my* responsibility. The sheriff is the one who ought to go, not me. If he decides not to warn the soldiers at the fort, that's his business."

Martha began busying herself with the bolts of gingham, silk, and other materials that were piled high on the scarred wooden table in front of her. As her hands deftly smoothed out wrinkles in the material and separated the bolts into different groups, she tried not to betray how disturbed she was by her husband's steadfast refusal to do what was right.

Frank was not deceived by her silence. He knew she disapproved and he was greatly annoyed by his inability to shrug it off. No matter how hard he tried, he couldn't get away from the fact that his wife's good opinion mattered. He tried once again to justify himself in her eyes.

"If I were to go to the fort with my report, the lieutenant would be bound to ask me why I didn't tell Sheriff Davis," he said in a strained voice, trying to be calm. "I would have to say that I did but he refused to act. That would get him into a lot of trouble. He might even be fired from his job, or what's worse, our town be put under military rule. Nobody wants that. I would be blamed," he said unhappily. "We have to live in this town, Martha. If I betray our friends by reporting to the soldiers, getting Sheriff Davis into trouble, and being responsible for placing our town under military rule, we'll be mighty unpopular. We may even have to leave after all the work we've put into developing this store." He paused long enough for his words to sink in, and then continued in a milder tone. "One of these days, Sweetwater will be big enough to interest the railroads, just like Ben Haskell says. When that happens, it will be clear sailing for us. In the meantime, we've got to be careful who we side with and what we do. Our actions determine the future. We have to think of our children, Martha," Frank reminded her, hoping the reference to their children's welfare would move her to agree with him.

Martha patted her husband's hand and said in a voice that did nothing to ease his conscience, "What really matters is that you do what you think is right." Before Frank had a chance to reply to this well-aimed shot, his two children burst in the door.

Leslie, at nineteen, was the exact likeness of her mother, although considerably slimmer. Beside her stood her younger brother, Luke, who was only eight. Although any casual observer could easily guess that the two were related, the difference between them was apparent at first glance. Leslie exuded bursting good health, energy, and an outgoing personality. Luke was shorter than most boys his age, thin and sickly. He caused his parents considerable worry by always being the first to come down with a cold or any of the childhood diseases, and taking the longest to recover. Periods of long confinement indoors, along with oversolicitous care by his mother and a clumsiness in athletics due to little practice, had made Luke Tilby shy with boys his own age.

Leslie, her eyes shining, said in a soft, musical voice,

"We saw them off. Michael looked real handsome," she declared, referring to Michael Mallory. He was her steady beau and the one boy she had worshiped all her life. "He promised me that as soon as it was over, we'd become formally engaged. Only think of it," she said excitedly, hugging her mother, "me and Michael married."

Under any other circumstances, the news would have delighted her parents. Michael Mallory was a good catch. Instead of warm congratulations, however, her parents exchanged worried looks.

Leslie lost some of her sparkle. "I thought you would be happy," she said in a puzzled voice.

"We are happy, child," her mother said slowly. "It's just that right now, things are a bit tense."

"Time enough to talk about weddings when Michael returns," her father said roughly, as he retired to the back of the store.

"I told you it was the wrong time to tell them," Luke joined in, taking the shiniest apple in the store and biting into it, as he made himself comfortable on a flour sack by the window. "Suppose Michael doesn't come back. Suppose he gets killed. Then you'd be without a beau."

Leslie's face turned white. Her blue eyes opened wide in horror. "It's not true. Michael will come back. He told me there was nothing to worry about. He said they'd teach the Indians a lesson they wouldn't forget in a hurry and that they'd be back before nightfall. Oh, Mama," Leslie said shakily, her eyes frightened, "you don't think Michael will be killed, do you?" It was obviously the first time such a horrifying thought had occurred to her.

Martha hastened to soothe her daughter's fears. "Of course he won't be killed. Everyone knows that the unfortunate Indians are unprepared for an attack. They won't have a chance to fight back."

"Are you sure?" Leslie asked hesitantly as the color slowly returned to her cheeks.

"Yes, I'm sure. It was very wrong of your brother to scare you like that." She frowned at Luke, who appeared to be absorbed with his apple. "But that doesn't give you any reason to rejoice," she added quickly in a voice loud enough to carry to the back room. "The poor Indians didn't do anything to us to warrant the attack. When our friends face their maker, they're going to have to answer for their crimes." She didn't add that she felt their father might have to share that fate, or that there was a possibility Michael Mallory would be killed in the ensuing battle.

There was one person in Sweetwater who would have tried to prevent the bloody massacre of the Indian villages by warning the soldiers in time. Unfortunately, Jim Carson, owner of the Sweetwater Saloon, had been purposely omitted from the town's confidence. He had left Sweetwater the day before, heading east to purchase a new piano, remaining oblivious of the heavy hand of fate that was rapidly closing about the throats of the townspeople of Sweetwater. Ordinarily Jim was not a man whose wits were slow to put two and two together. If he had not been preoccupied by waging a silent war with himself, he would not have remained blind to the increased tension and whispers in Sweetwater and might have altered its history.

Jim Carson, with jet-black hair, piercing gray-blue eyes, and a thick black mustache, dressed soberly for a professional gambler, except for his unlimited supply of imported patterned silk vests. His manners were exemplary. The only complaint the women of Sweetwater had against him was his habit of smoking three cigars a day. He was one of those rare individuals who are equally liked by both sexes. The men admired his unequaled marksmanship and were grateful for his openhanded generosity when their luck was bad. They also respected him for his refusal to back down in the thick of a heated argument, despite being vastly outnumbered. The women liked him for his charm, his graceful manners, his ability to laugh at himself, and his obvious good breeding. For the most part, they chose to ignore the fact that he also ran the only house of ill repute in Sweetwater. When he smiled at them, and inquired about their health, his soft voice, which retained the remnants of a Southern drawl, caused all resistance to melt. Even those women who were made of sterner stuff fought looking into the lazy eyes that studied them so carefully through half-closed lids. As though he had nothing to do with choosing his present occupation, the ladies often declared that he was meant for better things than being the owner of a saloon that served women as well as liquor.

Nothing could have been further from the truth. Five years previously, Jim had deliberately and with painstaking effort saved the money he earned from dozens of card games in hundreds of nameless towns and invested it in the Sweetwater Saloon. His house was honestly run, and while he reaped a nice profit from the sale of liquor, he was careful not to overcharge and cause his customers to abandon him for the Silver Dollar Saloon located at the edge of town. When he had offered his customers girls a year ago, he had not done so without grave misgivings. So far he had been lucky. The good women of Sweetwater hadn't kicked up too much dust about it, and their men flocked to his place in droves, causing the Silver Dollar to close down. Now the Sweetwater Saloon was the only saloon in town. He could afford to decorate it with tasteful pictures and a new piano that didn't sound like a death rattle. In another year, he might even be able to partition off the gambling area and install red velvet carpeting. He lit a cigar and leaned back in his seat, frowning, wondering why he felt depressed.

In Sweetwater, Jim Carson was known to have an

eye for the ladies and a heart of steel no woman could ever melt. His reputation did nothing to scare the women away. Their amazement and chagrin, however, would have been great if they had known that his apparent inability to fall in love was a result of his past. Once he had owned, not a saloon, but several fishing boats, and had been faithfully married to a woman whose smile had the power to make him weak even after two years of marriage. He was a different man then, a man who believed in the basic honesty and loyalty of his fellowmen, a man whose eyes had not yet begun to reflect the now perpetual smile of mockery brought on by treachery and despair. He had not been cynical about life, love, or friendship. That had all been before he came to Sweetwater, before his wife, Sally, her golden eyes overflowing with tears, told him she didn't love him anymore. The whole world came crashing down on him. He had held onto the headboard of their bed and asked in a stunned voice, "Why?" How could she not love him when he still loved her so much the possibility of her leaving him left him dizzy, the blood roaring in his ears. What had happened?

"I know I haven't been home much these last few weeks. But I've been working overtime for *you*. I wanted to buy you the things you should have. I didn't realize how lonely you must have been."

"No, please, Jim, it isn't that." Sally started sobbing, and he couldn't get any coherent answers from her. The next day, in desperation, he sought out his best friend for consolation and advice. Wade and he had been together a long time. They played cards together, drank together, and fought on the same side in brawls. They were like brothers. He could talk to Wade. Wade would understand how he felt. Maybe talking would help him to snap out of the numbness that had suddenly taken hold of him. Wade wasn't home. When Jim returned to his own home later that evening, after walking along the docks and staring at the silent black water until he felt exhausted, he found that his wife wasn't home either. Pinned to the big bed they had shared was a brief note from Sally telling him that she had left with Wade.

A cold rage replaced the numbness. He made up his mind to go after them. He would defend his honor by killing Wade. He immediately sold his boats, his house, and those private possessions he couldn't carry, and began tracking them down. It had been relatively easy, since the couple had no idea he was tracking them and so took no pains to hide. However, he always found himself just a little behind them. Along about the fourth town, Jim realized how ridiculous it was. If Sally and Wade wanted to be together, let them. His honor be damned! He had been blind. Now that he could see clearly again, he wasn't going to get himself killed or hung by following an antiquated code of honor. He wasn't fool enough to kill Wade, and then, if he remained free, drag an unwilling wife back to his bed. Not Jim Carson. He'd had no trouble finding a woman before he met Sally, and he'd had plenty of invitations sent out to him since. He'd let his adulterous wife and her lover fade into the sunset.

A cynical smile played about Jim's lips as he toasted the couple in the nearest saloon. At the same moment that Jim abandoned the chase and laughed at himself, he shut the door on any future close relationships. This did not include affairs he had with faceless bar girls, who eagerly shared his bed without asking for their usual fee. Nor did it refer to the occasional married woman who was bored or unhappy. Jim Carson wasn't through with lust, just love. He made it a practice never to make serious advances to any woman he knew to be a virgin. That was complicated as well as dangerous. All of Jim's women learned, to their bitter regret, that the one thing that caused him to suddenly turn cold as ice was a declaration of love. In any case, he never stayed in one town or with one woman long enough to give her encouragement.

When his money ran out, Jim didn't return to Louisiana. He wanted to forget all about that part of his life; he was a new man. He headed west, to the land of opportunities. For a while he worked on ranches as an extra hand. He soon found he wasn't cut out for that kind of work. Instead, he discovered a hidden talent that had lain dormant, and patiently developed it every spare moment he had. He had always considered himself fortunate where gambling was concerned, but he had never before seriously considered card playing as a career. The idea was slowly beginning to take shape, and the more he thought about it, the better it seemed. He sat in on card games in every dingy, dusty town he passed through, and almost always won. To some extent it was luck, but when, after hours of practice, he found his game to be vastly improved, Jim made up his mind he would make it his career. He would be a professional gambler. It was certainly preferable to back-breaking ranch work, where he was lucky to wind up with enough money at the end of the month to head for the next town. What really clinched it for him was that he enjoyed it. Other players sweated out a game, frightened of losing. Not Jim. He smiled when he won and smiled when he lost. The higher the stakes, the better. It was the thrill of not knowing when he sat down whether or not he would emerge triumphant or be ruined by the simple turn of a card that gave him his real satisfaction.

The life of a professional gambler was not without pitfalls, as Jim soon discovered. If a man was foolish enough not to know when to quit and lost too much, his anger turned on the winner, especially if the winner was a stranger he suspected of being a card sharp. He invariably accused him of cheating. If his friends backed him up, the gambler had to smile and hand over his winnings while he assured the enraged company that he hadn't cheated them.

If the gambler, however, also happened to possess expert knowledge in handling a gun, the situation was instantly altered. The angry man and his fellows were not so ready to challenge him when they knew they were in the wrong and might lose their life as a result. Discovering this to be the case early in his career, Jim rapidly developed his marksmanship, and another valuable asset, that of quickly and correctly assessing his fellow players' ability and personality.

For a while the life of a roving gambler appealed to Jim, but the idea of owning his own saloon began to take shape in his mind, and he started saving for his own establishment. That day arrived when he bought out the Sweetwater Saloon from its former owner, who had built it ten years back and wanted to return home to Chicago.

It had been nothing but a hole in the wall then, with a leaking roof and a dirt floor. He fixed the roof, put in a wooden floor, a mirror above the bar, and painted the place inside and out. Three years ago he had installed a roulette wheel. Last year the girls had arrived. He should have been ecstatic, pleased with himself and in a gregarious mood as he journeyed east to acquire his purchases.

"It's a lovely day," a middle-aged lady in a navy-blue cotton dress commented, hoping to capture the attention of the attractive gentleman sitting across from her, apparently fascinated by the floorboards of the jolting stagecoach.

"It's a bit too hot for my taste," her companion added loudly, mopping her perspiring face with a delicate white lace handkerchief. The two ladies waited expectantly for the man across from them to reply. Instead of making a polite comment or joining in their conversation, he remained silent and aloof. Suddenly he raised his eyes and scowled at them ferociously.

The two ladies turned pink with embarrassment and shifted uncomfortably in their seats as he continued to rudely stare at them without speaking. "Are you traveling far?" the first lady inquired timidly.

"Hell and be damned!" Jim muttered out loud as he threw the half-smoked cigar out the window, startling his fellow passengers and causing the second lady to remark in a scandalized tone of voice, "I beg your pardon!"

Jim failed to reply. His black brows drew together in a deep frown as he stared blankly at the two women across from him. He hadn't realized he had spoken out loud or that they had addressed him. In fact, he failed to see the women, although he stared straight at them. The two ladies shivered, exchanged frightened looks, and fell into an uneasy silence. They were convinced that if they had dared to address him again, they would have been physically assaulted, so menacing a countenance did he present to them. Neither of them would have guessed that this was far from characteristic, or that Jim himself was unaware of the unfavorable impression he was creating.

The cause of Jim's peculiar outburst and scowling appearance was that he had been thinking about the quiet, slim, chestnut-haired Charity Walker whom he had hired less than three months ago. He hadn't realized then that she would prove to be any different from the others. He carefully scrutinized her as he explained the rules when she came into his saloon.

"You'll get a small salary, plus room and board and a percentage of the drinks your customers order. Whatever else you make over that is strictly yours. There's to be no cheating the saloon, no fighting among the girls, and no stealing the customer's money when he's too tired or drunk to know what's going on. I run an honest house, and any disobeying the rules and you're out. There are no exceptions," he added coldly.

Charity stared back at him with a frozen face, a hard, calculating look he had seen on hundreds of women in her profession, and merely nodded. After he dismissed her, he wondered if he had made a mistake in hiring her. She was thin and much too quiet to suit his customers' general taste.

At first doubtful about her appeal, he soon discovered Charity possessed a quality that none of the other girls had. It was one that made her a distinct favorite with certain customers, especially the married ones. She was one of those rare individuals who really listened to other people's problems and then either gave her sympathy or offered various solutions that the other party had overlooked because he was too close to the situation. Those men who, after a drink or two, approached Charity with the idea of sleeping with her, ended up talking to her. In most cases, they came away greatly refreshed and with high praise for a girl so sensible and kindhearted. Jim had been amused and wondered how long it would be before she joined the others who slept with the customers, and was taken aback when she knocked on his door a few weeks after her arrival and inquired in a soft voice, "Is there an unwritten law that says I have to sleep with any man who wants me?"

"There's no law that says you have to go to bed with any man, unless you want to," Jim replied in surprise. "Why?"

"I've been approached and told I had to sleep with anyone who asks me. They said it went with the job. I wanted to find out if it was true, that's all."

"Would it have mattered?" Jim asked, raising one brow skeptically.

She met his gaze and without batting an eye replied, "No, it wouldn't. All the same, I like to feel I have freedom of choice."

Jim watched her as she closed the door quietly behind her, and found himself smiling. She had spirit, and he admired spirit in a woman. He made it a point to keep an eye on her after that to see what she had in mind. If she didn't sleep with the customers, she wasn't going to earn any extra money. He had an idea that this particular little bird, despite her soft voice and seemingly complacent manner, was one of the more ambitious ones. She wouldn't be satisfied with just enough cash to buy a new hat or dress. She was out to feather her nest with a nice large sum.

He soon discovered that his initial assessment was correct. Charity did indeed begin to bed down with some of the saloon's clientele. Unlike the other girls, she was particular. No run-of-the-mill dusty cowboy with a month's back pay and a good time on his mind. Her chosen few were the richest men in and around Sweetwater. Jim noticed that she didn't always end up sleeping with them, either. Even more interesting, the chosen ones treated her more like their own private mistress. They often bought her gifts—a bottle of French perfume or a pair of diamond earrings. They never seemed to take an interest in any of the other girls. Their loyalty intrigued Jim, and he began to pay flattering attention to Charity in order to win her over and see for himself what made her so different. It was about this time that the rest of the girls began to give him trouble.

"That bitch thinks she's God Almighty or the Queen of England, maybe," Lila muttered angrily one Monday afternoon at lunch, as she watched Charity open a newly arrived package from one of her preferred customers. The present turned out to be a long strand of pink pearls that shimmered in the dazzling afternoon light.

"Everyone knows why you're so upset, honey," Betty McAlister, one of the older women, said spitefully. "Until Charity arrived, you were it. Now you're just one of the regulars."

Several of the other girls laughed out loud. Lila wasn't very popular. She flushed to the roots of her flaxen hair, her blue eyes blazing. "You won't think it's so funny when Charity decides to take a fancy to one of your generous men friends."

"Her tits are too small." One of the other girls sniggered, her voice carrying across the room. Charity turned around slowly. Smiling, without saying a word, she slipped the pearls around her neck, twisting them twice. Putting on her new hat with the dyed green feathers, she left on her afternoon stroll.

Jim tried assuaging their wounded pride. He assured them Charity was only a passing phase. They continued to bicker and complain. Finally, in desperation, he threatened to fire them if they didn't stop picking fights with Charity and taunting her customers.

Eventually everything calmed down. The other girls gave Charity the cold shoulder and contented themselves with talking about her when her back was turned. Jim relaxed and invited Charity to dine with him in his private office. She accepted. He discovered she could be very pleasant company and could talk intelligently on a multitude of subjects. There was only one topic that she was reluctant to discuss—herself. This both puzzled and intrigued him. The women he had met had all been more than willing to talk about themselves at great length, emphasizing the wrongs done them in the past, their future dreams and ambitions, and usually ended up an evening by shedding a few tears over their lost childhood. Not Charity. When he asked her point-blank where she had grown up, she had disconcerted him by staring straight at him again, only this time her brown eyes were lit up by reddish sparks. They widened a little as she replied politely but firmly, "I don't wish to discuss it." He apologized and they spent the rest of the evening talking of other things.

Although Jim's original plan had been to wind up in bed with her, he changed his mind before the evening was half finished. He told himself it was because he wished to find out more about her. In the back of his mind, however, was the lurking suspicion that should he pursue such a course, she would ask him coolly if it went with the job. The thought that his advances would be unwelcome was something new for Jim Carson. Unlike some men, it did not anger him. It sparked his curiosity even more. He laughed at his original fear that she wouldn't be an asset to the business.

Charity Walker wasn't pretty; she was fascinating. He was going to find out more about her.

He set out to discover what Charity did in her spare time. The fact that she possessed a Bible surprised him, but not the fact that she ordered classics and read them too. She apparently received no correspondence other than books, and sent none. They began to have dinner in his office more and more frequently, and his earlier admiration of her grew.

One night, after several glasses of wine, she leaned back against her chair, her face flushed and her eyes soft. "I suppose everyone has a dream, something they'd like to do or be that they hold on to, no matter what."

"Everyone, young or old, has a dream. It keeps them going when things get to be too tough," Jim said slowly.

Charity smiled and nodded in agreement, her eyes beginning to sparkle like a good champagne. "I always wanted to earn enough money to travel and see other places."

"Europe, you mean?"

Charity sighed, her eyes far away. "Sure, I'd travel to Europe. I'd never stop traveling. It would suit me fine to be living out of a suitcase." She laughed.

Charity's open confession had started Jim to reminiscing. "I grew up in Louisiana. As a kid, I used to sit and watch the riverboats by the hour. I told myself that one day I'd have enough money to own one myself. It would be the biggest, the plushest, with gilt-edged mirrors on all the walls and the finest gambling and entertainment on board."

They both fell silent, lost in their own worlds, until suddenly the relaxed, open atmosphere between them began to be replaced by one of tension and embarrassment. Neither one had expected to reveal a secret part. After an uncomfortable amount of small talk, Charity excused herself and left. Occasionally she would mention an amusing incident out of her past, but with the exception of that one time, she remained basically aloof. Jim didn't press her, and he didn't make a pass at her, even though his attraction to her was rapidly developing. He noticed that she was beginning to warm to him too. When she stared at him, her eyes opened wide with the little reddish sparks dancing in their depths, and he saw the promise of true sensuality. It was the kind of sensuality born to few individuals and always visible to the opposite sex, no matter how unaware of it they themselves might be. He noticed, however, that Charity was well aware of it and kept her desires carefully under control. The closer she came to losing control, the more reserved and distant she became.

As Jim came to know her, the more obvious it was that she had been deeply hurt and kept submerged the natural fires that he felt must have once burned so strongly. There was an electricity growing between them that made for awkward silences. When they accidentally brushed against one another, they both drew back sharply and started talking nervously to cover their uneasiness.

Jim knew that should he make advances toward Charity now, she would not refuse him. The knowledge did not please him as it would have a month earlier. Jim was sensitive to other people's pain, and he saw that Charity had once suffered. He liked her and he didn't want to see her hurt again because of him. He wasn't a one-woman man, not anymore. He was afraid of disappointing her. That was the reason he gave himself for avoiding her the week before he left. That wasn't, however, the entire truth.

He had, within the past couple of weeks, been possessed by a tremendous urge to confide in Charity about his experience with Sally. It threw him into a panic. Should Charity let down her guard and confide in him as he felt she was on the verge of doing, it would indicate she not only trusted him, but was falling in love with him. That knowledge disturbed him, but not nearly as much as the thought that her situation also applied to him. Even worse, he was beginning to feel jealous whenever Charity went upstairs with one of her customers. Why should he care what she did? They were only friends. She was, despite her manners and education, still what his mother would have termed a painted woman. Jim was basically honest and couldn't continue to lie to himself. It was obvious he was becoming much too fond of Charity and she of him. He had made a mistake in cultivating her friendship. He should have left her alone, let her continue to be just one of the girls. He frowned. Now it was too late. Should he risk continuing with the relationship and let the cards fall where they may? If not, he might have to give her a month's pay and dismiss her. He couldn't continue avoiding her. He had almost gone out of his mind in that one week before he left. What bothered him most of all was that he had lost his sex drive where any of the other girls were concerned. They left him cold. Every time he looked at one of them, he saw Charity's brown eyes with the reddish flecks staring back at him. What the hell was he going to do?

Jim could not have known, as he debated with himself over what action he should take regarding Charity Walker, that outside influences would decide the matter for him. He would also have been surprised to learn that Charity's thoughts were very much in tune with his own. She, too, had remained oblivious of the events taking place in Sweetwater until that day. Torn between remaining in Sweetwater and succumb-

ing to feelings and desires she thought had died long
ago, she considered running away from the situation
by leaving town. In one way she hated Jim Carson for
reawakening her and exposing her so that she was vul-
nerable again. On the other hand . . . Charity allowed
her face to soften and was unaware she looked years
younger.

The disconcerting sound of Mayor Gady snoring
contentedly next to her brought Charity back to the
unpleasant reality of the moment. The mask of
hardness she had worn for so long reappeared. It
wouldn't work, nothing ever had. Not for her. The
week before Jim left, they had started to draw apart,
each one wary of the other, constantly on their guard.
She didn't think he cared if she slept with his customers or not, even though she found it increasingly
difficult. Mayor Gady's snoring became louder, and
Charity forced herself to look at him.

The Right Honorable Mayor Gady of Sweetwater
was rich and considered attractive by the majority of
women in town. Because he was also generous with
his money, he was a favorite with the girls at the
Sweetwater Saloon. In the past, Charity had not found
sleeping with him at all hard to take. Last night, the
only way she could stomach having sex with him was
to close her eyes and pretend he was Jim. It wasn't
that she needed the money, or even that she was
lonely for company with Jim away. She had gone to
bed with Mayor Gady to prove to herself Jim didn't
mean a damn thing to her. It had been a big mistake.
Mayor Gady wasn't Jim, she thought in disgust, as she
watched him breathe heavily. His skin was pale, so
smooth it felt like a baby's. He was getting flabby too,
especially around the middle. Jim didn't look like he
had an ounce of fat on him. Charity felt sure Jim
would be wonderful in bed. She crossed her legs as a
feeling of warmth spread between her thighs at the
thought of Jim's nude body. "Hell!" she muttered as

she climbed out of bed and reached for her silk robe. "What am I going to do?" She noted wryly that no illuminating reply appeared to be forthcoming.

"What's that, what'd you say?" Mayor Gady mumbled in a sleepy voice as he stretched and yawned.

"Nothing!" Charity mumbled as she brushed her hair. "Go back to sleep."

"That's impossible, honey. Once Arnold Gady is awake, he can't go back to sleep again. I thought," he added with a smile as he got out of bed and came over to her, fondling her breasts with his small hands, "we might linger in bed awhile longer."

Charity held her breath to keep from gagging as the smell of stale liquor assailed her nostrils. "Are the rumors true, Arnie?" she asked coldly, ignoring his attempts to rouse her.

"What's that?" Arnie murmured as his hands moved to the inside of her thighs.

"Is there going to be an Indian massacre?" she asked as she roughly pulled away from his embrace and walked over to the window.

"Oh, that," Arnie said with an air of dismissal. "Why talk of Indians? In fact, why talk at all?" he demanded, chuckling as he made another move toward her, his intentions obvious by the bulge in his nightshirt.

Charity turned away to keep from laughing. He looked ridiculous, wearing a nightshirt during one of the hottest spells they'd had in years. Winter or summer, he wore his stupid nightshirt to bed, regardless of whether he was having sex or not. "I was surprised," she said, once she had regained her composure, "that Sheriff Davis hasn't taken any noticeable action. Isn't that his job, keeping the peace?" she asked, knowing her talking, rather than submitting to his pawing, irritated him and that if she kept it up, he would shortly leave her alone.

"There's nothing to be surprised about," he said, frowning. "Andy Davis wants to run against me in the elections this year. He knows damn well it's the majority of votes that count. Besides, he has no love for the Indians. They killed his brother and his wife."

"Anybody who sides with the Indians in this town has got to be crazy," Charity continued, deliberately keeping her gaze fixed on the street below.

"I guess I'd better be getting along," Arnie said angrily. When Charity failed to protest, or even to turn around, he dressed more quickly than usual and intentionally slammed the door to let her know he was displeased. The other girls told him she was getting mighty uppity lately. He hadn't believed them. She had always seemed even-tempered. That was what he liked about her. Charity never seemed to have tantrums or moods. But it wasn't *that* time of the month. So the only answer was that the girls were right. She was getting too much above herself. If she didn't want him to make love to her anymore, that was her loss. It would be a month of Sundays before he picked her again. It was another scorcher, and Mayor Gady was in a foul humor. On his way out, one of the other doors opened and Julie stepped out into the hall, clad only in a loose-fitting robe, which she hastened to open wider, revealing a voluptuous pink-and-white body underneath.

"Surely you're not leaving without paying Julie a little visit?" she inquired in a soft, languid voice.

Julie was the newest member of the establishment, and from what Arnie could see, she was better-looking than the others, a lot better-looking than Charity. He had never been with Julie before. It was still early. He didn't have anywhere to go. What the hell! Why let a whore spoil his day?

Charity smiled when she heard the door slam, but didn't bother to turn around. The mayor was a good customer, and she knew she shouldn't have made him mad by wounding his ego. Charity wasn't really worried; he would come back. Right now, she didn't care if she ever saw him again.

Her interest in the attack on the Indian villages had
had been merely a ploy to get rid of the mayor. She
had heard men talking about wiping out the Indians
ever since she first arrived in Sweetwater, but never
dreamed it would amount to anything more than talk.
Now that the attack was under way, Charity was the
only one who had any doubts about the outcome. She
knew the Indians were unprepared for the onslaught.
But as she stared out at the deserted street below, she
felt an icy chill run down the length of her back, and
pulled away from the window shivering. Something
was going to go wrong.

Elizabeth Farrell, wife of Lieutenant Farrell, the
commander of nearby Fort Jubele, stepped down
from a buckboard driven by one of her husband's soldiers. The sergeant drove off. He had business elsewhere. However, he assured her he would be back in
time to return her to the fort that evening.
As he drove away from Sweetwater, Sergeant
Jared thought to himself once again that the lieutenant's wife was a fine-looking woman. He judged
her to be about twenty-two. Her shiny black hair was
always neatly parted in the middle and dressed into
two thick coils in the back. She had a friendly smile
and a waist so tiny a man could put his hands around
it and they'd meet. He did feel she dressed a bit drab-
ly, seeming to prefer the more somber hues. She had
beautiful, graceful hands though, a straight nose, and
clear, evenly spaced dark eyes with thick lashes. He
sighed. She always smelled of lavender water. As far
as Sergeant Jared was concerned, she had only one
serious fault. She was too religious.
Elizabeth had come to town to buy wool and some
black velvet ribbon she needed to finish trimming a
dress she was making for the Saturday-night dance at
the fort. The unnatural stillness hung over the town
like a pall, and the absence of men did not escape her
notice. As Elizabeth paid for her purchases in Tilby's

General Store, she put the puzzling question to Mrs. Tilby.

"I couldn't help but notice that the town seems unusually quiet and rather depressing for a Monday. It's almost like it's in mourning," she said jokingly. "Good heavens, I certainly hope that isn't the case," she added quickly, as Mrs. Tilby flushed and exchanged looks with her husband.

"No one's died . . . yet, as far as I know," Martha Tilby replied sharply.

Elizabeth thought the answer odd, to say the least, and noticed that Frank Tilby looked more and more uneasy. Her curiosity was piqued, and she turned to the only other customer in the store. "What is all the mystery about, Mrs. Gady?" she asked, addressing the mayor's wife. She knew Mrs. Gady's favorite pastime was indulging in harmless gossip with her friends, and felt sure she would fill her in. To her amazement, Mrs. Gady seemed equally reluctant to discuss the matter and exhibited unmistakable signs of a guilty conscience.

"I . . . I'm sure I . . . that is . . ." Mrs. Gady stammered. "It's so awkward."

Elizabeth's straight black brows rose slightly. "It is?"

"I had no idea myself until only a few hours ago. Arnold too," she added quickly, referring to her husband. "We were so terribly shocked by the news that we . . . we didn't know quite what to do. I mean . . ." she said, flustered by the puzzled look on Elizabeth's face. "It was all so sudden, and by now it must be all over, mustn't it?"

"I wouldn't know," Elizabeth said patiently. "What exactly is it that happened so suddenly and is almost over?"

"I . . . I . . ." Mrs. Gady shot a desperate look at the Tilbys.

Martha Tilby rose to the occasion, even though it was plain to Elizabeth that she had no desire to do so.

"What Mrs. Gady means is that it is an awkward situation because your husband is in charge of Fort Jubele."

Elizabeth frowned. "I'm afraid I still don't understand what you are talking about."

"It's the Indians," Frank Tilby put in so loudly and so suddenly that the women jumped.

"But they couldn't have broken the peace," Elizabeth said slowly. "My husband visited with their chief, White Mountain, only last week, and there was no sign of trouble."

"It's not the Indians who broke the peace this time," Martha Tilby said bitterly. "We're the ones at fault. The men left this morning to attack the two camps. They should be back soon. That is," she muttered, "the ones who haven't been killed."

"We felt it was the only thing we could do under the circumstances. A vote was taken, and it was approved unanimously," Frank Tilby said resentfully.

Martha Tilby, who had not heard this piece of information, turned to face her husband. "Unanimously?" she inquired in an accusing tone.

Frank Tilby's face twitched as another spasm of pain shot through his stomach. "We can never be sure of peace so long as we're surrounded by Cheyenne."

"Frank Tilby!" Martha expostulated in a stunned voice.

Elizabeth remained silent during the Tilbys' exchange. Long in the habit of obeying rules and regulations, she was amazed at such flagrant disobedience, especially on such a serious matter. Finally she managed to say, "If you were worried about the Indians attacking, you ought to have met with my husband and discussed it."

"It wouldn't have done any good," Frank Tilby muttered unhappily.

"Do you think our town will be put under martial law?" Mrs. Gady inquired timidly.

"I'm sure it will. My husband will be terribly angry

when he hears what you've done," Elizabeth admitted frankly. For that matter, she was angry too. By attacking the Indians without just cause, they had deliberately invited retaliation and had set back all the good work done on behalf of peace. The last four years were going to be washed away by a few hours of hysterical lawlessness. Everyone would live in fear again. No outlying ranch would be safe from attack. All the time and trouble Peter had taken to achieve and preserve peace would have been for nothing. It was dreadful. Since there was nothing she personally could do about it at the moment, she coldly excused herself and retired to the church, located at the edge of town, to pray.

She had gotten into the habit of praying a good deal lately. The women of Sweetwater and those at the fort praised her for her piousness. Elizabeth knew this and was embarrassed. She felt that if they were aware of the nature of her prayers, they would be shocked. She had always been a religious girl, reared in a good Christian home, and knew her Bible well enough to quote from it. Never before had she taken to spending so much time at prayer as she had this past year. She knelt on the hard floor, folded her long, slender hands together, and closed her eyes, breathing deeply. She wondered for the hundredth time if she was committing a sin by fervently praying to get pregnant. Elizabeth knew that wanting a child was not a sin, but the reason behind it was purely selfish. She desperately wanted a baby so that her husband would leave her alone.

Elizabeth had come to hate Thursdays. That was the night Peter picked to have sex with her. She dreaded his reaching out for her in the dark; the grunts of animal pleasure she did not feel left her sick to her stomach. She always ended up with a pounding headache. Lately she even recoiled from his morning peck on the cheek. Fortunately Peter was understanding about how she felt and promised her he would leave her alone once she presented him with a son.

It had been over a year since she had joined him at his post. A year of Thursdays, and still no baby. She wondered how much longer she could take it before she became hysterical and refused to let him near her. Elizabeth knew that was sinful. A husband had his rights. She was well aware that many women envied her. Peter was attractive in a clean-cut boyish way. He was always the perfect gentleman and extremely ambitious. She knew that one day he would be a general. None of his attributes seemed to make up for Thursday nights. What if she was barren and couldn't have his children? The sweat stood out on her forehead as this recent fear began to gnaw at her. Suppose she had to endure another five or ten years of Thursdays?

Elizabeth need not have worried. An alteration in her situation would shortly take place, but not one she would have willingly chosen for herself. Strangely enough, not even one she would prefer to Thursday nights.

Lorrie Gomber relaxed as she peeled potatoes for the evening meal. It was good to be alone, even for a little while. When she was alone, she didn't mind doing chores. As soon as her father came back, he would be starving and expect a complete dinner to be on the table. She paused to wipe the sweat from her face. When it was this hot, she lost her appetite, and if it was up to her, she wouldn't cook such a heavy meal. But her father would be hungry.

As she dumped the peeled potatoes into a pan of cold water and put the pan on the black iron stove so the potatoes could cook, she let her imagination stray. Imagination was one thing her father couldn't take away from her. He could punish her as much as he liked, but he couldn't make her stop dreaming. Lorrie dreamed of many things. She pictured how she'd look

...nd-new dress, not one of the shapeless ones
...ther forced her to wear. She could sew real
...l, and as she stared at herself in the cracked mirror
above the sink, she thought she might have looked
half decent, if her father hadn't insisted she make all
her clothes a size too big for her. He said she would
grow into them. Lorrie knew better. She was twelve
and big for her age. Her father was afraid some boy
would come along and take her away with him. She
sighed and wished that would happen. She'd go off
with any boy who asked her, just so she could escape
from her father. Lorrie frowned. Knowing her father,
he'd probably come after them, kill the boy, and drag
her back with him to cook and clean and suffer his
abuses.

She had once confessed to the minister in Sweetwater how she really felt about her father. "I hate
him. I always hated him and I always will."

The minister was shocked. "Nonsense, Lorrie. You
are naturally upset by his rough treatment of you," he
added gently, "as anyone would be. But he is your father."

"I don't care. I didn't ask to be born to him," Lorrie countered stubbornly.

"It's a sin to hate one's parents," the reverend ad-
monished her in a stern voice. "You have to learn to
forgive him. Jesus turned the other cheek. You should
take a lesson from the Master. He forgave everyone.
You, too, must learn to forgive."

"I'll try," Lorrie had replied reluctantly. She didn't
think she ever could, not if she lived to be a hundred
and eighty.

When she was younger and her mother was home,
it hadn't been nearly so bad. Her parents had argued
all the time and her father ended up beating her
mother as he now beat Lorrie. Her mother had run
off with that trapper man who was passing through
town. She didn't blame her mother for running off
with another man. Lorrie only wished her mother had

taken her. She looked at herself once again in the cracked mirror and smiled. She was getting to look more and more like her mother every day. Her hair was not as fair as her mother's. But her eyes were blue, just like her mother's, and the lashes dark. A few freckles dotted the top of her nose and cheeks. She wore her hair in braids because her father wanted it that way, and Lorrie didn't wish to anger him by dressing it differently. One day she would pile her hair up high on her head, just like her mother had worn it. She would be grown-up then, and she knew she would be pretty. Lorrie turned away from the mirror and poured herself a glass of milk. Maybe one day when she was free she would try to find her mother. She hoped her mother was happy.

A fluttering noise at the window startled Lorrie out of her daydreaming. She turned pale and jumped, spilling some of the milk onto the floor. When she opened the door, a startled robin flew away. For a minute she had thought it was her father returning home early. It wouldn't do not to have dinner ready. She began busying herself with the rest of the meal. If all went well, if her father had been able to kill a lot of Indians and the meal was to his liking, she knew he would in all likelihood fall asleep. That would mean she would be free for the rest of the evening.

If she was brave, she could take the opportunity to run away. He wouldn't wake up until tomorrow morning. By that time, she could be far away from Sweetwater. She had found some money her mother had saved hidden underneath the mattress, and she had never told her father about it. If he found out, he would beat her real bad, like that last time when she lost consciousness. Sadly, Lorrie realized she wasn't brave enough to run away alone, even though she had the money. It wasn't a great deal of money, she told herself consolingly. It would probably only take her through the next couple of towns. What would she do when she ran out of money? She was too young to work without someone becoming suspicious. She'd be sent back. Lorrie feared her father more than she hated him. She shuddered, thinking about his thick, hairy, ugly hands. When her father's hands balled into fists and started hitting her, Lorrie would do anything to get him to stop. That last time, he'd picked up a stick and beat her so badly other people had heard her muffled screams and interfered. That was when Judge Williamson had asked her if she wanted to stay with her father. She would have admitted the truth, admitted she would rather live with anyone else in the whole world, if her father hadn't told her about the rats.

"See that you keep your mouth shut tomorrow," he had said. "If you don't watch out, you'll get taken from me and sent to one of those workhouses. They'll beat you all the time, not just when you're bad. Worst of all"—he paused, smiling maliciously—"the place you get sent to will be filled with large, fat, hungry rats."

Lorrie still trembled whenever she recalled that conversation. It was the thought that her father might be right that decided Lorrie against admitting the truth. She suspected he was lying, only she didn't want to test him out. Lorrie didn't even like mice. Rats with their beady little eyes and long pink tails terrified her. She had once seen a pack of rats descend on a wounded bird and devour it. Some people said rats didn't eat meat. She had seen different with her own eyes. She even preferred living with her father over rats.

The four hundred men paused at the halfway point between the two camps of Cheyenne. Here they would separate. Half would attack one camp of Indians under the leadership of Joseph Mallory. The other half would attack the other camp at the same time, led by Ben Haskell. They agreed to meet back at the same spot when it was all over. No males over the age of ten would be spared, and the villages would be burned to the ground. They wished each other luck and rode off, confident of success and secure in the knowledge that God was on their side.

Several hours later they returned to the same spot. Both sides had lost a total of only eight men. Another twenty were wounded. They had burned the villages to the ground and covered their hands with the blood of their victims. Many of those that had prided themselves on the righteousness of their mission had stooped to unbelievable acts of barbarism. Men who were noted for their kindness became worse than animals as the screams of the helpless pounded in their ears. They tore out the hearts of women and children, sparing none that got in their way. There were, however, a few whose souls had been sickened by what they witnessed, who tried to stop the slaughter. It was impossible to turn back the tide. It continued on unabated, until they were left alone with the dead bodies and the charred ashes of what had only a few hours ago been a living, thriving community. It would appear that they had been successful. The handful of women and children that had escaped had dispersed into the hills and hidden trembling under the bushes and trees. Oddly enough, not one man among the victors uttered a word of congratulations.

From the east, a hot wind was beginning to blow. It carried the scent of death through the air, alerting the vultures to their prey. The men were silent, displaying signs of nervousness. On each man's face fear was clearly written, as though it had been branded on his forehead.

"Were the braves in your camp, Ben?" Joseph Mallory asked gruffly in a voice that plainly stated he already knew what the answer would be.

Ben Haskell frowned and shook his head. "No, Joe. I questioned one of the squaws and she said the men had gone off with White Mountain's braves."

The two old friends stared at one another in heavy silence. They didn't have to say another word. Each knew that when the braves returned from their hunting trip and discovered their women and children had been massacred, they would seek revenge.

"We could lie in wait for them," Ben offered half-heartedly.

"No good," Joseph Mallory said, sighing. "You know as well as I do that as soon as they catch sight of the smoke from their burning villages, they'll ride home expecting a trap. Besides, there's nowhere to hide, and our men are exhausted and wounded." He took a deep breath. "We'd better warn our families and bring them into town. It'll be safer than the ranches."

Ben nodded in agreement, and the group split up once again. This time, those men who owned ranches and had families waiting for them headed home to bring them to the town for safety. The rest went straight to Sweetwater with the disturbing news.

As Ben Haskell came in sight of his house, he saw that his wife, Sara, was waiting for him on the porch. She was still wearing the blue cotton dress she had worn that morning when he left. A few strands of her wispy butter-gold hair had worked loose and were blowing in the hot breeze. He knew her light brown eyes would reflect the worry and concern she felt for his safety. For once the knowledge that his young and pretty wife loved him and was worried about him did not cause a surge of warmth and pride to course through him as it usually did. He let his gaze wander over his property. He had some of the best grazing land in Minnesota and a nice, fat herd of cattle. His land stretched on farther than the eye could see, and it included good timberland too. He had maple trees and a stream that ran the length of his property. If things had worked out as he planned it, he'd have had a lot more. One day, his yet-to-be-born sons would inherit a vast cattle empire. Things hadn't worked out, he reminded himself bitterly as he pulled up in front of the house. He would be damn lucky if his house remained intact. He knew it was too much to hope for that any of his cattle would be spared. At least his wife would be safe.

"Ben, are you badly hurt?" Sara asked, turning pale as she caught sight of his bloodstained shirt and pants.

"I escaped with only a few scratches, nothing serious. What you see is their blood," he said grimly. As he dismounted he added, "You were right, Sara. We shouldn't have gone, leastwise not today," he said dryly.

"Oh, Ben, I knew something had gone wrong," she confessed nervously. "I couldn't concentrate on anything today. I even burned the chicken we were having for dinner."

Ben smiled. "Don't worry about that. We'll have something to eat in town. I need a fresh set of clothes, and you'd better pack some essentials. We're staying in town."

"Why, what happened?" Sara asked, turning pale again.

"Luck wasn't with us. The braves went on a hunt. Both camps. Only the squaws, old men, and children were left."

"Ben, you didn't kill them?" Sara whispered, horrified, as she followed him into the kitchen.

Ben frowned as he washed the blood off his face and hands. "We didn't know until it was too late. We must have wiped out three-quarters of them," he said slowly. "Not a single brave among them."

"Oh, Ben, no," Sara said, shocked. "Not the women and children!"

Ben dried his face and looked at his wife. In his eyes was an expression Sara found hard to interpret. It disturbed her even more than his words. "I can't describe to you what went on today. It was like noth-

ing I've ever experienced. All that blood." His voice
sounded weak to his own ears. "Men you thought you
knew, acting like wild animals. It turned my stomach."

"If the braves weren't there," Sara said suddenly,
the import of his words beginning to dawn on her,
"then that means the men . . . the men . . ." She
stammered, unable to finish.

"That's right," Ben agreed softly. "They'll be coming back to view the carnage, and we'll be involved in
another war with the Cheyenne." Seeing the terror
depicted in his wife's eyes, he hastened to reassure her.
"We may lose our cattle and even the house. But you
needn't fear for your life. We'll be safe enough in
town, once the soldiers are sent for."

"You mean they haven't been notified yet?" Sara
asked incredulously, her heart pounding in her ribs.
"The Indians could attack at any time. In fact, they
might be on their way to murder us right now," she
said, her voice rising.

Ben quickly disagreed with her as he put on a fresh-
ly laundered shirt. "We should have sent someone
for the soldiers right after the attack. I agree with you
there. But we were all upset, and a lot of the men
have wives and kids waiting on outlying ranches.
They have to be brought to town. The wounded had
to be taken care of, and the rest of us were exhausted,
as were our horses. None of the horses could make
the long trip to the fort in the condition they were in.
You have nothing to worry about," he added as he re-
loaded his shotgun. "Joe Mallory said he would send
one of his boys to the fort to alert the soldiers. In any
case, the Indians won't attack before dawn. They
won't fight in the dark. They're afraid of ghosts, and
the soldiers should be in Sweetwater long before
morning."

Sara didn't look relieved. She was recalling all the
old horror stories she had heard about the Indians and

how they tortured their prisoners before they killed them. She touched her husband on the arm. "We will be safe in town, won't we, Ben?"

He smiled and hugged her to him. "Sure we will, honey, everything's going to be fine."

Feeling his strength and hearing his assurances, she relaxed. "There's something I've got to tell you, Ben," Sara whispered against his chest. "I was going to do it last night, but you were so busy, and what with everything happening today, I forgot about it."

"What is it?" Ben asked curiously, knowing it must be important for her to be bringing it up now. She wasn't one to chatter about trivialities at a time like this.

"I know it will be hard on us if the Indians destroy our cattle and the house. We'll have to start all over again." She hesitated. "I was just wondering if you'll still be as happy over having a baby as before."

Ben looked down at his wife's anxious face, and there was no mistaking his feelings. "You know I will. Sara, are you pregnant?"

She smiled shyly. "I suspected for a while now, but I wanted to make sure before I told you. The doctor confirmed my suspicions the day before yesterday."

Ben caught her to him and kissed her. "You thought I might be upset?" He laughed, his eyes glowing with pride. "I've wanted a son more than anything else in the world. Not even the Sioux teaming up with the whole Cheyenne nation could make me unhappy about it. Sara, this will only be the first one," he said excitedly. "We'll have lots more, a whole dynasty of Haskells."

"What happens if they're all girls?" Sara laughed.

"They won't be, Sara. I feel it in my bones. They'll be boys, every one."

Sara had her doubts, but she didn't say so. She was glad to see him so happy. As she rode beside him in the wagon, listening to him rattle off various names for their unborn son, she was suddenly filled with a deep and piercing sadness she couldn't define. Ben's voice became faint. His words sounded monotonous and were in fact almost indecipherable to her ears. Perhaps it was the sun blazing down on her uncovered head, but for a moment she experienced the strangest sensation, as though she were slowly drifting, slipping away from reality. She felt lightheaded, and nothing seemed particularly important. She experienced a sense of well-being that bordered on euphoria. Fear immediately began to follow on the heels of the euphoria. It slowly tightened around her neck like a hangman's noose, making it difficult to breathe. When they reached the edge of their property, Sara turned and looked back toward the house. The top of it was still visible through the trees, and the blood began to roar in her ears. Panic gripped her, and she felt dizzy. She knew this was the last time she would ever see her house again. She was going to die!

"Ben, I'm frightened," she whispered, trembling, interrupting her husband's discourse on how he was going to teach his son to ride as soon as he could walk.

He patted her cold hand. "Trust me, Sara. There's nothing to worry about. The soldiers will take care of any Indians looking for trouble. You'll be safe in town." For the first time, Sara Haskell wasn't comforted by her husband's words.

Several miles away, Katie Mallory was trying to restrain an impulse to slap her sister-in-law across the face. "You must know where John and the others went, Nora. He tells you everything."

"I'm not saying I don't know where they went," Nora Mallory conceded reluctantly, "but John said specifically not to tell you or Sean. He said you'd find out when they got back."

"You guessed right, Katie," Sean said, frowning. "It looks like they decided to raid the Indian villages.

They didn't want us to know beforehand because they knew we'd argue with them and try to prevent their going."

"Is that true, Nora?" Katie demanded, her face flushed and her green eyes beginning to narrow.

Nora knew that Katie was fast losing her patience, and she wished her husband would return. She was aware that her husband's only sister had a temper that fully matched the reputation of people with red hair. At those times she was not to be crossed. In a few more minutes Katie would be in an ugly mood. There was no telling what she would do. Nora had once seen Katie throw a plate across the room. On several other occasions she had heard her use language Nora had not dreamed any lady knew. She supposed John was right when he said that his sister was spoiled because she was the only girl and used to getting her way. But when Katie wasn't in a temper, she was kind and always considerate, especially now that Nora was in such a delicate condition. She felt herself getting queasy again, and swallowed twice. "I suppose there would be no harm in admitting what you already know," she said slowly. "They ought to be back at any time."

"Well, I don't wonder that they didn't tell us, Sean," Katie said furiously. "What I can't understand is why Michael and Timothy went with them."

"You know how Michael is," Sean said dryly, "always up for adventure."

"Is that what you call it," Katie shouted, causing Nora to flinch, "butchering a bunch of unsuspecting Indians, an adventure!"

"Calm down, Kate," Sean advised, catching sight of Nora's pale face, "or you'll have Nora fainting on us. It's not what I call it, and I doubt very much of it's what Michael will call it when he returns. He just had to go and see for himself. He's like that. One of these days he'll jump off a cliff just to see if the ride down is exciting."

"I shouldn't be at all surprised," Katie admitted in a voice that was considerably less volatile. "I must say, I pity poor Leslie Tilby if she marries him. I only hope she doesn't turn out to be as poor-spirited as . . ." She blushed and caught herself in time.

Her sister-in-law understood her meaning. Nora did not feel angry. She did, however, feel she ought to say something to fill in the sudden embarrassed silence. "I know you think me poor-spirited because I don't argue with John," she said quietly, "but I believe that a man knows more about life than a woman, so it's only right she ought to defer to him. John acts for both of us, and believe me, Katie, I don't resent it."

Katie knew this was true, and it annoyed her all the more. "It isn't natural to always agree to everything he says, when his belief is contrary to yours. You used to love dancing until John insisted you stop, even though the church approves of it. The way he orders you about is disgusting," she continued, warming to her topic. "He tells you what you can wear and what friends you can have. I'm surprised he doesn't tell you what you can think."

Nora looked uncomfortable. "John is perhaps a trifle rigid," she allowed. "But you have to admit, Katie, he follows the same course he sets for me. John does try always to do what is right."

"I suppose going on that raid was doing what he thought was right?" Katie countered coldly.

"He did seem to think so," Nora agreed weakly, avoiding Katie's eyes.

"Timothy probably joined up to please Dad," Sean put in quickly, adroitly drawing the fire away from the cowering Nora.

Katie shifted her attention back to him and frowned. "Knowing Timothy, he'll get sick or faint and make Father dislike him all the more. Poor Tim!" she said, softening. "He never does anything right."

"I think they're returning," Sean said, peering through the window at a cloud of dust. "Unless it's a mirage, which it could be in this weather. I thought I saw a rabbit the other day. When I blinked my eyes, it was gone."

Katie was the first to run outside. "It does look like Father up front," she admitted. "And John, too. But I don't see the others," she added nervously.

"Michael is in back of John, with Timothy on the left. They're all right," Sean assured her, obviously relieved himself.

The closer they got, the more evident it became that something was seriously amiss. Their torn and bloodied garments all bore testimony to the day's activities. However, the words of rebuke and the scathing speech Katie had prepared died on her lips once she caught sight of their faces. Even Joseph Mallory looked frightened.

"Pack some clothes, Katie. Bring us fresh horses and the wagon, Sean. We're going into town," Mallory said roughly as he dismounted.

"The braves went on a hunt," Michael said in a dazed voice as he staggered toward them.

"There was only old men, women, and children," Timothy whispered thickly as he walked past his sister, his face ashen and his body shaking as though he was in the throes of a fever.

"It was terrible, Kate," Michael said, staring at her with eyes that had witnessed scenes he would never forget. "The smell of burning flesh was . . . everywhere." His voice cracked and he fled past her into the house, where she could hear him retching.

"If the braves weren't there," Nora said slowly, addressing her husband, "then they'll be coming back. Once they find out what you've done . . ." Her voice trailed off.

"That's why we're going into town, isn't it, John?" Katie said quietly. "For protection."

John winced as he dismounted. He was the only one who had been wounded. "Father's going to send someone to alert the soldiers," he muttered through clenched teeth as he held up his left arm to stop the bleeding.

"John, you're hurt bad," Nora said in alarm as she went to him.

"It's not as serious as it looks," John said faintly. "But I've lost a lot of blood," he admitted as he staggered inside, Nora half supporting him.

By the time Sean returned with the horses and the wagon, everyone was assembled on the front porch. Timothy was still trembling, only less violently. The dazed look was gone from his eyes. Michael was pale but apparently recovered. John's shoulder was bandaged and hung in a sling made from a cut-up sheet. His father ordered him to ride in the wagon with his wife and sister. Katie thought John must be worse than he looked, because he didn't protest.

"Michael," his father said, frowning, "how do you feel?"

"I'm all right," he said, flushing at the memory of his previous weakness.

"Good. Because I want you to ride to Fort Jubele with the news. Tell Lieutenant Farrell what happened and that all the ranchers have brought their families into town for protection. Tell him to send as many soldiers as he can spare, and as soon as possible. You'd better ride fast, and don't stop to rest."

"I could go, Father," Sean put in. "Michael's tired, and I'm as good a rider as he is."

His father hesitated, then shook his head. "Michael knows the terrain better than you do, and he's a more accurate shot," he added grimly after a slight pause. Handing Michael both a rifle and a pistol, he said, "They're fully loaded and I included an extra package of cartridges." He hesitated. "Take care of yourself, boy. Don't take any unnecessary risks. Hear me?"

"Yes, sir," Michael replied soberly.

As the Mallorys watched Michael ride away, there wasn't one among them that didn't harbor the suspicion he might be killed.

2

Red Turtle felt his heart tighten in his chest. He knew something disastrous had happened long before he spotted the greedy vultures on the way to their gory feast. Before the black clouds of smoke were sighted or the smell of burning flesh reached their nostrils, he knew what had been revealed to him in a dream that morning had come to pass.

The dream had caused him to awake with a start. His stocky broad body had been covered with sweat as he lay in the darkness trying to control the trembling. In his dream his village had been destroyed, his two younger wives had been killed and mutilated. His two young sons had met the same fate. Only Bright Eyes, his eldest wife, had survived the slaughter. Feeling uneasy, he rose and softly walked over to where his sons lay, listening for their even breathing. When he had satisfied himself that they were sleeping peacefully, he returned to his place in the lodge. Nearby he heard his youngest wife tossing restlessly in her sleep. His face softened as he stared down at White Dove. She was his favorite. She was a handsome girl and had been much sought after before he married her. She had the modesty and shyness that characterized a Cheyenne maiden. Her father was a man of considerable importance in the tribe, rich in horses. Her uncle was the leader of the Wohksehhetaniu, or Fox Soliders, who made up one of the influential soldier bands that acted as police forces for the tribe and helped to carry out the orders of the chiefs. White Dove had many admirers. He had not believed she would accept his suit, and tried to hide his unhappiness. Although he was a proven warrior, who had exceeded even her father in wealth of horses and counting of coup, he had seen many winters, while she was young. Her skin was smooth, her figure slender as the willow tree, and her movements graceful as a young doe's. Many of her other suitors were young, with strong, sleek bodies that glistened in the firelight, whose muscles were taut and firm, whose faces were not lined with age. Red Turtle had felt that there was little hope for success. He had tried not to think of White Dove's laughing dark eyes or her gentle smile. To his amazement, his offer had been accepted and the next day White Dove became his third wife.

He had worried at the time that his other wives, who were sisters, would quarrel with her. Everyone knew it was unwise to marry more than one woman, unless she was related to the others. It caused jealousy and dissension. He was fond of his first wives, but he had never loved them as he did this bride of his winter years.

Bright Eyes and Yellow Moon had been presented to him by grateful relatives when he was a young man. He had been the close friend of their brother, Blue Thunder. Blue Thunder was killed in a battle with the white-eyes. A year later, Red Turtle returned alone to the place where his friend's body lay and gathered up his bones to bring back to the tribe. It was a very brave thing to do. Grizzly bears and enemies roamed the prairie and were a serious danger. When the tribe learned what he had done, they all commended him and came out to mourn the dead man anew. The relatives of Blue Thunder rewarded Red Turtle's courage that very day by presenting the sisters of the dead man to him to be his wives. They had given him sons and had been good wives and mothers. He was still fond of them. But he was in love with White Dove.

He need not have worried about White Dove's position in his household. She went out of her way to please the older women, showing them the respect due first wives. They accepted her willingly. Because she was so much younger than they were, the sisters treated her more like a daughter than a younger wife, and pampered her as much as her husband did. His love for White Dove grew stronger with each passing day. When she whispered blushingly that she was with child, his heart was overflowing with gratitude to Heammawihio the Creator for bringing him so much happiness.

As he watched White Dove toss and turn in her sleep, Red Turtle frowned, wondering if she too were having a bad dream. When she moaned, he leaned down and gently touched her. Startled, she sat up, her eyes wide with fear.

"What is it, what is wrong?" he whispered uneasily.

"I had a terrible dream," White Dove stammered, her slim body trembling under the blanket. "There was blood everywhere. Our people lay dead and dying. There were only a handful of us left alive." She paused for breath. "Bright Eyes was one of those."

"I too had such a dream," Red Turtle muttered, feeling greatly alarmed.

"What do you think it means?" White Dove asked in a hushed tone after a momentary pause as she strained to see her husband's face in the dark.

"I do not know. It may be an omen of evil things to come." He gently touched his wife's face to reassure her. Her flesh felt cool and soft to his touch. He could feel her smiling.

"As long as you are here my husband, I do not fear dreams," White Dove said softly, as much in love with her husband as he with her.

The odor of tanned buffalo hides and the faint aroma of dead ashes mingled with the sweet, clean smell of White Dove. She was naked under the light blanket, and as always, he wanted her. But the similarity of the two dreams and the nature of them disturbed Red Turtle. All able-bodied men were to attend a buffalo hunt that day. The women and children would be left alone, unprotected. He forced himself to move away from her. "I will speak to Owl Man about the dreams. It is not good that we both had the same dream."

As he dressed, he could hear his other wives stirring. Soon all the tribe would be up. Owl Man was wise. He would know what the dreams meant.

The old man sat for a long time in silence after the ritual of the presenting of the pipe was completed. Finally he spoke. "Have you ever before experienced dreams or visions of the future?"

Red Turtle considered. "Only once. When I was a young man, a raven appeared to me in a dream and warned me that my brother would die in the next battle but that I would live until long after I had passed the middle years of my life. I fasted for four days before the dream came." He frowned. "My brother was killed by a Kiowa lance one moon from the time of the dream."

"That is the only occasion?" Owl Man inquired.

"Yes. That is the only occasion," Red Turtle admitted.

Once more Owl Man was silent. "Your wife has never experienced visions or dreams before?" Again Red Turtle assented. The old man looked distressed. "I will speak to the elders about it. What you fear may be true. While we are gone, our camp left unprotected, we will be attacked by enemies. It is possible. There has been no warning. None of those who are known to have dreams have done so, and the white soldiers have promised to protect us."

"The white soldiers do not care what happens to our people," Red Turtle said angrily.

Owl Man grunted assent. "Your dream and your

wife's dream are disturbing. But the people are still undecided. There is much tension and uneasiness among our people. Our chiefs may not want to threaten the goodwill of the two camps by canceling the trip. I will tell them about it all the same," he assured Red Turtle somberly.

Red Turtle thanked him and returned to his lodge. He soon received word from Owl Man that his dream had been reported to the elders. They had considered its importance. A handful of warriors had elected to stay behind. The buffalo hunt would not be canceled, and the majority of the Cheyenne would attend. All were eager to see friends and relatives once again. It would be a festive occasion. His friends urged him to go, and in spite of his own misgivings, he joined them. He wished to see his nephew Strong Heart again, and it would be good to be on a buffalo hunt.

All that day, in spite of his efforts to dismiss the dream, he worried about it. While the others were laughing, exchanging information and gossip with members and relatives from the other camp, he had been silent, apprehensive. There would be a big celebration that night in both villages. As they were about to part company with one another, one of the younger boys sighted a swarm of vultures. Silence followed as they shaded their eyes against the sun and followed the path of the flesh eaters to the approximate location of their villages. They exchanged nervous looks with one another. Several members of Red Turtle's band glanced at him, fear and horror clearly written on their faces. Then they saw the smoke. The dream was no longer a dream. It had become a reality.

Spotted Tail was also uneasy. If he had heard of the dreams of Red Turtle and White Dove, it would have confirmed his own suspicions. He did not belong to either camp of Cheyenne. His tribe had never made peace with the white-eyes. Instead, they had chosen to move farther north, where the footsteps of the white

men were too few to pose a serious threat to the
Tsistsistas, the Cheyenne name for themselves, meaning people. His cousin had married a girl from White
Mountain's band. He had not seen him since his marriage and had come for a visit with a small band of
men from his own village.

He was tall and impressive, overshadowing most of
the other Cheyenne. It was impossible to guess his age.
He could have been anywhere from thirty to fifty.
His long, straight black hair was stuck together with
pine gum, in a style that was still popular among the
Cheyenne. It hung down his back to well below his
waist, in a dozen different strings. His cheekbones
were high and exceedingly prominent and his dark
eyes were large and expressive. He was noted for his
agility as well as his great strength. Because of his
generosity and even temper, he was well-liked.

Spotted Tail and his people had been made welcome by White Mountain's tribe. He was urged to
feel at home. He had mingled with the tribe, sensed
their unspoken fears, and seen the restlessness of the
young men. He had listened in on the discussions of
the old men who worried about the uncertain temper
of the white-eyes and the smoldering hatred of their
own people for an arrogant, greedy race whose numbers could not be extinguished by disease, famine, or
war. Such feelings could never be contained for long.
They always erupted in war. His sister Half Moon
had lost both a husband and her only son in an encounter with the white-eyes after just such feelings
had exploded. The time was ripe for the breaking of
the treaty. The whites were stronger than ever, eager
to take the Cheyenne's land from them. The
Cheyenne had recovered their strength and were
yearning for combat and an opportunity for revenge.
It would happen soon. Spotted Tail frowned. Which
side would strike the first blow? When he heard the
boy's startled cry and saw the vultures and the smoke
coming from the two camps, he knew the answer.

Black Elk was among those who suspected nothing. He was preoccupied with his own thoughts. He was the youngest son of White Mountain, and had it not been for his deeply scarred face, he would have been a handsome man. He, too, was tall, with high cheekbones and serious dark eyes. Unlike Spotted Tail, he was slim. Not that he was weak. On the contrary, every muscle was taut and hard, through years of practice and steady exercise. He could run faster than many young boys and sit a horse lightly. What he lost in sheer physical strength he made up for in accuracy and speed. His aim with the bow and the gun were legendary. He won all tribal contests and games with these weapons. He was a notable warrior among his people, possessing no less than eighty horses of his own and counting coup many times since he had first gone on a raiding party at the age of fifteen.

Black Elk wiped the sweat from his brow and frowned. This was the first time the heat had persisted well into the moon of Seine, when the water usually froze on the edge of the streams. Many of the old men were saying it was a bad sign, foretelling a great disaster. He did not know. Voices did not speak to him, nor omens unravel themselves to him, unless he first fasted or made a personal sacrifice. For that he was glad. He did not want to know what the future held in store for him. He was a warrior and was content to be so. The hunting had gone well. He should have been pleased. Everyone else appeared to be happy. But he was recalling that it was in the time of Seine, several years ago, that he and Sweet Grass had broken their pledge to each other by returning the copper rings they had exchanged.

Sweet Grass was the only daughter of Gray Skies, in a household of six elder brothers. Because she was the youngest child and the only girl, she was greatly spoiled. When her brothers or father returned from a raiding party, they often presented her with a horse of her own. Before she was fully grown, she had become independently wealthy. Her chores around the lodge were simple and few, and her suitors many. Every day on her way for water or returning from a game of oassioph, the Cheyenne word for football, she would stop to talk to Black Elk and smile bewitchingly at him. Black Elk thought she was the most beautiful girl he had ever seen. Small and slender, she wore her thick, shiny hair in braids that were doubled up three times. Decorative quills or colorful beads adorned the deerskin rolls that were wrapped about each coil of hair, located behind either small ear. Sweet Grass wore earrings made of beads strung with sinew, and many bracelets and rings made of brass wire and copper.

It was common practice among the Cheyenne to court a girl from a year to five or even six years before he sent word to her relatives that he wished to marry her. Black Elk had been courting Sweet Grass for over a year before he joined the raiding party that claimed the lives of his companions and left him for dead, scarred beyond recognition. Until then, he had accompanied many raiding parties and war parties, always returning victorious. To show his sincerity and love for Sweet Grass, he would, when he returned to the village, lead a dozen or half a dozen horses to his prospective father-in-law's lodge as a gift. After he returned from a long journey, Sweet Grass would occasionally present him with a pair of ornamented moccasins or leggings and a horse of her own, to show her appreciation and affection.

This time it had been different. Black Elk and ten others went on a raiding party against the white-eyes. They were at war with them, but it was not a war party. Their mission was to steal horses. Many young warriors who had previously not had an opportunity to add to their wealth joined them. Black Elk and three other experienced men were to lead them. Stealing from the white men had always proved par-

ticularly easy in the past. They did not fear that they
would be caught. They would wait until it was dark,
and then, under cover of the night, lead the horses
away. The white-eyes were notoriously hard of hearing. The Cheyenne did not suspect a trap. They did
not stop to wonder at how few guards were posted
around the corral. Even the unusual stillness went un-
noticed. Black Elk, being more experienced, should
have been on the alert. His thoughts were elsewhere.
He was thinking of Sweet Grass and wondering if he
should wait another year before asking for her in
marriage, or if his suit would be accepted now.

It was only when they had entered the corral that
Black Elk's senses alerted him to the danger. The
horses were nervous and skittish. They would not be
still, and the smell of the white men was too close. Before he could warn the others and head back, shots
were fired. The bullets seemed to come from everywhere. His friends fell on every side. A few tried to
ride the horses out of the corral to safety. The white
men's shots cut them down. Some tried to hide behind
the horses until they could escape. Black Elk was one
of these. The white men moved in, coming out of
their hiding places with the rifles and shotguns smoking before them. As the Indians tried to break out of
the corral, they were shot down. When the white
men came upon a wounded Indian, they finished him
off with a second bullet or hit him with the butt of a
gun until he no longer moved. It all happened so fast
that Black Elk was stunned. The Cheyenne had barely
let loose with a half-dozen shots. Now only he remained alive. Realizing that sooner or later he would
be discovered and that he had no chance of survival,
Black Elk made up his mind to die killing as many
white men as he could before their bullets stopped
him. He was a Cheyenne. He would die with honor.
Picking out three men, he opened fire.

To Black Elk, it seemed that for years he stood
alone in the middle of the corral emptying his rifle

and feeling the returning bullets whiz by him as though he were invisible. He wondered fleetingly if he had been made invulnerable to the white men's bullets.

As soon as the white men had recovered their surprise at finding one Indian left alive, their shots found their mark. One bullet hit him in his right shoulder, ruining his aim and making it virtually impossible for him to continue shooting. Another bullet sank into his thigh and brought him to his knees. In a moment the white men were upon him. Drawing out his knife with his left hand, he leaped into their midst. He was thrown aside. Several men held him down while the one who appeared to be their leader pointed a gun in his face. Black Elk noted that he was a tall man with a fat stomach that extended over his worn leather belt. His head was without hair, although he had thick black hair on his face. He could see that the top of the man's round head was glistening with sweat. His small dark eyes were burning with hatred. Black Elk did not flinch. He awaited his end calmly. His attitude seemed to enrage the white men. They muttered and shouted at one another, apparently arguing over their prisoner. Since he could not speak their language, Black Elk did not understand what they said.

Suddenly he was dragged to his feet and pushed forward out of the corral to a clearing between two trees. Several men brought out ropes. At first Black Elk thought they were going to hang him. He knew the white-eyes favored hanging as a punishment to their enemies. He was not afraid. Instead, they bound his right wrist to a rope that was then tied tautly to a tree. They did the same with his right ankle and repeated this process with his left wrist and ankle, until he was spread apart between the two trees. A searing pain shot through his extended wounded arm and leg, but he was used to enduring pain and did not show it. The hairy fat one appeared in front of him with a long black whip. Smiling, showing several decaying

teeth, he demonstrated its use to Black Elk by striking
another tree, stripping off several layers of bark. Black
Elk felt sick. His courage faltered. He knew why he
had been momentarily spared.

He did not expect to live. His flesh ripped apart,
and the warm thick blood poured down his back. The
pain became unbearable. When he finally blacked out,
he could still hear the cracking of the whip in the air
before it touched his burning back. He had lost a lot
of blood and believed that when he lost consciousness
he would not regain it again. When the white men
could not revive him for their sport, they decided he
was near death. After a final surge of cruelty, they
cut him down. Tying him on a captured Indian pony,
they hit the animal so that he would carry his bloody
burden home as a lesson to the Cheyenne people. One
of the scouts from his tribe found him and brought
him back.

They all predicted he would die. After two weeks
they changed their opinion. If he had survived thus
far, he would not succumb to death now.

When Black Elk first regained consciousness and
learned his face had also been horribly scarred so that
his own nephew ran from him in terror, he wished he
had died. He could hide the scars of humiliation that
crisscrossed his back by always wearing a deerskin
shirt. He could not hide the thick gashes and mutilation that remained of a once smooth and handsome
face after the swelling and red welts had healed.

Once his strength returned to him, his thoughts began to dwell on Sweet Grass. He wondered if she had
seen him the day the scout brought him back to the
village. He had not seen her in a long time. He wondered if she still felt the same toward him. The following day he received his answer. He had walked
down to the lake to rest. Sweet Grass and her special
friend Bluejay strolled by and paused a few feet in
front of him. He knew they did not see him because
he was hidden by a large rock and the shade of a

maple tree. They were talking softly, but he could easily overhear their words. He would have revealed himself had he not discovered he was the topic of conversation.

"What will you do when Black Elk is well?" Bluejay asked curiously. "Will you marry him?"

"If he wishes it. There is little else I can do," Sweet Grass admitted with considerable irritation in her voice.

"Other couples have broken off their engagements," Bluejay reminded her friend. "No one has thought badly of them."

"Yes, that is true. But they were not near death. If I were to give Black Elk back his ring and ask for mine in return, everyone would say I had behaved badly. I spoke to my parents about it and they urged me not to shame them by breaking off the betrothal. After all, it was a miracle he survived. No one thought he would."

"Have you seen him since he returned?" Bluejay inquired.

"No, have you?"

"Yes!" She shuddered. "It is a great pity to think that he will never be the same. It would have been a different matter if he had not been so handsome before. Unfortunately the scars are not ones made from bullets or knives, so he cannot wear them with the pride of a great warrior. Poor Sweet Grass! I don't envy you." She sighed. "If only his face had been spared! It wouldn't matter so much about his back. He could always cover that up." She paused and added consolingly, "Well, perhaps you will grow accustomed to his face and content yourself with his wealth and ability as a hunter. Nevertheless, I am sure you must be very disappointed, especially since you are so popular. Everyone knows you could have your pick of the most eligible young men."

When Sweet Grass didn't reply, Black Elk felt a wave of anger and pain that caused him to tremble.

His dark face flushed with wounded pride. It was obvious that Sweet Grass no longer loved him, if she ever had. She would marry him anyway, to please her parents and public opinion. He overheard Bluejay say she would meet her friend later. Sweet Grass was alone. She paused, a frown on her pretty face. Before she had walked two steps, Black Elk appeared before her.

She gave a start and flushed, wondering if he had overheard the conversation. "You startled me," she whispered, trying not to cringe at the sight of his face.

He took off the ring that she had given him and handed it to her. "I do not wish to marry a girl who does not wish to marry me. Tell your parents that it was I who decided to end the engagement."

Sweet Grass stared at him, her eyes wide with surprise. He had heard her words. She felt embarrassed and did not know what to say. Being unable to reply, she meekly handed him the ring he had given her and tried to conquer a feeling of relief.

"You may marry whom you choose now, and I hope you will be happy," Black Elk said bitterly before he turned on his heel and walked off without once looking back.

That had all happened many years ago, but Black Elk still remembered it vividly. Sweet Grass had married someone else that year and was not happy. She had been spoiled by her family and done little work. Her handsome husband did not spoil her, and he often beat her for her laziness. They quarreled frequently, and after the birth of her first child, Sweet Grass became fat. Black Elk often saw her on her way to her lodge, her back bent under a load of wood, her eyes dull, no longer sparkling with mischief. Her husband was attractive, but he also possessed a short temper—and a second wife who was younger and prettier than his first.

After Black Elk announced the broken engagement

to his family, he informed them of his desire to set up his own lodge. He knew of an old widow named Reed Woman whose children had all died. She was distantly related to him and was willing to live in his lodge and care for his needs. His family was both upset and worried by his decision, but they didn't argue. They felt he needed to get away and be by himself, for they were not fooled by his words. They knew he still loved Sweet Grass. They believed he would eventually forget her and marry another.

Black Elk did not tell them of what really lay in his heart. He had made up his mind he would never marry. If Sweet Grass and Bluejay felt he was disgusting to look upon, others must think so too. He would never again put himself in a position where he would have to see the horror and revulsion that had been so obvious in Sweet Grass's eyes. As the winters and summers came and went without Black Elk taking a wife, his friends teased him about his unmarried state, and his father reprimanded him.

"My son, it is not fitting you do not marry and have children. You have a duty to your people to produce sons who will one day grow up to increase our ranks of warriors and girls who will grow up to be the future bearers of the Cheyenne race. Surely there is a girl among our people who pleases you?"

"I know you are disappointed in me, Father," Black Elk had replied sadly. "It grieves me to think I am the cause of your unhappiness. The Cheyenne maidens are handsome. I find no fault with them. The fault lies with me."

A burst of loud laughter behind him brought Black Elk back to the present with a start. He looked over to where his father was talking to his elder brother. He knew his father was right. There were many girls who would marry him in spite of his scarred face. The fact that they would do so only because he was an important warrior with many horses made him feel lonelier than ever. Still, he thought to himself, frowning, there were other people to consider besides himself. There were no single men in the tribe except for five Heemaneh, men with feminine traits, who directed the scalp dances and were the matchmakers of the tribe. His family had been made unhappy by his reluctance to marry, and he himself was lonely. He sighed. When they returned from the hunt, he would begin courting again.

Suddenly a boy drew their attention to the vultures.

Gray Sky was also unaware of any intuitive feelings of impending destruction. He stared in front of him with unseeing eyes, wondering why he had been cursed with barren wives. He stood a little over middle height with a deep, barrel chest, scarred from encounters in numerous battles. His thighs were thick, solid muscle, and his waist narrow. His nose was rather large and his lips wide. Gray Sky had married Lightning Woman eight years ago. At the time, she had been a slim, pretty girl who blushed and giggled whenever she found suitors waiting in front of her lodge. He had paid thirty horses for her and soon tired of her. He had not taken another wife until four years later. He had hoped she would give him a son, but she had remained barren. Because he knew it upset her as much as it did him, he had refrained from speaking about it. He married Little Flower, who was small and delicate, with tiny bones and a quiet manner that pleased him. She too had remained childless. Since she had entered his lodge, he had had no peace. The two women argued about everything. Their bickering could be heard at all hours. He could afford to take another wife, but he doubted if he could put up with *three* quarreling wives.

Once Lightning Woman and Little Flower had been pretty women. Now Lightning Woman had become too thin. Her clothes hung on her bony frame, and it seemed to Gray Sky that if a stiff breeze came along, it would carry her away. Little Flower had lost

her delicate beauty by overeating until she had lost all
resemblance to her former self. He no longer loved
them with the burning desire of his youth. In spite of
this, if they had given him children he would not have
considered taking another wife. A woman loses her
youth and beauty as a man does his strength. In time,
all that is left is the memories. He knew that if he
married another maiden whom he desired as he had
once desired his first wives, soon his passion for her
would also wane. He did not wish to hurt or humiliate his other wives by adding a handsome young wife
to his lodge. But more than long life he wanted to be
able to hear the sound of a baby crying in his lodge.
He wanted to teach his son to ride and hunt, to tell
his daughter stories and watch her grow into a beautiful maiden. He longed for grandchildren to grace his
winter years. Was he never to know the joy of a father as he held his firstborn in his arms and listened to
its laughter? he wondered bitterly. Would his hair become white as he watched the grass turn brown and
the leaves fall from the trees year after year, while the
only sound he heard in his lodge was his wives grum-
bling and complaining? For once the question that
had haunted him for so long was replaced by a more
urgent concern as he heard the commotion and
caught sight of the birds of prey hovering above the
two camps.

As the terrified Cheyenne neared their camps, the
stench of burning flesh became stronger. The only
sounds they could distinguish were the occasional
howling of a camp dog in pain. Otherwise all was
silent.

Red Turtle could feel his flesh crawl with the fear
that had settled in his stomach like a heavy rock and
was getting larger with each step. As he rode through
his village, he had to be careful not to trample over
the piles of bodies strewn throughout the camp. The
charred remains of the lodges with an occasional still-
smoking one were all that was left. Within some of

these enclosures were the now unrecognizable bodies of those that had been forced to stay inside and die in that manner. Scattered throughout the camp were the bodies of those that had tried to escape or fight off their attackers. Their positions were varied. Blocking Red Turtle's path to his lodge was the naked, decapitated body of a woman. The headless woman was still clutching her dead infant to her. Her flesh was riddled with bullets, and nearby rested her bloody head. The baby's face was smashed in.

Red Turtle dismounted and stared at the woman. She had been the sister of White Dove. Suddenly he felt dizzy and weak. He swallowed several times to keep down the sickness that had risen to his mouth. He could taste the bitter, metallic fluid and closed his eyes for a moment, gaining strength to go on. Lying in front of his lodge was the body of a woman. Her soft white deerskin dress was covered with dried dark blood. Ashes and blood stuck to her hair. Her face was turned away from him. He began to shake. Going over to her, he turned her around so that she faced him. Her face had been viciously butchered with a knife, so that it was hard to identify her. Trembling, he wiped the burning mist from his eyes and forced himself to study her. It was Yellow Moon. She had been dead for some time. Her body was cold. Where were Bright Eyes and White Dove? Where were his sons? Stumbling over a blackened lodge pole that instantly disintegrated into dust, he staggered off in search of his remaining wives and sons. Other men were doing the same. Occasionally they would come across a wounded woman or child who had managed to stay alive by crawling under others who were already dead. By this method they had been able to fake death. They all told the same story. The white men had come upon them without warning. They spared none.

Several Cheyenne were sent to the woods to give the call in case there were survivors who had by some miracle escaped the massacre and were in hiding. Gradually the lone stragglers wandered into the camp and were greeted with tears of relief by their relations. Their numbers were pitifully small.

Red Turtle and some of the other Cheyenne found a pile of dead bodies at the end of the village. They had been trapped and had taken a last stand. As their faces were uncovered one by one, White Dove and his two sons were found to be among them. His sons had been shot, one through the heart, the other through the head. The eldest one had seen only twelve summers. The youngest had seen barely seven. He gathered them to him and felt the silent tears streaming down his face. But it was seeing White Dove's naked body, her breasts brutally slashed off, and her once beautiful and tender body a mass of ugly cuts and bruises that caused sobs to rack his body. He released his sons and gathered what remained of her to him. Her face was frozen in horror and terror. Her lips were bruised, her mouth open as though she were screaming, even in death. He closed it with shaking hands and did the same with the sightless eyes that stared at him unseeing. He carried her to a place away from the sight and sound of others and gently laid her down while he returned for his sons and Yellow Moon. When they were all gathered there, he sat on the ground cradling White Dove in his arms for the last time. He stayed in that position, sitting among the dead, while racking sobs continued to shake him, until feelings of hate began to seep into his soul to replace the grief. Those that came upon him were quick to respect his sorrow and leave him alone.

As the hate dried his tears and filled his heart with bitterness that would not be appeased except through equal acts of pain and devastation, he buried his loved ones and began searching for Bright Eyes. In the dream she had been the only survivor. He hadn't doubted she would be alive, and was soon reunited with her. Bright Eyes had sustained only a superficial wound. Otherwise, she was not harmed. Neither one had cause for celebration. Their greeting was a silent affair. Yet each one knew that the other was glad of the reunion. Tenderly Red Turtle cleaned and cared for Bright Eyes's wound. When he had finished, he left her to join the others who were preparing for war.

It had been decided not to wait until morning. By that time, the white-eyes would be expecting an attack, so they would strike before their enemies had a chance to organize a defense, before the military arrived. The chiefs of Red Turtle's camp sent word to the other camp for aid in the upcoming war party. They had no doubt they would instantly accept, for they were sure the other village had not been spared the destruction they had suffered. The survivors amounted to less than half of their original numbers. Those women who had escaped the slaughter were instructed to get themselves ready for the move north. Whatever household goods could be salvaged were to be gathered together for the journey. In spite of the enormous loss of women and children, the unspoken agreement was that no white-eyes, man, woman, or child, would be left alive in Sweetwater.

Nevertheless, there were those among them who had other plans. Black Elk was one of these. He saw in the retaliatory attack a way out of his difficulties. If he took a white woman prisoner and made her his wife, she would bear him sons. His relatives would be content. It would not matter if she was repulsed by him. Her opinion of him would be of no importance.

Gray Sky was also considering the possibilities of taking a white woman prisoner. By a miracle, both his wives had escaped the slaughter. They had been among the first who had hidden in the woods, and they hadn't even been wounded. For that he was glad. Now, even if he should consider taking another Indian wife, it would be impossible. The women who were left were small in number, and the number of single maidens was half of that. It would be selfish of a man who had two healthy wives to court another when there were so many men who had none. If he were to capture a white woman, no one would complain. While his wives would resent a young Cheyenne bride, they would enjoy their status of first wives by bossing a white captive around. He would at last have another opportunity for children.

As they mounted their horses and started out to meet the other half of their tribe, Spotted Tail was also contemplating taking a prisoner. He had no use for other wives. He had a wife of his own, and several children. In his mind was his sister's face. She had lost both her husband and her only child. She had never remarried. He knew she was unhappy and lonely, and would not have been so, if only her son had lived. He made up his mind if an opportunity arose during the battle, when he could take a white boy prisoner, he would do so and bring him back to Half Moon, to be adopted into the tribe in place of her own dead son.

3

Elizabeth Farrell realized something was wrong when Sergeant Jared failed to return by late afternoon. When the men appeared in Sweetwater with their wounded, she learned what had happened at the Indian villages. She still didn't know what had prevented the sergeant from picking her up. Ben Haskell thought he might have run into trouble with the Indians. Elizabeth knew what that meant. He was dead. She shivered. At least she hoped he was dead. Since she had joined her husband at the fort, she had seen a great deal of violence. She knew that whenever the Indians captured a male adult, they usually tortured him before killing him. Elizabeth had viewed such bodies afterward. It was never a pretty sight. Poor Sergeant Jared! She had liked him. For the first time, she wondered if he had a girlfriend somewhere or a family who would mourn him. She hoped he did. It was a dreadful thing to be alone in the world. Nobody knew that better than she did, Elizabeth thought with a pang of self-pity. She wasn't alone, she reminded herself sternly. She had Peter. Somehow, the image of her husband in his stiff blue uniform and shiny black boots did nothing to alleviate the feeling of emptiness that suddenly made her feel like crying.

When she learned of the sergeant's probable fate, Elizabeth had illogically tried to borrow a buggy so she could return to the fort while there was still some light.

"It's too dangerous for you to try to get back

now," Mayor Gady insisted as he wiped the sweat off his fair brow with a polka-dot handkerchief and tried not to look as scared as he felt.

"The mayor's right, ma'am," Sheriff Davis agreed, frowning. He was silently cursing himself for being a jackass. If he had only stood up to the men that morning, done his job . . . He sighed. What the hell! I'm no hypocrite. I'd do the same thing again if the opportunity arose, he assured himself silently. His eyes fell on Elizabeth's anxious face. It was a damn shame the braves were away on a hunt. Our bad luck! he thought bitterly. Out loud he said soothingly, "There's nothing to worry about, Mrs. Farrell. Your husband's already been notified. You're safe in town."

Elizabeth nodded and quietly moved away. She wasn't afraid. She was used to towns and cities, having lived in them most of her life. She felt secure in such an environment, even though Sweetwater could hardly be compared in the same breath with New York or St. Louis.

Feeling she ought to take time out to pray for Sergeant Jared's welfare, Elizabeth walked slowly back to the simple white frame church. Here she felt she could recapture some of the peaceful serenity that consistently eluded her. There was only one other person inside. Elizabeth was surprised to recognize one of the saloon girls. The woman was sitting in one of the back pews, staring straight ahead. She didn't look up as Elizabeth passed her. She wondered why the woman was there. None of the saloon girls ever came to church. There was no law refusing them admittance. Elizabeth felt sure, however, that if they had attended, the other women would have complained. She felt such an attitude was unchristian. If the women wanted to pray, the church should be open to them. God never turned his back on the worst sinners. She knelt and closed her eyes. The prayer she had intended to compose for Sergeant Jared was lost in a flood of memories.

It was in a church not much larger than this that she and Peter had taken their marriage vows. She remembered the day clearly. She had felt so weak she was afraid she would faint and embarrass him. Her stays had been tied too tightly and she had missed half the service because she had been exerting every effort not to pass out. Once it was over, she recalled thinking: So this is it! I'm married now. She had looked down at the thin gold wedding band and told herself that she had done the right thing by marrying Peter. She had never pretended she was in love with him. Elizabeth had been fond of him and flattered by his constant attentions and proposal of marriage. He was her first suitor. According to her Aunt Hildegarde, he'd probably be her last. As she put it, "It's not that you're unattractive, Elizabeth. While you aren't as pretty as some, you do have a certain agreeable countenance and a sweet disposition. I've heard that dark looks like yours are enjoying a degree of popularity at the moment. But a girl without a fortune who is alone in the world ought not to set her aims too high. Your Aunt Louisa and I won't live forever. When we die, you'll get a small inheritance, but it won't last you long. And when an innocent girl like you is cast out into the world without friends or family to look after her, she's bound to fall by the wayside and get into mischief. I feel it is my duty to urge you to marry this young man and put our minds to rest."

Elizabeth smiled sadly in remembrance. Aunt Hildegarde had been right about one thing. She and her sister Louisa had both died within a fortnight of that speech. Happily they had lived to see her engaged and her future secured. She often wondered what would have happened to her if she hadn't married Peter Farrell. Would she have fallen by the wayside as her aunt suspected? She smiled wistfully. It was an intriguing thought. Heaving a sigh, she realized it didn't matter now. She had married Peter, even though Aunt Louisa had encouraged her to defy her strong-minded sister if she didn't love him. Louisa had always been hopelessly romantic. Unlike Hildegarde, she had once had an offer of marriage but had turned it down because her father disapproved of him, and had regretted her decision the rest of her life. It was the one topic the sisters had argued about ever since Elizabeth had first come to live with them.

Until she was fifteen, Elizabeth had lived with her parents in New York. Her father was a minister for the Methodist church. He worked and lived among the people he served in the slums of the city. She was an only child and often felt unwanted. She had always been of the opinion that her parents never should have had any children. They were too concerned with church work to devote much time to her. Because they were poor and the local schools were both inadequate and dangerous healthwise—the children being infested with lice and other vermin, as well as numerous diseases—Elizabeth had been taught at home by her parents. Neither of them had been particularly patient or affectionate. But they had been strict. Any disobedience had been instantly punished. Since the neighborhood children were not considered proper playmates for her, she had to content herself with dreaming and playing with her doll. In his spare time, her father taught her reading, writing, arithmetic, and religion, the latter subject being particularly emphasized. Her mother taught her needlework, cooking, and how to play the organ in church. Her parents were highly thought of by their parishioners and by the church hierarchy. Her father had turned down a better position in the country in order to remain among those unfortunate souls he served. Elizabeth often wished they hadn't been so pious and devoted to doing God's work. Anytime a little extra money came their way, instead of spending it on their family's needs, they spent it on those they considered less fortunate than themselves. As Elizabeth grew older, she discovered that there was always someone else who qualified for the extra money. The leaking roof was never repaired, the cracks were never sealed up so that the bitter winter wind was prevented from sweeping through the house, and Elizabeth never owned a new dress. She was forced to wear hand-me-downs from her mother. In their house, others came first. Elizabeth tried not to feel resentful over the meager meals, the faded clothes, and the dilapidated condition of the house. She knew that such wicked thoughts stemmed from a selfish heart. Nevertheless, she hadn't entirely succeeded.

When her parents died from scarlet fever within two days of each other and she had been sent to live with her aunts in St. Louis, Elizabeth had been embarrassed to discover she couldn't cry. Her father's friends all thought it was shock due to the loss of both parents within such a short time. They pitied her. Elizabeth knew it wasn't shock. Her parents had not been warm people in spite of their sacrificing for others. They hadn't neglected her education or her basic physical wants. Nevertheless, she felt they hadn't loved her. If they had, at no time had they ever openly expressed it. Now that they were dead, she couldn't bring herself to grieve over them.

Elizabeth soon found that living with her father's sisters was a big improvement. Living on a clean, tree-lined street where the sun always bathed the wooden floors of the creaking old house with light, unhampered by the shadows of ugly, damp, rat-infested slums, filled her with delight. The sisters did not have much money, but they owned the house they lived in. Although it was old, it didn't leak when it rained. To her relief, it was warm in winter, with fires blazing in all the rooms. They ate three hearty meals a day plus tea in the afternoon. A girl came in every day to help clean and cook. Both aunts had been horrified by the condition of her clothing and quickly remedied the situation by taking down their old silks and muslins and making her new dresses that were simple and yet at the same time more in style.

Aunt Hildegarde was the elder. At first she frightened Elizabeth. She was a tall woman with large gray eyes that could stare even the most arrogant, self-confident bill collector down and have him end up shaking and apologizing for inconveniencing her. She had mounds of soft white hair, was heavyset with an ample bosom. Unlike her timid sister, she had a rather severe countenance and was forever busy. Her stiff skirts could be heard constantly swishing through the hallways as she hurried about, bent on some task. She firmly believed in the motto "Idle hands do the devil's work." In some ways, she resembled her brother. Many fifteen-year-olds might have rebelled under her stern, autocratic authority. Elizabeth, long used to obeying her elders and possessed of a shy, timid disposition, felt not the slightest inclination to do so. Her life under her aunts' roof had been much improved, and underneath Hildegarde's gruff manner was a genuine affection for her niece, which the latter had not failed to detect.

Louisa was the exact opposite of her sister. She was a good head shorter than Hildegarde, and thin as a rail. Her eyes were a pale blue, and nobody would ever cower under their gaze. Louisa's high cheekbones and delicate pink-and-white complexion were still the envy of their few acquaintances. Unlike her sister, she was given to weeping over romantic novels, which Hildegarde referred to as pieces of trash, and reminiscing over the lost years of her youth. She adored Elizabeth and lavished all the affection on her she would have given her own children had she ever had any. Elizabeth returned their love and never dreamed she would ever leave them.

Although the sisters bickered continually, their one real bone of contention was Louisa's proposal of marriage. Hildegarde had little patience with her sister's romanticizing the past. She was also, Elizabeth felt, somewhat annoyed over the fact that she herself had never had an offer of marriage.

"You know perfectly well, Louisa, that Father was right about Andrew. He was a fortune hunter and would have made your life miserable if you had married him," Hildegarde would say severely.

Louisa would protest, a vague smile on her face. She would shake her head and say in between long sighs, "You're quite wrong, dear. Andrew was the noblest, most honorable young man. If I had married him, he would never have given me a moment's worry or concern. I'm sure I would have been blissfully happy."

At such unrealistic sentimentality, Hildegarde would either snort or throw up her hands and say in disgust, "Ha!" Such a reaction would usually set the two to arguing hotly for at least an hour. Elizabeth was at first upset by their battles. She soon learned, however, that they enjoyed it. In fact, that particular argument had developed into a tradition. If one of them failed to mention it at least once during the week, the other was sure to bring it up.

Louisa, being an ardent supporter of romantic love, was greatly disturbed by her niece's intention to marry someone whose appearance failed to cause her pulses to race. "You really ought not to marry someone you can't love, dearest. It would be terribly upsetting for you. Only consider spending the rest of your life with a man you don't care for!"

Hildegarde would interrupt, her lips tightly compressed. "Nonsense, Elizabeth. Peter is a nice young man. He is perfectly respectable and honorable. He holds you in high regard. There's no reason in the world why you shouldn't come to love him in time."

"Do you think that you could learn to love Peter, dear?" Louisa would inquire hesitantly. Elizabeth soothed her aunt's fears by admitting that she could. She believed it herself. After all, Peter was attractive.

He was tall and well-built, with light brown hair and evenly spaced gray eyes. He was courteous and always conducted himself like a gentleman. He claimed he loved her. Why shouldn't she come to love him, if he treated her well? She felt Hildegarde was right when she said that every wife loved her husband, and that romantic love of the type Louisa talked of existed only in cheap novels.

After the marriage ceremony, as she stared at the gold band on her left hand, Elizabeth began to experience doubts. Suddenly she felt trapped and terribly depressed, at a moment in her life when according to popular belief she ought to have felt deliriously happy. Later that night, long after Peter was sound asleep, she lay awake in the hotel room trying to overcome feelings of disappointment, revulsion, and guilt.

As soon as the ceremony was over, they had checked into a hotel and gone out to a concert and dinner. When they returned to their room, they discussed the future. Peter would be leaving in a week for a post out west. She would remain in St. Louis until he sent for her. His obvious concern for her welfare caused her to feel a surge of warmth and tenderness toward him that she had not experienced before. However, when they changed into their night clothes and got into bed, Elizabeth refrained from looking at her husband's face. Suddenly she felt shy and embarrassed. He snuffed out the candles, and they lay in the dark in an uneasy silence. Elizabeth was wondering nervously what would happen next when Peter startled her by leaning over, kissing her awkwardly on the mouth, and then immediately moving on top of her. His hot, sweaty hands pulled up the white lace bridal nightgown her aunts had made for her, while at the same time he freed himself from his own attire. When he entered her, he was rough. The tenderness and gentleness she had expected at such a time were missing. He both hurt and frightened her, and she begged him to stop. Instead, he pushed on until she felt herself tearing inside. The pain and fear stung her eyes with tears, and she struggled to escape. As quickly as it began, it was over. Peter grunted a few times and rolled off. She lay where she was in stunned silence, feeling the hot, sticky liquid roll down her thighs. Turning her head to the pillow, she began to cry.

"It's not unusual for women to feel as you do," Peter had said after a few moments of silence, broken only by Elizabeth's muffled sobs. He spoke stiffly, feeling embarrassed at having to discuss such a subject. "You have been properly brought up, and your reaction is perfectly normal."

"Why do women ever marry?" Elizabeth had asked, shuddering.

"To have children, of course," Peter replied, surprised. "I assure you, Elizabeth," he added as he reached over to pat her arm consolingly, "I am not an unfeeling man. I shall not bother you unduly. If you prefer it, as soon as you give me a son, I will leave you alone. In the meantime, you will have to bear with the pain until it subsides. You will grow used to it in time."

Elizabeth moved as far away from him as possible. She wanted to believe him. Deep in her heart, she feared he was wrong. Peter left the following week for his post out west, and she hadn't seen him again for almost a year. During that time, she had written him faithfully. Because she had no friends of her own, she had missed him. Loneliness set in, and when he sent for her to join him at Fort Jubele, she had been genuinely glad. The memory of those nights before he left were only blurs out of the past. She told herself she had expected too much. She was as unrealistic about love as Louisa had been. When she joined him, Elizabeth discovered one thing had changed. When he entered her, it no longer hurt as it had once. If she gripped the sheets and thought of other things, she could bear it. The revulsion she had first felt, however, had increased in intensity until she felt like screaming. Lately a burning resentment against Peter had begun to manifest, which she could barely hide. She knew now that she could never love him the way she had once thought possible. In fact, every little fault he had was magnified until his very presence irritated her. Poor Peter! Her dark brows drew together in a frown of concentration. He had said he loved her. He was certainly patient with her. They never fought, and he refused to argue. If she wanted something and it was within reason, he never denied her. He never questioned her about what she did with the money he gave her to take care of any extra needs the fort didn't provide. Did he really love her? Was he happy with her? Elizabeth had begun to wonder. How could he love her when he knew she couldn't bear his touch? And in all the time they had been married, she had never heard him laugh. It was one of the things that most annoyed her about him. If he was particularly amused, he would smile weakly. Peter took life seriously, and his career in particular. He had advanced far already. Elizabeth often imagined that the real reason he had married her was because he had felt it was time he took a wife and she possessed the right qualifications. She sighed. If he was a cold person, she ought to be relieved. At least he didn't bother her every night. He seemed to understand, and even sympathized with her aversion to having sex. Many men wouldn't be so tolerant. Occasionally she wondered if it would be any different with another man. At least Peter didn't drink like some of the other officers at the fort. She wasn't forced to put up with smelling alcohol on his breath as he grunted over her. She blushed and avoided allowing her thoughts to dwell on the most unpleasant aspect of her married life.

Elizabeth had once or twice considered leaving Peter. She wondered unhappily what good that would do. She had no money of her own and no family to turn to. How would she live? At least Peter provided her with a home, clothes, and food. For the first time she even had friends, women at the fort her own age whom she could talk to. She had never discussed her problem with them. They all seemed content with their husbands and children. She knew instinctively that should she attempt to do so, they would have been appalled. Such a topic was too personal to bring out into the open. Once again she sighed. If only she could have a child! She felt it would make all the difference. She could love the child. She knew she could. Peter would be happy. More important, he wouldn't bother her again.

Elizabeth's purse slipped off her wrist and fell to the floor with a soft thud, startling her. She noticed with amazement that it was already dark. As she picked her purse up, she realized with guilt she must have spent at least two hours wallowing in her own troubles, when she should have been praying for Sergeant Jared. Elizabeth immediately pushed aside her own unhappy reflections and concentrated on the sergeant.

Several pews in back of Elizabeth, Charity Walker sat with her hands clasped together in front of her, irony twisting her lips into a bitter smile. It had been a long time since she had been in a church. With all the things that had happened in between, she was surprised the roof hadn't caved in on her. She thought dryly that the only reason she had been spared was probably that Lieutenant Farrell's wife was up front. Mrs. Farrell came to Sweetwater weekly, most of the time to pray. Charity harbored a deep distrust of fanatically religious people. She considered anybody who spent as much time in church as Mrs. Farrell did a fanatic. She firmly believed, from past experience, that once you scratched the surface of such people, you always uncovered the rotten core of a hypocrite. Charity had cause to feel cynical. Her mother's rela-

tives had considered themselves good Christians. How
she hated the words "good Christians"! They evoked
painful memories, flashes out of the past that she
would have preferred to keep buried. She shook her
head in an effort to halt the flow of memories. It was
too late. The very fact that she was in church indicated a desire on her part to turn back the pages of
the past.

One she had been as pure and innocent as Mrs.
Farrell, she thought bitterly. If she happened to pass a
painted woman on the street, she felt a mixture of awe
and disgust. She certainly never dreamed that one day
she would join their ranks. Charity was glad her
mother hadn't lived to see what had become of her
only child. She sighed and brushed a wisp of hair out
of her eye. But then, if her mother hadn't died, she
wouldn't have gone to live with Betsy and Jonathan
Boggs. Betsy was her mother's cousin, and when her
mother passed away from a bad cold that developed
into pneumonia, Betsy had offered to take the orphan
in. Charity was thirteen, suffering from shock over
her mother's sudden demise and frightened by the
prospect of earning her own living. Her name hadn't
been Charity Walker then. She had chosen that ficti-
tious name after she decided to enter the shady profession of saloon work. In Layman, Pennsylvania, she
had been known as Diana Wilson. She winced. No
one in Sweetwater was aware of her real identity. Her
lips tightened. No one ever would be.

When Betsy made the offer, Charity had believed
her relative's motives for giving her shelter emerged
out of the genuine kindness of her heart. She soon
found out differently. Betsy had four children of her
own. The eldest was only seven, while the youngest
was still an infant. Her husband was incredibly tight-
fisted, and the money he gave her to manage the
household did not permit her to hire any servants.
Betsy had seen in Diana a live-in maid who would
work for her board and keep. Diana would have

borne the hard work better and the fact that she was
treated more like a slave than a member of the family,
if Betsy and Jonathan didn't feel it their duty to make
sure she turned out to be a "good Christian." For
some reason, the fact that she was an orphan and her
mother had defied her parents to marry a man they
felt was beneath her caused her relatives to consider
her to be of unsteady character. Not only was she
forced to attend church every Sunday, but she had to
go to the Wednesday-night services as well and read
from the Bible for an hour after dinner every night. If
she protested, it was taken as a sign of waywardness
and she would be lectured to not only by Betsy and
Jonathan but also by the minister of the church. The
latter was a pompous, self-righteous man who loved
hearing his own voice and heaped praise on the
Boggses for doing their Christian duty by providing
food, clothing, and shelter for a homeless orphan who
could otherwise expect to wind up a beggar in the
streets, or worse. Since she had no free time, she was
unable to make friends among girls her own age.
However, every evening, after the children were put
to bed and the housework done, she would sit in her
room and dream of the time when she could escape
from her life of drudgery. She smiled, but her eyes remained hard as she reviewed her half-forgotten youth
with a mixture of cynicism and sadness. As she grew
older, the escape always took the form of a handsome
man who would whisk her away with him into a life
of never-ending happiness. She laughed silently at herself now, wondering how she could ever have been so
naive.

As the years passed, Diana grew more openly rebellious. When she turned seventeen, Jonathan introduced her to a young man who worked for him. He
was at least a full head shorter than she, with pudgy
soft white hands. His name was Walter Simpkins. According to Jonathan, he was a smart lad and a hard
worker. Jonathan left her alone with him, and Diana

had found it difficult not to run out of the room. Walter stared at her with hungry eyes and licked his lips before he spoke. His voice was pleasant enough. With an effort, she kept her eyes riveted to a point just below his starched white collar and was able to relax enough to reply politely to his mundane questions.

"You are well, I hope, Miss Wilson?"

"Yes, thank you, quite well."

"The dark clouds foretell a storm, I fear."

"So it appears."

"I understand you are an excellent cook."

"I do my best," Diana muttered. She was left alone with him only a short time before Jonathan returned looking pleased and Walter abruptly left. As soon as Walter was out of earshot, Jonathan informed her of his intentions.

"I cannot help but feel, my dear Diana," he had begun as he paced up and down, his hands folded in back of him, "that you have become restless of late. Your sudden fits of temper and stubborn resistance to my wife's authority have caused an unnecessary amount of friction in the house. However, I do not intend to reprimand you for your behavior. On the contrary," he continued, his lips straining to form a smile, "I believe it is only natural for you to long for a home of your own. Believe me, we would like nothing better than to see you happily married." Here he paused to see what effect his speech had on her.

"I'm sure that would be very agreeable," Diana managed to say as she stared at him wide-eyed.

He nodded, and his false smile broadened. "Your reaction was as I imagined it would be. My wife especially has formed an attachment for you, and I feel she will miss you dreadfully." Diana noticed he had the grace to blush, and she smiled. "I have introduced you to Walter Simpkins, a respectable young man who assures me he finds you more than satisfactory. He will call for you every Saturday and accompany us to church on Sundays for a decent amount of time, after which he shall ask for your hand in marriage. I shall, of course, present you with an adequate dowry," he ended hurriedly, seeing the look of horror on Diana's face.

So that was it. Her eyes blazed defiantly. "I don't wish to marry Mr. Simpkins. The idea may be agreeable to you, but it isn't to me."

The battle began. If she had not met Gary Lawford a week later, she was sure her relatives would have thrown her out of the house.

Gary was tall and breathtakingly handsome, the hero of her dreams who carried her off into the sunset. She met him on an errand for Jonathan at a nearby bookstore, when he bumped into her and her purchases fell to the floor.

"Excuse me," he had said, smiling apologetically as he picked them up, showing white even teeth under a golden mustache.

She stared at him in a daze, unable to speak because she couldn't believe she had actually come face to face with the hero of her dreams. She never recalled what she said or how it happened that she went with him for tea. His friendly, easy manner and interest encouraged her to confide in him about her private thoughts and ambitions, recounting the years she had lived with the Boggses in amusing and poignant detail.

When she returned home, she discovered to her relief that she had not been missed. Jonathan was still at work, and Betsy had taken the children to visit a friend.

She never dreamed she would see Gary again. To her amazement and delight, he appeared on her doorstep one Friday evening. The Boggses were obviously impressed with his address and manners. When he explained that he had grown up with Diana and wanted to renew his friendship with her, they readily gave him their permission to pay his respects. Thus began some of the happiest moments of her life. She was permitted a great deal of freedom, and the Boggses, believing her to be almost married, allowed her to accompany Gary alone for greater and greater periods of time. Diana had fallen in love with Gary the moment their eyes met. She trusted him implicitly and never dreamed that his inability to find a job was based on laziness, or that his wanting her physically was anything more than an expression of his love. She tingled when they touched, felt a flush of pleasure when he held her against his chest.

"My little Puritan," he whispered in her ear, and then proceeded to prove his words wrong. His kisses, light and soft at first, deepened in intensity and aroused in Diana passions she had never known existed. When Gary took her to his lodgings on a false pretext and then proceeded to make love to her, she protested weakly and tried halfheartedly to keep him at arm's length. He laughed and pulled her close, smothering her protests with kisses. She didn't lie to herself. She wanted him fully as much as he desired her. Gary loved her. He would never hurt her. Diana knew that the church sternly forbade sexual relations between couples before marriage. She had little respect for church people. They were constantly preaching one set of values and acting out another. The vast majority were hypocrites. If she and Gary loved each other and they both desired each other, she was sure there was nothing wrong or evil about sex before marriage. When Gary held her against his chest, she could feel his every muscle taut with desire. The heat from his body seemed to sear her flesh. She trembled. His strong, sure hands moved over her body, loosening and unbuttoning her dress, exposing her naked flesh to his touch. Deep within her a fire began to stir, burning slowly at first and then rising to a white heat, blinding her to everything except the awesome intensity of her own feelings. She pressed against him, holding on to him for support. The room was spinning. Gary's face was only a hazy blur. She no longer cared about right or wrong. Jonathan and Betsy's disapproving faces vanished from her mind. Whether she lived or died no longer mattered. The only important thing in the world was touching Gary, feeling him close to her. The fire turned into a gnawing ache.

"You have a beautiful body," Gary whispered hoarsely as he took off the last piece of clothing from her body. She shivered at her nakedness and felt her pulse beating wildly. She stared at him with half-closed lids. She had never seen a naked man. A wild impulse to rip off his clothes shocked her, and she had to restrain a strong desire to burst into laughter. She watched him undress. He had trouble with the top button of his shirt and cursed at his clumsiness. When he finally stood before her disrobed, they stared at each other silently, shyly. The initial momentary embarrassment Diana felt at their nudity evaporated when he smiled and gently kissed her. There was no longer any barrier between them. Gary's body was lean and hard, his shoulders broad, and his waist slim. Diana ran her hands wonderingly over his back, feeling the length of his spine. Pulling him closer, she could feel his sex throbbing against her stomach and moaned with pleasure. He was kissing her again, biting her gently, teasing her with his tongue in her ear, on her neck, causing her nipples to harden. He loved her, wanted her, needed her. She longed to learn how to please him.

Diana could never have enough of him. Their hours together passed so quickly that it seemed to her as if they had just met when they had to part. She thought of him constantly. His handsome face with the golden mustache, the way he looked when he was naked and on top of her—his body covered with sweat and his face suffused with desire. Whenever she saw him, her heart began beating wildly and a deep red flush covered her face. She was sure the Boggses would notice her reaction and realize she was no longer a virgin. In fact, she was convinced everyone who saw her would know. The Boggses, busy with their own household, put her reaction down to maidenly embarrassment and left her alone with Gary, satisfied all was well. Diana would often stare at herself in the mirror, amazed it didn't reflect her new sensuality. The thought of him could start a fire in her loins. He taught her how to make love to him, and she looked forward eagerly to their stolen moments.

The weeks sped by. Gradually Gary's attitude toward her began to change. He saw less and less of her, claiming he had gotten a job and was working overtime.

She suspected nothing until the afternoon Jonathan returned home early. He looked annoyed and took her aside.

"Diana, this is very difficult. I had no idea. Indeed, I imagined all was aboveboard. His manners and attitude toward you led me to believe he had serious intentions."

"I don't understand," Diana said, frowning, feeling sudden qualms of apprehension.

"Your friendship with Mr. Lawford has come to an end."

"We're going to be married," Diana protested, her face flushing.

Jonathan avoided looking at her. "I'm afraid we were all deceived. He is a complete rogue, a fortune hunter. I blame myself for not checking into his background more thoroughly."

"That's not true," she shouted angrily, trying to convince herself of the falsity of his statement. Nevertheless, a sinking feeling in the pit of her stomach caused her to feel faint.

"I realize how distressed you are, but you really must exert an effort to control yourself." Jonathan spoke sharply. "I would have no reason in the world to lie to you. I have heard only this morning from Reverend Matthews that Mr. Lawford intends to

marry Miss Nora Sheritan next Sunday. She is an
heiress. Her father is extremely wealthy, and since she
is an only child, she will inherit a considerable fortune. It seems he has been courting her for the past
two months." Diana turned pale. "You will recall,"
Jonathan continued ruthlessly, "it was about that time
his visits here began to diminish in frequency, due to
an imaginary job. I'm afraid we have all been hoaxed.
He has been toying with you, Diana."

Charity leaned back in her seat, unaware of her
present surroundings. She was reliving the past. She
had screamed at Jonathan that he was lying, and had
run from the room. When she was alone, she burst
into tears. It was true. She knew it. She had felt the
distance each time they met. She believed he worked
on the nights he didn't see her because she had wanted
to believe it. He had used her—toyed with her, as
Jonathan had so aptly put it. She wondered if he had
ever cared for her at all. Charity smiled stiffly. She had
never been able to bring herself to hate him, in spite
of the fact that the only word she received from him
was a short note announcing his upcoming marriage,
wishing her well, and hoping she would understand
and find someone more worthy.

After sufficient time had elapsed, Jonathan began to
nourish hopes that Diana would be brought around to
reconsidering marrying Walter. As far as she was
concerned, that was a fate worse than death, especially since she had already experienced a passionate
relationship with Gary. In the beginning, Jonathan
left her alone, hoping she would change her mind.
When she continued to refuse, the house vibrated
with raised voices, threats, and slammed doors. During
a particularly violent quarrel, she felt faint and
blacked out. When she regained consciousness she felt
nauseous and began throwing up. The family doctor
was called in. Dr. Peabody, an elderly gray-haired
man, given to chucking his female patients under the

chin, gave her a thorough examination, after which he
began to hem and haw about her condition.

"I wouldn't exactly say that Diana is ill."

"She fainted, didn't she?" Betsy demanded. "Was
she faking?"

Dr. Peabody turned red. "No, she wasn't faking,
Mrs. Boggs. She certainly wasn't faking."

"Well, if she wasn't faking and she isn't ill, why did
she faint?" Jonathan pursued, obviously annoyed.

"It's rather difficult to put into words," Dr. Peabody mumbled, avoiding Diana's eyes. "She's so
young, and this is plainly a very, how shall I say, disturbing situation," he ended lamely.

"I insist you tell us the truth immediately," Jonathan said angrily. "What exactly is wrong with Diana?"

Dr. Peabody coughed. "Diana is in what is termed
. . . a delicate condition."

There was a full minute of stunned silence before
pandemonium erupted.

"I knew it," Betsy shouted triumphantly, "I told
you she was up to no good, and now we have the
proof."

"How could you behave so foolishly, Diana?" Jonathan spoke coldly. "If you have no morals yourself,
you could at least have considered how your waywardness would reflect on us."

Diana felt tears sting her eyes but refused to give
them the satisfaction of seeing her cry. "I loved
Gary."

"Your virtue was tested and Satan won," Betsy put
in maliciously.

"You might have waited, Diana," Jonathan began,
"but since you didn't, there's no sense in crying over
spilled milk. You have no choice now except to marry
Walter as soon as it can be arranged."

Diana stiffened. "I won't. I don't love him and I
never will."

"You have no conception of the word 'love,'" Jonathan said sarcastically. "Animal lust is the only emotion you're capable of."

"That's not true," she shouted, her lips trembling.

Jonathan ignored her protestations. "Walter is a respectable, hardworking young man with a generous nature. He has taken a particular liking to you, and I feel fairly certain that I can convince him to overlook your . . . mistake. You should be eternally grateful to him for being willing to make an honest woman of you instead of moaning about love."

"I hate Walter. I'll never marry him," she shouted hysterically.

"All this excitement is bad for Diana," Dr. Peabody interrupted. "I'm sure she'll come around to your way of thinking. She is a sensible girl."

"You can't make me marry someone I loathe," Diana had screamed at them all.

"If you continue to refuse," Jonathan said severely, "you will show yourself to be without hope of possible redemption and I shall be forced to wash my hands of you."

"You mustn't be hasty, Jon," Dr. Peabody exclaimed, much disturbed. "The child has no one else to go to. You and Betsy are her only relatives."

"We've always treated her like one of our own children," Betsy lied. "Even though she showed early signs of willfulness and an excess of pride."

"I would rather be thrown out into the street to fend for myself then have to stay here and listen to your filthy lies," Diana said bitterly.

"Our patience is at an end, Diana," Jonathan said in a tone of finality. "I shall leave you alone to think over the very generous proposition I offered you. In the morning I will return for your answer. If you still refuse, I shall be forced to dismiss you from my house. I cannot tolerate such immoral behavior in my household. Your aunt and I have our own children's welfare to consider."

Diana had not changed her mind the next morning

in spite of the fears that haunted her and kept her
awake. True to his word, Jonathan turned his niece
out at a time in her life when she was in desperate
need of help and comfort. Instead of being frugal
with the little money they grudgingly gave her, she
used it to travel to the next town. Diana couldn't bear
living in a city that reminded her of so much unhappiness. She wanted to make a new life for herself and
her child. She would pretend to be a widow and raise
her son or daughter in an environment of love and affection. Fortunately she had enough sewing skills to
land a job in a ladies' clothing shop. The job lasted
until two months after the baby was born. Due to a
customer's complaint, she had been fired without notice. The baby was a girl, and she called her Helen,
after her mother. She was a sickly child, constantly in
need of medical attention. After Diana was fired, she
did any work she could get in order to make ends
meet. With Helen's medical bills piling up, she found
it increasingly difficult to refuse the advances of men
who offered her money to sleep with them.

Two married men she worked for offered her more
money to sleep with them than she could make repair-
ing and sewing clothes in a week. In desperation,
when Helen came down with a high fever and developed a racking cough, she agreed to meet with one
of the men so that she could pay for more medicine
and another visit from the doctor. She was too late.
The reason for selling her body was no longer necessary. While she was away, Helen died of consump-
tion. She was alone. There was no one else to love and
no one else to worry about. She felt her heart shrivel
up as she watched the tiny casket being lowered into
the ground. If she had had the money when Helen
first showed signs of her illness, she might have been
saved. As Diana slowly walked away from the
graveyard, the minister's words, "dust to dust and
ashes to ashes," kept ringing in her ears. She felt bitter
tears welling up in her eyes. She refused to cry; now

that her baby was dead, she needed a new purpose for
living. Before she reached her run-down rooming-
house, she found it. Because of a lack of money, Helen
had died and she had worked herself to the bone
for a few pennies. Money was the magical key to happiness. It warded off sickness and prevented starva-
tion. Money was something she was going to have,
lots of it. She knew she could earn only enough
money by sewing to keep her head above water. That
wasn't what she wanted. Respectability be damned!
She had already sinned by sleeping with Gary and
getting pregnant. When she had slept with a man for
money, she had sinned even more deeply. As far as
her relatives were concerned, she was sunk beyond redemption. If Helen had lived, she would have tried to
lead a respectable life by working long hours and doing without, so she wouldn't feel ashamed. Now it
didn't matter. She had only herself to think of. Diana
had plans. She wanted to open her own dress shop
someday and travel to foreign cities. It was all possible
with money. The fastest, easiest way to make large
sums of money was to enter into liaisons with wealthy
men. She hadn't found sleeping with men she didn't
love particularly difficult. Neither had their caresses
excited her as Gary's had done. She felt nothing.

Diana Wilson, the trusting, passionate orphan, vanished. Charity Walker, cool, ambitious, and calculating, took her place. Charity slept with first one man
and then another. Her clientele increased. She learned
to use her intuition. When a man needed advice, comfort, or sympathy, she was quick to sense it and didn't
play up sex. She made it a policy to be honest with
her customers, and never stooped to stealing or black-
mail. Frequently she tried to cultivate friendship
rather than desire. If, however, lust was the only way
a rich man would part with his money, she accommodated him.

In her career as companion/whore, Charity never
made any ties she couldn't break. She laughed with

her men, listened to their problems, and advised
them when they asked. She never once surrendered
herself to any man. The inner core that was her
birthright, the essence that was Charity, was never relinquished. She became a master at deception. She exposed only the superficial, surface side of herself even
to those closest to her. She learned how to play the
game to perfection. It took no effort and little feeling,
only practice. She remained calm, unruffled, dispas-
sionate, until her arrival in Sweetwater.

Rumors about the enormous amounts of money to
be made out west in towns where the men outnumbered the women eight to one had intrigued her. The
first western town she was in, she made a small fortune. Gradually, as the town's population increased,
pressure was brought to bear on the saloon girls by
the influx of "good women." Charity decided it was
time to move on to another, less civilized town. When
an opportunity arose to work in the Sweetwater
Saloon, she took it, not realizing that once again fate
had stepped in to shatter her life.

Charity frowned and shifted in her pew uncomfortably. She hadn't been inside a church since she left the
Boggses' house. Today she needed the comfort and security of an environment that reminded her of a sim-
pler time. She had once believed in the power of
prayer and the existence of a benevolent God. She
didn't now, of course. Nevertheless, she was here, she
thought wryly. She was here because of Jim Carson.
If only she hadn't fallen in love with him. Verbalizing
the word "love" frightened her, and she began nervously to smooth out an imaginary wrinkle in her
green silk dress. What a laugh! Charity Walker had
fallen in love. The day her three-month-old daughter
had been placed in the rocky earth, she believed that
the last remnant of love had withered inside her. She
wondered how Jim felt. Had he suddenly withdrawn
from her because he didn't want to become involved?
Or was it because he was afraid? She closed her eyes

and inhaled deeply. She could only guess about the way Jim felt. She knew she had never been so scared in all her life. Kneeling down on the hard floor, Charity began to pray.

Lorrie Gomber, sitting alone in her house, was also afraid. She had been surprised when the men returned and her father didn't come right home for his supper. Everything was hot and the table was set. An hour passed, and she still didn't hear his heavy step on the porch. She never dreamed that something had happened to him. Lorrie felt her father was invincible. As the minutes ticked by, she began to worry that by the time her father did appear, the food would be spoiled and he would be angry. She knew the other riders had returned long ago, and she was tempted to go out and ask someone when he was coming home. She bit her lower lip. The trouble was, she was afraid that if she left the house, he would show up and be furious at her for not being there. Just as she was debating about what she should do, she heard a heavy step on the porch. To her surprise, instead of the door being flung open, there was a knock.

"Come in," she said, frowning, realizing it couldn't be her father.

Joseph Mallory stepped into the dimly lit room. He had his hat in his hand, and he was looking uneasy. "Lorrie, your father . . ." he began, and looked away when he saw the set table.

"Yes?" she said curiously, wondering why he looked so uncomfortable.

"He was killed in the raid," Joseph Mallory said quietly.

"Killed?" Lorrie repeated in disbelief. "You mean he's dead?"

Joseph Mallory nodded. "But you needn't worry. You'll be taken care of. Everything will be settled tomorrow, after the soldiers come. In the meantime, if

you'd rather not be alone, I'm sure the Tilbys will be
pleased to have you stay with them."

Lorrie shook her head. "No, I'll be all right. I . . . I
want to be alone," she said in a dazed voice.

"If you need anything," he added as he started to
leave, "just ask."

After he left, Lorrie sat down at the table and
stared at the cracked bowl of cold mashed potatoes.
Her father wasn't coming home again. He was dead.
Lorrie shivered. She wasn't sad that he was dead. She
was shocked. Her father had had the strength of ten
men. Only a few hours ago he had been alive. If he
could die as quickly as she could blow out a candle,
then death was more frightening than she imagined.
Lorrie had never thought much about death before.
Her mother hadn't died. She had gone away. She
didn't know anyone else who had died. Vaguely she
wondered what happened when you died. The minister said you either went to heaven or hell. Heaven
was where the angels were. They had golden wings
and sang songs. Everything was very nice in heaven.
You sat on clouds and sang along with the angels.
Hell was a terrible place, inhabited by the devil and
searing flames. If you went to hell because of your
sins, you stayed there forever. You burned for all
eternity. She frowned and shivered again. She was
sure her father had gone straight to hell.

Lorrie got up from the table and went over to the
mirror to look at herself once again. She was free
now, just like she had always dreamed. She looked
closely at her reflection and was surprised. She had always felt she would look drastically different once she
was free of her father's tyrannical hold. What would
she do now that she was free? Joseph Mallory had
said she needn't worry. She would be taken care of.
Lorrie returned to the table and began automatically
to clear it off. What did he mean? As she scraped the
food back into the pots, a terrifying thought began to
take shape in her mind. She was all alone. There was

no relatives who would take her in. Would she be
sent to that place her father warned her about that
was infested with rats? A plate she was holding
slipped out her thin hands and fell to the floor with a
loud crashd. She stared at the smashed bits in dismay.
What would her father say? Then she remembered. It
didn't matter. She could break every dish in the cup-
board and it wouldn't matter. Her father couldn't
hurt her now. He was dead, and Lorrie was alone.

A faint rumble was heard in the distance, which the
citizens of Sweetwater at first attributed to thunder. It
was not thunder. It was the pounding of horses'
hooves that signified the beginning of the Cheyenne
revenge.

John and Nora Mallory were leaving the doctor's
office when five hundred Cheyenne suddenly burst
through the town. The Indians dragged with them
burning wagons, which they pushed into doorways.
As they rode, they threw firebrands and shot flaming
arrows into the buildings they passed, delivering such
bloodcurdling war cries that the hackles rose on their
enemies' necks. Because of the complete suddenness of
the attack, the white men were temporarily paralyzed.
John and Nora Mallory didn't even have an opportunity to seek protection. Their bodies were riddled
with arrows and bullets before they realized what had
happened.

Joseph Mallory was inside the Sweetwater Saloon
when the attack began. As soon as the momentary
shock had worn off, he grabbed his gun and ran with
the other customers to the doorway. He was just in
time to see his firstborn son and daughter-in-law as
they fell lifeless to the ground and were trampled
over by hundreds of horses. Like the others, Joseph
Mallory shot into the gathering darkness at the fleeting forms. The Indians, being expert riders, had the
advantage. They used their animals for cover as they
galloped through the town. It was impossible for the

bullets of their stunned victims to hit home. Many of
the screeching Indians rode right through the windows of homes or shops, shattering the glass and
shooting as they went. Some of them jumped off their
horses and hid in town, stalking the terrified citizens
as they tried to seek better protection or get to their
loved ones. The Cheyenne watched and waited, attacking those inside while they were busy reloading
or treating the wounded. It seemed to the petrified
population of Sweetwater that the town was suddenly
overrun with thousands of Indians. Just as they imagined they were safe and their hiding place secure, ten
Indians would drop through a hole in the roof or
break through a back entrance.

Joseph Mallory's remaining children were all located at the Tilby house. He decided to try to make it
back so he could be with them. Since the Tilbys had
only one entrance and fewer windows than many
other places, half a dozen of the other customers
stranded in the Sweetwater Saloon went with him.
Only Joseph Mallory made it there alive, and he
wouldn't have made it if Sean and Timothy hadn't
rushed out to drag him in. He had been seriously
wounded in both legs and an arm.

Inside the Tilby house, pandemonium had broken
out. Frank and Martha Tilby were trying to put out a
fire the Indians had started. Leslie Tilby was hysterical, and Katie was trying to calm her. Luke Tilby sat
pale and wide-eyed underneath the table, reloading
the guns.

"Dad!" Katie screamed when she saw her wounded
father.

"Leslie, you help your father with the fire," Mrs.
Tilby ordered her weeping daughter sternly as she
joined Katie at her father's side. "Get me a bowl of
hot water and a clean sheet for bandages," she instructed Katie kindly. "He'll be fine," she assured the
frightened girl.

Katie immediately obeyed her instructions and

watched as the older woman struggled with the arrow
shaft lodged in her father's shoulder. The sweat stood
out on his forehead and upper lip. As Mrs. Tilby finally extracted the ugly weapon, he grunted, and to
Katie's horror, fainted from the pain. Martha Tilby
frowned. "I don't think I'd better remove this one,"
she said, referring to one of his leg wounds. "It's
deeply embedded in the flesh, and I'm afraid I'll rip
him up if I take it out. He needs a doctor. I'll just tie
up the wound so the bleeding stops."

"He'll be all right until we can get him to a doctor,
won't he?" Katie whispered, staring at her father's
white face and listening to his uneven breathing.

"You needn't worry," Mrs. Tilby said in a strained
voice.

Katie looked at her uneasily. Martha's tone of voice
had disturbed her. The older woman's eyes were fastened on her husband. As though he felt her gaze,
Frank Tilby turned around. Their eyes locked, and
they exchanged silent words. Katie read the fear and
doubt in their glances and knew her question
concerning her father's health had been foolish. None
of them would survive the Indian onslaught.

The initial full-scale attack had abated to only a
smattering of gunfire and an occasional war cry. The
fire had been put out, Leslie's sobbing had decreased
to occasional sniffles, and a stillness that was broken
only by the sound of heavy breathing pervaded the
room. In spite of the stillness, they all knew it wasn't
over. The Cheyenne would not give up. They would
regroup themselves and attack again and again until
they were all dead. The soldiers would not come in
time. Death would be their punishment for breaking
the treaty. Feeling suddenly weak, Katie sat down on
the floor next to her father. As though he read her
mind, Sean came over to her and put an arm around
her.

Luke stopped loading the guns. He had grown even
paler than before. "Are we going to die?" he asked in

a trembling voice that sounded unnaturally loud in the still room.

Martha went over and hugged him to her. She smoothed the fair hair away from his face and said, "Of course not. The soldiers will come. Everything will be all right."

Katie and everyone else in the room were not deceived by her attempt to soothe her son's fears. They all avoided each other's eyes, terrified of seeing their suspicions confirmed. Katie swallowed several times to force back tears of terror at the thought of impending death. In order to keep her mind occupied, she helped Luke to load the guns.

Suddenly the distant rumble was heard again. Everyone stopped what he was doing and stared at each other in mounting fear and panic. No one mistook the sound for thunder this time. It was impossible to know how many people had already been wiped out. Glancing out the windows, they could see that half the town was in flames. Only the church and a few houses down the street were left standing. The Sweetwater Saloon was a pile of smoking ashes.

The second attack appeared to the frightened survivors to be even more ferocious than the first. Two more fires had to be put out. Sean suffered a slight head wound, and Frank Tilby was seriously wounded in the chest when an Indian managed to break through their barriers. Timothy killed the Indian, but their protection had been pierced and another member of their party had been disabled. Katie watched helplessly as a powerfully built Indian emerged from the burning Gomber house, carrying the screaming Lorrie with him. The Indian paused for a fraction of a second outside the house. Swirls of thick gray smoke half shielded him from flying bullets, while the sound of crackling flames rose about him, before he disappeared into the night.

During the battle, Joseph Mallory temporarily

recovered his senses and insisted on participating in the defense.

"Give me a gun," he demanded in a thick voice laced with pain.

"But, Dad," Katie protested as he struggled to sit up, "you're not strong enough."

"I've got enough strength left to send a few of those bastards to hell," he muttered between clenched teeth. "Besides, you need me."

"He's right," Martha Tilby shouted over the gunfire, "we need all the help we can get."

Reluctantly Katie and Timothy propped him up against one of the windows and placed a rifle in his hands.

When the siege trickled off for the second time, they all sat back exhausted, knowing that the third attack would entirely wipe them out. Their defenses could not stand up under another onslaught. They had only a few more rounds of bullets left.

"The women and children ought to hide in the cellar," Joseph Mallory whispered hoarsely before he fell into a fit of coughing that left him weak and his face drained of color.

His suggestion immediately erupted into quarreling.

"I won't leave Frank," Martha Tilby insisted, her face pale but determined. "However, I think it's a good idea for the rest of you," she added as her gaze rested on her two frightened children. "The only entrance to the cellar is a trapdoor located at the far end of the room. If some heavy furniture were placed against it, the Indians might overlook it. There's enough supplies to last several days."

"I'm not leaving either," Katie announced in a strained voice. "I'm as good a shot as Sean, and if he stays, I stay."

"I won't leave if you don't, Mama," Leslie put in tearfully.

"Me either," Luke said in a voice so low it was barely audible.

"Besides," Katie added, "if they burn the house, as I'm sure they will, the wooden trapdoor will burn too, and we'll be discovered or die of suffocation. I'm sure the Indians know our methods of concealment better than we think. They fought us a few years ago. They would remember cellars and trapdoors. They'll search the house thoroughly and find us."

"I know it's risky," Frank Tilby admitted weakly, "but your father is right, Katie. You've got to take the chance."

Katie would have argued it further if the Indians hadn't immediately resumed their attack.

It was impossible to know from which direction they came. They seemed to descend on them from every corner. The Indians burst through their scanty protection as though it had been constructed of paper. They crashed through the roof, smashed their way through the door in spite of the heavy furniture placed in front of it, and shot their way through the windows. There was no letup. When one Indian was killed, twenty more took his place, and the horrifying screams of the Indians as they leaped into their midst, with their knives and hatchets swinging, struck terror into every heart. None of them had time to dwell on their fear or compose a last-minute prayer for their souls. Each individual was fighting for his life. Joseph Mallory and Frank Tilby had been killed by ricocheting bullets before the Indians invaded their defenses.

As Joseph Mallory lay dying, Timothy ran to his side. His face was streaked with tears. "Dad!" he said in a choked voice. "Dad!" he repeated again in a pleading tone as Katie joined him.

Joseph Mallory opened his eyes and stared at his son. He knew he was dying and that now was the time when he ought to make his peace with him. He had never loved Timothy, never been proud of him or understood his weakness. He made an effort to rise, and stretched out a hand toward him. The words he had meant to say stuck in his throat. Instead he muttered, "You see to Katie, boy," before he fell back dead.

Timothy wept unashamedly, and Katie gently placed a hand on his slim shoulder. "It's no use, Tim, he's dead." She hesitated. "He told me earlier to tell you he was proud of you. He was going to tell you himself, only he didn't have the opportunity or the strength," she lied.

Timothy looked at her doubtfully. "He really did?"

Katie nodded. "Sure, you can ask Sean."

Timothy wiped the tears away and got up. "Thanks, Katie," he said softly.

Katie watched him return to his place at the window. Tim's obsession to secure his father's love and approval had predictably failed once again. Her father was a stubborn fool. Tears came to her eyes. It didn't really matter anymore, she thought bitterly. We'll all be dead before morning.

When Frank Tilby had been fatally shot, Martha had run to her husband's side, only to be caught by a bullet in the head, shot by the first invader. Sean had killed the yelling intruder, but he couldn't stop the others that followed on his heels. Katie stood at one end of the room, facing an unoccupied window, and grimly shot each painted face that appeared. The room was rapidly filling up with smoke and dead bodies. Two Indians, enraged at the massacre of their village, furiously attacked Timothy and knocked him to the floor. Sean was struggling with another. Katie averted her gaze from the window in time to shoot one of the two Indians who had Timothy pinned to the ground and was about to scalp him while he was still alive. The other one managed to bury his knife deep in Timothy's stomach before her second bullet reached him. Leslie began to scream hysterically again and ran past them outside, despite Katie's pleading with her to remain where she was. Luke followed his sister, calling after her. He was blocked at the door by the sudden appearance of Spotted Tail, who deftly scooped up the startled boy in his arms and darted out again before the remaining two survivors could prevent him from carrying out his intention.

Katie heard Leslie's cries of pain and terror as she was dragged away by three Cheyenne. More Indians crowded into the room, and Katie aimed her gun at those that were closest. To her horror, she discovered it was empty. Grabbing the rifle by its butt, she held it up, poised ready to strike the first attacker. She was going down fighting. Before she had an opportunity to use it, a strong hand grabbed her arm from behind and snatched the rifle out of her grasp. It fell to the floor with a thud. She turned around to bravely face her assailant. What she saw caused the blood to freeze in her veins. She gasped with horror at the most terrifying vision she had ever beheld. Black Elk watched her fighting to the end against overwhelming odds and admired her bravery and courage. He had not abandoned his original intention of capturing a white woman. Since he was not surprised by the look of revulsion that appeared in her eyes when she saw his scarred visage, he pulled on her arm to indicate he wanted her to follow him. By this time Katie had recovered from the initial shock of seeing him, and began to struggle, striking out at his chest with her fists and clawing at his hand to force him to release her. Realizing she wouldn't willingly comply with his request, he didn't try to persuade her. Instead, he threw her lightly over his shoulder as if she were a dead animal carcass, and despite her struggles, carried her outside. She screamed out for Sean to come to her aid. Her pleas were useless. Sean had been wounded and taken prisoner by Tall Bull, who had lost his own son in the raid on his village and intended to take Sean to replace him.

Like the Mallorys and the Tilbys, Ben Haskell, stuck in the Laraby Café, had managed to repell the Indians in the first attack. He had been lucky, but Ben was not foolish enough to believe he could win successive battles. Unlike his naive wife, Sara, he did not for one moment entertain the notion that the Indians had given up. What troubled him considerably was that he had only a half-dozen bullets left. Two possibilities were open to him, neither one of which he particularly enjoyed contemplating. He was a realist, and if he had to die, he would die fighting. That was the way he preferred to go. Sara was different. He could see she was paralyzed with fear. She wasn't crying. She was too damn scared for that. Instead, she had seemed to shrink into herself when he told her that the savages would return. She knew how many bullets he had left, and the idea that she might not be killed instantly but live long enough to suffer the abuses and torture of those animals once they laid hands on her had driven her to beg him to spare a bullet for her. Just thinking about what they could do to Sara once they had her in their clutches caused Ben to suffer the torments of hell. He took a deep breath, trying to steady his nerves. It came down to making a decision. He knew she could never shoot herself. She knew it too, and had asked him to do it. His right hand, which held the gun, was burning with sweat, and he released the weapon long enough to wipe his hand on his pants leg. There wouldn't be much time left. The Indians weren't taking very long between attacks.

If Ben Haskell had been a different man, he might have regretted the decision that had been the cause for their present disaster. But Ben, like Joseph Mallory, was not a man to regret an action once taken. He was only sorry it hadn't worked out the way he had planned it. He didn't blame himself for being too greedy. To his way of thinking, there was nothing wrong with resettling the Indians' land with decent white folks. If a man who started out poor couldn't wind up rich in America settling the land and fashioning tiny holes into big cities, then America wasn't the land of opportunity it was reputed to be. Ben glanced

at his terrified wife. He did feel sorry for Sara. He
got up and went over to her. She searched his face,
and trembling, leaned against his chest. He enfolded
her to him in a tight embrace and kissed the top of her
head.

"I love you, Sara. You've given me more happiness
than I ever expected," he whispered softly, his voice
sounding hoarse and remote even to his ears.

"I love you too, Ben," Sara murmured shivering.

She smelled strongly of soap and water, and his
throat constricted. He wondered how in God's name
he was going to find enough courage to kill her. Suddenly Sara's grip on him tightened. The Indians were
returning for the second time on their murderous mission. He didn't move. Sara's embrace tightened. The
bitter memory of the brutal slaughter of his first
family suddenly materialized before him, and the
remembered atrocities of those days gave him the
strength to lift his gun to his wife's temple and
fire. The retort of the shot caused Sara's body to jerk
before turning stiff and falling slack against him. It
killed her instantly. He stared down at the black hole
in her head, from which a steady stream of blood was
flowing. He wiped away the sticky red liquid from
her small ashen face before he aimed the gun calmly
at the door, remaining where he was, with Sara still
against his chest. The first five Indians who tried to
enter were swiftly dispatched. The sixth found his
mark, and Ben Haskell, mighty empire builder, fell
back dead against the wall, an arrow piercing his
heart, the now-empty gun still in his hand.

Because of the solid structure of the church, Charity Walker and Elizabeth Farrell remained safe until
the third siege. When the firing started, Charity ran
to the heavy wooden door and bolted it. There were
only two windows, located too far up for the Indians
to reach. They had been shattered by bullets, and the
glass was scattered on the floor and in the empty
pews. Outside they could hear, above the shooting,

the Indian war cries and the screams of the dying, all the more frightening because they couldn't see anything. They could only listen and imagine what was happening outside.

Neither of them lacked imagination. They said little to each other during the time the raging battle took place. But within each woman's heart beat the faint hope that the Indians would overlook the church. They couldn't seem to break through the barriers of pews the two women placed in front of the big door. Their efforts appeared to be successful. Nevertheless, their attempts to protect themselves were futile and their hopes crushed by the third encounter. The Indians had gotten hold of a pole that at one time had belonged to the Sweetwater Saloon, and began ramming it against the door.

"They'll be in soon," Elizabeth whispered, her face white and her long slender hands trembling.

Charity looked around the one-room church with disgust. "A rabbit couldn't hide in this hole."

"What can we do?" Elizabeth asked, flinching every time the pole was rammed against the door.

Charity's gaze caught sight of the fragments of splintered glass on the floor. She picked up a particularly wicked-looking piece. Placing herself on one side of the door, she said in a determined voice, "I don't know about you, but I'm going to try to make it outside. If there are any survivors, they'll have guns."

Elizabeth gingerly picked up a piece of glass at her feet and joined Charity at her position by the door but she didn't think they had a one-in-a-million chance.

The door began to give. Chunks of flying wood shot off into the blackness. In another five seconds the door was completely demolished and the Indians rushed past them into the dark church, carrying firebrands. Elizabeth felt Charity touch her in warning, and followed close behind as she slashed at the last Indian in an effort to escape.

Red Turtle hardly blinked as the glass cut into his

arm and the blood gushed out. He grabbed Charity
and pushed Elizabeth backward so that she tripped
and fell. He roughly flung Charity to her knees, and
grabbing her by her hair, pulled her head back while
he raised his knife to slit her throat. He noticed with
pleasure the fear and terror in her eyes and would
have instantly completed his bloody act if the face of
White Dove had not appeared before him. She was
looking at him with a mournful expression, and his
hands trembled. The vision evaporated, only to reap-
pear once again as he was about to kill the white
woman. He frowned and decided it was a sign. She
was not meant to die. He jerked Charity roughly to
her feet. From what he could see, she was young and
strong. She would live a long life. He smiled grimly.
In the battle, he had been the most fearless fighter, entering into the thick of the fight, careless of personal
safety. He had nothing to lose. White Dove, Yellow
Moon, and his two sons would no longer be eagerly
waiting for his victorious return. The fighting was
nearly over, but the gnawing hatred still ate away at
him, refusing to be appeased by the merciless retribu-
tion. Death was not enough. He wanted the white-
eyes to suffer as he did, to feel the misery of utter
despair, to drink of the bitterness that had scalded his
throat, and to know there was no hope. His eyes
gleamed in the darkness as he stared down at his
prisoner. She would be his to do with as he chose, to
be a slave to Bright Eyes. He could wreak his vengeance upon her as long as she lived. She would live a
long time. He would see to that. With a painful pull
on her hair, he shoved her outside.

When Red Turtle had pushed Elizabeth backward
and she lost her balance, falling to the floor, she had
found two Indians hovering over her when she tried
to rise. One of them had a firm clasp on her arm. The
other was arguing and gesticulating. The first was
Gray Sky. He had seen Elizabeth fall, and rushed over
to her in order to claim her for his prisoner. He had

been beaten by another warrior, who wanted to scalp her. Gray Sky argued with Yellow Wolf until the other agreed to an exchange. He would give Yellow Wolf a horse if he would leave the woman to him. Yellow Wolf shrugged and left him alone with his prisoner. Gray Sky eyed her with satisfaction. She was young and would afford him another opportunity for begetting children.

Elizabeth never considered the possibility of being taken prisoner by the Cheyenne. Death had appeared to be the only result of an Indian massacre. Her first reaction was one of relief. She obediently followed her captor to his horse and allowed herself to be swung up in front of him. Her second feeling, which was much stronger, was one of dread. What did he have in mind? Did he intend to hold her for ransom? Or was he going to keep her as his squaw? Elizabeth shivered and tried to turn around so she could get a better look at him. She hadn't noticed his features in the church. Too much had been going on, and she had imagined herself near death. Perhaps he had a kind face and could be persuaded to let her go, once he understood that her husband would pay him handsomely for her safe return. Gray Sky grunted his disapproval at her movement and forced her to keep her gaze fixed straight ahead.

The six sole survivors of what would shortly become known as the Sweetwater massacre stared at each other with a mixture of horror and shock as the inky blackness was briefly illuminated by soaring flames that consumed the town. Katie noted thankfully that besides herself, her brother Sean had been spared. Luke Tilby, Mrs. Farrell, one of the saloon women, and Lorrie Gomber were, she discovered, also prisoners. Although she had last seen Leslie Tilby alive, she was not with them now. Katie forced herself not to think about what had befallen Leslie after the three Cheyenne had carted her off behind one of the burning buildings.

The Indians stayed only long enough to gather their wounded before they rode off to a prearranged meeting place, where they would pick up what remained of their families and disperse into the hills.

There was not one prisoner who did not feel the tentacles of fear constrict in his stomach to a hard knot as they galloped through the night into an uncertain future.

Joseph Mallory, the catalyst, was dead. His actions had erupted into death and terror for both sides. He had murdered his own flesh and blood in his quest for vengeance. Now all that remained of him was the record of his deed and the smoldering embers of the town he had inadvertently destroyed.

4

The occupants of Fort Jubele watched in silent apprehension as Michael Mallory galloped into their midst covered with dust and sweat. His favorite horse was foaming at the mouth. Instead of taking time to dismount, he jumped off the still-moving animal and forced his way into Lieutenant Farrell's office with the protesting Corporal Olsen close on his heels.

"What is the meaning of this intrusion, Corporal?" Lieutenant Farrell asked sharply as an angry red flush crept into his usually pale cheeks. "I gave specific orders not to be disturbed while I was conferring with"—his face stiffened—"Mr. Boone."

"Yes, sir. I know, sir," Corporal Olsen agreed. "But *he* took me by surprise. Do you want me to show him out?" he demanded, glancing at Michael Mallory meaningfully.

"I have to talk to you, sir," Michael interrupted impatiently, ignoring the corporal. "The Indians are on the warpath again."

Obviously startled, the lieutenant motioned for the now-fascinated corporal to leave them alone. When the door was tightly shut, he turned to Michael and spoke in a tone of considerable annoyance.

"Explain yourself, young man. What is all this about? The Indians are at peace with us. I personally paid a visit to White Mountain only last week, and everything was under control."

Michael paled and then flushed under the cool stare of the lieutenant as he slowly and with painstaking detail explained the situation. He added nervously as he finished, "and I feel there is no time to lose, sir. The Indians might decide to attack tonight instead of in the morning. In my opinion, troops ought to be sent out immediately."

An uncomfortable silence followed this speech. Lieutenant Farrell rose and approached Michael Mallory until he stood only a foot away from him. His blue eyes bore into the boy, and he spoke with biting sarcasm. "In your opinion indeed. Your opinion is of no possible worth to me. If what you say is true, I can only imagine that your family and the town of Sweetwater have gone mad."

The sudden unexpected sound of someone chuckling drew their attention to the third occupant of the room, who was leaning against the wall, his arms folded across his massive chest. Mr. Boone, or just plain Boone as he was known to the soldiers, was the scout for Fort Jubele. He had just turned forty, although he looked considerably older. His skin was dark and leathery from constant exposure to the elements, while his face still retained the faded marks of the smallpox he had contracted in his youth.

Boone's body was hard and lean from years of training in the outdoors. His voice was raspy from too much smoking and alcohol. He was the best scout west of the Mississippi, and the only thorn in Lieutenant Farrell's side.

The lieutenant was neat, precise, a teetotaler, the perfect gentleman, and a firm believer in rules and regulations. Boone was careless about the way he looked, refused to wear a uniform, indulged in all manner of sinful practices on his time off, spoke his mind, and frequently strayed from his superiors' orders. The lieutenant frowned and was in the process of reprimanding Boone when he caught sight of the mocking brown eyes challenging him and thought better of it. Before Michael Mallory had interrupted them, Boone and the lieutenant were engaged in another battle of wills. As usual, the lieutenant was losing. Boone had an insolent manner that enraged his superior officer. This, plus the fact that the lieutenant had tried and failed on numerous occasions to get Boone transferred to another fort, added salt to his wounds. Although the lieutenant was not a man to be ruled by his emotions, he had come close to hating the scout. It rankled deeply that although Boone openly showed contempt for him and flaunted his authority at every opportunity, he could not get rid of him. Now, because he feared losing another battle with Boone, this time in front of an audience, Lieutenant Farrell compressed his lips together and shifted his attention and hostility to Michael Mallory.

"There's no excuse for such shocking disobedience. The citizens of Sweetwater beg and whine about needing protection against the Indians. They plead for a fort to be built nearby that will make the savages stay in line. Then, without apparent motive, they deliberately break the treaty themselves and expect the soldiers to protect them from an Indian reprisal. It's absurd!"

The lieutenant paused for breath, and in the interim the jarring sound of Boone clapping filled the room. Lieutenant Farrell found his hands balling into fists, and had to fight down an impulse to physically assault the scout. Determined not to lose his temper, he ignored him, scowling at the embarrassed boy in front of him.

"Well?" he demanded coldly.

Michael shifted his weight and stammered. "Yes, sir . . . but at the time, we all thought—"

"You can't make me believe you thought at all," Lieutenant Farrell interrupted angrily as he began pacing up and down in front of his big oak desk, his arms crossed behind his back. "If any one of you had thought the situation out, you would have come to the fort for help. If you imagined that the Indians were beginning to pose a serious threat, you should have consulted me. After all, *I* am directly responsible for law and order. *I* would have seen that nothing happened." Abruptly he stopped pacing and returned to his chair behind the desk. He glared at Michael resentfully, as his long slender fingers gently pressed against his throbbing temples. He was beginning to feel the first signs of a headache, and winced. "You arrived with your news at a most inopportune time. We are at the moment severely understaffed. The majority of my men are out on other missions. However," he added quickly, as he saw the horror on Michael's face, "I fully expect them to return before nightfall."

"It may be too late by then," Michael shouted, paling slightly.

Lieutenant Farrell frowned and hesitated. His first duty was to protect the fort. On the other hand, if the boy was right, he would be held personally responsible for any harm that befell the inhabitants of Sweetwater. It was a ticklish situation, he thought, annoyed.

"The boy's got it straight," Boone put in quietly. "And your wife is in town," he added almost as an afterthought.

Lieutenant Farrell felt a momentary pang of guilt. He had forgotten all about Elizabeth. But he knew better than anyone that personal considerations ought not to enter into making professional decisions. He sat up stiffly in the wooden chair so that his spine felt rigid. It was easier making decisions that way. He felt more like a commanding officer, more like the general he had always wanted to be. "I am in charge here," he said icily. "The men will leave when I say so, and not one second before. My first duty is to this fort, and we will await the return of all my men so we can be sure the fort is not left unprotected."

"But, sir!" Michael begged.

"Good day, gentlemen," Lieutenant Farrell said firmly, averting his gaze to the pile of official-looking

documents in front of him, dismissing both Michael
Mallory and Boone.

It was late afternoon by the time the soldiers set
out, with Boone in charge. Michael Mallory, supplied
with a fresh horse by the fort, rode with them. After
his interview with Lieutenant Farrell, Michael had
fallen into a gloomy silence. The rumor of what had
happened quickly spread around the fort. Everyone
had pressed him for details, but Michael had not been
in a communicative mood.

Boone, idly studying Michael's troubled countenance from underneath his battered hat, speculated
about what was going on in the boy's mind. He was
pretty sure Michael hadn't experienced a twinge of
conscience about what he had done. His family's
safety—that's all that worried him. A bitter smile
slowly crossed Boone's face. In his experience, the
only time white people ever felt guilt over the death
of an Indian was when it caused trouble for themselves. To the majority of white men, Indians were
considered savages, beasts that were better dead than
alive.

Boone squinted against the sun's dying rays. Taking
a deep breath of the dry air, he choked. The air was
heavy, oppressive. His throat felt tight, constricted.
Another man might feel he was coming down with a
cold. Boone had never had a cold in his life. His
throat began to close up when death stalked his heels.
It was instinct. Most white men didn't even know
what instinct was. If they did, they felt embarrassed
about it and tried to ignore the unfamiliar feeling.
Boone knew that was just plain dumb. He had learned
years ago to listen to his instincts. The Sioux and
Cheyenne had taught him how necessary it was to a
man's survival. He frowned as a hot breeze stirred
Michael's golden hair. Boone had little respect for his
own people. He had spent most of his life among the
Indians, and thought more like an Indian than a white
man. From what he had seen of his own kind, he pre-

ferred the company of so-called savages. His eyes began to burn, and he rubbed them with a sweaty palm. He wondered how Michael would take it when he learned that his fears had been confirmed. Boone's throat felt like it was on fire. He tried clearing it again, and thought to himself once more how stupid Lieutenant Farrell was. The man was an ass. Boone wiped the beads of perspiration from his forehead with a wrinkled shirtsleeve and sighed. Asses were the only kind of man the military ever promoted. Lieutenant Farrell was another graduate from West Point. They arrived from the East, all looking exactly alike, with their starched uniforms, knowledge from books, and the gleam of ambition in their eyes. Without exception, they were greenhorns with no real understanding of the problems facing them, and little desire to learn. All they cared about was following rules and regulations to the letter. No deviations. Boone smiled grimly. Then they met him. He had given them all a hard time. He enjoyed their frustration and discomfort. It was his retaliation for their stupidities, their total ignorance. Boone had, however, another, much more ingrained reason for tormenting them. He felt that all men and women had the God-given right to do whatever they wanted, provided they didn't hurt anybody else. He despised anything or anybody that took away that right. Boone was an individualist. Restrictions on freedom and uniform behavior enraged him and brought out his worst traits. The army was no place for him. If he had been free, he would never have entered a fort, never seen a settlement. He felt uncomfortable in towns and cities, preferring the pine and birch trees for company. Tall, majestic, snow-capped mountains were his favorite type of scenery. The sight of church spires left him cold. He had grown up on the smell of sweet grass and maple trees. Soft deerskin moccasins protected his feet. He had known the company of birds and wild animals most of his life. He sighed. He had made a bargain, had given his word. Now there was no other choice. He had to act as a scout for the army. He had to wait it out. He took a deep breath. Soon he would be free, free to roam the prairies again, free to visit with his friends the Cheyenne and fish along the riverbanks where the water was clear enough to see straight through to the bottom, even in the deepest parts.

Boone had been born on a wagon train heading west, in a time when the only other white settlers were the bleached bones of those that had come before. His parents named him Samuel Jacob Dawson. His father had been an adventurer who should never have gotten married. He was always on the move from one place to another. He hated crowds. A crowd, to Abraham Dawson, was thirty people living in a hundred-mile radius. His constant wanderings must have disappointed his young, farm-raised wife. She followed her restless, handsome husband into unexplored territory, surrounded by naked red men who spoke in guttural tones when they spoke at all. As far as Boone recalled, she had never complained. When they paused for any length of time, she took the opportunity to teach her young son the Bible, which she always carried with her, and impressed upon him the importance of the ten commandments. His father taught him how to ride, hunt, fish, and swim. Before he was eight years old, he had learned to speak the language of the Sioux and Cheyenne.

In the summer of his tenth year, tragedy overtook young Samuel for the first time when they came across a white settlement stricken with smallpox. Because his father had been touched by the disease as a young man, he was immune. His mother died.

Samuel survived a long illness, retaining the scars of the terrible disease the rest of his life. By the time he recovered his health, his father, feeling guilty over his son's scanty education, insisted he remain in the settlement with friends and get an education.

"I ain't never had no book learning, and the way

we travel from one place to another, you're going to grow up as ignorant as I am, boy."

"I already know how to read and write," Samuel interrupted. "And I'm not ignorant about hunting and riding."

His father frowned, and forced himself to speak harshly, since he privately sympathized with his son and would have preferred having him with him.

"Education is more than just reading and writing. Your mama"—his voice trembled slightly—"was an educated woman, and she would have wanted you to have the opportunity to learn as much as you can. She took pride in the knowledge of books, and was worried about you growing up wild. She used to complain you were more Indian that white."

"What's wrong with that?" Samuel asked.

"I don't want no sass, you hear, boy?" Abraham demanded sternly.

"Yes, sir."

"You remain here through the winter, and if you apply yourself to learning what you can, maybe I'll take you with me in the summer when I return from trapping."

"Yes, sir!" Samuel agreed, with unaccustomed meekness.

Abraham Dawson hadn't counted on his son's stubbornness and resourcefulness. The ten-year-old boy came after him, leaving the settlement in the middle of the night and tracking his father down after several weeks until he found him. Impressed by the boy's frontier skills, his father overlooked his disobedience and kept him with him, nicknaming him Boone, after the legendary hero Daniel Boone. He was henceforth known simply as Boone.

All that summer and fall Boone and his father slept on blankets spread over soft, sweet-smelling pine needles, eating antelope, rabbit, buffalo meat, berries, and fresh fish. They trapped the beaver, mink, and rabbit for their furs so that they could trade them at the forts and settlements for canned goods, flour, sugar, blankets, and bullets for their guns. When the fall turned to winter, the soft white snow coming waist-deep and the rivers freezing over several inches thick, they could be sure of a warm fire, food, and good company among their friends the Cheyenne. It was a way of life not destined to last.

In the fall of the following year, the threat of war between the Sioux and the white men erupted into reality. The peaceful trading they had practiced for so many years was threatened as the Sioux painted their bodies and got their weapons ready for war. Abraham Dawson refused to believe the Sioux would turn against him. He was their friend, as he was a friend to the Cheyenne. Why shouldn't the trading continue on as before? The night before their planned journey into Sioux territory, as they sat before a Cheyenne campfire, their old friend Swift Arrow tried to warn them.

"The Sioux have lost many strong warriors. Women and children have been killed. The fire of hate burns steadily within the breasts of the Sioux. It is foolish of you, my friend, to ignore the inevitable. War has been declared, and in spite of your good intentions, you are white."

"But I had nothing to do with what happened at Cougar's Bluff," Abraham protested. "I have been a friend to the Cheyenne and the Sioux all my life. You know I speak the truth."

Swift Arrow spoke slowly, sadly. "I know you have never cheated us or killed a Cheyenne or a Sioux. You have been a good and loyal friend. But you are white. The Sioux want revenge and will not ask to see the purity of your heart. They will kill you and your son. Why not stay here with us, where you and the boy will be safe?"

Abraham Dawson was stubborn. He couldn't believe he was in serious danger. He knew the names of most of the Sioux tribe. To prove his good intentions, he took his young son with him.

Swift Arrow was right. The Sioux did not waste time with words. They opened fire as soon as they spotted Abraham and Boone. Abraham was killed with the first volley of shots. Boone's horse was shot out from under him, and he thought he too would be killed. It was only after much deliberation that the Sioux decided to adopt him into the tribe. He remained with them five years and was treated well. During that period, Boone didn't waste time nursing a hatred for the people who had murdered his father. He realized his father should have listened to Swift Arrow's advice. Boone lived among the Indians long enough to understand their philosophy. His father was white, and white men had attacked the Sioux. Revenge was something the eleven-year-old boy could understand. Since he had become one of them by adoption the Sioux did not hate him. He belonged to them. He was a Sioux.

Although the Indians were kind to him and accepted him as one of them, he never felt happy with his adopted tribe. He longed to return to the people he considered his own, the Cheyenne. An opportunity for escape arose when he was fourteen. He had gained a reputation as a fine hunter. Because he had never tried to escape previously, they allowed him to go out hunting alone. He never returned.

The Sioux had taught him more about life in the wilderness than he had known previously. During the succeeding years he spent with the Cheyenne, he learned even more. He mastered the Cheyenne language and customs so well that a casual observer would never have been able to tell him apart from the other Cheyenne warriors. He was valuable to the tribe as a hunter and tracker, and made many friends.

When he was twenty-one he took a bride. Her name was Laughing Girl. Boone courted her for four years before sending his adopted mother, White Rabbit, to ask for her in marriage. White Rabbit took thirty-five horses with her and tied them in front of Laughing Girl's lodge before making the announcement. She said simply, "Great Bear wishes your daughter, Laughing Girl, for his wife." Without waiting for an answer, she immediately returned home.

Gray Plume, Laughing Girl's father, summoned his relatives to ask their advice. This was a purely formal procedure, as he approved of Boone, whom the Indians called Great Bear, and had already made up his mind to agree to the match. The relatives shared his opinion, but if an unfavorable decision had been reached, the horses would have been turned loose and driven back to Boone's lodge. Until the decision was made, the horses stayed in front of Gray Plume's lodge. Once it was agreed that Laughing Girl could marry Boone, the horses were dispersed among her relatives. Her favorite cousin, Gentle Horse, received one, and her uncle, Big Mule, another. In return, they caught their best horse and sent it to Gray Plume's lodge to go with the horses he would send to Boone in return. They sent other gifts as well: blankets, robes, bowls, ornaments. Everyone had known ahead of time that the marriage was to take place and had prepared for it.

Laughing Girl was placed on top of one of the best horses. It was led by a woman not related to her. Her mother, Sun Woman, followed behind, leading ten horses, all of which wore ropes or bridles. The other thirty horses were led by female relatives and friends. Before they reached Boone's lodge, some of his adopted relatives came out and spread a new blanket on the ground. Laughing Girl was lifted from the horse and set in the middle of the blanket. The young men took it by the corners and carried her into the lodge. No one spoke.

When Laughing Girl set out, she was wearing new clothes, but after she had been taken into Boone's lodge, his female cousins took her to the back and removed her clothing. Laughing and giggling, they dressed her in clothing they had made, including a dress adorned with elk's teeth. Gently they combed and rebraided her long black hair and painted her face. In addition, they presented her with gifts, which she immediately put on. Among the ornaments she received were necklaces made of fish vertebrae, earrings of large blue beads strung on sinew, hammered silver pieces to be attached to her braids, and copper bracelets.

White Rabbit had prepared food. When Laughing Girl and Boone seated themselves side by side, she offered it to them. Laughing Girl's portion was already cut up into tiny pieces so that she need make no effort in eating.

The wedding lodge had been made for her in advance, and was pitched near her father's home. Because of the mother-in-law taboo, it was placed far enough in back so that Boone wouldn't have to see his mother-in-law too often. He wasn't permitted to speak to or even to look at her unless he had completed certain ceremonies. Once the lodge was ready, Sun Woman went to her daughter and said, "Daughter, there is your lodge. It is your home. Go and live in it."

Boone was a trapper, and absent from the village more than he was in it. Laughing Girl eventually succeeded in convincing him to allow her to accompany him into the mountains and plains. She waited patiently for him at the trading posts while he bartered for his catch of furs. The people at the posts and growing settlements eyed him with suspicion and hostility. They couldn't understand how he could prefer the Indians to his own kind. His refusal to answer their rude personal questions about Cheyenne customs angered them. His acting as the Indians' bartering agent so they would get a fair deal enraged them.

Laughing Girl bore him a son. The boy was given

two names, a white name and an Indian one. They called him Abraham after his father's father and White Bull after his mother's grandfather. Boone taught his wife to speak English. They were very happy.

When his son was seven years old, and while Boone was off trapping, a party of ten white men who had been away from civilization for several months searching for gold came upon his camp. Feeling a strong sense of uneasiness that morning, Boone trusted his intuition and returned to camp in time to see two of the men tie Laughing Girl down while another one ripped off her clothes with a hunting knife. His son lay lifeless on the ground nearby. He shot one of the men in the leg. Before he could do anything more, he was dazed by a bullet from behind. Strong hands bound his wrists with ropes while he was too weak to do more than feebly struggle. As he lay in a semiconscious state, he heard the cries and moaning of his young wife and the cruel laughter of the men. It appeared to Boone, lying helpless, that he heard his wife's screams of pain and terror for days before the final shot put a merciful end to her life. In reality, it lasted only one day. The men left him for dead and disappeared. By morning his head had cleared and the mist was gone from his eyes. The bullet wound had stopped bleeding of its own accord. Although he was weak, he was no longer helpless. He managed to free himself by shoving his hands into the smoldering campfire, until the hot coals burned the strands of rope away. His wrists still bore the faint discoloration where the fire had seared the flesh. Freed from his bonds, he staggered over to where his family lay and stared down at their battered, cold bodies, trying to comprehend what had happened. His body shook with a cold fury that left him weak. He had to sit down. Why? Why had they done this thing? He had done nothing to them to account for such brutality. At that time the Cheyenne were not at war with the white men, and Laughing Girl was a Cheyenne. He groaned. Didn't they know that? "Laughing Girl was a Cheyenne," he had shouted out, his voice echoing through the morning stillness. Boone could understand and accept the death of his father because it was an act of revenge in a time of war. He couldn't begin to understand what had happened to Laughing Girl and his son. His eyes narrowed to slits whenever he recalled that day.

The white men had only contempt for the Indians, looking on them as little better than wild animals. Of the two races, Boone knew it was the white men who were the more primitive, despite their enormous cities, superior weapons, and mighty ships. No Indian ever stole from his own people. No Indian would rape and kill unless he was at war, or waste his daylight hours keeping his eyes fastened to the earth searching for the yellow metal the white men called gold, while he was surrounded by the wonders of nature. White men were jealous of their possessions, hoarding them in locked and barred houses. The Indians shared their wealth with those less fortunate than themselves. The white men brought firewater, sickness, and death to the Indians. They smiled falsely at the chiefs while they secretly plotted to wipe the Indians out by deliberately butchering their herds of buffalo and removing them to other lands totally inhospitable to their continued growth. Ironically, the white men in their superior fashion also felt their religion was better than that of the Indians and tried to force it on them. The red men needed to be saved and brought to Christ. To Boone's way of thinking, it was the white men who needed to be saved from their own greed and lust, not the Indians.

Once he had recovered sufficiently from his wounds and his grief, Boone returned the bodies of Laughing Girl and his son to her people to be attended to properly.

According to Cheyenne lore, Laughing Girl and White Bull would travel to the home of the dead, which was where Heammawihio lived. All Cheyenne went there after death. It was reached by following the Milky Way. The dead lived as they did in life. The men chased the buffalo, hunted other game, and went to war. The women cooked, made clothes, and raised children. The lodges were all white and handsomely painted.

Laughing Girl and White Bull were tenderly dressed in their finest clothing, their bodies placed on robes, which were then folded closely, the bundles lashed with ropes that were passed many times about them. The bundles were finally lashed onto travois and carried to the designated place of burial, with Boone and Laughing Girl's relatives following behind. The women cut their hair short and gashed their heads with knives to express their sorrow. The men unbraided their hair and let it hang loose. There was much wailing. The bodies were placed together on the same scaffold on poles in the prairie. Boone remained by the grave in mourning for twenty-four hours. As soon as he had completely recovered, he set out alone on a mission of revenge. Many of the Cheyenne offered to accompany him. He refused their aid. He knew if the Indians joined him in his private quest for vengeance, it would start a war. Boone was not an Indian and could pursue his own path of destruction and let the authorities kill him if they could. Before they did, he would find every last one of the butchers if it took him the rest of his life.

Boone had no trouble tracking down the first man. He came upon him while he slept. He was small, slim and wiry, with mousy brown hair and a sallow complexion. Boone stood over his victim, watching him sleep unawares, the stinking smell of the man burning his nostrils as hate roared in his ears, making him dizzy. He muttered hoarsely, "Get up, you bastard."

The man sat up, wide-awake. Automatically he reached for his gun. It wasn't in its accustomed place.

The little man's face twitched. "What do you want? If it's money, you're out of luck," he said nervously.

"You don't recognize me, do you?" Boone asked softly.

The man blinked, feeling suddenly uneasy. "Am I supposed to?"

"Get up and slowly move toward the fire. Maybe the light will jog your memory."

The man licked his thin lips and stood up. Boone shoved him toward the fire. Suddenly the man stopped dead in his tracks and turned around to face him. Dawning realization drained him of all color. He trembled. "You ... you're alive."

Boone's eyes gleamed in the dark as he raised his rifle butt and knocked the man to the ground with one blow. He watched him, a look of disgust reflected in his eyes as the man groaned, covering his bleeding head, and tried to squirm in the direction of his weapon. Boone let the man get within one inch of it before he kicked him viciously in the face. Kneeling over him, knife at his throat, he demanded coldy, "Where are the others?"

"I don't know. I swear I don't," he croaked. Boone pressed the knife slightly against the soft flesh, drawing blood. The man winced.

"I want to know their names and where they have gone. You know!"

"No, I don't. I don't," the man lied. Beads of perspiration poured down his forehead and neck as the pain from the incision, which had at first felt like a thousand pinpricks, became more painful. "It wasn't my fault. I didn't want to go along with the others. They forced me," he pleaded, moaning.

"I can slice you up into a million pieces," Boone continued, unmoved by the man's pleading. "You won't die for a long time, maybe days."

"Jesus Christ!" the man shrieked as the knife cut into his chest and slit away a small chunk of flesh. "I'll tell you who they are. I'll tell you whatever you want to know if you let me go," he promised.

Boone paused, his knife poised just below the man's belt buckle. The terrified man quickly rattled off the names and where they had said they might be headed.

Boone smiled grimly. "You want to live, don't you?"

The man nodded.

"I will show you more mercy than you showed Laughing Girl or my son," Boone whispered. The man's eyes widened in horror. He tried to speak, but the words froze in his throat as Boone buried his knife in the man's stomach, until only the hilt was visible. The first murderer of his family was dead. He stood up. Brushing himself off, he spit in the dead man's face before he mounted his horse in pursuit of the others.

In this way, he was able to eliminate five of the men before the others knew he was tracking them. Because he had no set method of attack, appearing and disappearing at all hours of the day and night without warning, he struck terror into their hearts. The five remaining men separated, each taking a widely different route, hoping to lose him. Some tried to hide in cities. Boone was not so easily put off. Whether they hid deep in the woods or behind locked doors, he found them.

The military discovered the identity of the mysterious shadow murderer. They began hunting him down to punish him for the murders he had already committed and to prevent him from killing again. They set traps for him. Boone eluded them. He managed to avoid capture until he caught up with the last man. The sole survivor had become so unnerved by Boone's previous successes, he gave himself up at the nearest fort for protection. Boone discovered his whereabouts and silently slipped through the guards as though invisible, executing the tenth man before the army took him prisoner.

He was thrown into the fort prison to await trial. The threat of impending death didn't worry him. Now that his family was avenged, he didn't care what they did to him. Before a military tribunal, he was sentenced to death by hanging and awaited his end calmly.

Lady Fate laughed at him. She had a different plan and intervened on his behalf to snatch him from the jaws of death. The Sioux had all agreed to a new peace treaty except for a renegade half-breed named Dull Knife. Dull Knife had the color of his father's people, the blue eyes of his mother, and a gnawing hatred for the Long Knives. He was a Santee Sioux and he would prove it by not resting until the white men had been driven from the land or he was dead. Dull Knife attacked with unsurpassed ferocity, leaving the stunned white men without a shred of evidence as to his whereabouts. Boone, awaiting his day of execution, heard of the whispered stories concerning Dull Knife. Never before had a man behaved so savagely. The atrocities were worse than any committed before by either side. The settlers were screaming to the soldiers for protection, while the government was demanding to know why the soldiers were unable to capture one small band of men. In desperation they came to Boone, acknowledging his superior abilities as a tracker and asked him to help them locate Dull Knife.

At first he laughed at them. He was destined to die. Why should he help them?

General Allenham frowned. "You're a white man. In spite of what you have done, you are white. These are your people who are being killed. Can you stand by and do nothing while a maniac like Dull Knife roams free, butchering innocent women and children?"

"My people are the Cheyenne," he replied scornfully. "What would you have done to those ten men who massacred my family if I had reported the incident to you without taking revenge?"

"You would have gotten justice," General Allenham replied too quickly, without meeting Boone's eyes.

Boone laughed, a loud, biting laugh that jarred the soldiers present. "White man's justice!"

Their pleas fell on deaf ears. Finally General Allenham paused, taking a deep breath. "What if I make a deal with you? If you won't track down Dull Knife for the sake of your own kind, will you do it to save your neck?"

Boone studied the general with narrowed eyes. "I hang in four days."

"Not if you help us put an end to Dull Knife's reign of terror," General Allenham insisted. "I am quite sure I can get your sentence waived."

"But, sir!" Lieutenant Hansen had interrupted, shocked. "This man is a murderer several times over."

"Shut up, Lieutenant," General Allenham shouted, turning red. "Mr. Boone's crimes are understandable and even partly justifiable under the circumstances. He has been raised as an Indian and cannot help thinking like one. Well, what is your answer?" he asked impatiently.

"What are the terms?" Boone knew there had to be terms.

"If you act as our scout and successfully track down Dull Knife, you will be given your life in return. But," the general added quickly, "you will have to continue being a government scout for ten years. After that, you will be free to do as you please. Do you accept?"

Boone thought it over. "If I don't have to fight the Cheyenne, yes, I agree."

What he considered his years of servitude began. Although he could have reneged on his promise and escaped dozens of times during the years that followed, he never did. Other men made and broke promises lightly. Boone had given his word. Unless the white men proved treacherous, he felt honor-bound to fulfill his part of the bargain.

It took him a year before he finally succeeded in flushing Dull Knife out of hiding and into the arms of the soldiers. With his mission completed, he spent time at first one fort and then another. He hunted down the Sioux, Cree, Pawnee, and Assiniboines, but never the Cheyenne. He had agreed to lead the party to Sweetwater only because Lieutenant Farrell had thought there was still a chance he could talk the chiefs out of taking revenge. The lieutenant hoped the Indians would leave the dealing out of justice to him. Boone smiled grimly. He knew the Cheyenne better than that. Lieutenant Farrell had insisted. Boone smiled. He was well aware that the officer hated his guts. He realized at the same time that the lieutenant wasn't the only person at Fort Jubele who felt uneasy in his presence. He didn't think like a white man, and most white people resented it.

Boone was a loner, making few friends in the army. Out of his loneliness and grief, he had embraced the white man's vices. In time, his bitter memories faded and he no longer awoke in the night hearing the whimpering cries of Laughing Girl. In time, he also came to realize that while revenge had tasted sweet, now that he was no longer facing instant oblivion, it was empty. The burning fires of hate had long since withered. Only the loneliness remained. Laughing Girl was dead. His son was dead. Nothing would bring them back. He visited the saloons and spent time with powdered women in low-cut silk dresses who would sleep with him for money. The relief they provided only temporarily filled the gap of emptiness. The other women he saw avoided him. His appearance was disreputable, his manners rough and uncultivated. He made them nervous. Actually, white women did not particularly attract Boone. He preferred the smooth tanned skin, shiny black hair, and high cheekbones of the Cheyenne women. Only one white woman had ever really aroused his interest. She was married to Lieutenant Farrell.

"God damn!" Sergeant Patterson muttered thickly, bringing Boone back to the present with a nasty jolt. It had turned dark hours ago. The sky was a navy-blue carpet with only a smattering of stars and a pale half-moon peeping from behind gray clouds. As Boone followed the sergeant's gaze, he saw the reason for his muttered oath. Thick clouds of smoke rose into the coal-black night. The smoke was coming from the direction of Sweetwater.

Michael Mallory dug his heels into his horse and galloped ahead of the others, ignoring Boone's warning to remain where he was. Cursing the boy for his reckless behavior, when they might all be heading into a trap, he gave the order to proceed with caution.

No distorted nightmare could have compared with the gruesome reality that greeted Boone and his men as they rode through the scene of devastation. Bodies were scattered everywhere, men, women, and children. Most of the dead had been scalped. They searched for survivors. There were none. A group of five children looked like they had been hacked to death. Their arms and legs lay scattered over the ground. Boone felt his stomach tighten, and unconsciously held his breath. He had never grown accustomed to the stench of a battlefield after a massacre. He knew his men were thinking what monsters the Cheyenne were. He had seen with his own eyes the results of the white man's atrocities. They were no better, sometimes even worse. In this wave of nausea and rage that swept over his men, he knew they would forget it was the white men who had initiated the slaughter by attacking two defenseless camps of women and children. But it was impossible to be objective at a time like this. Feelings ran high. On the soldiers' time off, they had come to Sweetwater to unload their month's pay. They gambled and got drunk in the Sweetwater Saloon, pouring their troubles and loneliness into the ears of the girls the saloon provided. He had done it too, and knew the names of the girls would remain in the men's memories even if their faces were only hazy blurs. His gaze wandered painfully over the scene. The town was a graveyard. Dead bodies were all that remained of the citizens of Sweetwater. Their flesh was cold, their eyes glassy. Ben Haskell, the mighty empire builder, was dead. The kindhearted Tilbys were dead. Even old Joseph Mallory was dead. He had started the whole mess in the first place, Boone thought grimly. His eyes lighted on Michael Mallory's pale face. Joseph Mallory's one remaining son was left to face the ugly nightmare of his own complicity in murdering the Indians, having triggered the awful retaliation of the Cheyenne. That realization, Boone felt, was heavy enough to crush a boy's spirit, even a boy with as much pluck and courage as Michael Mallory.

Boone watched Michael stagger like a seasoned drunk over to where the Tilby store used to be. He had heard somewhere that Michael had been sweet on the Tilby girl. He couldn't remember her name, or what she had looked like. It was impossible to tell now. Michael fell down on his knees beside the staked-out body of a young girl. Her green-and-yellow gingham dress had been ripped to shreds. Her thighs were covered with dried blood where a knife had slit her open so she could be violated more easily. Michael began to sob uncontrollably. Boone felt sick and turned away. A deep sadness filled his soul. He longed to comfort the boy, to beg him not to follow in his father's footsteps. But he knew even as he heard the racking sobs being wrenched out of Michael's body that the boy would do as his father had done. He silently cursed man's legacy of cruelty and ignorance he imparted to his sons as their burden to carry into infinity. Michael would act as all men did. In order to purge himself of the misery he had helped to create, he would kill. God! When would the blood-letting cease? When would it all end?

"Sergeant," Boone shouted angrily in a voice he barely recognized as his own. "Bury them as best you can."

"Yes, sir," Sergeant Patterson choked.

"And try to get them identified. The Indians might have taken prisoners." Boone doubted this, but since the Cheyenne had lost so many women and children, a few of the braves bent on revenge might have relented. "While that's being done," Boone added, "you'd better assign a few of the men to keep watch in case the Cheyenne return."

"Do you think that's likely?" Sergeant Patterson frowned, his eyes nervously scanning the horizon.

Boone sighed. "No, Sergeant, I don't. But it pays to be safe." By now, he thought dryly, the Cheyenne were probably splitting up and heading as far away as possible.

It wasn't going to be easy identifying the bodies. Some had been disfigured beyond recognition. Even so, the majority would be recognized and named. The faces in Sweetwater and the surrounding ranches had all been familiar to the soldiers. Boone glanced over at Michael Mallory. He would be asked to help out, once he had recovered sufficiently. Boone found himself staring down at a woman in a bloodstained gray dress. He didn't recognize her and wondered why he was walking aimlessly when he should have been helping his men. Momentarily the face of Lieutenant Farrell's wife hovered in front of him. She had left for Sweetwater that morning and hadn't returned. No doubt she would be counted among the dead. He winced and shouted an order to a dazed soldier.

By the time the ordeal was over, the sun was just visible in the east. From somewhere nearby, Boone heard the raucous scolding of a family of blue jays. In the distance the muffled sound of a lonely wolf crying for its mate reached his ears. His head ached. A cool breeze ruffled his hair, and the threat of a storm lay thick in the air. Six people were unaccounted for, three women and three children. Elizabeth Farrell was among the missing. Except for Michael Mallory and Jim Carson, who had, according to Michael's account, left for another city the day before the massacre, those six survivors were all that was left.

Boone reined in his horse on the hill overlooking the town for the last time before returning to Fort Jubele with the horrifying news. In the faint light of morning, he caught sight of the bent wooden sign that lay on the ground nearby. It read: "Welcome to Sweetwater, Population 410."

5

The sun rose after the long hours of darkness like a magic shield casting an iridescent glow over the plains. A gentle breeze stirred the burnt stalks of prairie grass that felt cool and prickly to the touch.

"The Indians won't kill us," Katie Mallory muttered dully to Elizabeth Farrell as they sat facing each other, both too frightened and exhausted to move.

"How do you know?" Elizabeth trembled.

"They gave us moccasins to wear. The Cheyenne wouldn't waste a good pair of moccasins on prisoners they were going to kill," Katie replied woodenly as she stared down at her cream-colored satin-soft footwear adorned with fringe and colorful quillwork.

"What will they do with us?" Elizabeth whispered anxiously, her thin face pale and drawn.

Katie pretended she didn't hear the question as her eyes vainly sought out Sean's familiar features among the crowd of Indians. She caught sight of Lorrie Gomber's fair head. She was sitting stiffly next to an Indian girl about her own age. The girl was trying to communicate with her, but Lorrie appeared too terrified to respond. Katie's eyes traveled on, unable to discern another white face in the sea of hostile red ones. She blinked several times to hold back the tears and felt her throat tighten with fear. What had happened to Sean? Had they killed him like the others? What *were* they going to do with them? She shivered as the silent questions tumbled through her mind, each one echoing with the screams of the dying and the

Indian war cries of the night before. It was a nightmare, a ghastly nightmare, she thought numbly. Her eyes lighted on the tall figure of Black Elk only a few feet away. He was tending to his horse, unaware of her gaze. He stood a good head taller than the others, with prominent cheekbones and a long straight nose. His thick shiny black hair was cut off on one side. The other was fastened into a braid that had then been wrapped with brass wire. One ear was covered by the braid, while the other was exposed. The exposed ear appeared to possess no fewer than six large holes. To each one had been attached a ring of copper or a large blue bead tied by a deerskin string. His lips were full, sensual, and he moved with ease and grace. Katie stared at him, hating him, hating everything about him. Without warning, Black Elk looked up. His brown eyes met her green ones. Katie quickly turned away. It wasn't the deep, jagged, crisscross pattern that lined his dark face that had caused her to tremble and avoid him. Along the seams of his deerskin shirt were the scalps of his enemies, interwoven with the blue and green quills and beadwork. She shuddered. Her father was right. They were all savages.

Gray Sky suddenly appeared before the white women and motioned for them to eat the roasted meat and drink the water he placed before them. There wasn't much time. Soon they would be riding again, and they wouldn't stop to rest for a long while. Elizabeth crept as far away from him as she could get, as though coming into closer contact with him would contaminate her. Gray Sky tried once more to make the women understand his intention before he shrugged and left them alone.

"We ought to eat while we can," Katie advised after a moment of silence, feeling nauseous at the prospect.

Elizabeth shook her head vehemently. "I'm not hungry." She moved closer to Katie, deliberately avoiding looking at the crisp brown chunks of skewered deer meat lying nearby. "Do you think," she said so softly Katie had to bend to make out the words, "the Indians would trade us to the soldiers? My husband would pay them whatever they asked."

Katie gazed at her in amazement. Pity and scorn struggled for supremacy. Pity won out. She said gently, "I think we ought to be grateful we're alive, Mrs. Farrell."

Elizabeth nodded, looking miserable. "Yes, of course."

"We won't be together much longer," Katie continued, forcing herself to drink some water and eat a little meat. "The Indians are splitting up, and even if we eventually find ourselves in the same campsite, we won't be permitted to communicate."

After a momentary pause, Elizabeth asked tremulously, "How long do you think it will take the soldiers to locate us?"

Katie watched out of the corner of her eye as Gray Sky stopped to talk to two Indian women, one grossly fat, the other thin. The women stared stonily in their direction, and she shivered. Mrs. Farrell sounded as if she were on the verge of tears. Now that some of the shock had worn off, Katie wanted to cry too, but she knew the Cheyenne considered tears a weakness. Her green eyes hardened. No Indian would ever see her weep. She would be strong no matter what they did to her. Glancing over at the lieutenant's wife, Katie knew she hadn't accepted the reality of her position. Mrs. Farrell still believed their situation was a temporary one. Her husband and his men would soon be galloping into their midst, mounted on white horses, bugles blowing, their boots gleaming in the noonday sun. Without realizing it, Katie spoke more harshly than she intended. "I don't think we ought to count on being rescued any too soon, unless a miracle takes place, which I'm not betting on," she added grimly.

"You mean we might not be rescued for several days?" Elizabeth's voice rose.

"More like a few months or even years," Katie corrected bitterly.

Elizabeth was so shocked by this information that the tears of self-pity and fear froze into a small round ball, settling somewhere in the middle of her rib cage, making it difficult to breathe. She didn't have the courage to inquire further into their fate, but Katie felt compelled to add, "From what little I've learned about Indians, Mrs. Farrell, the less fear and weakness you show them, the more respect and consideration you'll be likely to get. Rebellious behavior will be punished. Force yourself to think like an Indian," she added rapidly as Gray Sky and his wives advanced toward them purposefully. "Learn their language as quickly as possible. Acclimate yourself to their customs. When you find yourself alone at night after everyone is asleep, only then allow yourself the luxury of tears and pray to God for your deliverance."

Despite Katie's warnings, Elizabeth held back from following Gray Sky until Lightning Woman picked up a sturdy switch and hit her several times. Katie looked away. It was the last time the women would see each other.

When Black Elk appeared leading two horses, a chestnut mare and a black-and-white stallion, Katie was almost relieved. Reed Woman followed silently on a spotted mare. As she mounted the chestnut horse, Katie wondered curiously if the older woman was Black Elk's mother or even his grandmother. She looked too old to be his wife. They joined a group of about sixty others. The pace was hard and fast. They barely stopped long enough to rest and eat before moving on. At the end of each day, Katie was so exhausted that every bone in her body ached. Although she inwardly groaned at the prospect of another day of hard riding, she knew she was lucky to be able to temporarily put off the inevitable. Black Elk didn't have any wives. Perhaps they had all been killed in the raid. Whatever the reason, Katie was only too well aware that she was now Black Elk's squaw. Once they were settled into a more normal life-style, he would begin to make sexual demands. Katie shivered and forced herself to think of other things.

As the days turned into weeks, Black Elk's admiration for the white girl increased. Not once did she complain, weep, or refuse to do one of the numerous chores Reed Woman assigned her. Besides being industrious and uncomplaining, she showed a willingness, even an eagerness, to learn the Cheyenne language and customs. As a result, she already possessed a working knowledge of the language. None of the occasional taunts or hostile looks of the women and children seemed to touch her. She walked proudly even under a heavy load of wood. Black Elk was pleased with her. He knew that Reed Woman looked with favor on the Green-Eyed Woman, as she was now referred to, and even some of the other women in the new campsite had begun to show her a grudging respect. Since her capture, and resulting constant exposure to the elements, her fair skin had burned and peeled, until Reed Woman applied a mixture of bear grease and herbs. Now she was almost as dark as some of the Cheyenne women. Her long thick flame-colored hair had been combed and twisted into two braids. Grease had been added so that the unruly hair would lie flat, and it had lost some of its brightness. Nevertheless, Black Elk could still pick her out in a crowd of Indian women by the reddish gleam to her hair. On the whole, his captive's conduct and attitude were a source of pleasure to him. Only one thing disturbed him. During the day, Green-Eyed Woman went about her tasks with patience and efficiency. Lately she had relaxed enough to hum some of the songs the women sang as they gathered roots or wood. But as soon as night fell, after everyone had eaten the evening meal, she fell silent and seemed to shrink into herself as though she were afraid of being punished. No matter how tiring the day's work had been, she lay wide-awake on the mat in her place in the lodge. Her breathing was rapid and uneven, her body rigid. Black Elk could smell the fear that came from her until sleep finally claimed her. Although she was his prisoner to do with as he chose, her nightly behavior and her attitude toward him hurt him. She might smile or try to converse with Reed Woman, but she was coldly polite and formal toward him. When he spoke to her, she listened respectfully and made an appropriate reply. Her eyes remained fixed on the top of his shirt or the ground at his feet. It was not shyness or modesty that caused her to avoid him. He felt sure his scarred visage must repulse her, as it had Sweet Grass, and this thought made him sad. His original motive for taking her prisoner was now obscured by feelings and emotions that puzzled him. He had not cared what his white prisoner thought about him when he captured her. Out of respect, curiosity, and kindness he had at first held back from sexual contact. He hoped as she came to know him she would like him, and his face would not matter. Now he realized he had waited too long. Her opinion of him mattered. She was no longer the enemy.

Katie discovered that her position in the tribe was greatly eased both by her resolution to faithfully follow the advice she had given Elizabeth Farrell and by an unexpected incident that occurred early in her captivity.

A permanent campsite had been decided on several weeks previously. The tribe was busily employed in replacing the kettles, mattresses, headrests, arrows, dishes, and other articles of daily use they had lost in the massacre. Katie, along with half a dozen other women, had gone to dig up the edible roots that were available at that time of year. Reed Woman had, on other occasions, instructed her in the use of the root-digger. There were several different varieties of the implement. The one Katie took with her was a long stick as tall as a man and forked at the upper end. It was painted red over the lower half and black at the handhold. The smaller root-diggers were worked from a kneeling position, but the one she now held was operated from a standing one, making the back-breaking work a little easier.

As usual, several of the women brought along their young children who were still too small to be on their own. One little boy about a year old was playing on the ground by Katie. Squirrel Woman, the child's mother, was laughing and gossiping with two other women as she dug out the tender shoots a few feet away. Although Katie now understood the greater part of what they said, she could speak only a few halting sentences and did not take part in their conversations. The women, hostile at first, now left her alone. Katie heard a soft, rustling sound nearby and looked up in time to see a rattlesnake coiled and ready to strike the unwary child. Without thinking, she slammed the root-digger down on the snake and at the same time yanked the child out of harm's way. As she did so, the snake, which had been pinned down but not harmed, struck her on the hand. The child began to wail at such rough handling, and the other women rushed over to see what all the commotion was about. The snake was still alive, but the women made short work of him.

Katie stared at her hand in mounting horror. Suddenly she started to laugh hysterically, until tears rolled down her face. Katie Mallory had survived an Indian massacre, only to die from snakebite.

The other women looked at her in alarm. Squirrel Woman, clasping the weeping boy tightly to her breast, pointed to Katie's hand. "She has been bitten."

The women escorted Katie back to camp, relating what had happened to those they passed.

"Green-Eyed Woman has been bitten by a rattlesnake."

"Little Chipmunk would have died from rattlesnake bite if Green-Eyed Woman had not saved him."

"Green-Eyed Woman has shown great courage and presence of mind. She rescued Little Chipmunk from a rattlesnake."

Katie had no time to feel embarrassed by their praise. By the time she reached her lodge, she had broken out in a cold sweat. The pain in her right hand had spread to the upper part of her arm and was so great it took all her strength not to cry out. The swelling had begun, and she felt sick to her stomach.

Reed Woman had been sitting outside the lodge making leggings when the party appeared. Taking charge of Katie, she half-carried her to her lodge bed. The bed, composed of a backrest and mattress was made soft and comfortable by coverings of tanned buffalo robes and other skins. Katie collapsed onto the bed, groaning with pain and shivering with fever.

"I will call one of the healers," Squirrel Woman offered.

Reed Woman shook her head. "There is no need. I will take care of her." At these words, she took out some dried medicine from a leather pouch, moistened it with water, and applied the sticky substance to the wound. To Katie's amazement, the pain ceased almost at once. Reed Woman took hold of her right thumb and shook it; then she took hold of her right little finger and shook it, and of the left little finger and thumb in succession, and shook each, saying to Katie, "Now you will see all sorts of snakes."

Katie felt as if a raging fire had taken possession of her body. The sweat poured off her, and she felt so sick she thought she would die. She saw her mother and father coming toward her and screamed out, "No, I don't want to die." Her brother John, his hair a mass of twisting multicolored snakes, all hissing and writhing, looked down on her severely. She was a little girl again, and cried out for her mother. A cool hand touched her forehead. She felt safe. Clutching the hand, she saw it was brown and belonged to Black Elk. The sturdy hand turned into a long brown snake with red eyes. Katie screamed and pushed it away. She tried to escape. She hadn't been captured by Indians. It was only a dream. She was home safe and sound in the great oak bed, the patchwork quilt covering her. It was winter. Looking out the window, she saw hundreds—no, thousands—of snakes jumping, flying, crawling through the snow. They were on the ground, in the trees, and even in the air. Suddenly she realized with revulsion that the quilt was also a thick mass of red, white, and blue snakes. Desperately she clawed at her body to get rid of the snakes. Strong hands held her down, Black Elk's hands.

Katie cried out again, and Reed Woman began rubbing her hand from the wrist up to the shoulder blade. The swelling and fever subsided, and Katie fell into an exhausted sleep. That night she was well enough to eat, and by the following morning was completely recovered.

When Katie awoke the next day, Reed Woman announced, "You now have a horse of your own. Blue Painted Robe presented it as a gift for saving his son from rattlesnake bite."

Katie turned red and felt uncomfortable. "I didn't think about what I did. I just reacted. It was what anyone would have done."

"Blue Painted Robe is a courteous man. He knows what is expected of him. The horse now belongs to you. It is a good horse."

Katie hurried outside to take a look. Reed Woman had been right. The horse was a magnificent animal, the color of dark honey, with long legs and a friendly disposition. She reached out and stroked him on the nose. He snuggled up to her as though he had known her for years. She laughed. "You belong to me," she whispered into his ear, and he licked her face.

"We have need of fresh water," Reed Woman called out.

"I'm on my way," Katie replied lightheartedly. She picked up the kettle of old water and dumped it before heading to the stream for more. No Cheyenne would use water that had stood all night, considering it dead.

The women she passed smiled and shyly greeted her. Squirrel Woman stopped to talk. "We are going to gather wood after the meal. Does Black Elk's wife wish to accompany us?"

"Yes, I would like that," Katie said, amazed at the friendly offer and at her own eager response.

"We will meet you in front of your lodge."

In spite of Katie's efforts to learn the Cheyenne language, obedience to Reed Woman's instructions, and natural industriousness, she had been, until the rattlesnake incident, an outsider. Part of her wished to keep it that way. But there was a much larger part of her that wanted to become one with tribal life. She was lonely in her isolation and wanted someone her own age to talk with.

Squirrel Woman was only a few years younger than Katie and became her particular friend. She was good-natured, lively, and popular. Her popularity eased Katie's reception with others. Whenever Katie found some free time, she asked Reed Woman's permission to join Squirrel Woman and the others in some of their favorite sports, such as swimming contests, football, and throwing sticks. Since Katie was naturally athletic and always conducted herself well, she was in high demand by the competing teams. With Squirrel Woman's aid, it wasn't long before she was speaking the language easily and fluently.

The different members of the tribe began to take on individual characteristics. Medicine Woman was serious, patient, gentle, and a hard worker. She almost never talked with the other women or joined in the games. Picking Bones Woman was quarrelsome and nagged her husband, Tobacco. Iron Shirt, whose fierce look had terrified Katie when she first saw him, loved little children and had a sweet tooth. Golden Eagle had a reputation for speaking and understanding the language of animals, especially birds. Turkey Leg was very handsome and well-mannered but had a terrible temper. It was rumored he abused his wives, which was why one disgraced him by running off with another man.

Soon Katie hurried outside in the morning as eagerly as the other women did, so she too could hear the village crier as he passed through the camp bringing the latest news, the commands of the chiefs, and the order of the day.

"The Dog Soldiers are having a dance tonight," the crier shouted out as he passed through the camp. "Crow Bed has lost one of his horses, a young black mare with two tan feet. The buffalo are not to be hunted today."

Katie learned how to cut moccasins, apply quills, and make beadwork. Once she had mastered these tasks and other various small ones, she began to learn how to tan hides, using the scraper to remove the blood, fat, and flesh, and the flesher for thinning them.

Although women's work was often hard and tedious, she enjoyed sitting in the shade of a maple tree, her hands busily engaged. A cool breeze ruffled the fringe on her deerskin dress while she listened to the soft voices of the women discussing a new scandal, a marriage, a birth, or an upcoming feast. At such times, Katie could believe if she closed her eyes for a moment that these were her own people. The women next to her could just as easily be wearing gingham dresses and ribbons in their hair as they laughed and chattered excitedly of a new celebration. The single maidens were looking forward to an opportunity to meet and dance with their favorite suitors, the married women to show off their new clothes. Katie sighed as she opened her eyes. She had been with the Cheyenne for five months. The bitterness and anger she had first felt had lessened as she came to know the Indians as individuals. Their way of life seemed primitive and at times was completely incomprehensible, even barbaric according to her standards. She had been horrified to learn that a woman sometimes cut off a finger joint in gratitude for a prayer being answered that her child survive a sickness or her husband return safely from battle. When Reed Woman boiled blood until it thickened to jelly, and ate it, Katie was sick and had to leave the lodge. And when the men returned home from war triumphantly bearing the sticky scalps of their enemies, she shuddered with revulsion.

Squirrel Woman's musical voice intruded on her thoughts. She was teasing her younger sister, Prairie Rose, about a new suitor. Katie smiled. She had at first been shocked to learn that when a girl had her first menses it was announced from the lodge door. Prairie Rose's father had proudly informed the tribe that his daughter had become a woman, and gave away a horse in honor of the event. Squirrel Woman had laughed at Katie's embarrassment.

"Why should you be ashamed? When a girl becomes a woman, it is a time to be proud. She is eligible for marriage and can add to the tribe's power and importance by giving birth to strong, healthy children."

Katie had by this time already undergone what she felt was the degrading experience of being forced to sleep in a separate lodge when her time of the month came, and was amazed by her friend's lack of embarrassment. "If it is such an important occasion, what happens to Prairie Rose besides being confined to the menstrual lodge?" Katie asked curiously. "Is there some special ceremony?" If there was, she had not experienced it.

"When I first felt the cramps and saw the blood," Squirrel Woman explained softly, "I told my mother and she told my father, who announced it as he did for Prairie Rose. I was told to unbraid my hair and bathe. My entire body was painted red. Naked, I was wrapped in a buffalo robe and sat near the fire. A coal was drawn from it and put before me. Sweet grass, juniper needles, and white sage were sprinkled on it so that the smoke rising from the incense swirled about me and covered my whole body. I felt very important and a little frightened," she admitted. "My grandmother led me to the menstrual lodge, where we remained for four days. She talked to me about the significance of what was happening. From now on I must stay near the lodge. I mustn't go wandering about alone. If I acted foolishly and ran off with a man without marrying him in the proper way, I would shame my family. She reminded me again and again that I must always think of my reputation, and what effect my actions would have on my family. Sometimes she told me stories about famous women who had brought honor to their tribes by their courage and goodness, like Day Woman, who rescued her brother Green Fire Mouse when he was attacked by Shoshones. Above all, grandmother stressed that now I must be very careful. As soon as I was aware my menses had come, I must remove myself immediately. If I was careless and did not do so and a man ate from a dish I used or drank from the same pot, he could expect to be wounded in his next battle. When I married, if I slept beside my husband while I was bleeding, he could be killed in his next battle," she added seriously.

Katie was strongly tempted to protest at this point, but refrained with difficulty from speaking out.

"At the end of four days," Squirrel Woman continued, "Grandmother took a coal from the fire and once again sprinkled on it sweet grass, juniper needles, and white sage. She then told me to stand over the smoke with my feet on either side of the coal. This was the ritual of purification, after which I was allowed to reenter the family lodge. Once I returned to my lodge, I was shown how to arrange the protective rope."

Katie frowned. She knew all about the rope. As soon as a girl came of age, the cumbersome cord was wound around her waist next to the skin, passing backward and forward between the thighs to the knee. All men respected it. At first Katie had thought the presence of a confining rope humiliating and was reminded of a chastity belt worn in the Middle Ages, but an incident in the tribe changed her mind.

Bluejay and her mother were the last of their line. There were no male relatives. Stinging Eyes, whose wife had died, sent forty horses to Bluejay's lodge in the hope of winning her as a wife, but was refused. He became angry and waited for her to come home from fetching wood. When she passed by, he attacked her and tried to throw her to the ground, but she was too quick for him. She grabbed one of the sticks she was carrying and hit him over the head, running away before he could recover.

The next day Bluejay and her mother hid in the bushes, lying in wait for Stinging Eyes. They were armed with heavy stones. When he came near, they took him by surprise and pounded him with the stones until he fell unconscious from the blows. After they left, no one went near him. Katie was astonished to learn that even his own family ignored his cries and groans. He had to crawl back to his lodge without help and tend to his own wounds. No one offered him sympathy. Katie knew he was lucky to get off so easy. If Bluejay had possessed male relatives, Stinging Eyes would have been killed. With such severe penalties, not many men would risk violating the protective rope.

Katie sighed. Some of the Cheyenne customs still seemed shocking and crude in her eyes, but she no longer judged them. Their way of life was not her own, but their laws supported and maintained tribal life. She respected this.

Although Squirrel Woman was her friend, their friendship was a superficial one from Katie's point of

view. There were topics she was afraid to discuss. She
had never given up the idea of eventually being rescued, and instinctively knew this subject was taboo.
Her people were white, her roots were firmly planted
in the white culture. She felt she could never be really
happy unless she was among her own race, speaking
her own tongue.

Black Elk joined a group of boys and young men
throwing arrows at a mark. Katie stopped applying
the dried black grass and beads to the shirt she was
making for him and watched. He was well-liked and
excelled at this game. She heard the crowd cheer as
his arrow found the center of the target, and was annoyed at the flush of pleasure this caused her. She
resumed her work. Black Elk was often gone for days,
weeks at a time on a buffalo hunt or with a war party.
When he was at home, he barely spoke to her. He
tended to his horses, spoke gently to Reed Woman,
laughed and joked with the other men, and played
with his nephew. The terrible scars that disfigured his
face and back were no longer ugly or frightening. She
was used to his savage appearance. To her relief and
considerable surprise, her original fears were unfound-
ed. He never touched her. Although she occasionally
felt his eyes watching her as she moved about in the
lodge, when she looked up he quickly turned away
or went outside. The sharp-pointed awl used to pierce
the leather so that the sinew or thread could be drawn
through the hole slipped and cut her finger.

"Green-Eyed Woman must be careful when she
uses her right hand," Red Bead warned. "Since the
snake bit her there, she will always be weak in that
spot. The hand will never be the same."

"Green-Eyed Woman's hand is not so weak as her
heart when she looks upon her husband," Squirrel
Woman teased. She had not failed to detect the direction of her friend's gaze.

The other women laughed, and Katie turned red
with embarrassment and irritation. She knew they all

thought she was in love with her Cheyenne husband, and modesty and shyness made her blush. She didn't dare tell them that Black Elk never came near her, spoke curtly when he addressed her, and never made sexual demands.

"Perhaps Green-Eyed Woman will soon have something to show for her husband's love," White Buffalo said boldly, causing the others to laugh even harder. White Buffalo was full with child and would soon give birth.

Katie's face burned. She frowned, keeping her eyes fastened on the shirt she was making, and said nothing.

"It is no disgrace to know your husband loves you," Squirrel Woman whispered when the other women turned their attention elsewhere.

"He doesn't love me," Katie whispered back fiercely, furious with herself at this outburst. Squirrel Woman stared at her in silent amazement, and Katie wondered if her friend's look would turn to scorn or pity if she told her the truth.

"Everyone knows how Green-Eyed Woman holds the heart of her husband," Squirrel Woman said softly. "Not since Sweet Grass has Black Elk loved a woman so."

It was Katie's turn to stare. "What do you mean?" She felt an uncomfortable jolting sensation in her lower abdomen, as though a hundred butterflies had suddenly burst into motion.

Squirrel Woman was staring at a fat woman with a pretty but unhappy face some distance away. The woman was trying to quiet a squalling child. Squirrel Woman looked guilty. "It all happened a long time ago, and she has suffered much. I should not speak about Sweet Grass's misfortune, now that her husband is dead."

The idea that Black Elk, who acted as though she wasn't there, loved her terrified Katie, although she didn't know why. "Black Elk admired Sweet Grass?" she ventured at last, unable to keep still.

"They were engaged to be married," Squirrel Woman admitted reluctantly.

Katie stared at Sweet Grass with interest. What had Black Elk seen in this beaten-down, overweight woman? she wondered.

"Sweet Grass was not always as you see her," Squirrel Woman said sadly, correctly interpreting Katie's thoughts. "She was one of the prettiest maidens in our village. She had dozens of suitors."

Katie knew the Cheyenne women were very handsome. This tribute puzzled her all the more. "What happened?"

"Black Elk was not as you see him either," Squirrel Woman added, her eyes downcast, not meeting her friend's.

"You refer to the scars on his face and back," Katie replied in ready understanding, hoping Squirrel Woman would not feel too embarrassed to continue.

Realizing Green-Eyed Woman was not upset or angry with her for speaking so plainly, she drew closer and lowered her voice even more.

"Sweet Grass was very beautiful, and the only daughter in her father's lodge. Her family spoiled her. She was very proud." Squirrel Woman paused. "At that time, Black Elk was also handsome. He was even more handsome than Turkey Leg," she assured Katie gravely. "He too was proud, and a fine hunter. Although Sweet Grass had many suitors, there was an understanding between them that they would eventually marry. Both families were in agreement." She sighed. "All this took place before the treaty between the Long Knives and the Cheyenne. Black Elk and the others went on a raiding party. They were to steal some horses from the white men. No one thought it was a particularly dangerous mission. The white men were not as vigilant as the Assiniboin or the Cree. No one suspected there would be trouble." Squirrel

Woman flushed, looking uncomfortable. She had lost
a favorite cousin in that raid and disliked bringing up
the past in this way.

Katie studied the soft white deerskin shirt that lay
in her lap. By mistake, she had attached two red beads
when she had intended to apply one red bead and one
white one. She frowned in annoyance. Why should
she care how Black Elk got his scars? Why should she
be so fascinated by whom he had once loved? It made
no difference to her, she told herself angrily. Squirrel
Woman sounded as if she would be relieved to end
the conversation. Katie had every intention of going
along with this plan by changing the subject. It was,
therefore, with mixed feelings of surprise and uneasiness she heard herself say encouragingly, after a few
moments of mutual silence, "It was on this mission
that Black Elk got his scars?"

Squirrel Woman nodded in agreement. "Black Elk
was the only member of the party who returned alive.
At first, no one thought he would recover from his
wounds or the mutilation." She looked at Sweet Grass
again, who was now stirring something in a black
kettle. "She was young and used to praise and compli-
ments. Everyone talked of how ugly and disfiguring
the scars were. Black Elk could cover his back with a
shirt, but not his face. The terrible humiliation at the
hands of the white men would remain with him forever. In the beginning, when people looked at him,
they lowered their eyes in shame. He was still a good
hunter and a brave warrior with many fine qualities,
but he was no longer handsome. Sweet Grass was
ashamed of him."

Katie was shocked at the outrage she felt at Sweet
Grass's disloyalty. "She couldn't have loved him."

"Sweet Grass never had to think of others before,"
Squirrel Woman explained. "She was spoiled and always got her way. In this, too, she got her way. Black
Elk backed out of the engagement when he learned
how she felt."

"Black Elk must have been very unhappy," Katie said after a slight pause.

"Not as unhappy as Sweet Grass," Squirrel Woman said slowly. "She accepted Roan Bear's offer of marriage. It was a bad choice. He was very handsome and a good hunter, but as soon as she became big with child, he took another wife without consulting her, and treated Sweet Grass harshly. In addition, he had an even worse temper than Turkey Leg. She wished to leave him, but her family urged her to stay and make the best of the situation. It was a good thing Roan Bear died in the attack on your village. She had started to nag him and be the cause of many fights with his second wife. He was thinking of divorcing her, and this would have created bad feelings with her family, who were very strict in such matters."

"Has she remarried?" Katie inquired after a slight pause.

"No, she has chosen to remain a widow. She has a lodge near her brothers, who supply her with meat."

"There must have been another woman Black Elk favored after Sweet Grass," Katie said incredulously, before she could stop herself.

"There was no one after Sweet Grass," Squirrel Woman insisted. "You are the only woman Black Elk favors."

Katie felt embarrassed. It was ridiculous. Squirrel Woman must be wrong. Black Elk didn't love her. He probably despised her. Her people had disfigured him, murdered his friends and relatives. How could he possibly love her?

"Green-Eyed Woman must be blind not to see the love her husband feels for her," Squirrel Woman said, smiling, touching her gently on the arm. "But even if she cannot see it, others can."

That night, as Black Elk sat before the fire sharpening his knife, Katie looked at him as she never had before. The orange and blue flames threw dark shadows onto his face. His hands moved lovingly over the hilt

of the blade, and she found herself following the
rhythmic movements of the knife almost hypnotically
as he sharpened it back and forth over the piece of
stone. She thought to herself that his hands were
deadly with the bow and the knife, gentle and firm
with an untamed horse, and soothing and comforting
to a frightened and feverish girl. She shivered, but not
with the cold.

Black Elk stopped working and looked up. Their
eyes met for a moment across the fire. Both were surprised at what they saw. In Katie's face there was tenderness and the beginning of desire. In Black Elk's
face there was love.

Once the fire had died down to glowing embers
and the lodge was still, Reed Woman slept, but they
did not. Katie knew he would come to her, if not that
night, then the next. It had been inevitable from the
moment of capture. Her mind said primly that she
must put up with it as best she could. She must not
fight him. She must not show fear. Her heart pounded
in her ribs, but she knew it was not from fear. She
wanted to be held in his arms, to be touched by his
hands, to feel his hard body next to hers. She closed
her eyes and turned on her stomach. She must be out
of her mind. He was a savage. His people had massacred an entire town. Her family had been killed.
Rivers of blood flowed between them, separating
them. There could never be any gentleness or love.
She should thank God he had left her alone for so
long.

Black Elk lifted the light covering and lay down
beside her in the dark. His naked flesh was warm. She
was afraid to move. His hand reached out and
caressed her satin-soft skin, sliding down her back,
stopping in between her thighs. She shuddered and
turned over, lying stiffly on the buffalo robes, her
eyes tightly shut. Her flesh was burning as his hands
moved slowly over her breasts, awakening the passion
she was afraid to acknowledge. Biting her lip to stifle

the moan of pleasure that was threatening to escape, she forced herself to keep her eyes closed. She longed to touch his naked body as he touched hers. She needed him, but her mind continued to torment her. She was his captive, his squaw, nothing more. He didn't love her. He couldn't love her. She had mistaken the look she had seen on his face. Squirrel Woman and the others were laughing at her. If he wanted her body, she thought angrily, she would give it to him, but only as a slave would. There would be no love, no tenderness, no desire. She would not respond. She felt the tip of his hard sex pressing on her inner thigh, urging her legs wider, for the mounting pleasure she fought to hold back. Her body ached. Her mind was shouting that this was sinful; her arching body assured her it was right. She reached out to Black Elk and embraced him. His breathing was as uneven as her own. They made love shyly at first, and then passionately. She flicked her tongue over his flat stomach, tasting his salty flesh, and kissed his strong upper thighs, feeling the muscles tense and his body quiver under her touch. He placed her hands on his sex, and she stroked it at his urging as he caressed her nipples until they stiffened. She begged him to enter her. The sharp pain that led to a throbbing sensation as he thrust deep inside her made her groan with a pleasure she had never felt. When his seed burst inside her a feeling of bitterness and resentment took possession of her. Not from disappointment or repugnance, it originated in the knowledge that Black Elk had the power to excite her, to arouse her to an erotic abandonment that she would be unable to resist.

Long after Black Elk slept, his right leg lying possessively over hers, Katie was still wide-awake listening to the gentle splatter of the rain outside. Her physical needs had been stronger than her intellect. She consoled herself with the thought that she had had no choice. Her surrender had been to lust, not love, and she silently vowed she would never betray her family by loving a man whose people had destroyed her own.

Sean Mallory scanned the horizon for a sign of his friend White Thunder. It was the end of winter, and they were out looking for bands of wild horses.

The day was crisp and clear. A year ago, Sean would have taken advantage of his freedom to escape. Today, plans of escape were far from his mind. He had been living with the Cheyenne for almost two years. Like his sister, Katie, he had hated them at first but also recognized the necessity of outwardly conforming to their customs. His wound, acquired during the attack on the town, was superficial and healed in a few days. Since he already possessed the rudiments of their language, it wasn't long before he began to speak it fluently. His adopted father, Tall Bull, presented him with his own bow and a set of arrows. At first he aimed at a mark. The boys his age laughed at him when he missed. Sean took their laughter and teasing good-naturedly and continued to practice diligently. His persistence paid off. He graduated from a mark to hunting sparrows and other small birds among the sagebrush and in the thickets along the streams. The next step in his education was to make excursions onto the prairie with a group of four or five other boys. They hunted rabbits, grouse, and turkeys. Almost unconsciously he acquired knowledge about where the different birds and animals could be found and how they acted under different conditions. Patience and endurance were gradually built into his character and were to become a permanent part of his nature.

On Sean's first buffalo hunt, he received the name Strong Right Hand and the respect and admiration of his companions. Excited by the chase, and having already killed one calf, he rode up alongside two others and shot an arrow with such strength that, to his surprise, it passed straight through the two calves, killing them both. White Thunder watched in amazement.

Everyone in camp talked of his achievement for days. Tall Bull was pleased. As soon as Sean's feat became known, he called out from his lodge, "My son has killed two calves with one shot, and I give the best horse I have to Little Man." In addition to giving away a horse to Little Man, who was poor, he gave a feast and invited other poor people to come and eat with him. At the end of the feast he made his guests presents of blankets, explaining once again, "My son is a fine warrior. He killed two calves with a single shot. He will be a good hunter." Little Man rode about the camp to show his horse to the people. As he rode, he sang a song mentioning Tall Bull's name and telling why the horse had been given to him.

"I have found the horses," White Thunder called out excitedly, bringing Sean back to the present with a start. "There are about thirty of them. They are thin and weak from the long winter. Several of the mares are heavy with foal. I am sure we will be successful in capturing at least two." Sean was holding a string of three gentle mares to be used in handling the wild horses they would take, and together they rode off to try their luck.

White Thunder carried a pole with a noose attached, which would be thrown over the head of the horse he had singled out, so that he and Sean could force the animal to ground. Once it was down, its feet were tied and a headstall was put on its head. A rope was knotted about its neck, passing through the headstall. One of the gentle mares was brought up, and after a knot was tied in her tail, the rope leading from the wild horse's head was tied about the mare's tail with a slack of three or four feet between the head and the tail. After making sure the wild horse could not injure the mare in its initial frantic attempts to break free, the feet of the wild animal were untied. When it sprang up, it plunged and struggled but very soon became quiet and followed the mare without trouble. Three or four days later, when it came to know the mare well, it was released, and having become attached to her, followed her about wherever she went. While the wild horse was tailed to the mare, White Thunder would occasionally go up to the mare, stroke her for a while, and then move on to the young horse, handling it and gentling it. The horse became accustomed to the sight and smell of man and no longer feared him. Sometimes, after the horse had become somewhat gentler, White Thunder would spring onto its back and at once jump off again. The wild horse learned from this that it was not to be hurt. White Thunder would shortly mount the horse and sit on it for a little while, and then the old mare would be led about by someone else while he was sitting on the wild horse's back. By this method, the breaking in of a horse was accomplished in a very short time. Occasionally a wild horse would attempt to drive the mare away from camp and out onto the prairie. This was prevented by hobbling the mare so she could only move slowly.

Now Sean and White Thunder joyfully returned to camp with the three new horses and proceeded to tame them in the manner described. On the boys' second day back, they learned that Red Eye, who was only a year or two older than they, had committed a terrible offense against the tribe and been severely punished. He had disobeyed the order of the chiefs and hunted the buffalo on his own.

When the buffalo were plenty, small parties or single individuals were not permitted to hunt alone. Sean learned the reasons for this were quite practical. Not only could larger numbers of men kill a greater number of buffalo at one time, but the animals would not be driven away from the reach of the people by one hunter. It was only when the buffalo were scarce and the elk and deer plentiful that the lone hunter was permitted to chase the herds.

The soldier bands who protected the tribe and enforced the laws dragged Red Eye out of his lodge af-

ter sighting the fresh meat drying on poles a few feet
away from his quarters. They beat him so severely
with their bows that he fainted and couldn't walk for
several days. If he was ever foolish enough to try
again, not only would he be beaten, his horses might
be killed, his weapons destroyed, and his lodge broken
up.

Red Eye was not popular among his people. He was
a poor loser at contests, boastful, and a practical joker.
At a short distance from camp he had hidden behind
some bushes one morning and fired several shots with
his gun, shouting, "The Long Knives are here. The
Long Knives are here." There was great confusion in
the tribe. The men rushed out half-dressed, some
naked, fully armed to fight the enemy. "The Long
Knives are over here," Red Eye shouted from a different spot. The men rushed over to the other place and
found it empty. "It must be Red Eye," one of the men
said angrily. The boy collapsed with laughter at the
good joke he had played on them. From then on,
however, many of the more serious men would have
nothing to do with him.

White Thunder had a much more personal reason
for disliking Red Eye. Both of them were courting
Shadow Woman, who was the youngest of three sisters, very pretty and merry. Shadow Woman was fifteen. White Thunder was seventeen, and although he
had been to war several times, he had never counted
coup. Red Eye had counted coup twice, and in addition, had captured five horses from the Pawnee and
driven them up to Shadow Woman's lodge as a gift.
White Thunder knew that Red Eye had the ability to
make her laugh, and feared his own suit was unsuccessful. When he learned about Red Eye's fate, he
couldn't hide his satisfaction.

Sean teased him. "I know you are not feeling sorry
for Red Eye's disgrace. Perhaps now Shadow Woman
will take more notice of you."

White Thunder smiled shyly and confided, "I'm

not taking any chances. I have asked Whirlwind to make me a flute."

Whirlwind had a reputation as a man who possessed extraordinary powers in love. If he made a flute for White Thunder, the music would charm Shadow Woman, causing her to fall helplessly in love with him. White Thunder practiced on the flute, which was made of juniper wood and ornamented with multicolored beads strung on a thread of sinew and wrapped close about the cylinder. He practiced his haunting melodies in the hills at night, and sometimes played until dawn. After several weeks of lonely playing, he approached Shadow Woman's lodge as he played, and she eagerly came out to meet him and talk. Sean did not believe in magic and spells of enchantment, but thought highly of his friend's playing and the sincerity of his affection. He was not surprised when White Thunder told him that Whirlwind's magic had worked. Shadow Woman confessed that she loved only him.

"You would not need Whirlwind's magic to win my sister's love," White Thunder kidded Sean not long after this. "She is fond of you already."

Sean shifted uncomfortably and avoided his friend's eyes. "She is too young for marriage, and I am not ready either," he said in explanation. He wished White Thunder would not talk about Mirror Woman. He knew that although Mirror Woman was only thirteen, it was not too soon to start courting. She already had a couple of suitors waiting in front of her lodge. Sean did not want to commit himself to anything as serious as marriage. His natural curiosity and common sense had enabled him to adjust to his captivity, and his hatred for the Cheyenne had dissipated. Even though Sean had made friends in the tribe and had a very real affection for his adopted parents, he knew he would not remain with them forever. The time would come when he must leave them to return to his own people. If he was a married man with a family, he wouldn't feel free to go.

"Well, you will see my sister tonight," White Thunder promised. "You are going to be invited to our house for a feast. Blue Lodge will be there."

Sean instantly forgot his discomfort. He loved to sit and listen by the hour to the Indian tales of adventure, mythical heroes, and stories about animals that in the old days had been half-human and half-beast. Blue Lodge, who derived his name from having painted his lodge blue, was one of the most popular storytellers in the village.

Since it was not a formal feast, they were invited by White Thunder's younger brother, who said simply, "My father calls you."

On entering the lodge, Sean turned to the right and paused. Walking Bear, White Thunder's father, sat on his bed at the back of the lodge on the west side. He welcomed Sean and his adopted parents and asked them to sit down. The place of honor was at Walking Bear's left and was occupied by Blue Lodge. Since it was very bad manners to enter that part of the lodge occupied by the family, or to pass between the fire and the owner of the lodge, or even to pass between anyone sitting in the lodge and the fire, Sean and his family walked behind the sitters, who moved forward to give them room.

The guest of honor was offered a pipe filled with tobacco mixed with red-willow bark. When he received the pipe, he raised and lowered it four times, touching the bowl of the pipe to the ground four times, and after he finished smoking, he went through the ceremonial motions of passing hands over legs, arms, and head. This was his promise to relate the stories as he heard them, and a prayer for help to do this. Only after Blue Lodge smoked was the food cooked. Before they ate the roasted ribs or boiled buffalo tongue, a little food from each kettle was offered to the spirits. The food was held up to the sky and then placed on the ground at the edge of the fire. All of the food offered to the spirits lay where it was until the lodge was swept clean. Once it was offered to the spirits and placed on the ground, it was believed to be consumed by them, and no one would touch it.

Many of the Cheyenne tales were the exclusive property of certain families and could be told only by the members of those families. Occasionally, at the close of the story, the storyteller would present the tale to some individual in the lodge, and after this had been done, that person might tell it.

Storytelling could go on all night long. If Blue Lodge chose to relate a short tale, at a certain point he might stop. After a pause he would say, "I will tie another one to it." There was a longer pause; the pipe was relit and smoked, and there was a buzz of conversation before he began again, telling another section of the story, ending as before. Very often the stories were told in groups of from four to six.

Thus, the long, often grueling and tedious hours of hunting were relieved by storytelling and participation in sports and feasts. Sean bet heavily with the other boys on the outcome of a contest or on competing teams of players. In a kicking match with the Sioux, Sean had been thrown twenty feet by one blow from his opponent's feet. Although he had been kicked in the back of the head, he had not been seriously hurt and laughed good-naturedly about it later. Like his friend White Thunder, he used a pair of tweezers to pluck out the hairs from his face, eyebrows, lashes, lips, and cheeks. After completing this arduous and painful task, he painted his face and dressed in his finest raiment. Together he and White Thunder rode through the camp basking in the light of admiration and envy.

The first winter Sean spent with the Cheyenne, he fell sick and nearly died. The illness started out as a sore throat accompanied by weakness and a mild fe-

ver. The weakness increased, forcing him to remain in
bed, while the fever soared, leaving him even weaker.
His adopted mother, Twin Woman, sent for the doctor, and when he arrived told him he would receive a
horse for his services. The doctor always courteously
accepted whatever was offered.

Before treating Sean, Badger purified both himself
and his patient. Sweet grass, juniper needles, and powdered bitterroot were burned on live coals. As the
fumes rose, Badger held his hands over the smoke, re-
ceiving on the palms of his hands the heat and the
odor. He then pressed them gently on Sean's throat,
which was the most painful part of his body. Shaking
a buffalo-skin rattle filled with little stones, Badger began to pray and chant over him, asking the Great
Spirit for help in curing Sean of his illness. When
Sean's fever caused him to toss and turn, irritably
throwing off the blankets from his sweat-drenched
body, Badger used the wing of a hawk to fan him. At
intervals, he moved about the lodge, singing loudly to
chase away the evil spirits that might be lingering in
the corners. After three songs had been sung, a pipe
was smoked. Sweet grass was once more burned, and
the pipe, having been cleaned, was refilled and placed
on the ground before Badger. He offered medicine to
Sean from a buffalo-skin sack. Attached to the bundle
was the claw of a badger. This was his particular
trademark of identification and possessed spiritual
power in treating illness. Before giving Sean the medicine in water, he stirred the bitter mixture with the
badger claw to strenghten its spiritual properties. Sean
was so sick he didn't have the strength to resist the
vile potion. Five new songs followed. Sweet grass was
again burned, and Sean was once more treated, this
time with a steaming tea that held traces of mint. The
pipe was smoked and filled as before. The buffalo-skin
rattle was held up, another pinch of sweet grass was
burned, and the rattle slowly passed through the

smoke. Seven songs were sung in succession. At the conclusion of the singing, the pipe was smoked again. Badger mixed the medicine with deer fat and rubbed the mixture on his hands, holding them out to the fire until they were warm; then he placed both hands firmly on Sean's aching limbs. Before resuming the singing, the rattle was held over the smoke once more. Nine different songs followed. Sean fell into a restless sleep before the third one had been completed. Badger finished all nine songs, and taking the pipe in his right hand, he held it up to the south, west, north, and east, to the sky and the ground in turn. He then switched the pipe to his left hand and smoked, ending the treatment.

The following day Sean felt a little better. The aching in his limbs had eased, but the fever remained and his throat was still swollen. Badger was consulted again and recommended a sweat bath, which succeeded in breaking the fever. In a couple of days the swelling had receded and Sean's appetite returned to normal. By the end of the week he was well enough to go for a short ride about camp.

The following spring Sean heard about the possibility of a new peace treaty with the Long Knives. He had just returned with a party of eight other boys from hunting deer and elk in the high country when White Thunder told him the news. Excitement at the prospect of a reunion with his own family quickened his pulse and lit up his face. There was no conflict of loyalties. He had adapted to the Cheyenne way of life with relative ease and had done so only partly out of necessity. Curiosity about Indian customs and culture had been the primary motivating factor. To Sean, the last two years had been a great adventure, not one without moments of tragedy and horror, but basically fascinating. Although he had made friends, he had been able to reserve a part of himself from becoming emotionally attached to his new surroundings. He was less volatile than Katie, and because he was a boy, had a much better chance of remaining aloof from direct involvement. Friendliness and amiability had been easily achieved, but deep ties of affection had never been fully forged.

Escape had been impossible in the beginning. He had been too closely watched. When freedom to escape finally arrived, he found himself unable to take it. The terrain was not only unfamiliar, it was dangerous. Along with wild animals, hostile Cree, Kiowa, Comanche, and Pawnee roamed the area. He doubted whether his new skills would keep him alive long enough to locate a settlement or a fort, provided there was one within a hundred-mile radius. Nevertheless, Sean had never doubted he would one day return to his own people. It seemed the moment had arrived.

"Has my son heard about the new treaty?" Tall Bull asked the next morning at breakfast.

"The village is talking of nothing else," Sean admitted.

"If the treaty is signed, all white prisoners will be returned to their people," Tall Bull said without expression.

There was a long silence during which Sean shifted uncomfortably and found himself unable to say what he had planned.

"Does Strong Right Hand wish to return to his people?" Twin Woman asked softly.

The answer to such a question was obvious, but Sean found it suddenly difficult to put into words.

"There is no need for embarrassment," Tall Bull assured him. "You were taken from your people at a time when the memories of your past were strongly planted in your heart. Do you wish to be returned to them?"

Sean looked at him gratefully. "I hope I have been a good son to you," he said sincerely. "I have tried to follow your advice and not break any laws."

"You have done well," Tall Bull said impassively.

Sean felt an overwhelming desire to explain himself.

"I have a brother who may be alive and looking for me. My sister was also captured," he added. "She may be among the prisoners returned."

Tall Bull and Twin Woman exchanged glances, and Twin Woman sighed. "If Strong Right Hand wishes to leave us, we do not hold him back."

The initial elation he had felt at the prospect of imminent freedom suddenly vanished. He frowned, wishing he could put his finger on what was troubling him. He had looked forward to this day since his capture and had dreamed about it almost every night for two years. The reality was sadly flat.

"We have been proud of your achievements and treated you as we would have the son who was killed," Tall Bull said quietly, placing his hands on the boy's shoulders. "Our pleasure would have been great if you had chosen to remain among us. We would have taken you far away from the sight of the white-eyes. But it is understandable that you wish to return to your people, and we respect your decision. When the Long Knives speak badly of us, calling the Cheyenne liars, thieves, and murderers, remember that we always treated you well, and speak out in our defense."

"I will," Sean promised, trying to swallow a lump in his throat.

"If you are to go, let these be our final words," Tall Bull said abruptly.

"How will I find the soldiers?" Sean asked with mixed emotions.

"Follow the river south until you come to the place where it branches off and turn right. Not long after this you will see the camp of the Long Knives."

"Take this with you," Twin Woman added as she handed him a parfleche pouch stuffed with food. "And may your reunion with your family be a happy one."

Sean found himself unable to say anything further, although there was a great deal he wanted to communicate. He left the lodge. On his way out of the village, he stopped to say good-bye to White Thunder, who insisted on riding with him part of the way.

"I shall take Red Cloud with me to hunt for horses," White Thunder said after riding in silence for some time. "He has not the strength of Strong Right Hand, but he is quick."

When Sean didn't reply, he added angrily, "Why are you going back?"

"I have a family," Sean said, frowning.

"You have a family here," White Thunder pointed out accusingly. "Have you been unhappy among us?" he challenged.

"No," Sean admitted truthfully.

"But still you would go back. Your white family may all be dead." White Thunder sighed. "I would probably do the same if I were in your place, but you will be missed. My sister cried when she learned of your going," he added.

They rode on in silence. Sean's memories of Tall Bull patiently teaching him how to improve his marksmanship with the bow and how to interpret the signs of the rabbit, deer, elk, and buffalo flashed through his mind. The long hours Twin Woman had toiled over his deerskin shirt so that it was white and soft as satin, as well as the pride in both their faces when he returned from his first buffalo hunt, having killed two calves with one shot, became vividly clear. He sighed, recalling the day White Thunder had defended him before two other boys' taunts; and the numerous other times when people had been kind and generous made Sean realize with a pang of regret that they all cared for him much more than he had cared for them. He had matched their love and affection with friendly interest and curiosity. A strong feeling of having missed something caused him to become depressed.

"I had better turn back now," White Thunder said, startling Sean out of his confusion. "I want you to have this," he added solemnly. "It has always brought me luck." White Thunder removed the prized bear-claw necklace and handed it to Sean. "It is unlikely we will ever see each other again. If we do, it may be in battle," he added, frowning. "Take this as a gift from a friend."

There were many half-formed thoughts Sean wanted to share with White Thunder, but he could not. It was too late for words. Instead, he handed him the knife he had just finished making. "I accept your gift with thanks and give you one in return. May you always be successful in hunting and live to see your grandsons grow into fine warriors."

It was only when White Thunder disappeared over a hill and the dust from his horse could no longer be seen that Sean continued on his journey.

Sprinkled across the prairie were clumps of golden asters that nodded sagely in the spring breeze. Reed Woman left early to help White Buffalo split the dry strips of sinew, twisting and pointing the strands to make them into thread in preparation for putting together a new lodge. Green-Eyed Woman had just returned from gathering fresh wood. Black Elk should have been off hunting with the other men. Instead, he lay still in his place in the lodge. His heart felt like lead. He was sick with fear.

Katie knelt beside her husband and felt his forehead. It was cool. She frowned. "What is wrong? Are you ill?" He turned his face away, and she felt uneasy. He had never stayed in bed so long. "Should I call one of the healers?"

"I will get up soon." His voice was harsh. She flushed and moved away.

Katie knew he was angry with her. He had not slept with her in over two weeks, not since the rumor about a possible treaty had spread around the camp. Squirrel Woman had brought her the news.

"Nothing is certain yet, but some of our people are talking about a new treaty with the Long Knives."

Katie was stunned. Two years had passed since she had been taken captive by Black Elk. She hardly ever thought of her own people anymore. "Why would they agree to a treaty now?"

"We are tired of moving. Every time a permanent campsite is located and the corn starts to ripen, the Long Knives arrive and we have to abandon it. The winter months have been especially hard."

Katie knew this was true. Several young children had died from the winter marches last year, and all of them were exhausted.

"The Long Knives promise if we sign another treaty and agree to certain things, we will be free to move farther north into the cold country without trouble. We have people there who would welcome us."

Thoughts of Michael and Sean caused Katie to sigh involuntarily.

Squirrel Woman eyed her friend with disappointment. "It is doubtful such a treaty will ever come to pass. We have not forgotten the treachery of the white-eyes." She spoke sharply.

Katie wisely remained silent, but when Black Elk joined Reed Woman and her for the evening meal, she couldn't restrain herself any longer. "Is it true that peace between my people and yours is a possibility?" she asked meekly, trying without success to keep the excitement out of her voice.

"It is being discussed," Black Elk replied coldly.

Katie knew she had offended him and wished she had not spoken so eagerly. For the first time he went to his own bed and did not come to her, although she waited for him until the gray light of dawn filtered through the opening at the top of the lodge. She thought his anger would eventually subside and he would forgive her. Although she never made the mistake of bringing up the peace treaty again, his coldness continued and he deliberately ignored her.

Katie was unaware that he had been waiting to see

what her reaction toward the news would be and was deeply hurt by her obvious joy. The secret fear that had eaten away at him every night as she lay in his arms could no longer be soothed by her eager responses to his lovemaking. She longed to return to her people and would leave him tomorrow if she could. He had been a fool to think he could get her to fall in love with him. He knew now she never would. Green-Eyed Woman was only biding her time until she could leave him.

Most of the Cheyenne would agree to sign the new treaty and be free to move north. The Long Knives would demand the return of all prisoners, but Black Elk knew some of them would not be returned. Their husbands, wives, parents, brothers, and sisters would flee with them before the white man could take them. Black Elk closed his eyes. He was sick with fear because he had three days in which to make up his mind what he should do about his wife.

"When there is trouble between husband and wife, all the people soon know it," Reed Woman said quietly as she worked diligently upon a robe she was making for Black Elk. She belonged to the Quilling Society and had a reputation for having decorated thirty robes, a remarkable achievement.

Katie frowned. She knew Reed Woman was right. Several of the other women had looked at her pityingly, and Squirrel Woman no longer teased her about Black Elk. She didn't care what they thought. Since she had spoken so impulsively, she had suffered loneliness and rejection. She missed the excitement of a night of lovemaking, the tender way he held her in his arms when they were finished, and the warmth in his eyes when he returned from the hunt and found her waiting for him in front of the lodge. It wasn't love, she reminded herself guiltily. She had only done what was expected of her, and if he had been kind and affectionate, it was in his nature to be so. Nevertheless, she bitterly regretted having upset him. Even though Katie had not gotten pregnant, she was certain Black Elk would never return her to her people. She was his squaw and realized the necessity of getting back on friendly terms with him, but didn't know how to do it. She had tried to please him in little ways, and had even considered going to his bed if he showed no sign of relenting, but abandoned this idea through a horror of further rejection. The thought that Reed Woman might be able to help her to make amends overcame Katie's shyness and embarrassment. "I have done what I could to create harmony between us," she said with a touch of irritation. "What more can I do?"

"Green-Eyed Woman cooks her husband's food, sews his clothes, and does not refuse him his rights. She is an admirable wife."

Katie glanced at Reed Woman suspiciously. Had there been a trace of sarcasm in the older woman's voice? "Then what have I done wrong?"

"Does Green-Eyed Woman love her husband?" When Katie turned scarlet and fell silent, she added gently, "A man may forgive a wife who is lazy or self-indulgent if he knows that she loves him. But no matter how hardworking and obedient a wife is, if she continues to be cold to him, he wearies of trying to win her love. Bitterness and humiliation force him to turn away from her."

"How can I love him?" Katie choked, suddenly overcome with emotion, her eyes stinging with tears for the first time since her capture. "My family and friends have been killed. My home was destroyed."

"Death must come to everyone sooner or later, and it has claimed as many Cheyenne lives as it has white. You have been accepted into the tribe. This is your home. It is time you buried the dead. Hate will not bring them back. You are surrounded by people who love you and who wish you to open your heart to them."

"You don't understand." Katie controlled herself with difficulty.

Reed Woman stopped working. Her dark eyes clouded over with memories of long ago. "When I was a young girl working in the corn fields, we were attacked by a band of Pawnee and I was carried off by Crazy Dog to be his wife. His two previous wives were dead. Because I was very young, only fourteen, and very beautiful, he was fond of me and treated me with respect and consideration. I hated him for taking me from my family and swore I would run away if an opportunity arose."

Katie listened with surprise, grateful for the time to compose herself, and ashamed of her outburst.

"Although he was considerably older than me, he was a handsome man, and I liked him in spite of my hatred. When I found I was carrying his child, I informed him of the event, but instead of making him happy, I could see it disturbed him. As the months passed, he became more and more depressed, until I finally asked him what was troubling him. In my ignorance I thought he did not want the child." She smiled. "He told me his two wives had died in childbirth and he was afraid for me. That night he held me in his arms and wept from fear. I knew he loved me. I will not say I loved him then, but tenderness and forgiveness were born that night." She looked at the robe she was making with fondness, as though it were for her Pawnee husband. "After I gave birth, I heard him ask if I was well even before he asked about his son." She chuckled. "He was very proud of his firstborn, and his great love for us and good qualities soon melted any traces of hatred I might have felt toward him for the abduction. We were very happy. Then one day I was out gathering roots and had wandered farther than the other women. I spotted some of my own people on a hunting party. They did not see me, and after a few moments I turned away and walked back to the others. By this time I loved my husband and did not want to leave him."

"But you are here now," Katie said slowly, trying not to think of Black Elk's many fine qualities.

Reed Woman's eyes cleared. "I spent many years among the Pawnee. They were happy years. I bore Crazy Dog two more sons. They were strong, brave warriors like their father. They died in battle. My eldest was killed by a Sioux lance. The youngest died trying to rescue his brother in a bloody battle with the Comanche."

"Your husband is still alive, then?" Katie asked curiously.

"Crazy Dog was wounded by white men's bullets, but he died of grief over the loss of three sons within the same year. I stayed for a while with my eldest son's wife. When she decided to remarry, I made up my mind to return to my people. I was old and wanted to see what had become of my family in the time I had spent with the Pawnee. My husband's family understood and let me go, urging me to return if I wished."

After a moment of silence, Katie said bitterly, "It's not the same for me. Even if Black Elk loves me, I shall never be able to love him in return."

Reed Woman shrugged. "Love cannot be forced. It must be given freely."

Shortly after this conversation, Black Elk rose one morning and issued instructions to Katie in a dull, hard voice. "Prepare enough food and water for two for a day's ride, and be ready to depart as soon as this is done."

Katie stared at him. "Where are we going?"

"I am returning Green-Eyed Woman to her people," he said abruptly, leaving the lodge.

Unable to move, Katie continued to stare after him. So many contradictory emotions coursed through her, she was temporarily frozen into immobility. Joy at the prospect of being reunited with her brothers was undermined by a deep sense of loss at the parting with Black Elk, Squirrel Woman, Reed Woman, and the others.

"I will bring the water and pack some pemmican and fruitcakes while Green-Eyed Woman gets herself ready for the journey," Reed Woman offered, disappointment in her voice. She too left the lodge before Katie had a chance to speak.

The possibility of being returned to her own people had been such a remote one that after the first year Katie had begun to think of it as only a dream. Even after she heard about the peace treaty, she had never seriously believed Black Elk would let her go. What had been a dream without hope of fulfillment a few hours before was now a reality. By the end of the day, she would be speaking English. She would be free. She felt slightly dizzy. It had all happened so fast. Katie frowned. If she needed proof Black Elk didn't love her, this was it. She knew that the Indian men who loved their white wives and adopted children were making plans to break camp and escape with their families into Canada. Katie had thought she would be one of them. A terrible feeling of desolation made her want to burst into tears. Reed Woman's return with fresh water forced her to control herself in time. She watched dismally as the older woman filled the parfleche pouch with the fruitcakes and pemmican. Katie looked at her helplessly. Reed Woman had always treated her with kindness. She would miss her, and wished she could think of something meaningful to say, but her mind was blank and she didn't trust herself to speak.

As Reed Woman handed her the food and water, she said slowly, "Now that Green-Eyed Woman is returning to her people, I hope she will be happy. I have come to look on her as a daughter and hoped she would choose to make her home among us. I see now that I was wrong. She must go back. Her heart is cold to the Cheyenne. I do not blame her for this. It takes great courage to release the past without looking back. I wish her well."

Katie wanted to hug her and admit that she was confused. She wanted to return to her people, but she also wanted to stay. Instead of expressing these feelings, she replied stiffly, "I shall think of Reed Woman with affection," before rushing outside, where Black Elk waited impatiently with the horses.

As they rode through the camp, those they passed quickly turned away. Although Katie looked for her friend, she did not see her. She wondered if Squirrel Woman had known about Black Elk's resolution and had deliberately avoided her, or if she would learn about it when she returned from gathering wood, roots, or water. Would Squirrel Woman miss her? Katie's eyes filled with tears. She would miss Squirrel Woman. She would also miss the dances, the games, and the town crier bringing the latest news. She sighed and wondered if Red Bead's fourth child would be the girl she longed for. Staring at her husband's broad back, she realized he was wearing the shirt she had made for him only two weeks ago. A sharp stab of pain made her bite her lip to keep back the tears. In desperation she pictured Sean and Michael and what she had to look forward to rather than what she would be missing.

They rode without stop until the sun was well overhead. Black Elk finally halted to rest and water the horses under the shade of a few elm trees, and Katie brought out the food. Neither of them was hungry. They sat in an uncomfortable silence and avoided looking at each other, until she asked with a heavy heart, "How much farther is it?"

"We should reach the soldiers before it turns dark," Black Elk replied stonily.

Realizing there would only be another three hours of riding, Katie childishly wished she was dead and didn't have to be put through such torment. The idea that she might possibly be in love with her husband

and this was the cause of her misery crossed her mind several times, but she ruthlessly ignored it. Memories of past tenderness and lovemaking couldn't be dismissed so easily, however. By the time Black Elk rose to go, Katie caught her breath and found herself saying, "Must we leave so soon?"

Black Elk heard the catch in her voice and slowly sat back down. He said roughly, "I thought· Green-Eyed Woman would be eager to join her people."

Katie forced herself to reply honestly. "I do want to return to my people. I want to see my brothers again, but . . ." She hesitated, trying to understand her own feelings. "Part of me doesn't want to go," she admitted reluctantly.

"In time Green-Eyed Woman will forget her stay among the Cheyenne," Black Elk said firmly.

"I have told myself the same thing," Katie said miserably, "but I don't think it's true." She stared at the fringe on his shirt. "I will miss . . ." She swallowed several times to keep back the tears. ". . . everyone," she ended lamely, looking away.

"You will make new friends," Black Elk insisted, refusing to weaken. Green-Eyed Woman would have to discover her own heart.

"Why did you take me for your wife?" Katie asked unexpectedly, looking directly at him for the first time.

Black Elk spoke coldly. "I admired Green-Eyed Woman's courage in battle and had need of a wife who would bear me sons."

"Oh!" Katie looked away. "I suppose that is why you are returning me to my people. I have disappointed you by not giving you children." Black Elk did not reply at once, and Katie looked at him more hopefully.

"My admiration for Green-Eyed Woman turned to love," he said, frowning. Katie felt a rush of pleasure at his words. "I thought in time she would love me in return. When the news of the new treaty reached my wife's ears, I waited for her response. She was overjoyed," he said harshly. "I saw how much she longed to return to her people. In that moment I realized how foolish I had been to think she would grow to love me. Her heart would never be touched by me," he said bitterly. "She had not yet borne me children, and this convinced me of the necessity of bringing Green-Eyed Woman back while there was still a chance for her happiness and my own."

Katie knew she had hurt him badly and that it had taken a great deal of courage to speak as honestly as he had. She vowed to do no less. Although she was still confused about returning to her people, his words had suddenly made clear one vitally important piece of information, which she felt driven to confess. "Black Elk has been mistaken in thinking he has not touched his wife's heart. His gentleness, patience, and strength have caused her to love him in return in spite of her stubborn resistance."

"Black Elk is grateful for his wife's kind words." His voice was still cold, but Katie was relieved to see the pain leave his eyes and his face soften as he longingly searched her own.

Ignoring a protesting voice within, Katie threw all caution to the winds and added, flushing, "We do not have to continue this journey. We can go home."

"And what of Green-Eyed Woman's brothers?"

"They may not even be alive," Katie said gloomily, voicing a fear that had only just occurred to her.

"If we were to turn back now, Green-Eyed Woman would later regret it. Her thoughts would turn toward her brothers and what would have happened if they had been alive and she had gone with them."

Katie wanted to shout that this was untrue, but the words stuck in her throat.

Black Elk stood up once more and spoke with determination, although his voice was gentle. "I will bring Green-Eyed Woman to the Long Knives."

Katie sighed. Perhaps it was for the best, she thought, depressed, as she mounted her honey-colored horse.

"There must be no looking back," he continued. "Green-Eyed Woman must have the opportunity to decide for herself which road she will take."

"But if you return me to my people, how can I choose?" she asked, puzzled.

"Does Green-Eyed Woman think she can find this place by herself?" When Katie nodded, he added, "I will ride here every day when the sun is directly overhead, for five days. If my wife does not join me by the end of that period, I will move farther north with the rest of the tribe."

Contenting herself with this alternative, Katie rode in thoughtful silence the rest of the way. A sentry posted along the road as a lookout intercepted them a mile from the rendezvous campsite where the exchange would take place. He rode up and demanded in broken Cheyenne, "Is this one of the prisoners?" When Black Elk assented, he added roughly, "You can leave now. I'll take charge of her."

Sergeant Bliss's rude dismissal of Black Elk, and the way he had imperiously grabbed Katie's reins and galloped off, preventing her from saying good-bye to her husband, caused Katie to take an instant dislike to him. The sergeant was not unaware of her hostility. He had expected it the moment he had gotten close enough to see her reaction. Instead of the joy and relief that should have been evident on any white woman's face at being rescued from savages, he had seen confusion and reluctance. Glancing at her again as he reined in the horses beside Colonel Mills's tent, he could see she was young and pretty. Once she was dressed in decent clothes and her hair washed and curled, she'd be a real beauty. Judging from the highlights underneath the grease, her hair was probably dark auburn. His eyes narrowed, and he tightened his hold on the reins. She looked to be plenty spirited, too. He decided to keep close beside her just in case she should try to make a break for it.

"Is this another captive, Sergeant?" Colonel Mills demanded wearily as they entered his tent.

"Yes, sir. She was brought in by a single brave. She was probably his wife."

Colonel Mills sighed. "I can't believe how many of the poor devils are starting to arrive. Trying to identify them and reunite them with their families isn't as easy as Washington seems to think. Do you have any idea what her name is?" he asked in a resigned voice.

"No, sir, I don't." Sergeant Bliss frowned. "She hasn't let out a peep since I took her from an Indian whose features would have made your blood run cold. Very likely she's one of those that was taken young and can't speak a word of English. My guess is she's going to give us trouble," he added grimly.

"My name is Katie Mallory," she said distinctly, and had the satisfaction of startling both men.

"My mistake, ma'am," Sergeant Bliss apologized, looking at her curiously.

"Yes, well, that will be all, Sergeant." Colonel Mills turned brick red underneath his tan. When the sergeant left, he added, "You have no idea how difficult and confusing this exchange of prisoners is, Miss Mallory. I hope Sergeant Bliss didn't upset you. The truth is, we often get prisoners who have been raised since the cradle in Indian homes and consider themselves Indians. They aren't happy about returning to their natural families and occasionally do try to bolt for it. It's a very awkward situation." When Katie continued to stare at him coldly without speaking, he shifted in his seat uncomfortably. "I gather you haven't been a prisoner long?" he continued uneasily.

"I've been with the Cheyenne a little over two years," Katie said quietly.

"I see. Two years." He stared at her with sudden

interest, his embarrassment gone. "You're not part of the Mallory clan that was wiped out in the Sweetwater massacre?"

She frowned and spoke rapidly. "My father, Joseph Mallory and my brother Timothy both died in Sweetwater. I think my brother John and his wife also perished. Sean was taken prisoner but my brother Michael may have made it to the fort in time to be spared, although I have no way of knowing that."

"Well, well, isn't that fortunate. What I mean is," he amended hastily, "both your brothers are alive and well. They'll be delighted to know you're safe and sound."

As if he had been waiting for the right cue, Michael Mallory burst into the tent. Katie only had time to notice with shock the deep lines etched on his handsome face, making him look years older, before he swept her into his arms, crushing her in a bear-like hug. Glancing over Michael's shoulder, she saw Sean, taller than she remembered him, smiling shyly at her from the entrance. She began to cry.

"I think I'll leave you to get reacquainted," Colonel Mills said, beaming. "I'll be nearby if you want me," he added as he discreetly left the tent. Her two brothers would take care of her now, he thought, breathing a sigh of relief. Recalling her resentful attitude at the time she was brought before him, Colonel Mills thought it extremely fortunate her stay among the Indians hadn't lasted a year or two longer and that she still had living relatives who obviously cared about her. They would encourage her to forget her experiences with the savages and return to her roots.

"Katie, it *is* you. Thank God! Thank God!" Michael mumbled in a choked voice, holding her tighter, as if he were afraid she was an apparition and would vanish once he let go. "You're safe now. Sean is here too. He arrived yesterday," Michael added shakily, reluctantly releasing her so that she could greet her younger brother.

Sean had changed his Indian clothing and cut his hair, but there was something about him, some subtle alteration in his manner that reminded Katie of the Cheyenne.

"You look great," Katie said warmly as Sean released her.

"Sean's fine," Michael said abruptly. "He was lucky. The savages treated him pretty well."

"I wasn't treated badly either," Katie said quietly, but Michael began talking to cover up his uneasiness.

"I've been staying with the Hendersons. They own a ranch ten miles out by Sugar Creek. Belinda and her father insisted we stay with them until we're all able to return home."

Only a few hours earlier, Katie had tried to persuade Black Elk to take her home, but she realized with a pang of guilt that the concept of home had meant something entirely different to her then. She knew Michael would be horrified if she told him how close she had come to remaining with the Indians and wondered hopefully if Sean at least would understand.

"As soon as we get to the Hendersons', Belinda will lend you some clothes and you can wash your hair," Michael said suddenly in a strained voice. When Katie blushed he looked away and mumbled, "Colonel Mills heard I was desperately searching for you and Sean and when the Indians agreed to return their prisoners in exchange for a peace treaty, he notified me in case you two were among them. I ought to thank him and say goodbye. You can stay here with Sean until I get back," he added awkwardly.

Katie was left with the distinct impression Michael was ashamed of her and would have preferred no one saw her until after she had changed her appearance. This left her feeling both angry and embarrassed. She wondered how it could be possible to feel so uncomfortable in the presence of her own family. Eyeing Sean's white clothing with a feeling of resentment, she said flatly, "I see you've returned to 'normal' very fast."

"What you see before you is Michael's handiwork," Sean said lightly. "He's acting out of the belief that the last two years never happened and I give you fair warning, the Hendersons are in on it. All talk of life with the Indians is taboo."

Katie frowned and said stiffly, "Is that so!"

"Was it really all right for you, Kate?" Sean asked hesitantly.

"In the beginning it was difficult, but I learned to adjust," Katie admitted cautiously.

"Did they give you an Indian name?"

Katie's face softened. "Green-Eyed Woman. What was yours?"

"Strong Right Hand." They exchanged smiles but Sean held up a warning hand against any further disclosures. "Michael will be back any minute. We can talk about it all later if you want, when we're alone." A look of amusement crossed his face as he added, "You needn't worry about what to say to Michael on the trip to the Hendersons. Just ask him about Belinda Henderson. He'll talk your ear off."

Following Sean's advice, Katie inquired after Belinda and had to restrain an impulse to laugh out loud at his overeager response. Belinda was an angel, perfect in every way, and later that evening, Katie discovered Belinda returned his admiration. Whenever Michael addressed her personally or her gaze happened to rest on him for more than a minute, she would blush furiously and lower her eyes. It was obvious she worshiped Michael.

As Michael sipped his second cup of coffee after a delicious supper, he said admiringly, "Belinda is the best cook in the world."

"This cake could easily win a contest at a church social," Katie agreed with sincerity. She was now arrayed in a faded muslin dress with mother-of-pearl buttons and puffed sleeves. Although she had meekly changed her comfortable Indian clothes at Michael's insistence and washed her hair, which was now pinned up and adorned with a blue satin ribbon, she refused to give up her clothes to be burned. A violent argument threatened to erupt between Katie and Michael, when Sean had taken his brother aside. Katie heard them whispering downstairs.

"Let her settle down. She needs time to readjust."

"I should think she'd be overjoyed to get rid of those filthy clothes. The sooner those rags go, the sooner the . . . the horror will fade and everything will get back to normal."

"Let her alone. She'll come around," Sean insisted soothingly.

Katie was grateful when Michael took Sean's advice, but felt an ominous pang of uneasiness at his words "everything will get back to normal." Two years couldn't be wiped out or ignored as though they hadn't happened, she thought bitterly. She had a great need to talk about her years with the Cheyenne and her feelings for Black Elk, but found little opportunity for doing so. In the next couple of days they all carefully avoided speaking about Indians and she suspected they were involved in a conspiracy to keep her and Sean from being alone together. If the topic of Indians was inadvertently brought up, Belinda blushed and Michael turned pale and changed the subject. They talked about what they would have for supper, the weather, the government, and the return to Mallory property. Katie thought she would scream if the tension wasn't broken soon, and decided to deliberately open that particular can of worms after supper that night.

"I understand your captivity wasn't all that bad, Sean," Katie said sweetly. The nervous clicking of knives and forks was the only sound in the room.

"I was treated very well," Sean admitted frankly, a smile of approval in his eyes. "How about you, Kate?" he asked gently.

"Now, now," Mr. Henderson said firmly, "there's no need to discuss the incident. I'm sure Katie would rather bury the past."

"No, I wouldn't," Katie said defiantly, her eyes beginning to flash. "I would much rather discuss it out in the open instead of seeing the curiosity as plain as day in your eyes. I don't mean to be rude," she added hastily. "It's only natural for you to be curious."

"Katie, for God's sake!" Michael pleaded.

"It's not fair for you to treat two whole years out of my life as though they didn't exist. I had bad times in the beginning, as I'm sure Sean did, but strange as it may sound, I eventually made friends."

"Friends!" Michael spat the word out and slammed down his coffeecup so hard half the coffee spilled onto the table. "How can you call those savages friends?"

"I made friends too," Sean said slowly. "You just don't understand how it was. I hated them at first, like you do, but after a few months, a year, the hatred loses its impact. They became individuals with their own personal characteristics. Some I liked, some I didn't."

"I suppose you thanked them for butchering your family," Michael sneered.

Sean paled and said quietly, "I never forgot that, or the fact that we started the massacre."

"Jesus Christ!" Michael muttered. "You're worse than you were before you were captured."

"If you'd only try to understand," Katie begged.

"No doubt you loved being a squaw," Michael snapped, flushing hotly.

Katie met his look without flinching. "I loved my Indian husband, and you might as well know now that I was reluctant to leave him."

A deathly silence followed this shocking admission. No one moved for the space of three minutes. Finally Michael got up and ran outside, slamming the door after him. A few seconds later, Belinda excused herself and followed him. Mr. Henderson coughed and said he thought he'd clear the table.

The tension in the house increased in the next couple of days and eliminated all but the most mundane conversation.

"I guess we really put our foot in our mouths," Sean said ruefully one day when they found themselves alone.

"Was I so wrong to break the taboo of silence?" Katie asked unhappily as they gathered blackberries for a pie Belinda was making.

Sean sighed. "No, Katie, not wrong. It's just that Michael will never be able to see what happened in the same light we do. In the first place, he wasn't taken captive. He never lived with the Indians and saw them when they weren't at war. To him they will always be screaming savages who murdered his family and friends and destroyed his home. Besides, if he didn't blame the Indians for everything that's happened, he'd have to shoulder some of the responsibility for the massacre himself."

"I know, but—" Katie began.

"Mr. Henderson told me Michael used to wake up with nightmares every night the first few months he stayed with them. He had to help the soldiers identify the bodies. That couldn't have been a pleasant task."

Katie shuddered. "You're right. Poor Michael." She hesitated. "Was Leslie Tilby killed?"

Sean nodded. "We were incredibly lucky, you know."

Katie put the basket down beside her and sat on the edge of the sloping hillside. "Were we? What is going to happen to us, Sean? I feel absolutely dreadful."

"Michael has plans for us at home. He wouldn't go back to work the spread until he located us. Now that we're all one big happy family again, I think he intends to ask Belinda to marry him."

Katie looked at him oddly. "Do you feel that we're one big happy family?"

"People can change a lot in two years," Sean admitted after a slight pause.

"Like me in particular," Katie said hotly.

Sean shrugged. "Both of us."

"It's different for you. You're a boy. You weren't married and you can't be carrying an Indian baby. That's what's bothering Michael, isn't it?"

"Michael loves you, Kate. You know that. But he's thinking about what others will say," Sean admitted, obviously embarrassed by the turn the conversation had taken.

"Even if I'm not pregnant," Katie said resentfully, "and I don't think I am, I suppose the best I can look forward to back home is pity and a lifelong dependency on my brothers."

Sean looked at her skeptically. "You can't fool me, Kate. You're not all that concerned about that. You want to return to the Cheyenne, don't you?"

"Maybe I do," Katie said softly.

"Are you sure?"

"I love Black Elk. I love him," she said passionately. "Do you find my loving a Cheyenne Indian horrible?"

"No, not horrible." He hesitated. "Only I don't think you should be so quick to make a decision. If you run off with him now, you could regret it later."

Katie sighed. "I know. Black Elk was the one who forced me to return. He said I should have the opportunity to decide for myself which road I should take."

"Sounds like he cared for you, all right."

"He did." Katie felt the tears start to well up in her eyes. She rubbed them and added huskily, "He does!"

"How long did he say he would wait for you?" Sean asked perceptively.

"Until the end of the week. If I don't meet him at the prearranged spot, he's moving on into Canada without me," she added miserably.

"That gives you only one more day to make up your mind."

"I don't know what to do," Katie said dismally. "I love you and Michael, but so much has changed. Since I've been back, I've begun to feel as though Katie Mallory was somebody else, a person who lived years and years ago. I don't think I can ever be that person again."

"You may not believe this, but in time the memories of your life with Black Elk will fade."

"I don't want them to fade. I want to return to Black Elk, only . . ." Her voice trailed off.

"Sounds like you're afraid to go and afraid to stay. Let's just say, for argument's sake, that you went off with Black Elk. We'd probably never see you again. You wouldn't just leave behind your family, you'd be leaving a whole way of life. Could you deliberately turn your back on the customs and culture of a people whose race you were born into? Would you be happy if you did?"

Katie wiped her eyes and took her time before answering. "There would be things I would find difficult to adjust to, but there are customs and laws I object to among my own people too." She smiled. "I would go without looking back, if it weren't for you and Michael."

"If that's all that's troubling you, don't let us hold you back," Sean said, smiling. "I may decide to work my way to Boston and go to sea. Michael could be dead inside of a week from some rare disease. Even if you stay, you might fall in love with a Southern planter and never see either of us again. Besides, we may be your blood relations, but you have another family."

"Another family?" Katie said, surprised.

Sean frowned. "I didn't realize until I was leaving the Cheyenne how much I had missed by keeping myself apart. In a way, I felt as though I had wasted those two years. I gained invaluable knowledge about Indian customs and culture and greatly enlarged my physical prowess, but I had missed an important point.

All those days and nights of loneliness, and self-pity could have been avoided. I had a family right where I was. There were people in the village who cared about me, but I resisted their efforts to get close." He sighed. "Your family isn't just blood ties. Wherever there is a mutual feeling of respect, affection, and trust, those are the people who belong to your family group. That means they don't have to share your customs, let alone be born into the same household."

Katie stared at her younger brother in awe. "You're right. But what about you? Why didn't you stay if you felt that way?"

"I was confused, and I didn't have the time to sort out my conflicting feelings until the moment of departure. If the peace treaty hadn't been proposed when it was, I might have been unwilling to go in a few more years," Sean added, recalling Mirror Woman. "At the time, I was dead set on returning. I saw my life up to that time as a temporary stopover. Now that I'm here, I don't want to return to the Indians." He smiled. "I guess I'm fickle. I'd like to help Michael rebuild our home. Each to his own."

"Michael would come after me," Katie said, frowning after a few moments of thoughtful silence.

"Since he left early today to examine the property back home, if you leave tomorrow morning, he won't hear about your disappearance for several days. Now that he has Belinda and I have every intention of staying, he'll let you go. He won't like it, and he sure as hell won't understand, but he'll let you go. And, Kate," he said, hugging her, "if things don't work out and you have another opportunity to change your mind, you can always come back."

Friday morning, while it was still dark, Green-Eyed Woman silently rose, went to the scarred bureau, and took out her Indian clothes. She dressed swiftly, enjoying the feel of the soft deerskin next to her naked flesh and the freedom of the garments. She braided her hair by the light of a single candle and afterward crept downstairs without making a sound. From the kitchen she took a square of cornbread and several slices of ham. Wrapping the food in paper, she stuffed the package into a leather-string pouch and slipped out of the house. Taking the canteen from the back porch, she filled it with ice-cold water from the pump and headed for the barn. Throwing a light blanket over her honey-colored horse, she led the restless animal beyond the house before mounting her. Hesitating, she glanced back at the house with its sleeping occupants, as yet unaware of her movements. From one of the windows on the top floor she thought she saw a flickering motion, as though a hand was raised in salutation, but in the next instant it was gone.

The sun was just beginning to break through the gray sky. A golden butterfly with dark brown spots on either wing fluttered by her right ear. It seemed to be whispering, "Hurry, your journey will be light and swift, hurry." Taking a deep breath, Green-Eyed Woman rode off to meet her husband.

6

Charity slipped out of her deerskin dress and knelt without flinching on the hard cold earth in front of Red Turtle. Her head was bowed in resignation. Her back was a mass of ugly black-and-blue welts and scars from previous beatings. Red Turtle thought of White Dove's mutilated body and those of his children and felt no compassion for White-Faced Woman. As the memory of the massacre returned to him in all its horror, the blows increased in intensity. The sweat rolled off him, and his breath came in gasps. Only after his thick arm was too tired to raise again did he finally throw the bloody switch down in disgust and leave the lodge.

The first few blows had merely stung, but the ones following burned, as though Red Turtle had thrown pot after pot of boiling water on Charity's back. New welts rose and blood oozed down her back, staining her white flesh with streaks of red. Through it all Charity was motionless, her eyes dry. As soon as she heard Red Turtle's command to undress and recognized the familiar look of hatred in his eyes, she had silently whispered the magical word "Abracadabra" and escaped to her secret place. He wanted her to suffer pain and humiliation, but she had discovered a way of outwitting him. He couldn't follow her to the secret place because it was in her own mind.

She found it quite by accident one day as he was beating her. The longer she remained in her own world and concentrated on the beautiful light, the less

189

pain she felt. Now she could completely divorce herself
from her surroundings at will. Only a very small part
of her viewed the cruel treatment as a disinterested
observer might. She was secure within the light. It en-
veloped her with its soothing glow of warmth. She
was safe because the light was inviolate. Nothing
could hurt her while she was there. Red Turtle could
torment her flesh as often as he liked, but he would
never be able to destroy her spirit. Charity smiled
from the safety of the secret place. It gave her a sense
of power to know that by retreating into her own
tiny world of light she was frustrating her tormentor,
cheating him of his vengeance.

"Lie down on the bed and I will treat your
wounds," Bright Eyes said quietly, bringing a bowl of
water and some dried roots to be used as a poultice.

Charity shrugged and lay on her stomach. Her back
was stiff, and she felt lightheaded. The pain on her
back had diminished to only a dull ache, but as soon
as she touched the mattress, her breasts felt sore and
she winced. She shifted uncomfortably and frowned.
It wasn't the first time she had felt that soreness.
There was something she ought to remember, something important about the soreness of her breasts, but
the memory eluded her.

Bright Eyes applied the poultice to Charity's back
in silence. She was worried. White-Faced Woman had
been taken over three months ago. When Red Turtle
had first brought her to his eldest wife to fetch and
carry and do the most difficult chores, Bright Eyes
had been relieved. She was not as strong as she used to
be. With Yellow Moon and White Dove dead, she
needed help around the lodge. Because her heart was
also filled with grief and hate, she felt no pity for
White-Faced Woman. Yellow Moon, White Dove,
and the two children had been viciously murdered.
White-Faced Woman was lucky to be alive. Bright
Eyes frowned. When Red Turtle was in camp, he savagely beat his prisoner, sometimes twice in one day.

His wife went about her tasks and did not interfere.
She understood his need to purge himself of his sorrow and rage. But he no longer came to her in bed.
He sat in brooding silence, staring at White-Faced
Woman until the gnawing hatred exploded in another
act of violence. Other men turned to their friends and
relatives for comfort. Red Turtle lived only to inflict
punishment on his captive. He took no interest in anything else. Bright Eyes gazed at Charity's back with
distaste. If her husband continued, he would either kill
White-Faced Woman or drive her mad. Bright Eyes
suspected she was already half-crazy. When Red
Turtle beat her, she sometimes hummed in tune with
the sound the switch made as it whizzed through the
air. Bright Eyes did not care what happened to White-
Faced Woman, but she was very much afraid her
husband was also losing his mind.

"I have finished," Bright Eyes said abruptly. When
Charity sat up with difficulty and winced again, her
right hand gently touching her breasts as though to
protect them from assault, Bright Eyes added uneasily,
"What is it?"

Charity dropped her hand. "Nothing," she said
dully.

Bright Eyes stared at her suspiciously. White-Faced
Woman had not had her menses in a long time. The
thought crossed her mind that perhaps she was carrying Red Turtle's child. He had gone to her bed in the
beginning, although he had not touched her except
for the beatings in almost two moons. The sound of a
baby laughing in the lodge might restore her husband's spirits. She sighed. He had always loved children. Perhaps the birth of a child would weaken the
evil spirits that raged within him. If he could hold a
new son or daughter in his arms, the madness might
leave him.

Red Turtle reentered the lodge. Bright Eyes
quickly whispered to Charity, "Go to sleep. You can
resume the chores in the morning." She watched her

husband walk to his bed at the back of the lodge and lie down on top of the robes. She went to him and took off his moccasins, gently rubbing his cold feet. Presently he opened his eyes and spoke to her.

"A party of Kiowa have been spotted a day's ride from here. They are hunting buffalo. I am joining up with Hatchet and ten others to steal horses. I will be gone for several days." His voice was weary, but as his gaze rested on Charity, his face hardened and his voice again became harsh. "Why is she sleeping? There is work to be done."

"I told her to rest," Bright Eyes admitted, a note of defiance in her voice.

Red Turtle sat up. He glared at Bright Eyes. "I spared her life so she could help you with the work. If I had known you were going to spoil her, I would have killed her."

Bright Eyes met his look squarely without flinching. "Husband, you cannot fool me. I know what is in your heart. You spared White-Faced Woman's life so you could vent your hatred on her for the deaths of our loved ones." Her voice softened. "This I understand. But now you must leave the dead behind and turn your attention to the living. There is no longer any love or joy in this lodge. You do not care about me." He started to protest, but she cut him off. "White-Faced Woman is the only one you think of." Red Turtle stared at her speechless. "Your heart is filled with hate," she continued. "Night and day you think of her and what new cruelty or torment you can inflict on her. You beat her until she is too weak to help me with the more difficult tasks. Soon the beatings will drain her of the will to live, and then she will be dead and I will have to do the work alone. It was not me you were thinking of when you spared her life." She paused for breath and was gratified to see her husband drop his gaze. "The punishment must stop."

"No," he said stubbornly.

"White-Faced Woman is carrying your child."

Red Turtle said nothing. His face remained a cold, rigid, unrelenting mask of hate. Bright Eyes stood up. Her voice trembled, but there was an air of finality about her as she spoke. "When my sister and I were given to you in marriage in gratitude for what you did for our brother, we did not know you very well. We were afraid that because we were not your choice of wives you would treat us badly. As we came to know you," she said softly, "we realized our fears were groundless. You always treated us with proper respect and consideration. Your kindness and gentleness awakened love in both of us." Her voice wavered. "Even after White Dove entered our lodge, we did not suffer from a lack of attention and affection. Your preference for her was obvious, but we did not begrude you your love for White Dove. We could see she returned your love, and any jealousy or resentment we might have felt was soothed by White Dove herself. There was always enough love to go around. We were very happy. Now all that has changed. My husband has become a stranger. This lodge is no longer a place of happiness and peace. You have chosen to retreat into your own private world of shadows and death. I do not exist for you except to maintain the lodge. Is it possible that my husband thinks I too have not suffered by the deaths in this lodge?" she demanded angrily, her voice rising. "Have you forgotten that I too lost a son? Yellow Moon was my sister. Her son was like my own. White Dove was like a daughter. I have need of my husband's support and comfort. I can no longer bear living in an empty, cold lodge with a man whose spirit has left him." She shuddered and took a deep breath. "Now that White-Faced Woman is carrying your child, you must let her alone. You have abused her enough. Her pain and misery cannot bring the others back to life. Perhaps the birth of a new child will ease your grief. If you continue to beat her, I will know there is no hope for future happiness, and"—her voice broke—"I will leave you."

As Bright Eyes turned away, Red Turtle grabbed her hand. His eyes were no longer burning coals of hate. They were full of unshed tears. His face seemed old and tired. When he spoke, his voice trembled as much as hers had.

"Your words have made me ashamed. I have neglected an old friend." His grip on her hand tightened. "You need not fear that I will kill White-Faced Woman. I will never touch her again."

"And what of the child?"

A spasm of pain crossed Red Turtle's face. He spoke fiercely. "I cannot promise to love the child. It will always carry the blood of its mother, and when I look upon its face I will see the murderers of my family." After a slight pause he added softly, "We have been together a long time, you and I. We have been partners in life. Do not desert me now, old friend." His voice trembled again, this time more noticeably. "I have need of you."

Bright Eyes bent down and embraced him warmly, comforting him like a child. She smoothed his hair and murmured words of reassurance, relieved at the silent tears that fell on her neck and shoulder.

The low, guttural tones were indistinct, but Charity could tell they were talking about her. A faint, sickly-sweet odor of malevolence filled the lodge and mingled with the burning buffalo chips and sweet grass. She immediately identified the scent. It originated with Red Turtle and usually preceded a flogging. She was surprised and puzzled. Red Turtle had just beaten her and had never before punished her so soon after the first beating. It wasn't his pattern. But there was always a first time, she reminded herself grimly. Closing her eyes tightly, she whispered "Abracadabra." She felt the warm golden light spread throughout her body and waited for the first sign of attack. Nothing happened. The unique scent of male-

volence gradually dissipated. She relaxed, realizing she
must have been mistaken. Reveling in her unexpected
freedom, she looked forward to the onrush of pleasant
dreams. To her annoyance, she was unable to fall
asleep. She tossed restlessly on the bed. Whenever she
felt herself slipping off into sleep, images of her infant
daughter rose up to torment her. Slowly she opened
her eyes and frowned. Why was she thinking about
her daughter now? She had been dead for years. Suddenly she recalled the look on Bright Eyes's face
when she had winced at the soreness of her own
breasts. A ghastly thought, too horrible to acknowledge, began to take shape in her mind and
caused her to tremble with revulsion. She was carrying Red Turtle's child! The sweat stood out on her
forehead, and she sat up, retching at the thought. She
was wide-awake now. God, could it be true? She
thought back and realized with disgust that it could.
The first few weeks she had been Red Turtle's prisoner, he had sexually assaulted her without warning as she lay sleeping. He had rammed his penis,
swollen with lust, into her, grunting with short, quick
breaths, his eyes gleaming in the dark. He wanted to
hurt her, humiliate her. If she struggled, he hit her
hard across the face and bored into her until his penis
felt like a battering ram. Charity's past experience in
sexual detachment saved her. Withdrawing from the
degrading act, she had lain passive, taking deep
breaths to relax and accommodate him. His cruel attempts to punish her had merely left her slightly sore,
not ashamed and quivering with terror as he had an-
ticipated. Cheated of his pleasure, he eventually left
her alone. Charity strained to remember if she had
had her menstrual flow since then. She recalled that
she had been confined to the menstrual lodge only
once, but it had been three moons since her capture.
Her throat felt dry. It was true then. She was pregnant with *his* child. Tears of rage filled her eyes.
There was no end to her suffering. Why hadn't she

guessed earlier? Her breasts had only been so sensitive
to the touch once before, during her pregnancy. She
frowned. She still hadn't experienced morning sickness
yet. A gleam of hope momentarily soothed her suspicions. Maybe she wasn't pregnant. Maybe her period
hadn't come in two months because of some other
perfectly logical reason. Maybe . . . No, she thought
bitterly, there was no use in pretending. She was pregnant. She knew the signs. Charity lay back down and
squeezed her eyes tightly shut. She tried to summon
the golden light for comfort. Her head ached. She felt
exhausted, drained. For the first time since she had
learned to direct it, the light failed to appear at her
command. Hopelessness and a sense of despair over-
whelmed her. What did she have to look forward to
except endless drudgery, brutality, and the birth of an
Indian baby conceived in hate? Life was meaningless.
God was dead, if he had ever existed at all. Her protective light had deserted her. She was alone.

Charity was so numb with misery the following
morning that she failed to exhibit the slightest surprise
when she inadvertently got into Red Turtle's way and
he allowed her to pass without so much as a slap. Automatically she picked up the buffalo paunch and
went to the lake for fresh water, as was her usual
early-morning chore. It was cold, and a slight mist
hung over the still water. She stood shivering by the
edge of the lake with the buffalo paunch hanging limp-
ly from one hand and stared straight ahead. The
sounds of life were all around her. Birds and insects
rustled in the nearby trees and brush. Spirals of smoke
rose from individual lodges. Camp dogs stretched and
yawned. Charity was only dimly aware of the activity. She took a few steps closer to the water. Her
moccasins sank slightly into the black mud. The icy
water gently lapped against the moccasin tops, soaking
them, but she felt nothing. She was recalling the time
when she and a wealthy customer had gone boating
on a lake similar to this one. They had taken along

chicken sandwiches and a bottle of wine. The wine had gone to their heads and made them careless. The flimsy boat had overturned, dumping them into the cold water. Neither one could swim. Charity remembered the shock she felt as the water covered her. She shivered at the memory. It had swirled over her head, blocking out the afternoon sun and the sounds of people rowing on the lake. The second time she had disappeared beneath the dark water, her dress caught on to a piece of wood from the boat and the wood held her under. Charity struggled, clawing at the water with her nails, holding her breath until she could hold out no longer and breathed in some of the water. She felt as though she were smothering. Suddenly something unexpected occurred. She stopped struggling for a moment and felt a deep sense of peace, an eternity of peace. Remnants of self-preservation warned her to fight. She must struggle to survive. But a curious lethargy had seeped into her consciousness. Resistance seemed senseless, foolish, when it was so easy to give in to the soothing, calm peace that wrapped itself about her like a warm blanket. There was no pain. A small voice way back in the interior of her mind whispered the word "death"—her death. Strands of loose hair touched her eyes gently. She remembered thinking, if this was her time to go, then drowning wasn't a bad death. At that moment a strong hand grabbed her, roughly snatching her from the water, and dragged her to the surface. It was only then that the pain began. Standing now by the lake, the icy water lapping at her feet, she made a decision. Dropping the buffalo paunch to the ground, she took a deep breath and began to walk into the lake.

"I will get the water," Bright Eyes said gently, taking hold of Charity's arm and firmly turning her away from the lake. The two women stood facing each other. For the first time, Bright Eyes felt the stirring of compassion for White-Faced Woman. "There is no need to end your life," she said softly, correctly guessing what was in White-Faced Woman's heart.

"What is there to live for?" Charity said bitterly.

"When my husband returns, he will never beat you again," Bright Eyes assured her. "He has given me his word."

Charity glanced over Bright Eyes's shoulder at a group of five small children playing house. Her face twisted into a grimace of pain and rage. "I am carrying *his* child." She spit the words out one by one as if she wanted to rip the unformed fetus out like a piece of diseased tissue.

Bright Eyes wanted White-Faced Woman's child to live. She felt sure it would heal her husband's spirit. But she could not be with her every moment of every day in order to prevent another suicide attempt. Bright Eyes felt she must say something that would make White-Faced Woman want to live. "The Great Spirit has been kind to White-Faced Woman. She has been given a child to comfort her in her loneliness."

"I don't want this child!" Charity shouted angrily.

"The newborn that grows within your belly has need of you. If you give it love, it will love you in return. It is half yours."

Against her will, Charity recalled the squalling red face and tiny hands and feet of her dead daughter and softened perceptibly. "When it is born, you will take it from me," she said accusingly.

"You are the mother," Bright Eyes reassured her quickly. "I will help you all I can, but the baby belongs to you."

Charity remembered what it felt like to hold the tiny warm bundle against her chest and hear its little heart beating loudly against her own. She wouldn't be alone anymore. She would have the child to love and be loved in return. She could even pretend the child was Jim's. She sighed, and Bright Eyes relaxed. She had succeeded. White-Faced Woman would not take her own life now.

"I will get the water," Bright Eyes repeated cautiously. "We have need of chokecherries to make more pemmican. Take one of the baskets and gather as many as you can carry."

As Charity picked the chokecherries, she felt strangely peaceful. She paused in her work, closed her eyes, and raised her face to the sun's early-morning rays. The warmth beamed down on her upturned face and spread throughout her body. For the first time since her capture, she felt good. There would be no more beatings. As long as she had the child, she could bear it if she remained a captive. She felt her stomach and smiled. The child was a part of her, and she would live for its sake. The other women's voices reached her ears.

"Look how White-Faced Woman sits in the sun. She is lazy and worthless."

"If Red Turtle hears of that one's laziness, he will beat her again."

Charity laughed. She opened her eyes and began talking in a low voice to her unborn child. "You're very lucky to have Jim for a father. He's very handsome and brave. And he loves you. He doesn't care if you're a boy or a girl. I don't care either. Just between us, I think you'll be a boy. You'll carry his name, James Carson. It's a fine name."

The other women watched suspiciously and whispered among themselves.

"See how she talks to herself."

"Perhaps she's crazy," one of them suggested.

The rest shrugged but kept their distance from White-Faced Woman.

Bright Eyes saw to it that White-Faced Woman drank the bark medicine she made for her from time to time during her pregnancy so she would have an easy delivery. In addition, Bright Eyes helped her make baby clothes and worked on a cradle, which she finished two days before the birth.

As Charity squatted on her haunches and bore

down hard for the third time, grunting with the effort, she was rewarded for her diligence by the appearance of a tiny, well-formed head.

"Good," Bright Eyes approved, "bear down again." As she spoke, she prepared the bowl of water for washing the infant and the knife for severing its umbilical cord.

Charity had to bear down twice more before the child was fully expelled. She then lay back exhausted and watched as Bright Eyes cut the umbilical cord short and dusted the inner surface of her son's legs and his navel with powder from the prairie puffball. The older woman then tenderly wrapped him in a cloth and placed him in his cradle. Ordinarily, another woman nursed the baby for the first four days after its birth while the new mother drank medicine to induce the free flow of liquid. However, none of the other young mothers offered to nurse White-Faced Woman's son, so Charity happily nursed him herself. They were afraid of her and did not want anything to do with her or her child. Red Turtle showed no interest in his new son. Several women and children swore they had seen White-Faced Woman talking to a river monster who was shaped like a giant green lizard. They whispered that he had seduced her. The child was his, and not Red Turtle's, which was why he took no interest in the infant. He ignored Bright Eyes's efforts to get him to name the boy, and Charity refused to call him anything except Jim. Out of necessity, Bright Eyes referred to him by the pet name Pot Belly, hoping that eventually her husband would take an interest in the boy and give him a proper name.

Charity was not put out by the way the other women avoided her. She preferred to be left alone. The only person she spoke to besides her son was Bright Eyes, and then only when absolutely necessary. Occasionally she would allow Bright Eyes to play with the child, but only when *she* was nearby. Since the baby's birth, Charity had withdrawn even more

into her own world. She took her son with her on all
daily excursions for wood, water, and roots. Sometimes she strapped him into the little wooden cradle
and carried him on her back. At other times she
wrapped him in a shawl slung in front of her. He was
a contented baby and seldom cried. He would look up
at his mother as she chatted to him in English, a frown
between his dark eyes as though he were trying to
make out her words. At night she insisted on keeping
him by her side. While he drifted off to sleep she
would whisper the only prayer she still remembered
from her own childhood:

> Now I lay me down to sleep,
> I pray the Lord my soul to keep.
> If I should die before I wake,
> I pray the Lord my soul to take.

Three moons passed before Bright Eyes began making demands of Red Turtle. Holding Pot Belly in her
arms, she approached her husband as he sat in front of
the lodge cleaning his weapons.

"See how quickly your son grows. He will soon be
walking. It is time he had his ears pierced."

Red Turtle frowned at the term "son" and muttered without looking up, "He is still young yet.
There is time."

Bright Eyes was disappointed by his answer and
continued coldness toward his offspring, but she had
not yet abandoned hope that eventually he would accept the boy. Two moons later she tried again.

"Your son is older now. Would you wait until he is
talking before you have his ears pierced?" she chided
him. The normal period for ear piercing was from
three to six months after birth.

"Very well," Red Turtle replied angrily. "If you
want his ears pierced, then you pierce them yourself."

Bright Eyes stared at him, scandalized. "People will
talk."

"I don't care what other people say," Red Turtle said coldly before leaving the lodge.

Bright Eyes began to wonder uneasily if she had been mistaken in assuming her husband would come to love little Pot Belly. He showed no signs of it so far. Piercing the boy's ears without the proper ceremony was unheard of and showed a complete lack of affection. Bright Eyes sighed. She would wait another moon before resorting to the ear piercing without the traditional ceremony.

This period was a turbulent one. The Cheyenne had to break camp suddenly and move farther north to escape pursuing soldiers who had not stopped hunting them. As they marched they attacked outlying farms, ranches, and small settlements. They stole horses, killed cattle for food and people for revenge. These acts only added to their numerous crimes against the United States government and spurred the soldiers on to stop them at all costs.

Charity showed no interest in the news that a party of sixty soldiers had been sighted only three days' ride away. In the beginning, she had believed the soldiers would eventually rescue her from her hell, but experience had made her feel cynical about the hope of deliverance. This wouldn't be the first time the soldiers had come within a hairbreadth of their enemies, only to find the village deserted and the campfires cold. Now that she was no longer physically abused and had her son, life was tolerable. When Bright Eyes instructed her to break camp again, she obeyed without protest or questions. Strapping Jim into his cradle, she carried him securely on her back while she helped load the travois with the household goods.

An unexpected early snowstorm forced them to set up a temporary camp after they had been traveling for four days. The snow fell steadily, blocking mountain passes and covering everything with a thick blanket of white. Successfully eluding the soldiers for so long, the Cheyenne were overconfident. They felt the snow would effectively hide their tracks and that the Long Knives too would find traveling in a blizzard difficult, if not altogether impossible. They had not counted on the dogged persistence of the officer in charge, who pushed on relentlessly, led by Comanche scouts. The colonel had been tracking the Cheyenne for six months, always one step behind them. Now that success was so close, he refused to halt. He was determined to bring the red devils to their knees before the week was out.

The morning stillness exploded with the crash of thunder irons as the triumphant soldiers charged into the camp. Like the others, White-Faced Woman awoke to screams of terror, the pounding of horses' hooves, and the discharging of weapons. Red Turtle snatched his bow and quiver of arrows and rushed outside. White-Faced Woman grabbed her baby. Together she and Bright Eyes hurried out, just in time to see Red Turtle fall heavily to the ground, the blood spurting from a gaping hole in his chest. It was still snowing, and thick flakes stuck to his shiny black hair and eyelashes. Bright Eyes screamed and knelt in the snow beside her husband, trying to rouse him, but he was dead.

Charity stared at him, shocked. Red Turtle had been her tormentor, a fiend out of a horror story who was bigger than life. Now he was just an old man who was dead. She tugged at Bright Eyes's sleeve anxiously as the bullets whizzed around them.

"We must get out of here. Leave him. Your husband is dead."

Bright Eyes stood up. Tears streamed down her face. Before Charity could prevent her, she snatched Red Turtle's knife and ran into the midst of the charging soldiers, shrieking wildly, "Die, soldier dog, die." Before she had taken three steps, she too fell, clutching her bleeding stomach.

Charity stood rooted to the spot, dazed, holding her screaming baby in her arms, unable to move. The scene before her was horrifyingly reminiscent of one she had recently lived through. The only difference was that this time the whites were the victorious ones. Lodges were slashes to shreds and set on fire. Men, women, and children were ruthlessly cut down as they ran for cover or tried to retaliate. The bright blue uniforms of the soldiers and the puddles of thick red blood that now freely intermingled with the snow had created a macabre effect. Charity stifled a laugh of hysteria that rose in her throat and choked her. The Indians didn't have a chance, not with such obviously patriotic signs as red, white, and blue. Anyone could see the logic of that.

A bullet came within inches of Jim's head, startling Charity out of her paralysis. She ran blindly with the others toward the woods. The soldiers were busy killing. Charity no longer trusted people, red or white. The sensible thing to do, as she saw it, was to get her baby to safety. If she could hide until after the battle was over and the soldiers had killed enough Indians, she might have a chance to explain she was a white captive.

Other women ran beside Charity, many hugging crying children to their breasts. A teenage girl carrying her five-year-old brother was cut off by two mounted soldiers who ran the boy through with their sabers and dragged the terrified girl through the snow out of sight. Standing beside her dead mother, still clutching her skirt, a three-year-old girl wept bitterly in the falling snow. Charity slid down an embankment and sought refuge among a clump of evergreens, only to find another woman and her son already crouching there. Their wide, frightened eyes stared at her as she joined them, fear, horror, and grief clearly evident on their faces. No one spoke. The killing continued.

Charity had no idea how long she remained huddled there, smelling the fresh pine scent of the evergreens and listening for the sound of crunching snow made by heavy boots or horses' hooves. It couldn't have been long. Suddenly the pistols and rifles were silent. It was over. Charity breathed a sigh of relief and hugged her son to her.

"It's all right. It's over now, honey," she said softly in English. Jim didn't move. She squeezed him tighter. His body felt stiff, rigid. It now occurred to her that he had not cried or moved for some time.

"Mama, look!" the little Indian boy whispered loudly. "The baby is hurt. Is he dead?"

His mother glanced at Charity pityingly. "Be still, child," she cautioned.

Charity stared with horror at the dark patch on the blanket that covered Jim, and felt sick. Slowly she turned back the blanket and saw a trickle of blood ooze down the left side of his head. As she ran, she had carried him against her chest protectively, but he had squirmed in her arms. His head must have been exposed to the soldiers' bullets. He was probably already dead when she slid over the embankment. She began to tremble. "Oh, God, please, no, not my baby. Please, God. I'll do anything. I promise." Charity's voice shook. Jim remained motionless, his little body cold and lifeless. She started to shake him gently, pleading, "Jim, please wake up. You can't be dead. You can't. I won't let you," she said fiercely, shaking him harder.

"Your son is dead," the Indian woman said gently, touching her on the arm.

"No," Charity moaned, snatching her arm away as though it were burned. "My baby is all I have. He can't be dead. He can't."

The sound of approaching footsteps made the Indian woman turn pale with fear and crouch even farther into the snow, pulling her son under her.

"That was quick work, Corporal," Colonel Caldwell said approvingly. "How many of our boys were hit?"

"Only five wounded, sir, and none dead."

"The general will be pleased," Colonel Caldwell

predicted. "When we get back to the fort, there will be plenty of cause for celebration. This is the first major hit we've made on the Cheyenne so far. I think the other bands might be willing to discuss a new treaty now."

"Yes, sir," Corporal Bates agreed. "This will teach the savages that the United States government never gives up."

Charity listened to the two men callously discussing the slaughter with smug self-satisfaction and shook with rage. Her son was dead. The only reason she'd had for living had been annihilated, wiped out, and they stood above her discussing it with pride. She laid her baby down and tenderly covered his face with the blanket. Her bare hands raked the snow and closed about a medium-sized rock. She pulled it up and held it tightly in the palm of her right hand, feeling a shooting pain surge up her arm from grasping the ice-cold object. Silently she moved away from her hiding place and started to crawl up the snowy embankment behind the soldiers. The two men were standing with their backs toward Charity, only three feet away. The brims of their blue hats were filled with a thin coating of falling snow. A small pool of blood had formed at Corporal Bates's feet. The blood dripped from a shiny steel saber he had not yet cleaned and replaced in its scabbard.

Colonel Caldwell was speaking in a low voice. "We'll take whatever survivors there are back to Fort Garth."

Charity threw the rock at Corporal Bates's head with all the strength and venom she could muster. The impact at such close range was immediate and powerful. Corporal Bates groaned and fell forward unconscious.

Startled, Colonel Caldwell drew his pistol and turned to face his assailant. He saw a wild-eyed Indian woman, fairer than most, her eyes burning with hatred, charge him. Her lips were parted in a snarl of

fury and her arms outstretched, as though she longed
to tear him apart with her nails, limb from limb. He
took aim with his pistol but never fired the shot.

"Bastard," Charity shrieked in English as she lunged
for him. "Murderers!"

Colonel Caldwell stepped aside just in time to escape Charity's attack. As she came for him the second
time, the colonel delivered a strong left hook, render-
ing Charity senseless.

"Broughty, McMillan, over here," he shouted to
two men within calling distance who had not
witnessed the assault. "On the double."

"Yes, sir," they answered, taking in the two unconscious figures with a grim look.

"Broughty, Corporal Bates has been wounded. He
may have a concussion. I want you to do what you
can for him."

"Yes, sir."

"McMillan, this woman is responsible for Corporal
Bates's condition. Tie her up securely so she can't do
any more harm, but keep her separated from the others. She's white."

"Yes, sir," Private McMillan replied uneasily.

When Charity regained consciousness inside one of
the still-standing lodges, she discovered her arms were
bound behind her. She was leaning against the side of
a lodge pole. An army blanket had been thrown over
her. It was very cold. Her arms ached, but she didn't
notice. They could have been someone else's arms.
She felt a creeping numbness take hold of her brain,
heart, and internal organs. Charity no longer cared
whether she lived or died. She could think about her
dead son and feel no pain, no sorrow, no tears, only a
bleak emptiness.

Colonel Caldwell entered the lodge and spoke
briskly. "Now, then, we know you're white, ma'am,
and we'd like to find out your name." Charity stared
straight ahead without responding. The colonel

frowned in annoyance. "When were you taken prisoner? Where?" Charity remained unresponsive.

Private McMillan entered the lodge and saluted.

"Well, what did you find out about our captive?" Colonel Caldwell demanded. "Did the Indians know anything about her?"

"It looks like she could be one of the survivors of the Sweetwater massacre, sir," Private McMillan said in an undertone.

"If my memory serves me correctly, there were three missing women," Colonel Caldwell mused. He turned back to Charity. "We'd like to help you, ma'am, but we have to find out who you are first. Private McMillan says it's possible you're one of the survivors of Sweetwater. Is that true?" Silence. The colonel lost his temper. "Take a good look, Private. In less than two years those savages turned a woman against her own race. She attacked me, nearly killed Corporal Bates, and continues to sit there staring blankly as though she doesn't understand a word of English."

"Sir, if I could have a word with you . . ." Private McMillan pleaded.

"Well, what is it?" Colonel Caldwell shouted in exasperation, allowing himself to be led out of earshot of the prisoner.

"In searching the area for survivors, we came on an Indian woman and her son hiding in the woods. She told us a white woman had hidden with her and that she had gone crazy with grief when she discovered her baby was dead."

Colonel Caldwell felt uncomfortable. He had been a widower for the past fifteen years. But even when he was married, he had never pretended to understand the opposite sex. One thing he had learned. When a woman loses a child, she can go berserk. His own wife had, and she was generally sensible. Men might feel the same sorrow, but they never broke down and did wild, unpredictable things. He eyed the forlorn figure with the hollow eyes that stared, unseeing, with a mixture of pity and scorn. He realized she couldn't help having an Indian baby, but he secretly despised her for loving it. "We'll take her to Fort Garth and let them worry about who she is," he said roughly, quickly turning away.

"Shall I release her for the trip back, sir?" Private McMillan inquired.

The colonel nodded. "Untie her, but don't take your eyes off her for a second. There's no telling what she might do," he added in final warning.

To Private McMillan's considerable relief, his charge exhibited none of the signs of hostility or resentment he expected. On the contrary, she was totally submissive. To prevent an escape, he had attached her horse's reins to a rope that was then affixed to his saddle. By the end of the first day of traveling, he had begun to suspect that if he hadn't controlled her horse's actions, the animal would have been left to its own devices. The woman seemed incapable of independent action. When he said it was time to ride, she mounted her horse without a word. If he said it was time to eat, she ate what was put in front of her, provided he reminded her from time to time. When they were ready to retire for the night, he had to tell her it was time to sleep. She would obediently lie down, but he had to cover her with the blankets himself. If he didn't, she would lie shivering with the cold, although the blankets lay in a neat pile at her feet. Except for meekly obeying his instructions, she showed no other signs of life. She never spoke, smiled, or wept. He finally confided to the colonel that he was worried about the state of her mind.

"It's all an act, Private. She'll snap out of it once we reach Fort Garth and the other women attend to her. There's no need to worry," Colonel Caldwell assured him confidently.

Occasional gusts of wind whipped the drifts of powdered snow into whirlwind activity, creating the illusion of a blizzard. Icicles formed breathtaking patterns on peeling birch trees, while stately rows of fir, spruce, and pine filled the valleys with their lush green fertility.

Jim Carson reined in his horse on the top of a rise and took a sip of brandy from a small silver flask he carried in the breast pocket of his overcoat. The smooth golden liquid took away the chill, and he stopped shaking. It was late afternoon, and the blue sky was streaked with ridges of deep purple, pink, and gold. Clusters of white clouds moved rapidly across the horizon as though they were being chased by invisible hunters. Jim's long, graceful hands felt like blocks of ice despite the leather gloves lined with fur. He took them off and rubbed his hands together vigorously to help speed up the circulation, totally oblivious of the great natural beauty of the scene before him. Jim's only concern was to reach Fort Garth before nightfall.

Two years of worry and guilt had altered Jim's appearance. His hair was as black and thick as ever, and underneath the bulky overcoat he still wore an impeccable suit and imported silk vest. It was his face that had changed. The hardness in his blue-gray eyes was more pronounced and the new lines in his forehead and around his mouth made him seem older, harsher. Unless he smiled, which he seldom did anymore, strangers were reluctant to approach him. However, there was an air of mystery and sorrow about Jim that was very appealing to women. He represented a challenge. They longed to take him in their arms and force him to forget everything else but the passion of the moment. If they succeeded, they were pleased with themselves, content to bid him good-bye in the morning, confident that their expertise and powers of

sexual allurement had been put to the test and that
they'd won out against great odds.

Jim had been in the town of Red River in the
middle of a steak dinner when news of the Sweetwater massacre had caught up to him. He had immediately set out for Fort Jubele, paying no heed to the
warning that he might be killed by marauding
Cheyenne. On the way, he fervently prayed that the
rumor of no survivors was a false one. Charity had to
be alive! His prayers seemed to have been answered
when he discovered she was one of six missing people.

At the time, he had naively imagined Charity would
be rescued in a couple of weeks. The weeks turned
into months. He spent sleepless nights recalling in
gruesome detail the horror stories related to him by
others of the brutal treatment of white captives. Like
so many people who have narrowly escaped the
destruction and death that claimed the lives of close
relatives and friends, he felt guilty. If only he had
been there, he might have somehow prevented the attack on the Indian villages. If only he had taken Charity with him to buy that damn piano. If only he had
told her he loved her. The "if onlys" were without
end or consolation. Whenever he heard that the
soldiers had raided an Indian village and discovered a
white captive, or signed a new treaty and been handed
white prisoners in exchange, Jim rode to the fort even
when he knew the women were too old or too young
to fit Charity's description. Three times he had met
Michael Mallory. Michael was searching for his sister
and brother. Neither of them had exchanged more
than a dozen words. Jim would have liked to offer the
boy some consolation, but he was busily engaged in
battling his own fears and bitterness. To offer another
something he himself lacked seemed useless.

Jim took a deep breath of the cold air before continuing on the last lap of the journey. His muscles
were taut with excitement. For some unaccountable
reason he felt this time would be different. He was

sure that when he was brought into the presence of the white captive, Charity's brown eyes with the reddish flecks would smile warmly at him before she ran into his arms.

The reception at Fort Garth did not go as Jim had planned. When he informed the sergeant he was there to see the white woman held by the Indians, he was taken straight to the army doctor.

Dr. Able Cook was short and stout, in his mid-fifties, with thin, nondescript hair, bulging blue eyes, a ruddy complexion, and long, startlingly beautiful hands. Dr. Cook's appearance belied the fact that he was an excellent surgeon had a passionate nature and a decided penchant for lost causes.

"Is the woman hurt?" Jim asked anxiously.

Dr. Cook scrutinized him carefully before answering cautiously. "She's been very badly treated, Mr. Carson, very badly indeed."

Jim paled. "What's wrong with her?"

"Sit down. Would you care for a drink? I have some of the best port in the world. Or perhaps you'd care for a whiskey?" he inquired politely.

Jim tried to hide his impatience and growing uneasiness. "The port is fine. Doctor, did she tell you her name?"

"We're still in ignorance as to her identity, but we have reason to believe she's one of the three missing women taken in the Sweetwater massacre," Dr. Cook said slowly, watching Jim's reaction.

Jim laid his untouched glass of port down on the table next to him. "What has she told you?"

"Nothing!" Dr. Cook said evenly.

Jim frowned. "She must have said something. She told you she came from Sweetwater."

"I'm afraid we learned that from the Indians," Dr. Cook admitted with a sigh.

Jim's body stiffened perceptibly. He felt suddenly sick with apprehension and swallowed half the port at one gulp.

"I gather the woman you're looking for comes from Sweetwater," Dr. Cook said compassionately. When Jim nodded, he added, "She's medium height, on the thin side, with brown hair and eyes. No distinguishing birthmarks. Does that general description ring a bell?"

"It could fit Charity," Jim agreed flatly.

Dr. Cook stood up. "I'll take you to see her, but I must warn you first, Mr. Carson. She was brutally abused. We may never know just how badly. The horror she went through, combined with the loss of her baby in the attack on the Indian village, caused her to go into shock. If she is the woman you're looking for, she probably won't recognize you."

Jim blindly followed Dr. Cook outside and across the yard to the quarters of the married personnel. The doctor's hints had chilled him to the bone. Could the woman he was about to meet be Charity, his Charity?

The door was opened by a middle-aged woman whose beauty, though faded, was in no way diminished. She was wearing a red plaid wool dress. Her silver-blond hair was piled softly on the top of her head, and dangling from her ears was a pair of garnet earrings. She smiled warmly at Dr. Cook, who took her dainty hand and kissed it.

"Lucy, this is Mr. Carson. He's come to see if our patient is the woman he's been looking for. How is she?"

"The same as usual." Lucy McKenzie sighed, closing the door after them. "She's sitting by the fire."

It was a comfortable room. An orange-and-brown braided rug covered the center of the scarred wooden floor. Bright curtains hung at the windows. Against one wall was a dark wood bookcase filled from floor to ceiling with leather-bound books. A rolltop desk of the same dark wood stood in front of it. Jim's eyes were instantly drawn to the roaring fire in the black iron grate and the figure seated in the rocking chair in front of it. He could see the top of the woman's brown head over the chair back. She didn't stir when Dr. Cook addressed her.

"How is our patient feeling today?" he asked jovially.

The woman remained motionless. Dr. Cook said softly, "I've brought you a visitor."

Jim stepped forward. The shock of recognition when it came stunned him into speechlessness. Charity looked emaciated, but it wasn't her physical condition that made his throat tighten in an effort to keep back the tears. Her face was smooth, clear, not a line on it. But her eyes. God, those beautiful, wondrous brown eyes with the reddish flecks that emanated sensuality, stared straight through him, dull and lifeless.

"Charity," Jim finally managed to articulate in a strangled voice. "It's me. It's Jim, baby, Jim Carson."

Charity's eyes did not light up with recognition or even with the faintest acknowledgment of his existence. Jim took her hand. It was limp and cold despite the heat of the fire. He wanted to hold her in his arms, but he knew she wouldn't respond to his embrace. Releasing her hand, he watched it fall lifelessly back into her lap. Dr. Cook gently touched him on the shoulder, and together they moved over to the bookcase. Lucy stayed with Charity, tucking the blanket around her legs.

"How long has she been like this," Jim asked, avoiding the doctor's face.

"When she discovered her baby was dead, she attacked Corporal Bates and gave him a mild concussion, but ever since then, she's been as you see her," Dr. Cook explained. "She does whatever we tell her to literally, but seems incapable of acting on her own. If Lucy didn't remind her to eat what is put in front of her, she'd starve."

Jim glanced back at Charity. Trying to keep his voice steady, he asked, "Can anything be done for her?"

"Why not return with me to my place?" Dr. Cook

invited. "Lucy doesn't approve of alcohol, and you look like you could use a shot of something stronger than coffee. We can talk at greater length," he added.

Jim left Lucy McKenzie's house without saying good-bye. He had never felt so depressed or helpless in his life.

"Lucy's a fine woman, Mr. Carson, but a trifle on the rigid side where liquor is concerned," Dr. Cook explained again as he handed Jim a double whiskey. "Of course, I can't really blame her. Her husband, Lieutenant McKenzie, God rest his soul, was an affable fellow when he was sober, but give him a couple of drinks and he was as mean and ornery a customer as you'd ever want to meet."

"I couldn't believe it was Charity," Jim said in a dazed voice.

"Swallow the whiskey, Mr. Carson," Dr. Cook advised kindly. "You've had a shock."

Jim downed the liquor. As it hit his stomach he shuddered, and some of the color returned to his face.

"I make it a practice never to give up on any of my patients," Dr. Cook confided. "Every now and then I come across a man or woman who's lost the will to live. I can't think of anything more tragic," he said sadly as he poured Jim another shot. "The poor devils are set in their ways, stubborn beyond reason. All they want to do is die in peace. But I'm every bit as stubborn as they are, and I'll do everything in my power to prevent them from recklessly throwing away God's precious gift of life. I'm like a gnat, Mr. Carson, a giant gnat that won't leave them alone. They hate me for interfering with their plans, and most of them live, if only to be strong enough to murder me." He chuckled and fingered the rim of his glass. "Of course, once they become actively involved with life again, they're eternally grateful that they didn't die."

"Were any of your other patients like Charity?" Jim asked in amazement.

Dr. Cook sighed. "I have to admit Charity is a very special case." He didn't mention the fact that he had seen a case like hers only once before, in an asylum in Chicago. "So far, every method I've used to try to reach Charity has failed abysmally," he confessed. "But now that you're here," he added cheerfully, "I'm beginning to feel optimistic."

"Why?" Jim muttered miserably. "She didn't know me. I don't think she was even aware of her surroundings."

"I'm sure you're right," Dr. Cook agreed amiably. "Nevertheless, young man, I have a theory. It doesn't in any way have the support of the medical profession. It's just my own pet belief, about which I feel strongly. Charity's reaction is more severe than the others' because she has completely cut herself off from the outside world. But that doesn't mean she can't be reached."

"How?" Jim asked eagerly.

Dr. Cook smiled. "I'm a great believer in the healing power of love, and that's where you come in. If I'm not much mistaken, you're in love with her."

Jim frowned. "Yes, I am. But how does my loving Charity help her if she's unable to recognize me?"

Leaning back in his chair, Dr. Cook poured himself another whiskey. Like the rest of his stock, it was excellent, and he was thoroughly enjoying it. "If Charity loved you once as you so obviously love her, she still does, and your presence is going to make a difference. I want you to remain at the fort. I'll put you up. I have plenty of room," he said generously. "Take Charity out, spend time with her, talk to her as if she were perfectly normal. Tell her you love her and want her to get well. If my theory is correct, she'll begin to respond."

Jim looked doubtful. "What if it doesn't work?"

"You have nothing to lose by trying," Dr. Cook reminded him. "But don't worry. I told you once be-

fore I never give up, absolutely never," he assured Jim
with more confidence than he felt.

Ghostly shadows flickered in and out of Charity's
vision. The low, pleasant hum that had rung in her
ears since she had first been sucked into the cocoon of
golden light was now as much a part of her as an arm
or a leg, perhaps more so. She wasn't sure that this
light was the same one that had aided her on other occasions, but she didn't care. Charity and the beautiful
light were now permanently one. It was safe and
warm and peaceful. The humming sound was her protection against hostile outside elements. Formless
shadows tried to make contact with her in an attempt
to lure her back to the world of pain and grief. The
shadows frightened Charity, but she was also curious
about them. Occasionally she tried to distinguish features and individual characteristics. The humming
sound saved her. It rose to a piercing scream that
forced her back to a state of passivity. Lately she had
lost all interest in the shadows, but tonight something
strange had happened.

Whenever one of the phantoms wanted her to obey
it, it would hover before her without moving.
Tonight when one of the shadows hovered in front of
her, she was startled to see, instead of colors, pink
roses pulsating out of the center of its being. She
didn't know what that meant, but it bothered her.
Charity liked to know at all times what was expected
of her.

It had rained heavily during the night, and the
ground inside the fort was knee-deep in gray slush
and mud. A month had passed since Jim Carson had
come to Fort Garth. He glanced over at Charity, who
was sitting in a chair by the window in Lucy McKenzie's quarters. Little progress had been made as far as
he could see. She still hadn't uttered a word or shown

the slightest recognition. Looking at her now, sitting there with her hands demurely in her lap, Jim thought that if a stranger entered the room he wouldn't realize at first that anything was wrong with her. Her appetite had increased, and she now looked the picture of glowing good health. Lucy was visiting Dr. Cook. Realizing Jim was embarrassed about speaking aloud to Charity when someone else was in the room, she always tried to leave them alone. Lucy was an angel. She never complained about her charge, but Jim knew Charity must be a burden. A decision would soon have to be made. General Steagall had broached the undesirable possibility of putting Charity in an institution, but Jim was adamantly against it. When the time came, he would pay someone enough to look after her as Lucy did. Jim looked out the window with bleary eyes. He hadn't slept much in the last couple of weeks. The sun was making a feeble attempt to escape from behind dull clouds. Soldiers marched single file across the yard. Peaceful Indians had come to trade. Visiting civilians in their buckboards arrived and demanded to speak to General Steagall. Business as usual. He turned dismally away from the window. For Charity the world had stopped. He put his arms around her waist and urged her to rise. She stood obediently in front of him, her head reaching the top of his shoulder, her arms slack against her sides. He drew her unresisting body toward him. Lucy had washed Charity's hair the night before, and it smelled fresh and clean. He kissed her forehead and brushed a wisp of hair out of her eyes.

"What do you think about? Or do you think at all?" he murmured. "Is there a small part of you that knows me? I wonder!" He embraced her limp form. "I love you, darling. I always have. It's ironic," he whispered in her ear, "but if you were perfectly healthy, I would find saying I love you more difficult." He clasped her fiercely. "Hell, if you'd only get well, I'd say it twenty times a day."

Charity was now used to the dark shape whose center pulsated pink roses. She no longer tried to figure out what it meant. She only knew that when this particular shadow went away, she was sad. Several times she tried without success to see more, but the humming sound interfered. For the first time she was annoyed with it. She had begun to feel that the hum was more of a hindrance than a protection. There was no reason why she shouldn't be able to see the features and form of the rose shadow. Charity didn't think she was being unreasonable. She had never exhibited such persistence before, and it was only this one time. The hum was being unfair.

"Time is running out," Jim said softly. "I have to make a decision about you by the end of the month. It's not fair to Lucy to keep you here. I promise you, darling, I'll find a woman who's as competent and kind as Lucy to take care of you. I'll visit you whenever I can. Maybe someday . . ." Jim's voice wavered, and tears filled his eyes.

Charity sensed something was wrong. The rose shadow would vibrate with intensity one moment and then fade the next. This new activity disturbed her. She was afraid the beautiful rose shadow was going to go away and leave her alone. She had to keep it with her somehow. If only she could see what it looked like! Charity exerted a tremendous effort to break out of the golden cocoon of light. The humming sound, low at first, became louder and louder until it shattered her eardrums with shrill echoes. The pain was unbearable, all-consuming, agonizing. Charity felt like screaming, but held on until the outer fringes of the shadow began to lighten to gray. Finally she could stand it no longer and gave up, exhausted with the struggle.

"What a filthy day," Dr. Cook commented cheerfully as he and Lucy returned arm in arm.

"It certainly is messy," Lucy agreed as she reminded Dr. Cook to remove his boots before taking another step farther into the house.

Jim released Charity.

"Anything new?" Dr. Cook inquired while Lucy was off preparing lunch.

"Nothing!" Jim said gloomily.

"It takes time," Dr. Cook began consolingly, but suddenly stopped, a startled look in his eyes.

"What is it?" Jim asked. Dr. Cook was staring at Charity.

"She's sweating," Dr. Cook said excitedly.

Jim looked puzzled. "I don't see . . ."

Dr. Cook turned a beaming face on him. "It's not hot in here, and Charity is always cold. She never sweats. Take her hand and feel it."

Jim was surprised. "It's burning hot. Does that mean she's sick?" he asked anxiously.

"It could be illness, of course, and I'll take every precaution," Dr. Cook assured him, "but I think she's sweating because of some inner stress. We've never seen the slightest hint of it before. I don't want to get your hopes up, but this is the first promising sign we've had. I think you may be getting through to her at last, Jim."

Two weeks passed without any further developments, and Jim was beginning to feel depressed again. Dr. Cook urged him to go into town for a few days.

"Get away from it all. Relax. Besides, I'd like to see if your absence creates a reaction in Charity."

Jim wearily agreed.

Charity was angry. Rage bubbled up inside her like molten lava. The rose shadow was gone. She wanted to sob her heart out but couldn't. Tears were not allowed inside the cocoon of golden light. Charity had come to hate the light and the hum. They were now her enemies. She knew that somehow she would find a way to destroy them even if she was destroyed in the process.

Jim returned after three days. He went straight to Charity. She sat in her usual place by the fire, wearing a dark green dress. A velvet ribbon kept the rich chestnut hair out of her face.

"I'll be in the other room if you need me," Lucy said, smiling, leaving them alone.

Charity couldn't believe it. The rose shadow had returned. Before it went away again she had to see what it looked like. She had to! The battle between her and the forces that imprisoned her began. This time she knew she had to win out against the humming sound. It was imperative she prove to herself that she was in control of it, and not the other way around.

Jim kissed Charity lightly on the cheek and sat down on a chair next to her. He was about to tell her of his trip to town when he noticed that she was sweating again.

The high-pitched deafening hum reverberated off the walls of Charity's mind like chalk screeching on a blackboard. There was no end to it. Waves of sound traveled through her. Charity couldn't breathe without feeling searing pain shoot through every fiber of her being. An inner voice pleaded for her to stop now; she could always try again. No, she wouldn't give in, not this time. She had never come this far before. The impenetrable darkness had slowly changed to gray and was now beginning to get lighter. Lines were forming into more discernible shapes. There was another kind of light beyond the one that enclosed her. She must reach it before the sound destroyed her.

"What is it?" Jim said excitedly, studying her. Gone was the serene, placid mask that cut her off from others. Charity was sure as hell feeling something. She was not only sweating profusely, she was trembling. "Whatever it is, let it out. Come on, Charity," Jim muttered as he squeezed her damp hands in his. "Tell me what's wrong. Say something, anything!"

Charity began to scream and scream and scream.

Lucy rushed back into the room to find Jim holding a hysterical Charity against his chest.

"Get Dr. Cook right away," Jim shouted with relief. Hysteria was better than that horrible silence.

Dr. Cook gave Charity a sedative and put her to bed, but not before she had asked for Jim.

He sat on the side of the bed holding her hand.

"I recognized you, Jim," Charity mumbled thickly as the drug took effect. "You were the rose shadow."

"You're going to be all right now," he said, stroking her hair.

"Don't leave me," Charity pleaded, clutching his hand. "Promise you won't leave me alone." She shuddered.

Jim kissed her tenderly on the mouth before answering fervently, "I'll never leave you alone again. Never!"

Charity sighed and relaxed her grip on his hand. "I love you," she muttered sleepily.

"I love you too," Jim assured her.

"She'll sleep now," Dr. Cook whispered. "Lucy and I are going to celebrate Charity's recovery with a glass of sherry. Care to join us?"

"I'll be out in a minute."

Dr. Cook nodded, and he and Lucy left Jim alone with a peacefully sleeping Charity.

As he sat holding Charity's hand in the slowly gathering shadows, Jim realized he was beginning to exhibit all the aftereffects of shock. His body was wringing wet and he felt as weak as a kitten. But never in his whole life had he felt such peace. He watched with satisfaction as Charity breathed deeply in and out. Her flesh felt warm and alive under his touch. She had recognized him and said she loved him. Tomorrow would be time enough to discuss the future. "I've always wanted to go to California," Jim mused out loud. He had whispered, but his voice sounded unnaturally loud in the still, dark room. "I think you'd like San Francisco," he added softly, and smiled happily when Charity mumbled his name in her sleep.

7

The sky was gray and overcast. Five days of steadily falling snow had finally let up, but the occupants of Fort Jubele were not deceived into thinking this was a sign of continuing clear weather. They knew it was only a temporary breather. The snow would start again that night or the next morning. The inhabitants were restless and irritable, their tempers short.

Outside the fort, the tracks made by the soldiers' horses coming and going were clearly etched in the stark white panorama. Inside the fort, mountains of snow were hastily shoveled against the walls. The area most frequently traveled over by boots and horses had turned to dark slush. It was bitter cold. Situated in one corner of the compound stood half a dozen tepees. Armed soldiers stood guard, but there was no sign of the Indians.

Boone flicked his half-smoked cigarette down and made a point of crushing it under his heel. He frowned and took a deep breath of the cold air before turning the corner and heading for Lieutenant Farrell's office. The lieutenant had ordered him to appear on the double, and for the first time in their mutually disagreeable association, Boone had complied without protest. He knew why the lieutenant had sent for him. The previous evening one of the guards had been murdered. His throat had been cut with a knife that had later been traced to one of the Indian prisoners. Boone was needed as an interpreter in the interrogation.

Lieutenant Farrell was furious. He glared at the two other people in the room, Sergeant Patterson and an Indian boy about fifteen. Ever since the Sweetwater catastrophe he had been edgy. The massacre had almost lost him his post. He had tried to make up for it by hunting the Cheyenne down and forcing them into a position where a new peace treaty would be called for. Lieutenant Farrell knew if he could pull that off, all would be forgiven. When a small hunting party had been captured after a slight skirmish over a week ago, he hadn't wanted to keep the prisoners at his fort but had received word to hold them until spring. Now this! The sweat stood out on his forehead at the thought of being replaced, or even worse, demoted. He stared with loathing at the Indian in front of him. The boy's gaze seemed to be fastened to a spot just above the lieutenant's left shoulder. His dark face was impassive, devoid of expression. Lieutenant Farrell wasn't fooled by the boy's youth. He knew Indian boys were taught from the time they could walk how to pillage, murder, and scalp. It was their nature to be brutal, untrustworthy, and ruthless. Lieutenant Farrell's mouth hardened. He would be just as ruthless in dealing with them.

"You wanted to see me," Boone drawled, entering the office without waiting for Corporal Olsen to announce him.

"I want you to question this Indian. Find out why he killed Private Evans," Lieutenant Farrell said sharply.

Boone turned to the boy and spoke softly in Cheyenne. "The soldier chief wants to know why you murdered one of his men."

The Indian boy continued to stare straight ahead. When he finally spoke, his voice was disdainful. "I killed no one."

"Your knife put an end to his life," Boone pointed out.

"I did not kill the Long Knife," he repeated firmly.

"What does he say?" Lieutenant Farrell demanded.

Boone shrugged. "He says he didn't kill him."

"That's ridiculous." Lieutenant Farrell was annoyed. "It was his knife, wasn't it?"

"He admits it was his knife," Boone agreed. "But anyone could have used it. The knife alone is only circumstantial evidence."

"You're here as an interpreter, Boone," Lieutenant Farrell reminded him, flushing, "not as a lawyer."

"Maybe one of the other heathens did it," Sergeant Patterson offered.

Lieutenant Farrell frowned and began drumming his fingers on the wooden desk. "If he didn't kill the soldier, ask him who did," he instructed Boone.

"Do you know who murdered the Long Knife?" Boone asked the boy.

The Indian shifted his gaze to Boone and hesitated. "You will not believe me."

"Tell me," Boone insisted. "If it's the truth, I'll believe it."

"None of my people killed the Long Knife."

Boone raised his eyebrows and with a trace of a smile on his face repeated what the boy had said to the impatient lieutenant.

"He must think we're fools," Lieutenant Farrell said contemptuously.

"Lieutenant . . ." Sergeant Patterson interrupted apologetically.

"If you have something relevant to say, Sergeant, out with it," Lieutenant Farrell muttered irritably.

"Private Evans had a particular grudge against the Indians," Sergeant Patterson began. "There was talk he was . . . well, that he was a bit hard on the prisoners, sir," he ended uneasily.

Lieutenant Farrell stopped drumming on the desk and stared at the sergeant coldly. "Elaborate, Sergeant!"

"Yes, sir." Sergeant Patterson looked decidedly

uncomfortable. "Private Evens lost his whole family in an Indian attack. He hated them with a passion."

"Most people around here have lost families in Indian attacks," Lieutenant Farrell said stiffly. "Get to the point."

Sergeant Patterson turned red with embarrassment. He knew the lieutenant's wife was still missing. "I heard he used to take pleasure in tormenting the Indians whenever he could. In other words, sir," he continued miserably, "Private Evans might have been a bit too harsh in his treatment of the prisoners, and one of them decided to take revenge."

"Private Evans's behavior should have been reported to me," Lieutenant Farrell said in exasperation. "If I'm not told what's going on, I can hardly be in a position to prevent an incident like this one from breaking out."

"Yes, sir," Sergeant Patterson agreed weakly, breaking out in a cold sweat, "but . . . but I didn't have time to confirm the rumor, sir," he explained desperately. To the sergeant's considerable relief, Lieutenant Farrell shifted his attention to the scout.

"It's now perfectly obvious what happened," Lieutenant Farrell said, trying to hide his indignation. "Private Evans went too far and was killed. A regrettable incident, but no matter what provocation the Indians might have had, they shouldn't have taken the law into their own hands. Their knives were generously returned to them so they could work at their daily tasks as usual. They weren't returned so they could commit murder." Lieutenant Farrell glanced at the Indian boy with obvious distaste. "These Indians must be cured of their savagery. They must learn how to obey rules and regulations like everyone else. I'm afraid I shall have to make an example of the boy."

"He claims neither he nor his people had anything to do with the death of Private Evans," Boone commented quietly.

Lieutenant Farrell stared at him. "Naturally he would say that."

"The Indians weren't the only ones Private Evans had a grudge against," Boone remarked cryptically.

Lieutenant Farrell eyed him uneasily in silence for several seconds before asking grimly, "What are you talking about, Boone?"

"Private Evans had a running feud with Private Bellows. They couldn't even sit at the same mess-hall table without winding up in a fight. Last night they had guard duty together."

Lieutenant Farrell turned to the sergeant, who stammered, "It's true they weren't on the best of terms, sir, but—"

"Never mind, Sergeant," Lieutenant Farrell broke in hastily. "It isn't important. We know who killed Private Evans." He glared at the scout. "We also know how you feel about the Indians, Boone, but there is no doubt at all that this one is responsible for Private Evans's death, and he is the one who is going to pay for it."

Instead of the snide comment Lieutenant Farrell had expected, Boone asked softly, "What do you intend to do with the boy?"

"He's to be put in the guardhouse for safekeeping. Tomorrow he'll stand trial for murder, and if he's found guilty, as I'm sure he will be," Lieutenant Farrell added, "he'll be hanged."

Sergeant Patterson started forward to take charge of the Indian, but Lieutenant Farrell stopped him with a wave of his hand. "Let Boone escort the prisoner, Sergeant. I want to have a talk with you," he said sternly.

"Yes, sir." Sergeant Patterson sighed and steeled himself for the tongue-lashing that lay ahead.

Once they had reached the prison, Boone told the guard, "I'm going to spend some time with the prisoner. Lieutenant Farrell asked me to question him at greater length."

The guard saw nothing odd about this, and locked Boone in the cell with the captive. Boone turned to the boy, who was standing underneath the barred window with his back to the scout. "The soldier chief thinks you lied to him. He believes you killed the Long Knife because he treated you badly."

The boy turned around. He shrugged. "It is true that the Long Knife used to jeer at us and challenge us to fight him, but we ignored his taunts."

"Tell me what you know," Boone urged. "I will help you if I can."

The boy looked at him skeptically. "Why should you wish to help me?"

Boone frowned. "I work for the soldier chief, but I refuse to hunt down my old friends the Cheyenne." As he spoke, his face softened. His own son would have been approximately the same age as this boy if he had lived.

The boy's skepticism turned to curiosity. "My father used to tell me of a white man who lived with the Cheyenne and was one with us. He was a great hunter and took a Cheyenne bride. When white men murdered his family, he took revenge on them and was taken prisoner by the Long Knives. Instead of hanging him, they made him work for them as a scout, but he refused to fight us. This all happened a long time ago," he added.

"In those days," Boone said gently, "I was known to my brothers the Cheyenne as Great Bear."

The boy's eyes widened. "I am Porcupine, the son of Two Feathers, who was a good friend of your wife's brother."

They gazed at each other in silence for several minutes. Porcupine had heard a great many stories concerning this tall white man, and was impressed. Boone recalled that Two Feathers was one of the men who had offered to accompany him on his mission of vengeance. "Your father was a good friend of mine," he said finally. "If I can help his son, I will. What happened last night?"

"It was very cold and we stayed inside the lodges. Much later, we heard two white men talking. Their voices were raised as if in anger. The sound of a struggle followed, and one of them cried out. Then there was silence. We did not look to see what had happened. If the Blue Coats argue among themselves and kill each other, it is none of our business. We went to sleep. Toward morning we heard cries and shouts. We were dragged outside. The Long Knife who had taunted us was crouched in a sitting position with a blanket wrapped around him as if he had fallen asleep, but we saw the blood and knew he was dead. When I recognized my knife lying next to him, I knew I would be blamed."

"You're sure no one saw the man who had argued with him?" Boone insisted.

"I am sure. Do you think there is a chance the soldier chief will believe my story?" Porcupine asked hesitantly.

Boone's eyes narrowed. He knew Lieutenant Farrell only too well. "I don't think he'd believe your story if you pointed out the soldier who did it and he had bloodstains on his uniform," he said glumly.

"I thought as much," Porcupine admitted.

"It's not likely my talking to him will do any good either. In fact, it might make things a lot worse," Boone said dryly, "but I'll repeat what you told me to the soldier chief." Before calling for the guard to release him, he promised, "No matter what the verdict is tomorrow, if you're innocent, you'll not hang. You have my word on it."

Lieutenant Farrell listened politely to what Boone had to say and then smiled thinly. "I've already questioned Private Bellows. He says he spoke briefly to Private Evans when they went on the second shift. Bellows acknowledges they weren't very friendly and he left Evans alone. Bellows was standing guard at the other end of the area and freely admits he dozed on and off. He didn't hear any signs of a scuffle, although he did hear a groan, and even attributed it to Private Evans, but had no reason to be suspicious. I can't blame him. It must have been an uncomfortable night for guard duty."

"I suppose you believe his story," Boone said flatly.

"Yes, I believe it," Lieutenant Farrell replied curtly. "I have no reason to disbelieve it."

"Even after what I just told you?"

"Mr. Boone," Lieutenant Farrell said stiffly, "I realize as well as you do that it's a question of Private Bellows's word against that of the Indian, and I should hope that as a commanding officer I would accept the word of one of my men against that of a savage."

"I see!" Boone snapped. The knuckles of his clenched fists were white with rage.

"I assure you, everything will be done to see that the Indian gets a fair trial," Lieutenant Farrell added hurriedly, but Boone had already stormed out without asking permission.

Once he was alone in his quarters, Boone made himself a cigarette. His hands shook. Gently pouring out the tobacco, rolling the small cigarette tightly, and licking the paper to seal it always succeeded in calming him down. He lit it and took a deep drag, enjoying the taste of the strong tobacco. He concentrated on relaxing. By the time he had finished the cigarette, his head was clear and he no longer felt like smashing his fist into Lieutenant Farrell's face or the nearest window. Leaning back on the narrow cot, he turned his thoughts to Porcupine. Even if the boy was lying, which he didn't think likely, he intended to help him, if only to upset Lieutenant Farrell's smug self-righteousness. Besides, he had given his word. He realized, however, that any scheme he devised to help Porcupine escape would have to include the other Indians as well, otherwise the dumb-ass lieutenant would probably hang them all in retaliation. He was halfway through his second cigarette before the plan evolved in its entirety. Carefully he turned it over in his mind. It was risky. He estimated his chances of success as about one in a hundred. Lighting another cigarette, he smiled. What the hell!

The moon was full and the snow had started to fall again in large soft flakes. Wolves howled in the distance. The lonely guards tried to keep warm by stamping their feet and walking briskly back and forth at their posts. A tall shadow detached itself from the rest and moved stealthily toward the tepees. The two guards who were posted there were wide-awake and nervous. They jumped at every sound and warily watched for any sign of movement from the tepees. They didn't want to get *their* throats cut. Because they were concentrating on the Indians, they failed to detect the movement of the silent shadow as it weaved its way in back of them. A sudden noise startled them, and they turned around, guns cocked. The shadow quickly slipped behind the tepees out of sight.

At intervals other shadows appeared and silently slipped over the fort into the darkness below without alerting the guards. One of these shadows moved toward the guardhouse. The soldier on night duty there heard a noise and went to investigate. That was the last he remembered for several hours.

Early Tuesday morning Lieutenant Farrell sent an armed guard to escort Boone to his office.

"What seems to be the trouble?" Boone queried innocently as the lieutenant dismissed the guards.

Lieutenant Farrell's cold blue eyes blazed with hatred. A muscle in his right cheek twitched convulsively. "You're in serious trouble, Boone."

"What did I do?" Boone asked with interest.

"You know perfectly well what you did, and you're not getting away with it." Lieutenant Farrell's voice shook with fury. "You deliberately and maliciously helped the Indians to escape last night. I'm going to personally see to it that you hang."

Boone smiled. "I retired early last night. Is there somebody who says they saw me fraternizing with the Indians?"

Lieutenant Farrell mastered his seething emotions with difficulty. "Private Henderson is being questioned right now. He was guarding the Indian prisoner. You lured him outside and then knocked him unconscious with your gun."

"Is that what he says?" Boone asked, feigning surprise.

"You also made sure the other Indians escaped," Lieutenant Farrell added bitterly, ignoring the scout's question. "The knife slashes in the back of the tepees were made by someone on the outside. All the Indians were accounted for earlier."

"Sounds as if word got back to the Cheyenne that their people were being held here and they organized a rescue party," Boone commented.

"That's what you'd like us to think," Lieutenant Farrell said acidly, "but the person who helped them escape was someone who knew the movements of this fort pretty well. In addition, none of my men were killed, as they certainly would have been if an Indian rescue party had been responsible."

Sergeant Patterson knocked and entered.

"Well, Sergeant," Lieutenant Farrell asked eagerly, "what did Private Henderson have to say?"

"He didn't see his assailant, sir."

Lieutenant Farrell turned pale. "He must have seen something, recognized someone?" he insisted.

"No, sir. He says he heard a noise and went to investigate. When his back was turned, someone knocked him over the head. That's the last he remembers until Corporal Olsen discovered him this morning."

"What about the other guards?" Lieutenant Farrell demanded.

"The guards heard a few noises, but nothing particularly suspicious. The noises turned out to be false alarms, an animal moving in the bushes, the wind rattling a couple of twigs, things of that nature, sir," Sergeant Patterson explained apologetically.

"Escort Boone to his quarters and see that he stays there," Lieutenant Farrell ordered grimly. "I want to question the guards personally, and, Sergeant, spread the word that anyone who was awake late last night should report to me immediately."

"Yes, sir." Sergeant Patterson eyed Boone suspiciously as he led him back to his quarters.

Three days later, Boone was still confined to quarters. Lieutenant Farrell had reached a dead end. Incredibly, no one had seen or heard anything. Word quickly spread around the fort that Boone was suspected of freeing the Indians. Most of the men respected the scout's abilities, but no one felt any real liking for him, and everyone looked with suspicion on his loyalty to the Cheyenne and his belief in the Indian boy's innocence. On more than one occasion, Lieutenant Farrell got the strong impression that if he had encouraged it, any of the soldiers being questioned would have admitted seeing Boone near the guardhouse or the tepees, even though it was a lie. Lieutenant Farrell frowned. He was convinced of Boone's guilt, but due to lack of concrete evidence, the scout would get off scot-free. Outraged at this miscarriage of justice, the lieutenant had been momentarily tempted to take advantage of the temper of his men, but a quirk in his personality prevented him from following through. Whatever his faults, Lieutenant Farrell was too proud to besmirch his reputation by encouraging his men to lie. He was, therefore, faced with a dilemma. He could either bring Boone to trial and watch him be exonerated of the charges, or he could forget the whole thing. Neither one of these solutions appealed to him. His men were beginning to congregate in groups and mutter about taking the law into their own hands if the lieutenant didn't act soon. He realized with horror that all he needed now was an insurrection to end his military career permanently. Miraculously, a way out of his difficulties arrived by special messenger the next morning.

General Harty, commander of Fort Garth, urgently requested Lieutenant Farrell to send him his best scout. Bands of Sioux and Cheyenne had moved into his territory, and he needed help in tracking them down and coming to terms. Boone was undoubtedly Lieutenant Farrell's best scout. If he sent Boone to General Harty, he would be relieved of the awkward situation at Fort Jubele and rid of the troublesome scout forever. That thought cheered him so much, he didn't even suffer a pang of guilt in dumping Boone on the general. Since the lieutenant had no desire to see Boone again, he instructed Sergeant Patterson to deliver the new orders for him. The sergeant could barely conceal his hostility as he handed Boone his notice of transfer. The majority of men at Fort Jubele felt as he did. The Injun lover had gotten off too lightly.

Boone was aware of the resentment and hostility generated by his departure, but as was typical of him, he didn't give a damn. Let them think what they liked. He felt as if a heavy burden had just been lifted from his shoulders. He was free of Fort Jubele and Lieutenant Farrell. In another year he would be free of all forts and soldiers. Ten years of servitude were finally drawing to a close.

Even though he knew Lieutenant Farrell must have been delighted to lose him, Boone had been somewhat surprised to discover he was free to reach Fort Garth on his own. Maybe the lieutenant had had the brains to realize he wouldn't run away now, not with only a year left, or what was more likely, he thought dryly, Lieutenant Farrell didn't care. Boone wondered what General Harty was like, and laughed out loud. No matter how rigid or dogmatic the general turned out to be, he couldn't possibly exceed Lieutenant Farrell in stupidity. As he rode, his thoughts turned suddenly to the lieutenant's wife. He had thought about her quite a lot since the massacre. She was a graceful, pretty woman, and he hoped she had had the strength and intelligence to stay alive. He grinned. Not that coming home to Lieutenant Farrell could be much of an incentive.

The frozen rivers changed seemingly overnight into rushing torrents of white foam. Tiny green buds blossomed on trees that had been stripped of their foliage. Animals were suddenly more plentiful and offered the promise of an abundant and easily accessible food supply. The earth was still hard and sprinkled with patches of snow, but spring had arrived.

A clearing had been fashioned among the timber. Lodge skins were strung on branches in a wide circle. They acted as an effective shield against the biting wind. The heat generated from the roaring fire in the center of the compound warmed the enclosed area so that the women could work at their tasks in relative comfort and among friends. Elizabeth Farrell was busily applying the tanning mixture that consisted of brains, liver, soapweed, and grease to the buffalo hides that were to be sewn together to make a new lodge. Lightning Woman worked silently beside her. Little Flower had chosen to remain at the lodge. Elizabeth heard her son's laughter and looked up to see him trying to communicate in his own mysterious baby language with a fat worm who was desperately trying to escape his reaching fingers by hiding underneath a hollow log. Stone Forehead's chubby little body was encased in a white deerskin jacket adorned with green quills, bright blue beads, and pieces of mirror. The inside of the jacket, as well as his tiny moccasins, was lined with fur. Around his waist he wore a beaded belt Little Flower had labored over for three days, and around his neck hung a necklace of hammered silver and blue beads made for him by Lightning Woman. He laughed again as the worm escaped, and

Elizabeth caught Lightning Woman's eye. Together they smiled and resumed their work.

Life hadn't always been so peaceful. Elizabeth had resisted the Indians at first. She saw them as half-naked savages whose language appeared to consist of unintelligible grunts. The Cheyenne seemed brutal and unfeeling, their customs barbaric and indecent. Gray Sky's two wives, Lightning Woman and Little Flower, punished her with sharp slaps accompanied by shrill screeching when she was slow to obey their commands. Now she could recall the memory without flinching.

"What took you so long?" Lightning Woman had demanded impatiently.

"You have not collected enough wood," Little Flower complained, slapping her as Elizabeth went by bent over at the waist with her heavy burden.

Gray Sky tormented her with sexual demands almost every night. He crawled inside her blanket and rolled over on top of her, his heavy body covering her, grunting as Peter had. She closed her eyes and tried to block out the sight of his dark, stocky body and the smell of bear grease and sweat. Sometimes he lingered with her and toyed with her breasts. She lay rigid, refusing to relax, until he had returned to his own bed. Elizabeth pleaded with a frighteningly unpredictable God to be returned to Peter. She would never complain again. Never! Peter and she had been married in a church of God. Physical contact between them, no matter how unsatisfactory, had been legal and decent.

Elizabeth's pregnancy came as a severe shock to her. She had been barren for so long she had imagined pregnancy to be an impossibility. Her second feeling was one of revulsion. She felt nauseous at the very idea of carrying an Indian baby and all that implied in her society. Guilt was followed by despair. By giving birth to an Indian baby she felt she had cast her lot with the savages and would never see civilization again.

Gray Sky was overjoyed at the news of her pregnancy. He had the unborn child's ears symbolically pierced at the next celebration by his old friend Standing Elk, who recited the story of an important act he had performed in war. For this service, Gray Sky gave him a horse, and everyone remarked on the deep affection he had for his coming offspring. Lightning Woman and Little Flower stopped quarreling and no longer struck Elizabeth. They became solicitous of her, urging her to drink the bark medicine for an easy delivery, and other herb teas to quiet her nerves. As her grasp of the Cheyenne language became more proficient, Elizabeth learned that this was to be Gray Sky's first child. He seemed to think of nothing else and didn't care if it was a boy or a girl. She was amazed at his continued excitement and happiness over a half-breed child, and surprised by his tenderness and consideration toward her. He presented her with her own horse, made sure she had the choice parts of the meat, and promised he would not demand sex of her in the future.

When Elizabeth was told to do a task that was particularly repugnant to her, such as strangling dogs before a feast, her increasing understanding of the language and customs of her captors helped her to cleverly avoid it.

"Among my people," Elizabeth said softly, "there is no taboo against dressing the hides of the bear, wolf, beaver, or coyote. We may do this with complete freedom and without fear. I will gladly be responsible for this chore myself, because I know you cannot touch them without breaking your taboo. However, I am forbidden to kill dogs."

"There is a taboo against this?" Little Flower asked, surprised.

Elizabeth kept her eyes lowered as she replied meekly, "We have a taboo against killing dogs and eating them, because they are the friends of man. If I were to break this taboo, the spirit of the dead dogs would haunt me. It would be very unfortunate," she said sadly.

"You must not break your taboo," Lightning Woman said quickly. "Little Flower and I will kill the dogs and prepare them for the feast. You may eat other food."

Because everyone around Elizabeth was deliriously happy about the baby, she began to feel better about the child she was carrying, but was worried about complications. Elizabeth was used to relying on doctors in starched white shirts and dark suits, carrying little black bags. They spoke to her soothingly, reassuringly. The Cheyenne doctors shook snakeskin rattles filled with colored stones, chanted ferociously in guttural tones, and painted their naked bodies with bold colors. They sounded more like they were going to scalp their patients than soothe them. Little Flower and Lightning Woman would be with her at the birth, but they were almost as nervous as she. Gray Sky had asked Spider Woman to assist at the delivery to be sure nothing went wrong. She had had six children of her own and had helped to deliver thirty others. Spider Woman frightened Elizabeth more than the medicine men did. She was very old and blind in one eye. Her face was lined with age, and she had only two teeth left in her mouth. Her hands were shriveled and they shook. She cackled and she smelled bad. Spider Woman was, however, knowledgeable in the use of herbs and medicines and had never lost a child or its mother. The fact that she had accepted Gray Sky's invitation was considered a great honor.

According to custom, Elizabeth worked up until the very moment of the baby's birth. She had just finished preparing the evening meal when she was stricken with severe cramps and sickness.

"Where are you going?" Lightning Woman inquired. "We are about to eat."

"I don't feel well," Elizabeth said, breaking into a cold sweat.

"Go inside and rest," Lightning Woman commanded. "I will send Little Flower to fetch Spider Woman. Your time may have come."

"It isn't the baby," Elizabeth said in annoyance. "I just feel sick."

"Don't argue. Go inside," Lightening Woman insisted.

When Little Flower returned with Spider Woman, it was determined that the baby was due. Two hours later, Elizabeth let out a final agonizing scream and gave birth to a boy. When they laid him beside her, Elizabeth stared at him in wonder. His mouth was scrunched up, and tears were pouring down his little face. She took him in her arms and awkwardly tried to comfort him. Being a mother took a little getting used to. Lightning Woman and Little Flower looked on enviously. Gray Sky glowed with pleasure. Later that night, after everyone including her son was sound asleep, Elizabeth lay wide-awake. Traces of guilt lingered on, but mostly she felt proud of herself. In the last two years she had survived an Indian massacre, slavery, petty abuses, rape, and now the birth of a perfectly healthy child in primitive surroundings, without the slightest complication. A sudden surge of strength that was rooted in a new sense of self-respect and dignity flowed through her as she lay on a bed of buffalo skins in a Cheyenne lodge on the open prairie. She might cry, be fearful, and tremble again, but she would never doubt her ability to cope with any situation. Elizabeth smiled in the dark. She was a lot stronger than she had ever given herself credit for, and was only just beginning to recognize it.

Elizabeth's son started chattering in a high voice to a sad-looking sparrow that had stopped to rest on a nearby tree, and her thoughts were drawn back to the present.

"See how little Stone Forehead speaks to the sparrow," Lightning Woman remarked. "Perhaps when he grows up he will understand the language of birds."

Elizabeth nodded and continued with her work. She had once looked down on the Indians' beliefs, considering them superstitious. Now she wasn't so sure. There was a man in the camp who claimed he could speak and understand the language of ravens. Whenever the buffalo were scarce, the people would ask Thunder Ridge to locate their whereabouts by asking a raven. Sometimes he left the village and returned with his answer, and sometimes a raven was captured and brought to him to question. His instructions were often quite detailed and infallible. The rational, practical, materialistic side of Elizabeth said the idea of communicating with birds was ridiculous. On the other hand, Thunder Ridge was unerringly accurate. She sighed. There were so many customs and beliefs the Indians held that were in direct conflict with their white neighbors'. Young boys were taught it was more honorable to die in battle than to be felled by sickness or old age. Stealing from their enemies was something to be proud of, while stealing from their tribe a disgrace. The Cheyenne had great respect for the earth and the creatures that inhabited it. They took from the land only what they needed for their survival and looked with horror at the white men, who killed animals for sport, destroyed forests for profit, and blew up mountains searching for gold and silver. It was no wonder the two races clashed. The naming of children was one of the few customs they had in common. White people often named their children after relatives. The Cheyenne did the same. Stone Forehead received his peculiar name from an uncle of Gray Sky's.

Elizabeth vividly recalled the day a week after her son was born when Gray Sky's uncle sent for the infant. He took the boy in his arms and said, "I give to you my name, Stone Forehead." He then presented him with a horse. Because of the old man's fine record as a hunter and reputation as a fierce warrior in battle, it was considered an honorable name. Shortly after this, Elizabeth took a new name herself. She had always been referred to as Woman, or White Woman. The implications of such terms were derogatory, and she had an overwhelming desire to free herself of the past. She wanted a new name to symbolize the changes taking place internally, and hesitantly approached Lightning Woman and Little Flower on the subject.

"I would like to take a Cheyenne name," Elizabeth announced shyly one evening as they were preparing for supper.

"What name did you have in mind?" Little Flower asked curiously.

"Since I have been among you," Elizabeth said cautiously, "I have had the sole responsibility of dressing gray eagles, because of your belief that you will turn gray if you handle them. I would like to be called Gray Eagle Woman." She did not reveal that the real reason she had chosen the name was because of the enormous sense of power and freedom the bird inspired in her. The Cheyenne revered the bird, using its feathers in war bonnets, confident they would protect them from bullets and arrows.

"It is good that the mother of Stone Forehead wishes to take a Cheyenne name," Lightning Woman said thoughtfully. "I am sure our husband will be pleased," she added.

Gray Sky was delighted.

"The mother of Stone Forehead shall be called Gray Eagle Woman from this moment on," he assured Elizabeth, patting her on the shoulder. "I shall give a horse to Stands in the Road. He will spread the news throughout the village."

Elizabeth sensed approval from the other Indians. They saw her desire for a Cheyenne name as a wish to shed her white identity and become one with them.

"Come quickly," Little Flower shouted as she burst into the compound, startling Elizabeth out of her reverie.

"What is wrong?" Lightning Woman asked sharply.

Little Flower's fat cheeks trembled. "Our husband has returned. Something is wrong with him," she said anxiously. "He sits in front of the fire without moving or speaking. When I ask him what is the matter, he does not answer. I have never seen him this way before," she added, sounding really frightened.

"I will go with Little Flower," Lightning Woman informed Elizabeth, "but there is no need for you to come."

Lightning Woman returned alone a few minutes later, looking puzzled and upset. "Our husband is sick," she said in a tight voice.

"What is wrong with him?" Elizabeth asked, surprised. She had never known Gray Sky to be sick before.

"I do not know," Lightning Woman admitted. "He sits and stares without seeing. When I asked him what was troubling him, he shook his head and would not speak. I thought perhaps the sight of his son would restore his spirits."

"Of course," Elizabeth said quickly, folding up her work. "You may take Stone Forehead yourself," she said gently. "I will bring the hides."

When they reached the lodge, Elizabeth saw that Little Flower was trying without success to get her husband interested in a bowl of soup she had made.

"It is rabbit, your favorite. There is plenty of meat in it, and onions. Try some," she urged, a note of desperation in her voice.

Gray Sky remained motionless. His face looked stiff and pale in the firelight. An air of grief hung about him like a heavy blanket.

"Look who is here," Lightning Woman said lightly. "Stone Forehead has come to greet his father."

Elizabeth watched as her son crawled over to Gray Sky, laughing, and pulled at his pants leg. He wanted to be picked up and swung in the air. When his father failed to respond, Stone Forehead frowned, obviously puzzled at this lack of interest. He tried another tactic. Climbing into Gray Sky's lap, he began playing with the beaded necklace that hung around his father's neck. Suddenly Gray Sky shuddered and clasped his son to him in such a tight embrace the boy cried out in protest. Gray Sky tenderly kissed his son's forehead. With tears in his eyes he handed him back to Lightning Woman.

"I have seen my shadow," Gray Sky said flatly. "Soon I will die."

Elizabeth was shocked. "What do you mean?" she asked hesitantly.

"I was on my way to take horses from the Pawnee," Gray Sky explained in a rasping voice, "when it happened. I saw my shadow and turned back. When a man sees his shadow, it is certain he will die."

"There must be men who have seen their shadows and lived," Elizabeth said practically.

"No man has ever been known to see his shadow and live," Gray Sky insisted. "My time has come. I am going to die."

Elizabeth glanced at Lightning Woman and Little Flower. Much to her surprise, they seemed to be equally convinced his death was imminent. Little Flower was silently weeping. Lightning Woman was pale and looked genuinely frightened.

Gray Sky stayed at home for the next three days. He spent the time playing with his son and visiting old friends. Most of the time he seemed abstracted. When the town crier called for volunteers to attack a small party of Long Knives heading toward the village, Gray Sky notified his wives he was going. Lightning Woman and Little Flower wept and clung to him, begging him to stay.

"Even if I remain here at the lodge, I will not be safe," Gray Sky said in resignation. "A wild animal may attack me, or an unseen sickness strike me as I sleep. When a man knows he is going to die, it is futile for him to try to escape. I am a warrior, and prefer to meet death on the battlefield." He briefly embraced Elizabeth and his two sobbing wives. Taking his son in his arms, he spoke in a soft, low voice that vibrated with emotion. Elizabeth had to strain to hear the words.

"Stone Forehead has given his father much joy. It was Gray Sky's fondest wish that he live to watch his son grow to manhood and teach him the things a warrior should know. But the future holds no such pleasures," he said sadly, "and the time draws near when he must follow the Hanging Road to the place of the dead." Lightning Woman and Little Flower began to moan, and Stone Forehead frowned. He seemed to be considering his father's words and finding them distasteful. "When you grow up, my son," Gray Sky continued gravely, as though Stone Forehead understood every word, "never disgrace your family by doing anything foolish or cowardly. Do not be lazy. Live up to your excellent name, and like your father before you, do not be afraid to die." With these final words of advice Gray Sky handed his son back to Elizabeth, who was considerably touched. Mounting his horse, dressed in his finest raiment, Gray Sky rode off to battle.

The trick was an old one. Once the battle was in full swing, the small troop of soldiers suddenly materialized into seventy men. The Indians didn't have a chance. After eliminating the war party, the soldiers marched on to surround the camp. When the Cheyenne discovered what had happened, a few impulsive boys rushed out to defend their village but were cut down by rifle fire. Captain Marshall, a reasonable man, offered the remaining Indians a chance to surrender. Unprepared for an attack, and badly outnumbered, they accepted. The men were instructed to give up their weapons to the officer in charge. The women were told to take what household goods they could carry. The horses were taken by the soldiers. The lodges and remaining goods were burned.

Some of the smaller children began to cry, but their parents stared straight ahead, stony-faced and dry-eyed. They watched in grim silence as their homes and worldly possessions went up in flames. The armed soldiers went about their tasks efficiently, the spurs on their boots making a clicking sound as they walked. The horses were jittery and restless. Officers issued orders in belligerent tones to passing soldiers, as though the pressure of those silent, watching eyes made them feel the necessity for a show of aggressive behavior.

Elizabeth wrapped her son in a blanket and blindly followed Lightning Woman and Little Flower. It had all happened so fast, she felt dazed and frightened. She found herself on a long, slow-moving line of women and children. Before they could join the men, the women were searched for hidden weapons. Elizabeth was near the front of the line. A knife was discovered hidden in the baby cradle of a woman being searched. It was added to the rapidly rising pile of guns, bows, and hatchets already discarded. The woman was roughly shoved aside. Elizabeth felt a sudden exhilaration as the officer shouted, "Next!" These were her people. They might even be soldiers attached to her husband's fort. They weren't going to hurt her. She was about to step out of line and announce that she was a white captive when a party of twenty new soldiers rode into camp. They were led by a middle-aged man who was obviously a scout. He wore moccasins instead of military boots and was dressed in deerskin pants and a military jacket. Elizabeth watched him approach the officer in charge of searching prisoners. His face was rugged, dark as an Indian's, and he had obviously once had a bad case of the pox. She frowned. There was something vaguely familiar about him.

"What are you doing here . . . sir?" Sergeant Ferris demanded uneasily. He knew of Boone's love for the Cheyenne and was suspicious. Boone was unpredictable and difficult to handle. He had refused to accompany any of the missions against the Cheyenne. There was no reason for him to be here now. Sergeant Ferris didn't want any trouble and tried smiling in a friendly manner that came across as strained.

"General Harty has new instructions regarding the prisoners," Boone drawled.

"New instructions, Boone?" Captain Marshall said in surprise as he joined them. "What new instructions?"

"You're to take them to Fort Williamstone. My men and I will escort any white captives back to Fort Jeremiah." He handed the captain an official-looking document.

"Damn!" Captain Marshall muttered in annoyance as he read the letter over. "Fort Williamstone is twice the distance. Some of my men are wounded, and I'm afraid the prisoners will try to escape if I allow them to ride. What's the point of all this anyway?"

"Bureaucratic red tape," Boone said, smiling. He liked Captain Marshall better than most. "I'll be glad to take your wounded with me. Any white captives?"

"None that will admit to it, at any rate," Captain Marshall said gloomily. "And the Indians aren't talking."

Elizabeth stepped out of line, and a nervous young soldier pointed a gun at her.

"Go back. Stay with the others," he shouted, drawing the attention of the officers.

"I'm one of the white captives," Elizabeth explained, blushing as they stared. Her hair was black and shiny, and her skin was as dark as the other Indian women's. Captain Marshall thought to himself that he would never have known she was white if she hadn't spoken up.

"Will you come with me and Mr. Boone, ma'am?" Captain Marshall said politely. "There's a few questions we'd like to ask."

"Yes, of course." Elizabeth turned to say good-bye to Lightning Woman and Little Flower, but they ignored her.

"This way, ma'am," Captain Marshall urged, leading her to a single remaining lodge.

Elizabeth reluctantly followed him inside. She had wanted to speak to Gray Sky's other wives before leaving. She knew they would miss Stone Forehead, and in her anxiety to communicate with them, she failed to catch the fleeting expression of recognition in Boone's eyes.

"How long have you been a prisoner?" Captain Marshall began.

"Approximately two years," Elizabeth said, considering.

"Is that your son?" Captain Marshall inquired hesitantly.

Elizabeth hugged Stone Forehead. "Yes, that's right."

"I gather his father is . . ." Captain Marshall looked uncomfortable. He hated interrogations. ". . . an Indian."

"He was. He's dead now," Elizabeth said coldly.

"What is your name, ma'am?" Captain Marshall asked quickly, changing the subject.

Elizabeth hesitated. Would Peter be glad to see her? She tried to summon up an image of his face, but all she could picture was a dim shadow inside a stiff blue uniform and shiny black boots. She felt Stone Forehead tugging at her dress. Would Peter accept her son? She had lived at the fort long enough to know the ostracism a white woman with an Indian baby faced. Peter was the head of the fort, and ambitious. Would Stone Forehead be a constant embarrassment to him? Elizabeth sighed, realizing suddenly that even if he accepted her son, she didn't want to go back to a loveless marriage. She had made a choice to leave the past behind and wouldn't back down now. Taking a deep breath, she said, "My name is Amanda, Amanda Kirby," choosing the first because she had always liked it and the last because it was a family name.

Boone raised an eyebrow but remained silent.

"Do you have any relatives we can notify?" Captain Marshall continued.

"No, there's no one," Elizabeth said, looking away.

Captain Marshall frowned. "I don't seem to recall your name on the list of missing persons. Were you traveling with a wagon train when you were captured?"

Elizabeth nodded. "My husband and I were heading west from St. Louis. We started out with a wagon train, but quite a bit south of here, my husband came down with scarlet fever. According to the law, we were cut out from the rest of the train. We were told we could go back or join them later on after . . . after Peter had completely recovered." Elizabeth blushed at the blatant lie. "My husband died from the fever, and one morning I awoke and found myself surrounded by Indians." She was amazed at the ease with which she had related the fabricated story.

"It must have been a terrifying experience," Captain Marshall said sympathetically.

"Yes indeed," Elizabeth replied weakly. The tale was one she had heard at Fort Jubele, and was relieved Captain Marshall had accepted it so readily.

"Boone will take you to Fort Jeremiah," Captain Marshall said, smiling, glad his part of the interview was at an end. "You needn't feel alarmed about the future. Until more permanent arrangements can be made, you'll be accommodated at the fort."

As Elizabeth rode past the silent, hostile crowd of Indians, she recognized Lightning Woman and Little Flower near the front. Lightning Woman glanced at her with blank eyes and quickly looked away. Little Flower stared after Stone Forehead longingly, tears in her eyes. Elizabeth felt sorry for them, but tightened her grip on her son. She knew they would have taken Stone Forehead if she had left him, but he belonged to her. She had come to love him passionately as the only truly joyous experience that had happened to her since she had gone to live with her aunts.

Later that evening, after a meager supper, Boone lay back against a tree and watched Elizabeth play with her son. After a few moments of silent observation he remarked, "It's a pity you don't have any relatives to take you in."

Elizabeth didn't look up as she replied, "I shall get along quite well without them."

"All the same," Boone persisted, "it's unfortunate. You're going to have a pretty rough time all alone, saddled with a half-breed child."

Elizabeth stiffened perceptibly and raised her eyes to meet his squarely. "We will manage well enough, thank you."

"Yes, ma'am," Boone said softly. Although it made no difference to him, he was glad she wanted to keep the boy. He wondered if she would change her mind once she was back in civilization. How long would she continue the charade of being Mrs. Amanda Kirby? It had surprised him when she had lied so convincingly to Captain Marshall. He hadn't thought she had the courage to strike out on her own. He didn't think it would last. She was the dependent type. Eventually the realization of her position as a single woman without relatives and an Indian baby to support would throw her into a panic. She'd run back to that ass of a husband of hers. He sighed. It was a damn shame.

The following evening, Stone Forehead crawled over to where Boone was sitting and began pulling on his jacket to be picked up. His mother was busy set-

ting up the blankets for bed. Boone took him for a
ride on his shoulders.

"I'm sorry if he's been annoying you," Elizabeth
apologized when Boone returned. Her son was
squealing with delight.

"He's no trouble at all, ma'am," Boone said, smiling
one of his rare smiles. "I like kids." As Elizabeth took
her reluctant son back, he added, "What's your son's
name?"

"Stone Forehead," Elizabeth replied after a moment's hesitation.

"The Indians have some pretty interesting names,"
Boone remarked, obviously amused. "I've no doubt
Stone Forehead was named after some famous rela-
tive."

Elizabeth nodded. "Yes, an uncle of . . . of his father's," she explained, flushing, unable to refer to
Gray Sky as her husband.

"A name that serious-sounding doesn't fit a little
tyke like that. Why not give him an English name? It
would be more appropriate now that he's returning to
his mother's people," Boone added, apparently oblivious of her embarrassment.

Elizabeth relaxed. "Yes, I've already thought of that.
I'm partial to the name David. It means 'beloved,' "
she said softly.

"David's as good a name as any," Boone agreed, sitting down to clean his weapons.

"Tell me, Mr. Boone," Elizabeth said, joining him
after making sure David was fast asleep, "is Fort Jeremiah very far?"

"Another full day of riding," Boone replied indif-
ferently.

As Elizabeth made herself comfortable beside him,
she said with a sigh, "The very first thing I'm going
to do once I get settled in at the fort is take a hot
bath. I've dreamed about it for months."

Boone laughed. "I'm used to taking a dip in the
rivers and lakes like the Cheyenne. I cut a hole in the

ice in winter. It wakes you up, but I have to admit a nice tub of steaming water has its merits."

"I gather you've spent a good deal of time with the Cheyenne, Mr. Boone," Elizabeth said, smiling.

"I grew up with them," Boone said shortly. Polishing the barrel of his rifle, he added, "My hitch in the army ends this year, and I'll be free to return to the Indians."

Elizabeth frowned. "But the Cheyenne are at war with us. Won't they kill you?"

"I have friends and relatives who'll take me in," Boone said confidently.

"But you've been working for the army as a scout," Elizabeth pointed out. "Won't they be angry about that?"

"The Cheyenne know my reputation," Boone replied grimly. "They know I won't fight against them."

"Did you say you have relatives among the Indians?" Elizabeth asked impulsively, allowing curiosity to overcome good manners.

Boone stopped polishing. "Relatives by marriage," he said briefly.

Elizabeth recognized the underlying tone of bitterness and was irritated. She wished she had restrained herself from prying into a stranger's life and stirring up unhappy memories. She was about to say good night when he startled her by speaking again.

"Her name was Laughing Girl," Boone said hoarsely. "We had a son," he added, as though driven by some mysterious compulsion to speak against his will. He frowned. What the hell was wrong with him? Why was he suddenly bringing up private matters he had never discussed with anyone, to the lieutenant's wife? He stared at her resentfully, as if she had used some magical power to get him to betray a confidence.

"You sound as if you loved them very much," Elizabeth said gently.

"I did," Boone replied curtly. "Just like you must have loved your husband," he added unexpectedly, watching her reaction with a peculiar intensity.

Elizabeth rose hastily, considerably disconcerted. "It's been a very tiring day, Mr. Boone. I'd better get some sleep. Good night." Drawing the warm army blankets around her, Elizabeth shivered. There was something very unnerving about Mr. Boone. When his brown eyes held hers, she suddenly panicked, overcome with mortification at the irrational thought that he knew all about her life with Peter. She even suspected he knew about her practiced deception. But that was impossible. She had said nothing incriminating. And if he knew who she was, why hadn't he said so? Elizabeth soothed herself with the thought that she was just overreacting.

Boone gazed up at the dozens of stars that crowded the sky and felt a twinge of uneasiness creep into his soul to disturb his usually relaxed attitude before sleep. Being naturally honest, he knew he had awaited Elizabeth's reaction to his statement with a curious excitement that turned into a deep sense of satisfaction when she turned pale, abruptly rose, and excused herself. What bothered him was why he should feel the least pleasure in her response. If he was any judge of people, she had probably never loved her straitlaced husband. So what! Unable to arrive at an answer that provided relief, Boone finally fell into a troubled sleep.

Fort Jeremiah had been built high on a hill overlooking the surrounding countryside. On a clear day and from his station on the lookout platform, a man at his post could easily spot the silver fish doing somersaults in Lake Sarisito, several miles away. The returning party of soldiers was spotted early, and shouts went up that Boone was back.

When Elizabeth entered the fort, she became acutely self-conscious that every eye was focused on her and her son. The majority of occupants of Fort

Jeremiah were well aware that Boone's mission had been to return white prisoners, and those that did not know it were quickly informed in hushed whispers. Embarrassment made the men look discreetly away. In the faces of the women Elizabeth detected a mixture of pity, scorn, and resentment.

General Harty, the commander of Fort Jeremiah, was a small man with a shock of prematurely white hair, clear blue eyes, and a pink-and-white complexion that was the envy of many young girls. His appearance, coupled with a dazzling smile, was guaranteed to put people at their ease. He was an agreeable man and an able officer who was well-liked by his men. He almost never lost his temper, which was fortunate, since on those rare occasions when he did, it took four strong men to pull him off the offending individual. When he learned that Boone was returning with a female captive, he lost no time in notifying his wife to join him in his office.

Clara Harty had thick black ringlets, bright hazel eyes, and a dimple in her left cheek. Of diminutive stature, she came up only to her husband's shoulder, and like him, she was held in affectionate regard by the fort personnel.

"I want you to be here when the unfortunate woman is brought in," General Harty informed his wife as soon as the door had closed. "Until we can find out exact details and locate her relations, I think the best thing to do is to keep her with us. We have room, and I'm sure you'll be able to put her at her ease. She can have the study," he added hurriedly as the sounds of approaching footsteps warned him the conversation was about to end.

"I shall do all I can to make the poor woman forget her dreadful experience," Clara assured her husband sincerely.

Boone knocked once and entered. Elizabeth was directly behind him, carrying David.

Once the introductions were over and Boone had

delivered his report, General Harty turned to Elizabeth, a look of genuine concern on his face.

"You're positive you have no living relatives on either your side or your husband's that we can contact?" he inquired anxiously as his eyes rested on David playing at her feet.

"None!" Elizabeth answered firmly, finding her deception easier to practice as she went along.

General Harty seemed momentarily dismayed but smiled reassuringly. "Well, everything will work out eventually. In the meantime, my wife will see that you're comfortable. You'll be staying with us until more permanent arrangements can be found." As everyone rose simultaneously and prepared to depart, he motioned for Boone to remain. "It's a pity Mrs. Kirby doesn't have anyone to turn to," he remarked musingly.

"I wouldn't be overly concerned, sir," Boone said dryly. "There's no telling what long-lost relatives might turn up unexpectedly."

General Harty stared at him, frowning. Boone was an excellent scout. He had no regrets about having assigned him to his post, but there were times when he found communicating with him exceedingly difficult. Boone succumbed on occasion to a strange tendency to talk in riddles and be evasive when a straightforward reply would have better served the purpose. In addition, General Harty frequently suspected the scout possessed superior knowledge to himself, which touched his pride and was one of the few things that annoyed him. "If you mean something pertinent by that speech, Boone, speak up, man," he said, nettled.

Boone shrugged. "I wouldn't worry about Mrs. Kirby," he advised. "Like you said, everything will work out eventually."

Mrs. Harty let down one of her own dresses for Elizabeth to wear. Underclothes, shoes, and a set of children's attire were generously donated by the other women and altered to fit her and David. To all intents and purposes, Elizabeth was shown every kindness. Nevertheless, inwardly she cringed every time she had to pass a crowd of people. Elizabeth felt the disapproval in the way they stared at her, in spite of the frozen smiles and polite greetings that issued from their lips. As soon as her back was turned, the whispers began. If David was with her, it was worse. Women with small children would clutch their little ones to them as if coming into contact with David would somehow mar them for life. In the past, Elizabeth had always followed the line of least resistance, out of an overwhelming fear of incurring condemnation, mockery, and isolation. She had never attempted anything without first discovering if her actions would displease those around her. If the answer was yes, she abandoned the plans, no matter how much she longed to carry them out. Acceptance by others was of vital importance to Elizabeth. The horror of becoming a social outcast had never entered her mind, except perhaps in nightmares. She found dealing with the reality of her position a constant strain, far worse than facing outright cruelty and terror with the Indians.

The ugly situation came to a head at one of Mrs. Harty's dinner parties. In a voice loud enough to be heard at the other end of the table where Elizabeth was sitting, Lavinia Bourke exclaimed maliciously, "I for one would not permit myself to be captured by savages."

A deathly stillness characterized by acute embarrassment settled on the table like a pall. Trembling with anger and humiliation as every eye discreetly avoided her, Elizabeth asked, "And just what would you have done to prevent it, Mrs. Bourke?"

"I should have found the courage to do what any woman of character and breeding would have done," Lavinia replied superciliously. "I would have put an end to my miserable existence and gained the satisfaction of cheating the devils of their amusement."

Elizabeth stared at her in amazement before she was able to respond. "How fortunate for you that you are not faced with that decision momentarily. And since you are not, you can hardly be in a position to defend your remarkable statement. What's more," Elizabeth continued hotly, tears coming to her eyes, more from frustration and anger than hurt, "it seems to me, Mrs. Bourke, that your eagerness to relinquish life while there is still hope indicates you to be an unusually foolish and ignorant woman." Rushing from the room, Elizabeth missed the commotion that resulted from her brazen speech.

After the guests had departed, General Harty and his wife knocked on Elizabeth's door and apologized for Mrs. Bourke's breach of manners.

"I can't understand how Lavinia could have behaved so rudely," Clara remarked, greatly upset. "Her conduct was inexcusable."

"It seems to me," Elizabeth said bitterly, "that Mrs. Bourke's conduct, inexcusable though it was, appeared to adequately express the silent opinion of those who were too polite to give vent to their private thoughts."

"My dear Amanda!" Clara protested, a pained expression on her face.

"Nonsense, Amanda," General Harty said gruffly. "You mustn't think badly of us. Lavinia is a dreadful troublemaker if ever there was one," he declared darkly. "She positively delights in mischief-making, and I do assure you she in no way speaks for the rest of us."

"I apologize!" Elizabeth said stiffly.

"Nothing to apologize for," General Harty insisted. "As a matter of fact, I don't know when I've spent a more enjoyable evening."

"William!" Clara said, shocked.

"My love, I wouldn't have missed hearing Lavinia Bourke called an ignorant, foolish woman to her face for the best shot of whiskey west of the Mississippi," General Harty declared, chuckling at the memory.

"You should have stayed to see the results of your handiwork," he told Elizabeth, who had begun to smile. "I thought she was going to have an attack of apoplexy."

"Really, William," Clara exclaimed, obviously having difficulty restraining her own amusement. "You shouldn't make fun of poor Lavinia."

"Poor Lavinia, indeed," her husband retorted.

"You've both been very kind," Elizabeth said, feeling ashamed of her outburst. "I know David and I must be a burden on you. If only you could get me a job, General, any job. It wouldn't matter what," she insisted eagerly.

General Harty shook his head. "I'm afraid all the jobs are filled by men. I'll send out word to Baxter, the nearest town. It's fifty miles away, but if you insist . . ."

"Yes, please do," Elizabeth urged.

"If I were you, I wouldn't hold out much hope," General Harty warned. Studying Elizabeth for a few minutes in silence, he said suddenly, "I hope you won't take what I'm about to say to you the wrong way."

"No, of course not," Elizabeth answered automatically, feeling a qualm of uneasiness grip her as the general exchanged nervous looks with his wife.

"I've been meaning to speak to you about it for some time, but . . . well"—he cleared his throat before continuing—"I've been extremely busy lately, and the right moment to broach the subject never came up."

"Yes?" Elizabeth said, forcing herself to smile encouragingly, all the while feeling more and more uneasy.

"You're a sensible girl, Amanda," General Harty said hopefully, "and Clara and I would like to feel that you'll eventually forget the past and make a new life for yourself."

"That is my wish too," Elizabeth admitted cautiously.

"There's no reason why you shouldn't fall in love and get married again," Clara broke in impulsively.

"Women in this part of the country are at a premium, and no man worth his salt is going to hold what happened against you. However . . ." General Harty hesitated before proceeding with the most delicate part of the conversation. ". . . a woman with a half-breed child is at a decided disadvantage."

"I realize that," Elizabeth said stiffly.

"We've learned that your captor had two wives who are still living," General Harty continued hurriedly, ignoring Elizabeth's flashing eyes and the inflexible set of her jaw. "They would be willing to raise him, and it would be far better in the long run to return him to his father's people."

"We know how much you love your little boy," Clara chimed in quickly, "which is why we knew you'd want to do what's best for him."

"I'm not giving him up," Elizabeth said fiercely.

"We only want you to think about it," Clara begged. "Try to understand. It would be the most beneficial course for both of you."

"Thinking about it won't change my mind," Elizabeth snapped. "David is my son and I'm not giving him up."

"I'm sorry if we've upset you by speaking so frankly," General Harty said nervously, alarmed at Elizabeth's high color and vehement manner.

"We never meant to offend you," Clara added unhappily.

"It's all right," Elizabeth assured them coldly. "I know you meant to be helpful, but I've had a very hectic evening and I'm exhausted," she said truthfully enough.

Clara and her husband took the hint and left her alone.

Elizabeth rarely got headaches, but that night she had one of the worst. Her sinuses and the back of her neck throbbed with pain. She winced and vowed to go straight to bed, putting off thinking about what had happened until the following day. She slept fitfully and awoke early, feeling depressed, dimly aware of something most unpleasant crouching on the edge of consciousness. As she began to recall the events of the preceding day, Elizabeth felt something akin to panic. She had been at Fort Jeremiah for almost a month and had not made any friends. The general consensus seemed to be that if she relinquished David, her social status would improve, but she had no intention of doing that. Unfortunately, Elizabeth had no money and no relatives she would acknowledge to take her in. She had naively imagined that because she was willing to do any honest work, she would eventually find employment and be able to support herself and her son. Judging from General Harty's reaction, securing a position seemed extremely remote.

"Out, out," David squealed.

"All right, David, all right." Elizabeth sighed as her son jumped on top of her for the third time. "We'll get dressed and you can play outside."

Carrying David into Mrs. Harty's miniature backyard, Elizabeth sat on a low wooden bench and contented herself with watching him play in the sun. The air was crisp without being cold. She thought to herself that it was a shame the pleasant weather would all too soon give way to the pounding, unrelenting heat of summer.

"Nice day, isn't it?" Boone remarked behind her.

Elizabeth jumped. "Mr. Boone, you startled me," she said, smiling. Making room for him beside her, she added, "Won't you join me?"

"Boone," David cried out happily, crawling with remarkable speed over to his friend. Lifting up his little arms, he shrieked, "Up."

As Boone swung him high in the air amid screeches of joy, Elizabeth said warmly, "I've been meaning to thank you for spending so much time with David."

"It's my pleasure, ma'am," Boone said gruffly, setting David down and joining Elizabeth on the bench.

They sat in companionable silence for several minutes, enjoying the warmth of the sun and watching David's antics with amusement. Boone finally broke the silence.

"How was General Harty's party last night?" he asked casually.

"An unequivocal disaster," Elizabeth replied flatly.

"What happened?" Boone asked, a trace of a smile at the corners of his mouth.

Elizabeth made a face. "Among other things, in front of all the guests I called Lavinia Bourke a foolish, ignorant woman."

Boone burst out laughing. "Can't see as how anyone's going to hold that against you. You spoke nothing but the truth."

"You may laugh, Mr. Boone," Elizabeth said, frowning, "but it wasn't very funny at the time. And that's not all," she added miserably. "I'm afraid I antagonized General Harty and his wife," she said, feeling her throat constrict with an effort to keep back the tears.

"Don't tell me they stood up for Lavinia Bourke," Boone said in amazement. "She probably goaded you into speaking out as you did."

"It wasn't because of Lavinia," Elizabeth said angrily. She hated to cry in front of him. "They wanted . . . they suggested that I give David back to the Indians," she explained resentfully, waiting for him to add his opinion to theirs.

"And your answer was no?" Boone inquired curiously after a slight pause.

"Of course it was no," Elizabeth shouted, the color rushing into her face. "I love my son. He's the best thing that's ever happened to me." She was trembling with emotion. "I don't care who his father was, I'm his mother. He belongs with me."

"There's no need to get all riled up," Boone said

gently. "If you want to keep David, you have my support."

"I'm sorry if I misjudged you," Elizabeth said hastily, wiping her eyes. "It's just that I didn't think anyone would be on my side."

"Friends stand together," Boone said slowly. "I'd like to think of you as a friend."

"Thank you, Mr. Boone," Elizabeth said gratefully, holding out her hand. "Your friendship is much appreciated."

"How is the job hunting coming along?" Boone asked, quickly changing the subject.

Elizabeth sighed. "I'm afraid my prospects look very poor. General Harty doesn't hold out much hope."

"What kind of work did you have in mind?" Boone queried.

"Believe me, Mr. Boone," Elizabeth said sincerely, "I'm not fussy. I would be delighted to take in laundry if the opportunity presented itself."

"You know," Boone said woodenly, "I knew of a woman who was taken captive by the Sioux several years ago. She had a small child like you, and when things looked bleak, she suddenly remembered a cousin living in Ohio."

Elizabeth gave a start and turned pale at this speech, but remained firm. "I'm afraid there really is no one in my case," she said steadily. "I am quite alone."

Boone smiled again, the smile lighting up his face and transforming the harsh, bold features into more attractive lines. "I've never seen it fail," he remarked upon rising, "when a situation looks its worst, something always turns up. I'll be going now," he added, tipping his battered hat and leaving before Elizabeth had the chance to thank him for his kind words.

The next morning General Harty sent for Elizabeth. When she entered his office, she saw that Clara was already there, standing beside her husband's desk looking considerably ill-at-ease. Boone was leaning against a wall. He looked up as she entered, and smiled.

"You sent for me, General?" Elizabeth asked curiously.

"Yes, my dear, I did. Won't you sit down?" he added, indicating a straight-backed chair in front of him. When Elizabeth was seated, he continued in the tone of a man who was unsure of himself. "Mr. Boone has presented me with a proposal which I feel I ought to pass on to you for consideration."

"A proposal!" Elizabeth said, surprised. "What sort of proposal?"

"I've told William I don't think it's at all suitable," Clara interrupted.

"I can't help but feel, Clara," General Harty said with a trace of annoyance in his voice, "that your sentiments are a little out of place in this situation."

Elizabeth was by now fascinated and wished he would get to the point.

"You needn't accept the plan that Boone has suggested," General Harty hastened to reassure her. "However, I think in the circumstances, it is an adequate solution to your difficulty."

Elizabeth looked interested, and he continued with more confidence. "Mr. Boone has said he is in great need of someone to look after his needs, few though they may be, and he is willing to provide you with a small salary if you are amenable to the idea."

Elizabeth gave Boone a look of gratitude and said instantly, "Indeed, General, I would be delighted to accept his kind proposition."

"But, Amanda, dear," Clara said unhappily, "you would be living in the same quarters with an unmarried man." She blushed. "It would be most improper."

Elizabeth knew how improper it was, and the reception she was likely to receive from the other women, but didn't care. "I'm afraid I don't have much choice in the matter. I can't afford to obey the proprieties and earn a living at the same time," she said practically.

"Very sensible attitude," General Harty approved. "Besides, Clara, Boone is gone more than he's here, and it's a temporary situation. He'll be leaving the army in about six months. During that time Amanda can put aside a little nest egg to start life anew."

Clara frowned but silently reassured herself with the thought that there was no chance of real danger. Amanda would have the protection of the fort, and as far as the scout was concerned, she wasn't worried. Clara had always found Boone most unappealing and felt that Amanda would see nothing attractive about him to pose any real threat. A point in his favor was that he seemed to be genuinely attached to her little boy. "I suppose if you are quite sure . . ." she began.

"My mind is made up," Elizabeth insisted, elated at the prospect of earning her own living.

Elizabeth wasted no time. She moved into Boone's ramshackle quarters after supper. Taking a look around the two rooms, she was satisfied. Mr. Boone hadn't just asked her to be his housekeeper out of the kindness of his heart. He truly needed one. In addition to the piles of discarded dirty clothes, the place was grimy and looked as though it hadn't been thoroughly cleaned in years. The narrow windows were bare of curtains and streaked with dirt.

"I'm sorry it's so messy," Boone apologized, looking embarrassed. "Living alone makes a body careless in personal habits."

"On the contrary, Mr. Boone," Elizabeth said, smiling. "I am enormously relieved to see that you didn't take me on purely as a charity case. I can see my work is cut out for me, and I'm not at all daunted by it."

Boone relaxed and grinned. "You and the boy can sleep in the bedroom," he said simply. "I'll fix a cot for myself out here."

Elizabeth found it necessary to straighten the bedroom and change the sheets before permitting herself to fall asleep. The next day she rose bright and early to fix Boone his breakfast. After he left, Elizabeth rolled up her sleeves and began cleaning the place in earnest. When Boone arrived home late that night, he walked into a spotlessly clean room with sparkling windows that peeped out from behind colorful patchwork curtains.

"Amazing," Boone said, awed, "how a woman's touch can transform a place."

"I'm glad you approve," Elizabeth said, pleased.

During the next several weeks their friendship blossomed rapidly. Elizabeth went out of her way to prepare Indian dishes because he particularly liked them. In appreciation, Boone made a point of shaving every morning. Since they were almost totally ignored by the fort personnel, who looked on their arrangement as highly suspicious, they were thrown together constantly. Whenever he was free, Boone took her and David out beyond the fort to a beautiful green valley for picnic lunches. While she was with him, Elizabeth never worried about being attacked by Indians. She had great respect for his abilities. In the evenings Boone would clean his weapons, whittle a piece of wood into a new toy for David, or play with him until it was time for the boy to go to bed. Elizabeth often joined them. She had never felt so contented. Although there was something undeniably frightening about Boone at times, which Elizabeth put down to his wild upbringing, she discovered many qualities she liked. She appreciated the way he spoke his mind, his sense of humor, the warmth of his smile, and the real affection he bore her son. Because their relationship appeared to symbolize an almost perfect scene of domestic tranquillity, Elizabeth was never sure just when she became aware of the change. She only knew she was suddenly conscious of a subtle tension between them. Perhaps it had been there all along and she was simply unaware of it. Elizabeth later wondered if her insatiable curiosity had finally revealed it for what it was.

"David reminds me of my own boy," Boone said softly one evening. "He has the same loving, happy nature."

Elizabeth had promised herself never to pry into Boone's private life again, but she was unable to conquer her curiosity. "How old was he when he died?"

"He was five, just five," Boone said stiffly.

"I'm sorry," Elizabeth apologized, seeing it still hurt him to discuss it. "I shouldn't have asked."

Boone gazed into the empty space in front of him as if mesmerized. "He was shot by white prospectors and died instantly. His mother wasn't so lucky. She lived long enough to suffer their abuses."

Elizabeth stared at him horrified. "How ghastly! Were the men ever found and brought to justice?"

Boone smiled unpleasantly. "Not one of them lived to boast about the kill."

Elizabeth shuddered. It was obvious from his words that Boone had had a hand in their destruction.

Boone watched her reaction with amusement. "I didn't get away with my revenge scot-free. I forfeited my freedom. The only reason I work for the army is because I gave my word I'd work for them in exchange for my life."

"You mean," Elizabeth demanded incredulously, "the army actually pardoned you on the condition that you agree to scout for them?"

Boone shrugged. "They needed Dull Knife, a renegade Sioux, more than they needed to hang me."

Digesting this most irregular proceeding, Elizabeth doubted if her husband would have agreed to such a deal, no matter how desperate the situation, and for some unaccountable reason this annoyed her. Elizabeth found Boone's retaliation for his family's deaths understandable, if not justifiable. "Did your revenge satisfy you, Mr. Boone?" Elizabeth asked, fascinated.

Boone frowned. "At first."

"Then you later regretted what you did?" Elizabeth pursued eagerly.

"No, ma'am. They deserved what they got."

"I don't understand," Elizabeth began.

"Revenge tasted pretty sweet at the time, but it didn't bring my wife and child back to life," Boone said bitterly.

Elizabeth again regretted having spoken out. A few minutes later she regretted it even more.

"It all happened a long time ago," Boone said slowly. "I loved my wife. We had fun together." Studying Elizabeth's face from underneath half-closed lids, he inquired softly, "Did you have fun with your husband Mrs. Kirby?"

"I beg your pardon?" Elizabeth stammered, flushing hotly as he continued to stare.

"I asked you if you ever had fun with your husband," Boone repeated.

"Of course we had fun," Elizabeth said quickly. "We had lots of fun," she added, desperately trying to avoid his searching gaze.

"You almost never talk about him," Boone pointed out. "And when you do, you don't look happy. You don't have the look of a woman who was loved."

Appalled, Elizabeth was about to retort it was no business of his when she recollected it was at her urging Boone had revealed the story about his family. "You certainly have a way of plain speaking, Mr. Boone," Elizabeth said nervously. "I admire you for your forthright attitude, but I'm afraid I'm not used to being so open myself. However"—she hesitated—"we are friends, and since it was at my instigation you revealed a confidence that was obviously painful for you, I will endeavor to be equally honest. You are quite correct in thinking I wasn't very happy with my husband."

"Why did you marry him?" Boone asked.

"I don't know. No, that isn't true, Mr. Boone. I am being evasive with you," Elizabeth said suddenly. "I married my husband for reasons of security, and he married me because it was time he took a wife and I was suitable."

"Occasionally the parties in a marriage like that can grow to love one another," Boone remarked impassively.

Elizabeth remembered how it had been—the unspoken frustrations, resentments, and fears that were smoothly covered by layers of boring, polite conversation that made life bearable and at the same time stifling—and stated conclusively, "Believe me, Mr. Boone, there was never any love between us. The only people I've loved were my two elderly aunts and my son."

A heavy silence fell between them. When Elizabeth finally glanced up, she noticed with considerable uneasiness that Boone was still watching her with the curiously veiled stare. His buckskin shirt was tight around the chest, and she resolved to make him another. She noted that his straight black hair needed a trim and that his legs were longer than she had thought. The tension she had only recently become aware of was suddenly pulsating in the room. Elizabeth seemed unable to look away from Boone. She could almost hear him breathing from where she sat. The passion that flickered in Boone's eyes as they held her own frightened Elizabeth. With an effort she rose and, trembling, excused herself. Her cheeks burning, she hurried to the safety of her room, locking the door behind her with a shaking hand.

Although Elizabeth was grateful to Boone for giving her a job and was even fond of him, sexual contact was out of the question. In addition to its being sinful with any man but her husband, Elizabeth had never found it an enjoyable experience. Occasionally she had wondered if sexual relations with a man other than Peter would be pleasurable. While Gray Sky was not what she had had in mind, the result was the same. She found it degrading. Crawling deeper under the covers, Elizabeth vowed to discourage Boone from thinking his advances would be welcomed.

As fate would have it, Boone commanded a mission the following day that lasted two months. When he returned, Elizabeth was so overjoyed to see him, she forgot all about her vow to discourage him. Impulsively she embraced Boone and even kissed him on the cheek.

"I think I'll bribe the general to send me on the next difficult mission that looks like it might be extended," Boone said, smiling, refusing to release her, "if you promise to greet me this way when I return."

Elizabeth blushed and broke away. That night after David was fast asleep, they sat up laughing, exchanging stories and news. Elizabeth was completely relaxed and in the middle of a tale about Lavinia Bourke when Boone interrupted.

"I haven't had an opportunity to thank you yet," he said, his eyes sparkling with mischief.

"Thank me for what?" Elizabeth asked, taken aback.

"For greeting me in my favorite dress. You look beautiful," he said admiringly. "The gold brings out the warmth of your skin."

"My . . . my other dress needed fixing," she stammered helplessly, knowing full well there was nothing wrong with the dark brown check.

"There's no need to feel ashamed about wanting to please someone you care for," Boone said seriously.

Elizabeth wanted to deny that she cared for him at all in the way he meant, but the words wouldn't come.

"Why are you so afraid to admit you care for me when your eyes tell me the truth?" Boone continued gently.

"I . . . I . . . you don't understand," Elizabeth protested feebly. "You mustn't say such things. We're just friends, that's all, and we can never be anything more."

"Why not?"

"Why not?" Elizabeth repeated wildly, standing up and nearly knocking the dining table over. "Because!" she shouted desperately.

Boone rose and pulled her to him, despite her outraged demands to be released. Whispering softly, he said, "You remind me of a frightened deer who is so panicked by the sound of hunters in the woods that it runs without direction, without purpose. Be still," he urged soothingly, pressing her against his chest. "I'm not going to hurt you."

Elizabeth continued struggling for a few seconds more before she shuddered and was still. The feel of Boone's strong arms about her and the smell of his leather shirt relaxed and comforted her. She felt safe, warm, and peaceful. He began stroking her hair.

"I love you," he said softly. "And I need you," he added hoarsely. "I think you care for me enough to love me in time. What could be wrong about two people who care, giving of themselves?" he demanded, kissing her as Peter had never done.

Elizabeth automatically responded to the deep passionate kiss, but as his hands moved down her body, she became fearful and broke away. She was shaking. "No," she said breathlessly. "I can't."

Boone took her hand. It was burning hot. Her cheeks were flushed as though with fever, and her eyes were wide with fear and longing. He frowned. "I won't force you against your will," he promised. "What's wrong? Are you afraid of what others will say? Or is it because we're not married?" he asked, studying her. "Is that it?"

"Those things matter," Elizabeth admitted, "but . . ." She turned away, humiliated.

Forcing Elizabeth to face him again, Boone insisted, "What is it? Tell me!"

Boone's shirt had pulled open at the chest. Elizabeth stared with fascination at the exposed part. The stiff black hairs stood out against a background of nutty-

brown flesh in a tantalizing manner. She was physically attracted to Boone as she had never been to any
other man, but would that be enough? "It's no good,"
she explained sadly. "It never was any good. Don't
you see," she said tearfully, trying to break away
from him, "sex was always an ordeal for me. I only
participated in it because I had to. I never enjoyed it."

"Listen to me," Boone said, shaking her. "You never
loved your husband, you said so yourself. And I'm
not your blundering idiot of a husband," he shouted
angrily.

"What difference does that make?" Elizabeth
mumbled miserably.

"By God, I'll show you what difference it makes,"
Boone said grimly, crushing her in an embrace from
which she could scarcely breathe, let alone struggle.
Raising her face to his none too gently, he kissed her
again.

Elizabeth felt Boone's warm mouth pressing down
on hers in a slow, deliberate kiss. She could feel every
inch of his tall, hard body against her own. His hands
caressed her, moved over her with infinite skill and
patience, until the fear they inspired gave way before
a stronger emotion. Elizabeth moaned without realizing it and clutched him even tighter. Boone relaxed
his hold on her. He was breathing heavily, his eyes
full of laughter and tenderness.

"Let me teach you what it is to make love with the
right person," Boone said huskily, kissing her lightly
at the corners of her mouth. "All I ask is that you trust
me enough to relax." He opened the top of her dress
and kissed the throbbing pulse in her throat. "Close
your eyes and only permit yourself to feel," he whispered softly as he carried her to the bed.

Squeezing her eyes tightly shut, Elizabeth lay rigid
on the bed. She heard the sound of clothes rustling
and knew Boone was undressing. The sharp clink of a
metallic object hitting the floor indicated to Elizabeth
that Boone has dropped his belt. I must be mad, she

thought to herself. I must be mad. Suddenly the bed moved, and she shivered as Boone began to undress her. His kisses and murmured words of reassurance did nothing to quell the terrible apprehension that was rapidly building as each piece of clothing was removed and added to the pile on the floor. When her final undergarment was discarded, Elizabeth took a deep breath and waited. Instead of forcing himself on her as she half-expected he would, Boone began stroking her breasts and thighs. Elizabeth felt his naked flesh as he drew her to him, and she began to tremble. She could feel his hard member, long and thick, quivering against her thigh. His kisses burned her flesh as his caressing became rougher and at the same time more exciting. Her nipples began to harden. Liquid fire raced through her veins, burning up any lingering pockets of fear. She groaned with pleasure. A primitive urgency that knew nothing but its object made her pull Boone even closer. He hesitated before entering, but she pleaded wildly, "Yes, yes." She was ready, and his erect member slid in easily. She gasped as he moved to a rhythmic beat, slow at first and then faster. As if she had always responded, Elizabeth moved along with him. Just as she was convinced she could stand the exquisite agony of her pleasure no longer, Boone grabbed her shoulders roughly and began to move in deep, long strokes, gaining momentum until he spilled his seed inside her. For a few seconds they lay exhausted, unable to move. Boone finally raised his head and kissed her. Elizabeth smiled shyly, her eyes wide open.

Basking in her newfound happiness, Elizabeth radiated a beauty that made the other women raise their eyebrows and exchange knowing looks. She no longer cared what they thought. Boone looked years younger. The officers were amazed at his even temper and easy camaraderie. When their womenfolk commented acidly on the possible reason behind such altered behavior, the men turned a deaf ear. "Live and let live" was their motto.

The joy of being in love made Boone indulgent toward Elizabeth's continued silence on the nature of her identity. She would tell him who she really was when she was ready. As the months passed and Elizabeth showed no signs of revealing her secret, Boone felt hurt at her lack of trust. It also annoyed and upset him that although Elizabeth responded to his lovemaking with growing ardor and freedom, she had never actually said in words that she loved him. He had begun to wonder if she ever would. The new plans he had made for the future centered around Elizabeth, but he was reluctant to discuss them. She never questioned him about what he would do once he left the army, and since she showed no interest, he was too proud to tell her. Boone also feared that Elizabeth, who despite being captured by the Indians was used to the relative comforts of civilization and the laws of conventional existence, wouldn't want the kind of rough pioneer life he had to offer. Fort living was rugged, but it was a veritable den of luxury compared with what lay ahead. Deep in his heart Boone feared that if she accompanied him into the wilds, it would be because she lacked alternatives, not because she loved him.

"What's wrong?" Elizabeth asked softly one night after they had made love. "You've been brooding over something these last few weeks, and don't say you haven't," she challenged.

"I won't deny it," Boone admitted grimly.

"Well, what is it?" Elizabeth prodded curiously.

Boone frowned in the dark. "I haven't been honest with you," he said quietly.

"What do you mean?" Elizabeth asked startled.

"I wasn't always a scout for Fort Jeremiah," Boone explained slowly, trying without success to make out her features in the dark. "Before I came here, I was a scout at Fort Jubele." He felt Elizabeth stiffen, and added, "I recognized you right off."

"Why didn't you say something?" Elizabeth asked in amazement.

"If the wife of Lieutenant Farrell wants to change her name, it's none of my business," Boone said coldly.

"But you could have mentioned it later," Elizabeth pointed out, "after we became friends."

"Yes, I could have," Boone agreed harshly, stung by the term "friends," "but I figured it was up to you to tell me."

"I wanted to forget about Peter and everything that happened." Elizabeth spoke defensively. "I wanted to make a new life for myself and David."

"What are you going to do once it's time for me to leave Fort Jeremiah?" Boone demanded suddenly.

"I . . . I don't know," she replied faintly, taken aback. "I thought perhaps we might go somewhere together, but if you don't want to," she said quickly, stumbling over the words, "you needn't feel obliged."

"Elizabeth," Boone said gently, taking her hands, "the sort of life I have to offer is a hard one. We'll be facing periods of great loneliness and isolation, with only the bare necessities of existence. It's a life that has its rewards and pleasures, but without love it would be unbearable." He paused. "Because I loved you, I rushed you into a relationship you may not have been ready for. Knowing you cared for me, I was confident you would grow to love me. Was I wrong?"

"No, you weren't," Elizabeth said tearfully. "I love you very much, but I was terrified to say so. I . . . I had to be sure of your feelings," she explained, embarrassed.

"I told you how I felt from the first," Boone said incredulously.

"Yes, I know," Elizabeth admitted, "only I was afraid you might have said you loved me in a passionate moment and later regretted saying it. You had once told me you intended to join the Indians when you were released from the army, and never afterward even hinted at other plans," she said accusingly.

"Elizabeth!" Boone protested.

"I've been feeling absolutely horrid for weeks," she confessed. "Tonight when you admitted something was bothering you, I was convinced you were going to say our arrangement was only a temporary one and you would be leaving me at the end of the month to join the Indians."

Boone drew Elizabeth into his arms. "This experience ought to teach us a valuable lesson," he said, smiling. "If ever we find ourselves at loggerheads, we should sit down and state how we feel in no uncertain terms, leaving no room for dangerous assumptions or speculations."

"I quite agree," Elizabeth laughed.

"Just for the record," Boone said, kissing her, "are you going to let your husband know you're alive?"

"Do you think I ought to?" Elizabeth asked softly, playing with the hairs on his chest.

"It's all the same to me," Boone said thickly, running a hand down her leg, which was entwined with his.

"Maybe I'll write him a letter once we get to wherever it is we're going," she whispered.

"Good idea," Boone replied softly, reaching for her.

Epilogue

Sweetwater lay exposed to the elements. Sun, rain, wind, and snow eventually disintegrated the rubble. Weeds covered the ground. Flocks of whitetail deer, rabbits, field mice, short green snakes, and porcupines became the new transient occupants of the town. Wolves roamed freely at night, howling their discontent. Birds flew overhead during the day and paused to rest and ruffle their feathers among the tall weeds.

The massacre acted like a catharsis on the lives of the survivors. Charity Walker began a new life in a distant place where the pain of remembrance would gradually fade and the concept of love would grow. Elizabeth Farrell and Katie Mallory each followed the dictates of their own hearts and led lives full of hardships, but also rewards. Little Luke Tilby and Lorrie Gomber had no say in the way in which their destinies were shaped. Cut off from their own culture and separated even from the company of each other, their lives were forever altered. In time, the memories of Sweetwater seemed more like a dream than a reality. They grew up, married, had children of their own, and died speaking a language other than the one they were born into. Joseph Mallory's seed was firmly planted in the soil and his two sons, Michael and Sean, returned to the land he loved and were among the first to help to rebuild the town.

Relatives of murdered residents who had inherited the land slowly filtered into the abandoned area. Thin streams of restless, hungry pioneers fleeing from con-

'gested cities and towns in the East drifted west with
small bands of wagon trains armed with a few precious belongings and a multitude of dreams. Soon the
demand they created initiated an influx of doctors,
storekeepers, saloon owners, lawyers, and dentists,
who joined their ranks. Like the previous builders,
they chose the old site of Sweetwater to be their own.
It was a logical choice. The land was easily built on,
and water was accessible. More important, Sweetwater was situated smack in the middle of the surrounding reaches and within a day's ride of Fort
Jubele. Horror stories of the Sweetwater massacre
rapidly faded before the lust for land and dreams of
material security. The Indians had either moved north
into Canada or been settled on land far away. They
posed little threat to the new residents. The iron
tracks of the mighty railroad were moving farther
west. A new golden era of prosperity awaited the citizens of Sweetwater, and they knew it.

Twenty-five years after the massacre, Sweetwater
was again a thriving, buzzing community of industrious individuals working toward a common goal—
success. Whether or not they would be victorious lay
in the uncharted future. For the present, Sweetwater
lay like a giant womb, nurturing, giving birth to the
men and women who would shape the destiny of
their community with their thoughts and feelings.
The trend of their thinking would attract either the
success they craved or the annihilation of their ambitions. The decision, as with their predecessors, was up
to them.

ABOUT THE AUTHOR

Roxanne Dent's writing career began at age 16, when her poem, THE DEVIL'S DISCIPLE, was chosen to be included in a National Anthology of High School Poetry. Since then, she has contributed magazine articles and short stories to *Womancraft*, *Caper*, and *Ultra*, and has had several books published.

Ms. Dent, whose interests include astrology, travel, and cooking, lives in Manhattan, where she is presently at work on her next novel.

Introducing a new
historical romance by Joan Wolf

DESIRE'S INSISTENT SONG CARRIED THEIR PASSION THROUGH THE FLAMES OF LOVE AND WAR . . .

The handsome Virginian made Lady Barbara Carr shiver with fear and desire. He was her new husband, a stranger, wed to her so his wealth could pay her father's debts, an American patriot, sworn to fight Britain's king. But Alan Maxwell had never wanted any woman the way he wanted this delicate English lady. And a hot need ignited within him as he carried Barbara to the canopied bed, defying the danger of making her his bride tonight . . . when war could make her his enemy tomorrow. . . .

Coming in July from Signet!